twochubbycubs
The Second Coming

James and Paul Anderson

DEDICATION:
IT'S ALL ABOUT EMMA, ISN'T IT?

Our last book – Saturated Fats – was dedicated to my dear old nana who died in 2015 and who would have been tickled pink to see her face in a book that wasn't 'Button Thieves of the 1920s'. However, she's still dead, and although she's always in our hearts, we thought we'd dedicate this book to another – someone who is most dear to us.

El Ehma is our muse. Whenever we're sitting trying to think of a witty analogy or some antiquated word to use to sound clever, there she is, wind whistling through her ears. She provides a natural distraction, like some wonderful lava-lamp clad in eighteen buckets of whatever perfume they had out in Boots that day. There will be times when Paul and I are watching Only Connect and struggling to think of the exact lineage of the House of Liechtenstein and we're reassured that El Ehma's whirring mind is only ever a call away.

This book, of course, is also dedicated to all of you – I'd write stories even if no-one read them and I was putting them straight into the shredder – but all the thanks, lovely comments and warm feedback fair makes my heart swell. Thank you! Now let's get to the knob gags. Oh and be gentle – this is a published from home book, we've really tried our best to iron out any wrinkles!

CONTENTS

This is a tricky one to write, actually – do I type as though we've never met and you've happened across us by accident like a dog-walker finding a corpse, or do I talk to you like old friends talking over a cup of tea? Hmm.

If you're familiar with us (perhaps you've read our blog or previous books) please be assured that we're still fat, still fairly foul-mouthed, still blundering from one embarrassment to the next and still happily married. Our cats are one year older, we're both slightly fatter but we have managed to win most of the neighbours round. Phew.

If you're a Cubs virgin, I feel I must apologise profusely. Some of the language in this book is rather coarse, but I like to think there is a great big heart beating in there, even if I'm drowning it in saturated fats. These articles come from our blog which we set up in 2014 on a whim – essentially a place for me to dump my verbal nonsense – but that blog has become a beast and we couldn't do without it. We now have almost three years of perfect memories all typed out, meaning we can look back over them and laugh and smile like we're on a regional news bulletin about losing a member of our family.

I'm not quite sure how we come across in these posts: I'd hope that underneath the sheen of sarcasm and rage you can see that we're actually two decent fatties. We mean well! Oh and we're not one for photos, but I've slipped a few in where I can!

Three things left to say:

- please remember that these posts are mostly from our blog, and thus, very occasionally, there may be references to photos / links / other blog content that doesn't scan quite right now it is in a book – I've tried my best to edit it the best I can but please, forgive a fat bloke his minor indiscretions;

- if you're picking this up and have never seen our blog, take a look – we started out as a food blog and now have over 400 recipes on there. We aren't allowed to publish the recipes otherwise powerful men will come and rearrange our faces, but hopefully the funny stories will keep you going;

- if you read this and you enjoy it, please leave us a review on Amazon and recommend us to your friends. I'm like a big jowly puppy who craves a kind word every now and then and your love will only make me stronger!

Enjoy!

James and Paul

x

Long-time readers may recollect a particularly disastrous trip to a wedding in the last book where, in no particular order, I forgot my tie, our suit hiring folks forgot to remove the massive security tag on my suit jacket and, after a particularly bouncy bit of drunken sex, Paul and I fell asleep and missed the entire reception.

Since then, we have managed to avoid weddings, which is probably for the best given our ability to embarrass ourselves at any given notice, but we were invited to a New Year's Eve wedding at the start of the year before and given it was someone who I a) like and b) strongly suspect would cut my face if I had turned her down (I mean, she's from Worksop, they use a headbutt like one might use a comma), we had no choice but to go.

A bit about the bride: I've been her PA at various points in my life. I follow her around like a persistent dose of thrush. I joined her team as a fresh-faced young man full of innocence – she then systemically ruined me over the course of the next few years. I'd seen her blossom from a cantankerous, foul-mouthed, cock-hungry hussy to a slightly older cantankerous, foul-mouthed, cock-hungry hussy. It was with a great sense of pride that I was to see her down the aisle, her flaming Rebekah Brooks hair trailing behind her.

A bit about the groom: Paul and I both would.

Paul hates weddings so it was a case of promising him that it was going to be a fun event, there would be delicious food AND it was to be held up in Otterburn so there was a slim-to-maybe chance the night could end with one or both of us being tumbled around a field by a gang of rough-handed, drunken squaddies. It's exactly the same way I get him to go to family BBQs.

Usual pre-wedding promises were made: lose plenty of weight, get a decent suit, pick a decent present. Usual pre-wedding promises were then completely ignored: we put more weight over Christmas, our suits came from Marks and Spencer's 'GOOD GOD MAN YOU'RE OBSCENE' range and the bride wanted cold hard cash, which was something I could immediately get behind. The cash that is, not the bride. I feel that may have been a tad inappropriate during the service and anyway, the groom looked like he could take us both in a fight.

Paul drove us the 50 miles there. You all know how I feel about his driving – there's still three fingernails lodged in the passenger side door from my grip.

We'd booked ourselves a fancy suite in a gorgeous old country hotel – just the thing to pick our arses in, clip our toenails into the carpet and watch The Chase in. We know our place. The receptionist was a delight – he looked exactly like a tiny version of Paul, and well, Paul's pretty miniature anyway. I wanted to reach over and pick him up, half expecting there to be an even smaller version of Paul inside, played by Hervé Villechaize in a fat-suit. The receptionist was definitely one of us and there was more than a hint of '*anything else you need; you just ask*'. I told him that we were good for now but if I woke up at 3am fancying a Mexican Pancake, I'd ring down.

I had a quick bath, mainly to rid myself of the fear-sweat that soaked me through following Paul's 'driving', then, after a change into our court outfits, we were ready.

The wedding was a mile or so away at an absolutely beautiful hall (Woodhill Hall, if you please) and so we piled into a people's carriers lest I got my shoes muddy. There was just time enough for a quick drink and a look at everyone's pretty clothes and Sunday best shoes before we were directed to take a seat in the sunroom. The service was terrific – not all fussy and old-fashioned but some custom lyrics and a fair bit of crying. I begged Paul to let me hurtle down the aisle screaming "It Should Have Been Me" like that bit in Vicar of Dibley but he told me to behave myself. Boo. You have no idea how difficult it is for me not to cause a scene.

Rings fingered and kisses given, we were all put in another room to enjoy a gorgeous meal of local delicacies and whatnots before listening to the speeches which, for once, were actually funny. There's nowt worse than people thinking they're funny (although to be fair I've created quite a sideline from it) but these got more than a few titters from me.

Bellies full and hearts singing / straining, we nipped back to the hotel room to get changed into slightly less strained shirts – there's only so long I can sit fretting that my collar is about to burst open and blind someone with a stray button – and the excellent news is that we managed not to fall asleep like we did at the last wedding. I'd hate to get a reputation as someone who just turned up at weddings for the sandwiches and free drinks and then buggered off away to bed before my wallet came out. I mean, that IS exactly who I am, but I'd hate to have a reputation.

Anyway, back at the hotel we bumped into El Ehma (who the book is dedicated to) and, after dressing, we headed down to the bar for a quick drink before nipping back to the venue. Emma's idea of a 'quick drink' turned out to be a triple Tanqueray and tonic, which seemed to cause the barman great consternation. She had to explain several times over that a triple was three shots, and it was with a very shaky hand that he set about the optics for the third time. I didn't care, I was already fairly tipsy at this point. After more gin we set off back to the wedding venue, with El Ehma promising hand-on-heart that we'd meet again at 1am to get the car back to the hotel, with the offer of a 'chocolate Baileys' as a nightcap.

I write as a hobby and like to think I have a good handle on most euphemisms but even I wasn't sure what a chocolate Baileys entailed. Would I ever find out?

The rest of the evening's festivities were held in a giant tent in the gardens of the hall. There was a roaring fire in the middle and thankfully, I was too drunk to entertain my catastrophic thinking that the whole place would go up like the school in Carrie. At some point in the evening the DJ started playing the songs that each guest had requested months prior to the wedding – because this was a more alternative wedding there was a lot of rock music and loud noise, but the atmosphere was great. I had completely forgotten what I had put down on my reply.

Anyway, seeking some "fresh air" and "time to ourselves" (seriously though, there's something about weddings that gets us both hilariously frisky – I've only got to hear the first few seconds of the Wedding March and the old cock-clock jumps straight to midnight), we ventured outside behind the venue, eventually finding a little shed that we could "rest our feet" without fear of interruption.

Let me tell you this – naughty outdoors wedding sex is great fun, it really is, especially when the air is crisp and cold and there's the distant sound of people having an amazing night, but it doesn't have put you off your stroke when you're near the point of climax and you hear the DJ shout your name over the crowd followed by the words "…specially requested this all-time classic – OOOH AAAH (Just A Little Bit) by Gina G".

Listen, I've had sex under pressure, I've had sex in dangerous places, but there was no possible way I was going to be able to paint the town white under these circumstances. Having a barely successful Eurovision singer annotating your thrusts is a recipe for disaster. We zipped up and headed back inside, putting our flushed faces down to musical embarrassment. Sort of true, I suppose.

The rest of the evening passed in a blur of food, liqueur, dubious dancing and actually, everyone just having a bloody lovely time. I've never been to a wedding before where everyone who mattered was smiling and laughing and do you know, it was grand. When people are there not out of obligation but out of friendship, well, you know you're on the right track. The evening finished with a midnight fireworks display set to Pour

Some Sugar On Me (some Canestan might have beenb better) and sparklers and then everyone slowly made their way to bed.

Not us, though. No, despite El Ehma's promises of keeping the car ready for us, piloted by her lovely sober husband, and us turning up at dot on the time we said, she was away, leaving us stranded. Bah! We could see her brake lights snaking away down the road. Clearly she was in a rush for that chocolate Baileys / anal.

There was no chance of us walking back because by this point I was seeing six legs when I looked down, so we threw ourselves on the mercy of the lovely lady behind the bar. She was probably struck with the frightening idea of seeing our swimmy eyes and moon faces leering at her gin collection all through the night and so it was that we found ourselves packed into the back of her Fiat Uno, being driven all the way back to our hotel. I could have kissed her. Hell, I was that pleased (and blue-balled from earlier) that I would have fathered her children had she given me a bit of keen-eye.

We tumbled into bed (just Paul and I) and were straight off to sleep. Things came to a lively head at about 4am when Paul tumbled drunkenly out of bed, setting the very posh and old bedside table crashing over, which in turn knocked a chest of drawers asunder, which then set a lamp crashing to the floor. It was like Total Wipeout, only with more gin fumes and Paul trapped in sheets on the floor. We inspected the antiques with all the care and concentration you'd expect from two burly men who at that point were more gin than human, and hastened back to bed.

The cold light of day revealed that, somewhat surprisingly, there had been no damage done, save for a mobile-phone shaped bruise on Paul's arse where he had landed on his phone. If only he'd been charging his electric toothbrush then at least one of us would have seen some action round the back. We quite literally staggered to the breakfast room where we were met with El Ehma's fresh face ("eee we waited! We did! We did!") and a fry-up that came on two plates. Across the way from us were a couple visiting from down South and who had ordered a tiny bowl of muesli and a cup of smugness and by God were they repulsed by my alcohol fumes and unshaven face. I'm just glad I don't smoke anymore – if I had lit a match at that point I would have gone up like a dry forest fire.

We couldn't leave at this point because we were still tipsy so we had to walk around Otterburn until we were safe to drive. You know when people say the best thing to do for a hangover is to get some fresh air? Balls to them. I've never felt rougher than I did when I had my face lashed by the cold Northumberland air and soaked by the type of rain that gets in every single gap in flesh, clothing and soul. When we could eventually drive home, we did so silently, green-faced and gingerly. What a truly amazing wedding, though.

FAIR WARNING: this opening post is very rude indeed and contains graphic talk about knobs. Skip ahead one if you're unsure! They're not all this rude but I like to open with a bang.

There's definitely a few sentences a man doesn't want to hear, but a doctor telling him 'well, it's going to have to come off' whilst he holds my cock in his hands with all the nonchalance of a bored prostitute is definitely high up there.

Let me explain. This entry wasn't published in the blog last year because frankly, I don't believe every Tom, Dick and Harry needs to know about the ins and outs of my penis. But, I needed an opening entry at least on par with the colonic irrigation of the last book, and so here we are. You've paid £5 for this, might as well get your money's worth!

A few weeks prior to this incident I'd had the most unfortunate accident. See, I had been out at a Christmas party was having a piss in Possibly The Worst Pub Toilet In Existence. I was rushing it along before I passed out from the stale urine fumes, fell face-first into the trough and was found later by friends with a urinal cake up my nose and third-degree burns on my face. In my haste to leave quickly, I shook off the drips, tucked him away and pulled my zip up, like I've done so many times before in the 31 years I've been on this Earth.

Only, things are never that simple, are they? No, this time around, in either my haste or my drunken state, I managed to not tuck him away entirely and as a result, got a good chunk of my foreskin entangled up in the closed zip. You know when you're on a train and someone makes a dash for the closing doors only to get halfway through them and squeezed as a result? Yeah, that. There was so much blood, I nearly hobbled next door for a Tampax and a cuddle.

Anyway, zip forward (ouch) a week or so later and I'm stood in my doctor's surgery with my on-the-flop cock out whilst he turns it this way and that like he's trying to get Radio 4 to come from my bumhole. It was healing, yes, but because scar tissue is thick, it also meant that 'movement was restricted'. To give you yet another analogy, imagine putting your arm into the sleeve into an old woollen jumper only to find it has shrunk considerably. He tutted and murmured and was down there for a good couple of minutes before announcing that, indeed, it would have to come off.

I have to say, I thought it was drastic – I like my cock very much, it's served me well through the many years that I've paid interest in it – and a life without him would be grey indeed. He must have saw the shock sweep across my face because he immediately followed it up with a little chuckle and said 'no no, just the foreskin', as though I was meant to laugh and slap him on the back with relief. It would still involve someone setting about my genitals with a sharper blade than I'd ever want down there.

This meant a quick visit to a urologist who confirmed the news. I sat in the urology department, never desiring more a t-shirt that said 'I DON'T HAVE THE CLAP', until I was called in and, but of course, the man who wanted to look at my knob was incredibly attractive. Of course! In any other circumstance I would have been lubed and prepped before he'd had a chance to put his gloves on, but it was hard to get frisky when you know that he's deciding the fate of your manhood that very day. I mean, I was quite literally an NHS cutback.

This decision didn't take too long at all – he, like the other doctor, had a bit of a roll around with it, had a quick taste (I'm kidding, I didn't go private) and then sat me down to discuss options. Options! With a circumcision! Apparently you can have a tight cut that makes everything prim and proper or you can have a loose cut which makes the whole thing look like an ice-cream cone that's been left out in the rain. I asked if he could perhaps use pinking shears for a festive, fun twist but apparently not. Bah. The operation was scheduled for a few days away (it would not be the first time in my life someone's tried to fit my penis into a tight spot) and, it gets better, it was on Paul's birthday! Poor bugger.

That day soon rolled around, unlike my foreskin, and

once I'd given Paul his birthday presents and he'd kissed my poor penis goodbye, we were off to the hospital. I had to change into one of those awful gowns that show your arse to every passing patient but hey, no time to be fashion conscious. I did plan on asking if Paul and I could have a couple to take away for our 'trips to the lorry park to see the lorries' but the anaesthetic put paid to that. The nurse asked if I'd had anything to eat or drink and I mentioned I had had a coffee in 1996, meaning I had to wait another few hours for that to leave my system. Bah! Time moves very slowly indeed when you know you're going to be put under!

I admit I was nervous: I'm a big guy and the thought of going under anaesthetic troubled me. I have a weak heart and I'm a light sleeper. I didn't want to a) die or b) come around halfway through the operation only to see them helicoptering my cock about or taking pictures for the staff newsletter. When it was time for the operation I relayed my concerns to the nurse prepping me for theatre who explained something which I can't remember because I was out like a bloody light. It was as if someone had just switched me off.

The next time I woke up I was in an entirely different ward with what looked like an entire roll of dressing around my knob and an uncomfortable amount of dried blood. My gasp of shock must have roused the nurses because they came over with a cheery hello and, after asking if I was OK, they wheeled me back to Paul. We embraced and he had a look for himself. I've never seen a face go grey so quickly. It's a bad job when I'm the one who has had the operation and Paul's the guy who ends up on oxygen. Pfft.

They told me to rest for a bit but that I'd be out of hospital that evening, once I'd had some toast and a piss. The glamour! The very last thing I wanted to do was urinate but I never say no to toast. I had hoped it might be like when you have your tonsils out and you get ice-cream, but no. Eventually, the moment came when I did need a slash and so it was, with steps more ginger than my first as a child, I hobbled to the loo.

I can't begin to tell you how uncomfortable it was getting there, every brush of my gown tickling the end and setting my nerves on fire. Having eventually managed to get myself to the bathroom, I, so very delicately, flopped him out, bandages and dressing included, and started to urinate.

Well fuck me. You know if you squeeze the end of a hose-pipe the jet of water goes much further? That was me in this tiny hospital bathroom. The swelling at the end was acting like a firm grip and good lord - I aimed for the toilet but hit the wall behind it with so much force I'm surprised I didn't bust straight through into the ladies and piss in some poor woman's handbag. I couldn't stop because it would hurt too much so I stumbled back, eventually managing to hit the toilet only when I was stood right at the other end of the room, pissing a good 10ft or so into the toilet. All I could think is what would happen if I had a wank – I'd blind myself!

The nurses, content that I wasn't pissing blood, let me go. I did ask if I could take my foreskin home with me but they said no. That's a shame. I could have fashioned a wallet with it, with the added benefit being if you rubbed it just right it would swell to fit your chequebook in.

We stumbled slowly, oh so slowly, to the car, and it was then I knew bringing the Micra – with its absolute lack of suspension or finesse – was a mistake. It was enough having my knob drag on my trousers but every speed bump felt like someone was kicking me in the balls. Paul did his best, bless him, but Christ did I not feel every square inch of that drive home.

After that, it took a good couple of weeks to heal. Some comical asides – for a good week or so I had to stand in the doorway to our bathroom and piss right across the room because the pressure didn't calm down for so long. We had to sleep apart, as Paul has a tendency to get frisky in his sleep and the last thing I needed was a stitch catching on his teeth, and to top off the indignity, I had to sleep with a bloody salad bowl over my crotch to stop the duvet dragging on my knob until everything has healed.

Even now when I make a salad I wince.

But you know what the worst part was? Being told to try my best not to get an erection because doing so could pull the stitches out. Men get erections so easily – sometimes for no good reason at all. I could be washing the dishes and suddenly have to stand back with my back arched until it goes back on the flop. There's no rhyme or reason to the whole business. Luckily, the fact that my cock looked like it had been run over for a good week or so meant it generally behaved, but I was flicking through the TV one day, salad bowl placed over the area, when I absent-mindedly starting watching the rugby.

Big mistake (oh I'm a boaster!) – the pain! Christ almighty – and the bloody thing was being resilient, too, working right through that pain barrier. The things I had to think about in order for it to beat a retreat doesn't bear thinking about now. Bleurgh.

Thankfully, it all healed very nicely. It looks great, even if I do say so myself – I've avoided that Neapolitan ice-cream look that sometimes happen with a late circumcision. It works well too, but you don't need to know that, I'm sure. I'll also add in a footnote – if there is anyone out there with a partner who needs the chop, tell him to go for it – despite my hyperbole above, it really wasn't that bad. Uncomfortable yes, but I've had more painful craps. If he's unsure about whether he needs it, just send him down to Cubs Towers and we'll be more than pleased to take a good, hard look at it for him.

Gosh, I really feel like we know each other well now, don't you?

twochubbycubs go to Iceland: part one

We decided on Iceland for three reasons:

- Corsica taught us that two fat men in very hot climates equals rashes, sweating and uncomfortable levels of public nudity;

- it looks fantastically ethereal and unlike anywhere we've ever been before; and (perhaps crucially);

- we envisioned the place being full of hairy, mountain men who could club a polar bear to death with their willies.

We actually almost ended up in Iceland three years ago but we had to cancel the trip to fund the remodelling of our kitchen – it was certainly more important, the place looked like a museum exhibit, all foisty and fussy from the previous old biddy who shuffled around in there. Broke our heart though to cancel for something so mundane, even if I do have a fabulous cerise stand mixer like old cokehead Lawson and a whole load of Le Creuset. Flash forward several years later and, after watching a ten-minute video on YouTube, we had the whole holiday booked within ten minutes.

Fast forward to December, you know the drill. We shuttled our way up to Edinburgh and arrived at the hotel.

We ate a perfectly satisfactory (damning with faint

praise) meal in the hotel bar, where we were served by an entirely lovely young waitress who baffled us with menu choices but steered us towards the money-saving options with aplomb. Clearly one look at our tattered shoes and my Donald Trump haircut elicited a sense of pity from her. She did respond to our chat about Iceland with a question we'd hear surprisingly often both before and after the holiday:

"Iceland…is it cold there?"

I mean the clue is in the name. I was faultlessly polite, resisting the urge to tell her that they only call it Iceland to lure unsuspecting penguins there to sell them timeshares, and demurred that it was indeed rather nippy. Perhaps she knew that as hard-bitten Geordies we only feel the cold when our heart stops and our fingers turn black.

That's a faintly true stereotype – take a look out in Newcastle on a Friday night in winter and you'll see plenty of bubbling and rippling masses wearing less material than I use to wipe my bum. Only when both sets of lips turn blue does the *cough* Prosecco get put down. Anyway, yes, we were asked many times if Iceland was cold to the point I developed a tic in my eye from inwardly wincing so much.

I wish I could say there was anything eventful to write about from finishing our meal through to getting on the plane, but no – it was the usual perfect Premier Inn service. I should be on bloody commission; I tell everyone about Premier Inn. Just saying, if you're reading this PI, a free night in a London hotel wouldn't go amiss. We don't mind if Lenny Henry is in there, he looks like he'd be a cuddler. We did, however, manage to deviate from our normal practice of turning up at the airport eight days early 'just in case' by instead spending the day shopping in the salubrious Livingston Centre. I say shopping, we minced in, fannied about in the Le Creuset shop, bought a salt pig and a honey pot and then walked around looking at all the shops that cater for people of less corpulent frames than us. We decided to have a game of mini-golf in Paradise Island. Paradise Island? More like Hepatitis Inlet. No I'm sorry, I've been to America and I've seen how they do mini-golf over there – carefully crafted courses, erupting volcanoes, accessibility ramps for the fatwagons. What do we get? A shoddy animatronic of Paul's mother appearing out of a crate of MDF, a vinyl recording of a door creaking and some torn artificial grass. I felt like I was having a round of golf in an abandoned IKEA. We plodded around with all the enthusiasm of the terminally bored, finished under par and didn't dare have a pop at the 'WIN A FREE GAME' final hole in case we were actually victorious.

Unusually, we did manage to get lost on the way to the airport carpark – we normally have an excellent sense of direction, but somehow we missed the giant planes swarming around over our head. I pulled over to ask someone for directions and I've genuinely never stared into such an empty face. I asked for directions to the airport and he gazed at me like I was speaking tongues. My exasperated eyes met his watery eyes for a moment or two, then, realising he was clearly as thick as the shite that killed Elvis, we barrelled away in the car. He was still stooped over 'looking at the car' as we turned a corner 100 yards away, somewhat ironically onto the right roundabout for the airport. Ah well. It'll have given him something to use his brain for other than absorbing the wind.

Having parked the car in a car-park that looked exactly like the type of place you'd see on Watchdog where they tear your cars up and down the country, touching everything with oily hands and merrily hacking up phlegm into the secret camera, we were on our way. I told Paul to 'remember where we had parked' and he replied with 'Berwick upon Tweed'. He does come out with the jokes occasionally you know. Edinburgh Airport remains as charmless as ever, with the only place to eat that didn't necessitate filling out a loan application being the little Wetherspoons up by the gate. I had four gins and a tonic, Paul had a beer and after only an hour or so, we were boarding the plane. I've typed many words about the way people board planes so I won't bother you with them now, but for goodness sake, the pilot isn't going to set away early, you don't need to crowd on like they're giving out blowjobs and cocaine. Bastards.

The flight was uneventful but packed – the mass wearing of winter clothes meant everyone took up slightly more room than normal and the air was soon steamy with sweat. To squeeze past someone in the aisle involved so much personal intimacy that I automatically lubed myself up. Lovely. I can handle flying but struggle with feeling boxed in, so I just shut my eyes and dozed for the two hours it takes to travel from Edinburgh to Reykjavik. Being the caring sort I also kept hold of the iPad just in case, but it did mean poor Paul had nothing to do other than gaze at the cornflakes of dandruff gently falling off the scalp of the slumbering mass in front. I'm a sod, I know.

Oh, there was a moment of interest when the overhead cabin across from us starting leaking something at quite an alarming rate, necessitating the decampment of the passenger immediately below the leak into the only spare seat available on the plane. Seems sensible? No. The woman (who was somewhat...large) next to the vacant seat kicked up such a stink that the stewardess had kick up a stink in return, and a veritable hiss-off occurred – too much make-up vs too much circumference. How selfish can you be, though, to make someone sit under a dripping leak for two hours? I feel guilty just making Paul sleep in the cuddle puddle after sex. Don't think us gays have a wet patch? You're wrong, though ours is mainly lube to be fair. Still, makes getting up for an early-morning piss that much easier when you can just slide to the bathroom like Fred in the

Flintstone's opening credits.

Also, I'm no expert on aircraft, despite all my many hours of sitting slackjawed in front of Air Crash Investigation watching reconstructions of plane crashes brought to vivid life via the graphics card of a Nintendo 64, but is a major leak not worrisome? Surely water sloshing around amongst the electrics is a VERY BAD THING. The stewardess opened the locker, moved around a couple of the many bags crammed in there then decreed the leak to be a mystery. A mystery! That helped my anxiety – I had visions of it being hydraulic fluid or jet fuel and us being mere moments away from landing via someone's front room on the Shetland Isles. I still don't like getting up for a piss on the plane because I'm worried I'll upset the balance. A rational mind I do not have. We landed safely, obviously, and the leak was plugged by about 1000 blue paper towels. Keep it classy, Easyjet.

Let's be fair, actually – easyJet continue to be fantastic to fly with. I have no problems with a company that will fly me around Europe for less money than I pay for my weekly parking ticket in Newcastle. Everyone from their check-in staff to the onboard team always seem to be smiling, and as a nervous passenger, that really helps. Their planes are comfy, although I noted with alarm that I wasn't too far off needing a seatbelt extension. Not that there's any shame in that, but I'd sooner be strapped onto the roof and flown that way than ask across a crowded cabin for a bungee-cord sized seatbelt. I'm shy!

We touched down into Keflavík Airport in the early evening and, yes, it was cold. Bloody cold – minus one or two degrees. The airport is small as it only serves a few flights a day in winter, and we were through security and bag-drop in no time. You know the drill by now – I had to wait ten minutes whilst Paul dashed into a toilet and released his Christmas log. Any airport, any time. I think the air pressure changes associated with flying does something to his bowels – I can genuinely count the seconds from getting our bag off the conveyor to Paul turning to me with an ashen face clutching his stomach and bemoaning that he needs to go for a crap. Some people tie fancy socks to their suitcase or have a favourite towel to take on holiday as tradition – my holiday tradition is looking furiously at the closed door of a gents' toilet.

As Keflavík Airport is around thirty miles from the centre of Reykjavik, you'll need to take a bus or hire a car. I didn't fancy Princess Diana-ing my way through the icy roads, so we opted for the bus. It's all terribly simple and you don't need to book in advance, rather just bustle your way to the ticket office, purchase a ticket and step aboard the idling bus, which then takes you to your hotel. It's all exceptionally civilised. One of the many good things about Iceland is that it doesn't seem to attract the SKOL-ashtray-and-red-shoulders brigade, so you're not stuck on a bus hearing fifty different English accents bellow about lager and tits for an hour. Good.

We were dropped off at the Grand Hotel first, and as it was pitch-black outside, we decided to stay in the room to drain our swollen feet and order room service. I tried to order something Icelandic but the closest we could see was a SKYR cheesecake. Oh imagine the pains. I did my usual hotel trick of hiding in the bathroom when they bring all the trays of food in so that Paul looks like a giant fatty, though I was fairly restrained this time – I didn't make my usual 'straining' noises from behind the door.

Stuffed full of food and tired from all the sitting down, we were off to sleep in no time, accompanied by the only English channel we could find – Sky News. Under normal circumstances I wouldn't watch Sky News if a nuclear bomb was stuck up my arse and they were telling me how to defuse it, but you know, needs must.

twochubbycubs go to Iceland: part two

We awoke the next day nice and early – not out of any special keenness to make the most of the day...somehow, that never occurs to us, but rather because the breakfast buffet was open and we didn't want to miss a single bloody crumb. We're classy Brits, what can I say? I barely had enough time to do something about my Germaine Greer bedhair and have my morning piss before Paul was pushing me into the lift and down into the lobby. We had a very pleasant surprise with the lady who ushered us through to the breakfast area, who, as I detected immediately underneath her posh 'how do you do' voice, was a fellow Geordie! You can always tell – the strangulated vowels and elongated syllables, the eight bottles of Dog clinking in her handbag, the fact that as soon as both our façades were dropped we were 'NAAA NO MAN'-ing and 'DIVVENT'ing away like the poshest remake of Auf Wiedersehen, Pet ever. Honestly, I wouldn't have been surprised if Denise Welch herself had come tumbling down the stairs with her knickers around her ankles, 'icing sugar' on her nose shouting on about cheap bathrooms and kitchen deals. Anyway, we stopped and had a pleasant chat about Iceland and then were allowed through.

Well, how lovely. Everything you could possibly want, and more, all steaming hot and plentiful. Good work, Grand Hotel. We immediately developed Buffet Anxiety

– what to have, how much to slop onto a plate before people took us to one side for an intervention, where the hell the full fat milk was because god-damn-it I'm on holiday and I'm sick to death of eating my thimble of Puffed fucking Wheat with what looks and tastes exactly like Tesco Everyday Value White Emulsion. There was a wee glass of oil with a label in Icelandic (the Icelandic language is beautiful, but written down, it looks rather like how you'd spell out the noise the bath makes when it's draining the last of the water). I filled up a tiny portion and took it to Paul as olive oil for his bread and cheeses. It was cod liver oil. He wasn't happy, not least because he spat it out like it was curdled cum. Mahaha – that would be the second time I'd managed to get him to eat something awful, with my minor victory of getting him to eat a dog chew in the car on the drive up to Edinburgh only a day or so ago. I told him it was beef jerky. He finished it mind, so it can't have been that bad, and it's reassuring to know that if times get tight, I can put him on Pedigree Chum and crack on. Poor Paul. Let me say though – normally the things I do put in his mouth don't taste like cod liver oil or dog food. Well, maybe cod liver. If it's a warm day.

After breakfast, we nipped back to the room to review our options. We were booked on a bus tour later that day (the glamour!) but the morning was ours. It doesn't get light until around 11am in December, but that suits us. Darkness flatters our faces. We spotted that the famous Iceland Phallological Museum was only a thirty-minute walk from the hotel, so we decided to set out in search of all that knob. The website stated they opened at 10am so we had plenty of time to dawdle. One of our main concerns with Iceland is that we'd fall over on the ice and crack open our heads or split our trousers, so Paul had been dispatched a few days before to buy some suitable boots. I had my Dr Martens, so of course, I was fine – and effortlessly stylish.

He came back with a pair of boots that looked exactly like something an old lady would wear to bingo so she didn't tumble over outside when she was having a fag. They were awful. Square, boxy, 110% polyester. But he loved them. They worked, mind, though if you're worrying about falling over on the ice, don't be. The footpaths and roads are exceptionally well-gritted and Paul only went arse-over-tit once, right into a puddle. Which was hilarious.

Central Reykjavík is a doddle to get around on foot, with long straight roads and well-marked streets, and we arrived at the Knob Museum (sorry, my wrists hurt and phallological is just too much) just as it was supposed to open, hanging back for a few minutes because well, it doesn't do to look too keen for a museum about knobs to open. We waited nearby…waited…waited…no. No, turns out it wasn't going to open that day because the owner needed a rest, presumably from cramming willies into glass jars and making carriers bags from foreskins (what a great idea though – if you rubbed them just right, they'd turn into bin liners!) We went back to the hotel.

On our way back, I remembered that we had asked for a deluxe room, and that our current room, although perfectly serviceable, didn't quite marry up with the word deluxe. It was very standard. The view we were afforded was of the service entrance around the back and plus, we were only three floors up. This hotel had many more floors than that! I pitched up to the front desk and enquired whether, because see it's our honeymoon (cough), we could have a nicer room. Good old monobrow Aðalsteinunn behind the counter was having none of it and icily told us that we'd 'already been upgraded'. I resisted the urge to ask whether we were originally going to be bedding down on a soiled mattress under the lifts, and pushed on politely. She crumpled a little and then offered us a room upgrade for a mere £100. Meh, fair enough. At this point I could see Paul's ashen face and knew that his breakfast was already knocking on the escape hatch, and time was tight. I handed over my card, she disappeared for roughly five days, and came back with a new key for a room on the 10th floor. Marvellous! We rushed up, Paul left a goodbye skidder in the toilet only to find there wasn't a brush to clean it away with, and off we went to our new room.

Well, let me tell you this – had I not physically pressed the button in the lift for a new floor, I would have bet the house that we were in the same room. Not a thing was different, bar the toilet pan no longer looking like the starting grid at Brand's Hatch. Yes, they'd moved us up a few floors, but no difference to the room. BAH. We did, however, have a much nicer view.

I didn't dare go down and ask for another room in case housekeeping had visited our previous room and reported us, so we did what all young, happy couples do on holiday and had a quick nap. Our bus for the Golden Circle tour was due for 12.15, so we had plenty of time.

The way most tours work in Iceland is simple – you book them in advance either online or through your hotel, and a small shuttle bus will come and pick you up from the hotel and take you to the bus depot, where you will board a waiting coach. It works brilliantly. We used Grey Line for all of our excursions and they were terrific. The Golden Circle tour (well, the small one) encompasses a visit to Thingvellir National Park, the Strokkur geyser and Gulfross waterfall. All very pleasant. We were pushed out of the way whilst boarding the coach by some frankly gargantuan American lady who was inadvisably wearing leggings and showing everyone her business, but aside from that it was all terribly civilised. The tour guide, Lorenzo (a good strong Icelandic name right there), gave an interesting commentary on Iceland between the three places and it was one of the very few occasions where I've been on a bus and not immediately started snoring in the ear of the person next to me. You do have to wear your seatbelt, mind – it's the law, even if, as in my case, it pushes up your coat to give you the appearance of having a colossal rack. There's not much point in me waxing lyrical about how beautiful Iceland is – you really need to see it for yourself, but know that it is so alien and snow-covered and different that it really will take your breath away.

We stopped here for around half an hour to allow everyone to take pictures and gaze at the scenery. Paul and I managed to walk into around ten different family photos so that's not a bad average – I always try to pull a face in the vain hope I'll end up going viral on a South Korean You've Been Framed but it hasn't happened yet. The main attraction, other than the view, is the giant crack (story of my life) where the tectonic plates are pulling apart. Paul and I walked down a fair way before realising that we'd need to walk back and endure the shame of gasping and spluttering our way onto the bus. We stopped in the gift shop to buy a ridiculously awful teddy bear and some more cocoa.

The bus trundled on to Strokkur geyser, which is one of Iceland's most visited hotspots. Literally. Essentially a bubbling pool most of the time, it'll suddenly go off, spurting up to 40m into the air with an almighty splash. It's great fun, until you remember the water is superheated and, because it contains so much sulphur, smells like death. Seriously, it's one of the few tourist places I've ever been to where I can fart with gay abandon (is there any other kind) and actually improve the smell of the place. We took a video, as you'd expect, but it's really just two minutes of me going 'I reckon it's going to blow, it's gonna blow, any second now...' followed by Paul going 'FUCK ME IT'S AWAY' at the top of his voice. It's like our videos on xtube, really, only you don't need to pay the Amateurs fee.

After we'd all have a good gawp and made sure to spend a billion trillion krona on a Kitkat, hot chocolate and surly attitude from the small onsite restaurant, we were back on the bus and heading into the dusk to Gulfross waterfall. Lorenzo kept us informed as to how Iceland grows vegetables (in greenhouses), warm their houses (heat from the ground) and er, how much unemployment benefit you get. It all sounds like a utopia. The roads were very icy in places, with the bus slewing around at the back, but it all felt very safe, albeit the loud look-at-me chuntering from the aforementioned American lady got a little grating. We arrived at Gulfross around an hour later.

CATASTROPHE. The bus parks about 500m away from the viewing platform, but that 500m is down what felt like 499m of rickety, wooden stairs with no room to go side by side. Now as fat blokes, stairs are fine when you're going down them, although they did creak and bend alarmingly underfoot, but we knew that once we were down there, we'd need to climb back up. Agony.

We braved it anyway and it was absolutely bloody beautiful. Again, photos can't really do it justice – it was just getting dark and this colossal waterfall is cascading busily just in front of you, cutting its way through the Earth.

We did spot an opportunity for mischief and to get our own back on the brash, burly American lady who had pushed us out of the way at the beginning, however. See, she had come down behind us and we knew she would be just as weary going up the stairs as we were. So, naturally, we waited until she had seen that there was no-one else on the stairs going up and could therefore make her very slow ascent. She began, and we immediately started up behind her, meaning she had to do it all in one without stopping. The fact that her heavy, laboured breathing masked our own was a bonus, and let me tell you, climbing behind this lady and looking up to see her lycra-clad gammon flaps not a moment away from your face sure as hell makes you concentrate on looking down and finding your footing. We all made it, though, and how we chuckled to ourselves as she was taken away on oxygen.

The tour finished with everyone dozing lightly on the bus as it made its way back to the capital, and we were back at the hotel for around 7pm. We decided, given our feet looked like slabs of corned beef from all the walking, to have a gin and tonic in the bar downstairs and rest a little, given it was "Happy Hour".

I think they need to look carefully at their definition of Happy. The barman was obnoxious and disinterested. We asked him what he'd recommend and he replied by telling us what he drinks when he's out for 'real fun' as opposed to 'hotel fun', but in an intensely condescending fashion. I'm always wary of people who have to big themselves up like that – I rather got the impression he'd be home away to bed with a hot Vimto and a cold wank. Nevertheless, we ordered two gin and tonics and my recollection is £36. £36! I hadn't asked for a bottomless glass! It was nice gin, yes, but I'm fairly sure it was just Bombay Sapphire. Of course I couldn't lose face so we paid up without comment, but fuck me, never again. For the rest of the holiday our interaction with the dour barman was limited to us trying to figure out who he looked like, until Paul got it in one with 'Tyrone from Coronation Street after receiving a poor health diagnosis'. Mahaha. We planned to go out in the evening but once we were back in the room, we were out like a light and didn't wake up again until 1am. Thank god for room service!

twochubbycubs go to Iceland: part three

Tired from yesterday's day of looking into cracks, dealing with spurting geysers and admiring a foamy gush, we decided to spend the day mincing about in Reykjavik, seeing the sights, buying tat. As you do. We filled up on an early breakfast and walked the thirty or so minutes along the seafront into the town centre. It feels so peculiar to be shopping and walking around with everyone at 10am, with the sky still inky black and the very first fingers of sunlight just poking through. We could cheerfully live there – we don't need the light – already got arthritis, might as well go for rickets and get the full-house. We stopped (shamefully) for a coffee in Dunkin' Donuts. I know, I know, eat local, blah blah, but in our defence they had a gorgeous selection of donuts and we wanted to nick their Wi-Fi. The hotel Wi-Fi was crap – almost like being back in 2000 and trying to watch porn on a dial-up modem. That was an awful experience, let me tell you – by the time I'd typed and sent my A/S/L I'd had a birthday and grown pubes. We decided on a rough schedule of the National Museum, the church, shops and then Escape the Room. After finishing our coffee, tutting at children and other tourists, we were on our way.

We walked through the parks and headed up to the National Museum of Iceland, full of vim and joy and wonder from the beautiful snow-filled parks and the frozen lake, pausing only briefly to try and find a toilet. There were signs everywhere but no visible toilet block – presumably because, if Iceland was anything like England, as soon as you enclose three toilets in concrete and asbestos, you'll have a seedy man with a hand-crank drilling a glory hole and putting his name on the wall. After much looking, we eventually found one of those tiny automatic toilets that look like a TARDIS, with the spinning door and scary buttons. Unlike England, you didn't need to pay 20p for the privilege of pissing, and Paul was soon merrily enclosed in this tiny metal tube having a wee. He didn't bank on me hiding around the back and screaming in his face as he emerged, but well, we like to keep things fresh. You'll see these all over Reykjavik. We were at the museum in no time at all.

Well, let me just say this – for all that we heard that Icelandic folk were friendly, welcoming and pleasant (and, to be fair, they were for the most part), every last member of staff in the museum had a face like they'd seen their arse and didn't like the colour of it. Clearly smiling and pleasantries were off the menu. I've never felt such guilt for asking for a bloody welcome leaflet.

I have a bit of a love/hate thing with museums. See I want to be one of those people in coats that smell of eggs that will stand and ...hmmm and ...*oh I see* over every exhibit, but try as I might, I just don't have the attention span. It was all so very dry and boring for a country forged from fire and ice. I was captivated by the sight of some hipster twatknacker doing warm-up exercises in the 'Vikings' section. Why? He was making sure all eyes were on him as his silly little man-bun bobbed up and down. The only time I want to see a man-bun bobbing around if it's perched atop a man drowning in a turbulent sea.

We did happen across a mildly interesting exhibition on women in the workplace, which afforded us the chance to titter at some exposed breasts and make blue remarks, but that was it. There was an old style Bakelite phone sitting on a plinth – Paul picked it up, looked grave and then shouted 'NO DEAL', much to the obvious hatred of the stern looking curator. We make our own fun, at least. We took a moment to look around the gift shop but again, the staff seemed so unwelcoming that we put down the little bottle of pink rock salt that we were going to buy and hastened on our way. You'd think judging by her pinched face and obvious expression of blistering hatred that she'd mined the salt herself using her teeth.

In Reykjavik, your eyes are always drawn to a church high up on the hill called Hallgrímskirkja, and despite misgivings about how steep the hill was vs how fat our English little bodies were, we set out to have an explore and a look. Perhaps it was the promise of an exceptionally large organ that enticed us. Forty minutes and much swearing later, we arrived, took the obligatory photos, marvelled at the fact that this church smelled exactly like an English church (foist, farts and cabbage soup) and had a reverent look around.

It was wonderful, it really was. I'm not a religious person – I'm not going down on my knees unless it's to pick up change, give a blowjob or a bizarre combination of the two – but even I was captivated. The lighting, the architecture, the ten million Chinese girls shrieking into their hands and milling around – all wonderful. It was prayer time, so everyone was head-bowed and silent, bar for the vicar who somewhat ruined the placidity by bellowing urgently into his phone from high in the eves. He could have been giving a sermon, I suppose, though it rather sounded like he'd been stabbed in the throat and was calling urgently for help.

We waited until most of the tourists had filtered back out before walking up to the altar. I noticed that neither of us had burst into flames for our wicked sodomising ways, leaving me comfortable enough to inch forward to look at the ornate work on the lectern. I'd barely taken in a detail when a tiny mobile phone on a stick crossed my vision, close enough to part my eyebrows. Well, honestly. A tourist with a selfie stick. I find them pointless at the best of times – why would you go on holiday just to take a photo of your face gazing blankly into middle distance whilst blocking out anything pretty? That happens to me every time I look in the mirror to shave. That, and tears of sadness.

Naturally, Paul and I were so aghast that we spent the next fifteen minutes subtly following this poor lady around the church, making sure we were just in the background of all her shots, grimacing and gurning away. She eventually caught on when I tripped over the edge of a pew in my haste to get the top of my head poking into her shot of the font and her face. We made a sharp exit. I like to think we'll be on a Facebook page far away – the two fat menaces of Iceland.

As we left, we noticed a lift that we'd missed in our haste to get inside – a lift which took you right to the top of the church tower (and that's high – the church being the sixth tallest structure in Iceland). Perfect! After paying a small charge to keep the church going, we were in the lift and away, with only a momentary and startling stop halfway up, when the lift stopped and the doors opened on a solid brick wall. I've seen Bad Girls, I know this is how it ends, but before I'd had chance to scratch 'FENNER' into the bricks the lift rattled away and we were at the top.

Taking photos is actually quite difficult, as the little openings which provide the view have bars across them (presumably to stop you hurling yourself out through the shame of ruining someone's photos), meaning you have to undertake a nail-biting manoeuvre of holding your phone in your hands over a 70m drop. I get the jitters stirring my tea, so seeing Paul waving his phone around had my arse nipping. Mind, not as much as the fact that, completely and utterly oblivious to where I was, I took a moment for quiet reflection and leant against the central column, only to have my eardrums blown through my skull by the giant bell no more than 3ft above my head ringing in 2pm. I said an exceptionally non-church friendly word at the top of my voice, removed my trousers from my sphincter and, somewhat dazed, went to find Paul, who somehow *hadn't* managed to either drop his phone or shit himself. Truly, a miracle. Cheers Big G.

The next couple of hours were spent looking around the many, many stores that fill Reykjavik's main shopping streets, though I'll say this right now – if I never see another stuffed fucking puffin again I'll be happy. Or a t-shirt that suggested fat people were great because they can't outrun polar bears (yeah, but we can eat them, so you overlooked that one). We bought two figurines for the games room and, thanks to Paul leaving my iPad chargers in the old room and the maid being dishonest enough to keep it, a new charger from a knock-off Apple shop where again, we were met with abysmal customer service – waiting almost ten minutes for the bespectacled little spelk to finish his conversation and address the only customers for miles. Listen, don't take my moaning as evidence that the Icelandic are a frosty (ha-de-ha) bunch, they're not – aside from the odd knobhead, everyone was charming.

We partook in a couple of traditional 'street food' items

which were just bloody amazing – fries at Reykjavik Chips and a hotdog from Bæjarins Beztu Pylsur. The fries place we happened across just off the main shopping street and it was amazing, even though it was just fries and Béarnaise sauce washed down with beer. You get the fries piping hot in a paper cone with sauce dribbled all over them, and you take a seat at a tiny table with a hole drilled in to hold your cone, all served with beer. Something so simple but done right. The hotdog was a weird one – it really was just a bog-standard hotdog – delicious, but I couldn't understand the fanfare bar the fact that the stand had apparently been there since time immemorial. Perhaps it was the fact that the guy serving officially had Dreamboat status – not our type, heavens no, but he had one of those faces that moisten knickers just with a glance. Bastard.

Once we were full and our wallets empty, we decided it was either time to Escape the Room or go back to the hotel for a Fat Nap. After a bit of deliberation, we decided our time would be best spent walking along to Reykjavik's version of 'Escape the Room', where you're locked in a room by a sinister figure and told you will never escape. I believe Josef Fritzl developed the prototype. After a short but arresting diversion via the offices of the Chinese Embassy, we arrived. The woman in charge was wonderful – full of good cheer and welcoming bonhomie. We were given a choice between prison, curing cancer or escaping the clutches of an evil abductees. Naturally, we chose prison. The rules were explained – no breaking things, no wresting lights from the ceiling or sockets from the wall, no oil fires – and then we were led into the room.

At this point, the lady in charge told us to get into character and act like we were in prison. Paul look suitably chagrined whilst I immediately skittered a bar of soap along the floor and bent over with a 'what **AM** I like' leer. What can I say, I'm like Pavlov's dog. Once I'd straightened myself up, tucked my trouser pocket back in and scrubbed off the 'WING BITCH' tattoo from my neck, we were on our way.

I **can** tell you that we escaped, but it was close, with only a few minutes left on the clock. Paul derailed us immediately by finding a key, deciding it wasn't relevant and putting it away, not realising it was a crucial part of the first clue. We had been given a phone so we can text our 'captor' if we got stuck – we only used it three times, and one of those was Paul accidentally ringing her with his buttocks. To be fair, she probably thought the sound of his cheeks slapping together and the odd, low, rasping fart was just his attempt at speaking Icelandic.

After emerging victorious, we were made to stand for a photo with some 'AREN'T WE CLEVER' signs – we didn't buy them because of course, we look awful. We're not the worst looking people in the world but we just can't get a good photo together. Between my chins spilling down my chest like an armadillo's back and Paul's barely-tuned in eyes, we're a mess. If we had children, they'd come out looking like Hoggle from Labyrinth viewed through the bottom of a pint glass. Ah well. She did at least have the good grace when taking the photo not to back away too far to get all of our bulk in.

Tuckered out, we headed back to the hotel, dispensed with all our flimflam and ate a very passable meal in the hotel restaurant. Dangerously, we ordered drinks and put them on our room bill rather than paying for it upfront, which made for quite the unpleasant surprise at the end of the trip. REMEMBER: ICELAND = EXPENSIVE.

We slept like logs that night.

twochubbycubs go to Iceland: part four

I wish I could tell you that we spent the day doing all sorts of thrilling things, but instead, we just mooched around the city, taking our time with food and nonsense. Listen, people who say they go on holiday and proceed to tell you they spent every waking moment doing activities, undertaking the local customs and enjoying the national food is an outright fibber. Sometimes you need to take it slowly, like a fibre-packed jobbie.

Having enjoyed 'Escaping the Room' once, we went back and tried the other two scenarios available – curing cancer and escaping a creepy haunted bedroom. I've never cured cancer, so of course we failed on that one, but we did manage to escape the bedroom, after somewhat embarrassing ourselves...

We walked from the hotel up to Reykjavik's main shopping centre, Kringlan, partly because it was within stumbling distance and also because I needed to buy the vilest sweets I could find for the office. Not because I hate the people I work with, you understand, but simply because nothing says 'GLAD TO BE BACK, LOL' like salted liquorice balls that look, taste and smell like something you'd shovel out of a hamster cage.

Perhaps I'm spoiled by having the Metrocentre so nearby (where retail goes to die), but it really wasn't worth the trip. Perhaps due to the fact it's an island, the 'stock' of stuff to buy seems to be very similar wherever you go. Once you've smiled politely at a stack of neon pigs or a collection of ashtrays, you've done your bit. We did find a shop called Minja which tickled us pink, though neither of us really fancied going in. We looked at it hard, but despite the many people entering it, we sloped off.

More interesting was the fact that Florence and Fred from Tesco seems to be rather big, where it is sold as a high-end range in a department store rather than the shameful secret in amongst the crisps and the beetroot faces as is the case over here. They even had shirts in our sizes, which was surprising given we normally have to buy our shirts from garden centres, but the fact they wanted the equivalent of £55 for a shirt I can buy (and hide under my groceries) for a tenner at home was too much to bear #tightarsegeordie (ah my former gaydar name).

After a bite to eat where they gave me a sandwich and took half of my salary as payment, we were on our way back to the hotel and onto grander things – a Northern Lights bus-tour. The sky didn't look promising – thick cloud and low visibility. I was reminded of the air directly above Paul's mother's chair when she starts on her knockoff Rothmans. The bus driver said we should give a try anyway, so on we went to a very comfortable coach accompanied by around fifteen or so other folks.

We had chosen the deluxe tour, meaning we were to

receive snacks, hot chocolate, a footrub and a personal apology from Jesus if the Northern Lights didn't appear. Sadly, we hit an immediate problem. See, on our tour a couple of days earlier, there had been a somewhat overbearing woman – the double of that wailing banshee from Everything But The Girl – who sat near us with her mother, and every time we stopped anywhere she'd drift over and attempt to make conversation.

Listen, I've got time for anyone, I really have, but deep down, I'm incredibly antisocial. My face screams talk to me; my mind is saying please die. Perhaps I exaggerate. Anyway, every single sentence she said was a really poor joke – it was like making polite conversation with a box of crackers – and then she did this really weird, far too familiar 'lean' into our personal space, perhaps to check the volume of our forced laughter.

And, of course, here she was again. Luckily, we had had the wherewithal to dump our bags on the seat in front of us, so she sat in front of those – champion, no talking needed. No, but every single quip, gag, remark or gasp that the chap commentating the tour made was met with her turning around and pushing her face in-between the two seats to see if we were laughing. We started off with the polite smile and a 'can he say that' shake of the head, but we weren't even out of Reykjavik before that had downgraded into a 'stare straight ahead, don't even acknowledge her', the type of stance you might take if you'd stumbled across a man wanking in a phonebox.

Perhaps this comes across as mean, it really wasn't meant to, but I stopped babysitting in my teens, I didn't need it on my holiday. She eventually got the message and stopped turning around, and we were able to concentrate on the fact the coach was busy barrelling down a twisty, turny road in the snow and a very dramatic snow-storm. Excellent driving, absolutely, but I'm not going to claim my arse wasn't busy unstitching the seat fabric through fear.

After an hour, we stopped off at this little restaurant in the middle of nowhere and were told that we'd be the first people to experience their new attraction, a quick movie about the aurora borealis. Bemused, we were shepherded into the arena where they usually put a live-action horse stunt show on and asked to take our seats – all twenty of us, in this little area that probably held 1,000.

The movie started, projected onto the back wall. And just didn't finish. I love the Northern Lights as much as anyone, honestly, but it's hard to maintain a rictus throughout half an hour of stolen footage from YouTube accompanied by Icelandic Enya caterwauling away in the background like she's shitting out a pine-cone. I'm not exaggerating when I tell you it was almost twenty minutes too long, and every time the screen went black and we thought it was finished, up it would start again, leading to a few more taxing minutes of footage of a wispy green cloud. It wouldn't have been too bad if we had been sitting in proper seats instead of on long wooden boards, at least then we would have been comfortable, but no. It's a bad job when someone has to turn you to prevent pressure sores halfway through.

We eventually stumbled back to the coach and were on our way into the night. The commentator mentioned that there had been a sighting of the lights on the other coastline, so we were to head there. Absolute fair play to the tour company, they weren't going to give up – and I had free Wi-Fi and a fully charged phone to keep me occupied. Paul had gone to sleep almost the second his seatbelt clicked on. There wasn't much to see out of the window – a black cloudy sky above a bleak desolate landscape outside, much like driving through Southend during the day.

After another hour or two, the bus slid into a tiny village and attempted to reverse down a very steep, ice-covered gradient to our restaurant. That was soon stopped, and we were told we had to walk / slide down ourselves. We had been promised a meal to fill our bellies so naturally Paul and I were the first ones off the bus, sliding down the hill to certain satisfaction. Sadly, our weird friend was immediately behind us, and of course, naturally, without any doubt, sat at our table with her mother.

What followed was two things – almost an hour of

unbearably awkward, strained conversation, and something that was definitely not a filling meal. The waiter came down to take our order, insofar as he drifted down, put some bread on our table and told us we were having soup. No choice. Meh, I don't mind soup, and well, it was a restaurant, so how wrong could it go?

Very wrong. The vegetable soup looked like something our cat sicked up when we had her fanny butchered by the vet. It had the consistency (and taste) of one instant tomato soup sachet, divided between twenty. I poked around with a spoon to see if I could find anything to tax my teeth with and happened across one tiny cube of swede. Naturally, Bus-Friend piped up to express her jealousy that I'd at least found some vegetables HA-HA-HA and how I'd need ROLLING BACK UP THE HILL I'M THAT FULL HO-HO-HO. Being the gentleman, I resisted the urge to put her and her Connie Clickit haircut into her tomato water, and grimaced on. I expected dessert, a mint, hell, they could have spread some jam on the tablecloth and I would have gobbled it up, but no, that was it.

I will admit to something terrible, though. And this is terrible, mind, so please don't think any worse of me after reading. Before we all decamped to the bus, we all got a chance to use the restaurant's facilities. Naturally, there was only one tiny cubicle, and Paul and I were 9th and 10th in the queue respectively. There was an exceptionally posh lady behind me. Everyone went in and did their business and by the time I went in, there was piddle all over the seat and floor, and, putting paid to my plan for a quick poo, no loo roll to be seen.

Again, ever the gentleman, I didn't want the lady behind me to think I'd pissed on the floor and seat, so I grabbed a little tiny grey towel that was sitting near the sink to mop it all up with. I hadn't factored in that the water on the floor wasn't piss but rather, piss mixed with the melted snow from so many shoes, and as soon as I used the cloth, it was covered in brown streaks and yellow stains on one side. Was there a bin? Of COURSE not.

So, I did the only thing I could do, finished my piss and very gingerly folded the towel back up in such a way to hide the heavily streaked and piss-soaked side. And popped it back on the little radiator. There was literally nowhere else to put it other than down the toilet and well, I'm not a bastard, I didn't want to block their toilet, not least because they'd have nothing to serve for dinner to the next unfortunate bastards who rocked up on the coach. I pity the poor madam who went to dab her lipstick or wash her face with that towel and got a load of pissy flannel in her face. I'm sorry, I really am. I'm not a monster.

I did cackle a tiny bit; I'm not going to lie.

With our hunger unsatisfied and our tummies rumbling, we headed back to the coach, drove on a bit and stopped in the middle of nowhere in a deserted carpark. Listen, I've been here enough times to know what was happening, but before I'd even had a chance to flash the reading light off and on and put my lip-balm on, we were off again, the driver sadly telling us there would be no chance of seeing the lights at this location. No, we needed to get higher.

I was all for that, though it's been a while since I've skinned up anything more exciting than a social cigarette for a co-worker, but no, he meant going higher into the mountains. Bearing in mind it was pitch black, icy and knocking on past 10pm at this point, everyone reacted in quite a subdued manner. Bus-friend let out such a huge sigh that Paul and I deliberately voiced loudly our desire to go on. Hell, you're only on holiday once. Or four times a year, in our case. On we went.

The next stop, knocking on at around midnight, was another carpark in the middle of nowhere. We got out, braced ourselves against the absolutely bitter and very strong wind, looked hopefully at the sky, but sadly, the clouds never quite parted. I did see a faint green ethereal glow in the distance, but it turned out to be the driver's e-cigarette. The commentator opened up the side of the bus and, god bless him, pulled out the world's flimsiest trestle table and a giant urn of hot water, announcing hot drinks were now available.

Crikey, what a comedy of errors. The wind was so strong that whatever he picked up, be it a paper cup, a sachet of whatever the Icelandic for Options is or the sugar, it either blew out of his hands or he spilt it. We watched from a distance before approaching. For giggles, I asked for a grande mocha Frappuccino with no cream, mint syrup and could he use soya, I'm lacto-tolerant. He looked like he was about to stick me in the tea-urn so I immediately gave him a gracious 'BRITS ABROAD EH' face and got back on the bus. Hmm. Paul eventually brought me a coffee and tutted at me.

Once everyone was on board and had been treated for their second-degree burns, it seemed inevitable that they'd call it a night...but no – one more roll of the dice. He knew a church with excellent viewing possibilities...on a clear night. I looked out of the window into the abyss and dozed for an hour, having drained my battery streaming fail videos on YouTube.

This is the bit where I tell you the bus pulled up, we got out and saw the best god-damn Northern Lights we'd ever seen.

Nope.

But we DID see them, for almost five minutes, albeit through the faint wisps of clouds barrelling all over. It was like God, noticing our bus parked outside of the church (and er, if he existed), parted the clouds as best he could to make our almost seven-hour journey worth it. It was. Not much can be said about the lights that you can't imagine yourself, other than what will be obvious to you but didn't occur to me until I saw them myself. They're huge, and they're silent. I was expecting a whoosh or a flutter, but nothing, although the wind would have covered anything. You can't just look at them because they're all around you, above you, and they're magical. Worth seven hours on the bus with a cup of watery coffee and some instant soup? Yep. Worth dealing with a socially awkward lady? Yep. Recommended? Wholeheartedly. It's something to tick off the list, for sure.

Once the clouds covered them up again, I went for a quick piss around the side of the bus. Sadly, thanks to the wind, it was like that moment in Apollo 13 where he vents his piss into outer space in a giant cloud. I'm a classy guy, what can I say.

The bus took us back to the hotel, with both Paul and I succumbing to the sweet caress of sleep on the journey home, which in turn meant no-one else would get a moment of rest thanks to the cacophonous snoring coming from the back. I'm surprised the driver didn't pull over to see if he had a reindeer stuck under his tyres. We were back at the hotel for around 2.30am and straight to bed.

Listen – this might have come across as an awful experience, but it wasn't, it was hilarious, and nothing but top marks to the tour company for so much effort in getting us to see the lights. Yes, the food was pap and the movie abysmal, but we'd do it all over again.

There's something genuinely romantic and exciting about chugging through the darkness in the hope of seeing something so wonderful!

twochubbycubs go to Iceland: part five

Our trip to The Blue Lagoon, then. The Blue Lagoon is possibly one of Iceland's most recognisable places – a large man-made pool created from the water output from the nearby geothermal power plant. They take super-hot water from the ground, spin a few turbines with it and then let the rest pour into the lagoon, keeping it toasty warm. I admit I was surprised – I thought it was a natural pool thanks to all the tasteful photography and talk of 'lagoon', but then I suppose 'come and have a swim in the run-off water from our power plant' doesn't sound quite so grand. I mean, I don't worry about my fertility at the best of times, but I do like to know my *snake tears* could still do what they are supposed to do if the situation required it. Luckily, obviously, it's not radioactive. They also completely replace the water every two days, meaning that even if someone sharts in the far corner of the pool, you're unlikely to be bothered by it.

Let me start by saying that this quick tale will be bookended by two bus-woe stories, both equally vexing, but only one where Paul and I redeemed British folk for all the world.

We booked our trip well in advance and, yet again, were picked up at the hotel by a minibus and then shepherded to an idling coach early in the morning. This is pretty much the start of every single tour you'll ever do in Iceland by all accounts. If you're a fan of looking hopefully at the horizon, you'll be in your element here. The buses are clean, comfortable and have free Wi-Fi, which is handy if the endless beauty of Iceland holds no appeal for you and you've got Candy Crush to dribble over.

Like class swots, we took our seats at the front of the coach, only to have the two biggest, boring, most vacuous young ladies sit immediately behind us. They were lawyers from London and by god did you know about it by the time the bus had climbed into third gear. Every word was strained like they were running out of air, every sentence pronounced so loudly that I could have stayed in the hotel and still heard all about her stupid landlord who wouldn't let Gareth (Guuur-*raaaaaath*) stay over. Everyone else feigned sleep – it was 8am after all – but no, this pair of braying donkeys kept up their schtick all the way to the Lagoon, a good forty-five minutes away. Paul and I were terribly British about the whole thing – coughing, giving side-eye, sighing like the oxygen on the bus was running out, but there was no stopping them. Never have I thought about crashing off a mountain road into an abyss with such longing.

The bus drops you off seemingly in the middle of nowhere (actually, a lava field in Grindavík – not active lava I needlessly add – there's nothing especially relaxing about third degree burns), with a tiny visitor centre and a rock exclaiming that you've arrived.

There's very little to indicate that you need to walk further on, but, despite being spherical, we bravely continued, not letting the 400m walk to the entrance faze us. Heroes the both of us. We had booked our tickets in advance online and I'd heartily recommend you do the same – the queue, even at that time in the morning – was through the door. We chose the 'Premium' ticket online, which allows you to queue jump and gets you a free drink within the Lagoon. It's worth it for not having to wait, plus you're given a pair of slippers and a robe. Sadly, the Body Beautiful behind the counter looked at me and handed me an XL robe with a *very* 'that won't fit' look. **It was Paul in the Austrian mine all over again.** For the record, the XL robe fitted *perfectly*, although it did say 'FOR RENT ONLY' in big letters on it. That took me back to my college days, I can tell you. You're also given a wristband (mine said **HERALD OF FREE ENTERPRISE** on it) (no it didn't) which acts as both your key for the locker and a card of sorts for any drinks or food you purchase. Handy. On we trotted.

Now, let me cover something off – you absolutely do need to change and shower with other people. In order to keep this facility clean and hygienic you're expected to give yourself a good soaping. Fair enough, no-one likes to swim drinking in tagnuts, holehair and winnits. If you're like me and couldn't give the shiniest shite about what other people think of your body, you can whip everything out, have a blasting hot shower and be done in a few minutes. If you're shy, though, that's also accommodated for by way of little changing cubicles which you can hide your modesty behind, though it's that frosted glass so if you have a particularly hairy growler people can still see it. I'm not a fan, I'm always worried my arse-cheeks will press up against the glass as I take my socks off and someone will think it's a magic eye puzzle of a hot-air balloon disaster. There's a handy chart on the wall showing the special areas you must wash – your face, armpits, fanny and arse, though presumably you're not expecting to use the same cloth. Again, if you're shy, you'll face a wait for the privacy cubicles – so there's another reason to get there nice and early.

Once you're showered to the point where someone could eat their dinner off your bumhole (and they'd have a handy place to keep their napkin, certainly), you pop your clothes in the locker, use your wristband to secure the door and out you go, carefully dodging all the willies flapping about as others change (though presumably, that doesn't happen in the ladies' changing room, not least because everything is so generously tucked away). I pity the poor bastard who is given a locker closest to the ground because inevitably you're going to look up from putting your shoes away and find yourself peering into someone's arse-crack. Anyway. The lagoon is just at the bottom of some stairs and, being so early in the morning, was lit by soft blue lights under the twinkling stars. It was magic. You can wade in like you're on a Lidl Baywatch, or, perhaps more sensibly, you can swim out into the lagoon from the building itself, getting yourself used to the water.

A few quick observations. It's hot. Durr, I know, but it really threw me quite how hot it was. You know when you're in a bath and you're letting more hot water in with your toe, and you're about five seconds away from it being too hot? It's like that, in places, and even hotter still if you swim near to the vents where the hot water bubbles out. You're not going to burn – they're 'rocked' off – but expect everything to be soft and sagging when you get out. It's the first and only time in my life where I've been able to scratch my balls with my big toe. The rest of the lagoon is around the same temperature as your body, but, being Iceland, you just need to stand up to cool off, given how cold the air is. It's a wonderful feeling.

It's also surprisingly large. Although it's crowded at the entrance to the pool, you can swim out into the steam and lose yourself. I never felt like I was in anyone's way, besides Paul, but that's only because he wanted to cuddle in the water and I was alarmed that we might stick together like a cheese toastie in the heat. It's not so deep you can't stand up in it, but it's deep enough to swim around should you desire. There's a cave to swim through (where I naughtily found the switch to change the narrator from gentle, soothing English to booming German, much to the consternation of a few bathing

Chinese ladies who were probably already confused by the apparent sight of two beluga whales swimming towards them. There's also a waterfall which cascades lovely hot water all over your body with such force that my fat rolls started playing a disco beat from slapping against each other. I probably looked like an oil slick viewed through a heat haze. Don't care. You can book a massage where you float on a pad in the water but we never got around to sorting this out. Of course, we both immediately regretted it when we saw the masseuse – a giant muscly mountain man who could have put us both over his shoulder and had his wicked way with us. We'll put down the wistful tears in Paul's eyes to a reaction with the sulphur, shall we.

Ah yes, the sulphur. Look, you can't get away from the fact the place has a certain eggy smell to it. In places, it smells like a freshly cleaved poo. But it's a natural smell, like when they spread muck on the fields or when the sewers overflow. You get used to it, which is handy, as you'll be smelling of eggs for a good while afterwards. Dotted around the lagoon are pots of the silica mud that naturally forms on the bottom of the lagoon – it's apparently an excellent face-mask. It's also a brilliant white, leading to some frightening experiences when some of the more…aged folks in the pool come swirling out of the mists looking like Heath Ledger as the Joker. Paul and I covered ourselves in it and had a whale of a time. I swam up to the swim-up bar (well, it seemed like the right thing to do) and ordered us some drinks – I had a plastic pint of beer, Paul had a strawberry iced drink. Luckily I have the chest hair to carry off such manliness, even if I did scream when Paul accidentally spilt his slop down my back. Well, wouldn't be the first time.

After an hour or so of floating about, we got out, had a sandwich and a sit down (it's tiring being lazy) and then went back in for another hour or so. You don't really need a full day here. Oh! One more observation. So many selfie sticks! But worse, so many unprotected phones being carried out in the water. Why?! If you drop that bloody phone in the water, it's not coming out again working, let me tell you. You might get a final kamikaze shot of someone's legs uploaded to your iCloud but that's it. I don't know how people hold their nerves, I get anxious brushing my teeth with my phone in my hand.

We got changed and walked back to the bus, stopping only for a couple more photos and a Calippo. Keeping it real. Vexingly, we had missed the hourly bus back by about thirty minutes, but we were happy enough to sit and wait.

Unlike the beast I'm going to call Sandra – for that was her name. Sandra and her very, VERY henpecked husband had missed the bus by only a minute or two, seemingly by the husband not sprinting ahead to stop it. She apparently would have ran herself but 'what would have been the point, given how slow you were'. Let me tell you, the only time this woman was running anywhere was if a vending machine had been left unlocked. She was absolutely dreadful – she sat and very loudly explained to her husband all of his faults and why she could do better. My heart went out to him – I almost asked Paul if I should nip over and give him a blowjob just to lift his spirits. I rather got the impression she wouldn't have done that either.

And, typically, with all the inevitability of day following night, when the bus did come, she sat behind us – and the forty-five-minute bus-ride from hell in the morning was nothing compared to this. She had this incredibly irritating way of trying to sound like she was better than everyone else, both Icelandic and English, and that, in her words:

- *"Iceland is shit because you have to get a bus everywhere"* (you don't, you can get a taxi, unless you can't afford it but you want people to think you can)

- *"what's the fackin' point of Wi-Fi if it doesn't FACKIN' WORK"* (who'd have thought it? Wi-Fi on a bus in the middle of nowhere being patchy!)

- *"…place would be so much better if it wasn't for all the FACKIN' tourists"* (it would certainly be better without one of them)

- *"aren't Icelandic houses shit"* (because that two-up-two-down in some piss-pot village is the classier choice)

- *"who'd stay in a FACKIN' shit 'OTEL like this"* (not you, my love, because you're staying at a cheaper hotel down the road)

and so on and so forth. She was embarrassingly crass and vocal and all her husband could do was 'yes dear' and 'no dear'. She was loud so EVERYONE could hear her. Here's the fun part though. The bus, dropping everyone off in 'random order' (but clearly based on how luxurious the hotels were...i.e. the more expensive hotels got their passengers back first) and ours was second on the list. This pissed her off and on she ranted.

So, naturally, as we got off, I turned around on the steps of the bus and, loudly, called her a '**common, classless tart**' before proper dashing into the foyer in case the rancid old bag or her wispy husband followed suit. They didn't. That split second I saw of her face avalanching in anger was more than enough for me and I'm not joking when I say that gives me a chuckle even now. Probably shouldn't have said anything. Don't care though.

twochubbycubs go to Iceland: part six

OK, confession. At this point, our holiday was lots of little snippets of activities, so I'll cover them off briefly. I can't remember the chronology but look, I don't claim to be a travel writer, so don't bust your buns getting in a flap about it.

First, the Phallological Museum. We made it on our second visit and it was...interesting. Essentially a few rooms filled with all sorts of knobs, from tiny little mouse knobs to big old American knobs holding giant cameras who think that they are the only ones interested in taking photos. Silly man, you'll find the c*nt museum is next door. Yes, I'm asterisking that, but only because I'll get a phonecall from my mother saying I can't use that word on the Internet without going on a register.

It's no secret that Paul and I are both committed fans of the penis, but even so, there's only so many you can see in one place before they all start blending into one. There's precious little in the way of human willies, although there *is* a fine metal casting of all of the knobs of the Icelandic ice hockey team, covering everything from the goalie to the puck, who seemingly had enough foreskin for the rest of the team. The whole display would make for a unique present for a lady to hang her necklaces, that's for sure. We learned that the biggest penis in all of the world belongs to the blue whale, measuring over 16ft long. Gosh! The biggest cock I've ever seen was 6ft 3", but I stopped dating him after a couple of weeks. Boom boom. After twenty minutes of stroking our chins and various wooden willies, we hastened to the gift shop where, out of a mixture of British politeness and a love of tat, we bought a wooden ashtray shaped like a giant willy. We don't even smoke. It's currently sat in our games room, where doubtless when our house burns down it'll be dragged from the rubble and held aloft for the papers as a sign of our deviant lifestyle.

Second, we went out drinking one night, which was great fun though FUCK ME was it expensive. I'm by no means an expensive date but hell, we ended up emptying my wallet twice over and all we were drinking was their local beer and vodka. We found a bar which gave us flights of beer, essentially four different third-pints and a shot of vodka in order to "try them out". Well, we were absolutely wankered in no time at all. At some point in the evening we ended up in a sports bar hollering at the TV with all of the locals at some sport of the TV that even now, with a sober mind, I can't tell you what they were playing. We bumped into another couple of blokes who recognised us from the hotel (presumably we flashed up on their radar as the fat fuckers who kept eating all the bread at breakfast), immediately agreed we'd join in with their pub-crawl, and then almost as immediately Paul and I buggered off around the corner and lost them. We stopped for a crêpe from one of the many food trucks scattered around (because, let's be honest, adding cream, eggs and chocolate onto a belly full of dark beer and vodka is always a clever idea) and Paul asked to use her toilet. It took almost five minutes of her explaining that there was no toilet in her tiny food-truck before Paul stopped looking at her owlishly and staggered off to find one of the many loos scattered around the streets, a big chocolate smear halfway up his face. I apologised for us, called us typical Brits, and hastened off after him.

After many more drinks we decided to stagger back to the hotel along the seafront (a 50-minute walk when sober) and, on the way, spotted a Domino's pizza. Well, we had to try an Icelandic Dominos, surely, so in we went, ordering two large pizzas with the strict instruction that they couldn't deliver back to the hotel until after forty minutes had passed, giving us enough time to saunter back cool and collected. Nope. No, realising that the walk was altogether much further than we had anticipated (not least because we were both careering around drunk), we had to really pick up the pace, and that's how the good folk of Reykjavik were treated to the sight of two large, fat blokes, drunk as all outdoors, staggering, sliding and powermincing along the icy roads. I tumbled into a grass verge at one point and Paul *might* have been sick in a bin. What can I say, we ooze class. Once we stumbled into the hotel lobby, the pizza guy was waiting with a scowl – clearly the sight of us wheezing and lolling about didn't amuse him. Poor sport. I slipped some notes into his pocket like he was a ten-quid prossie, apologised profusely in that earnest drunken voice that we all hate, and retrieved Paul from the concierge office, which he'd mistaken for a lift.

Oh, and those two pizzas? Cost us £70 by the time we'd tipped the poor bloke standing in the lobby. But they tasted *delicious*.

We spent our final day shopping, eating chips, walking around and just soaking in the place. It's truly remarkable. A slightly bizarre moment in a tiny little coffee shop where I witnessed a young, buxom lady having a coffee with what I presumed to be her father until she stood up, almost straddled him and gave him the wettest, longest, most committed French kiss I've ever seen. I'm not sure if she had a real thing for the taste of Steradent but it was so unexpected and bizarre that I barely had time to pull my phone out. Good on the old chap for getting some, I suppose, but it sounded like someone had pulled a plug out of a bath filled with wet hair. We made a swift exit and carried on. Paul fell on his arse again into a large puddle and I knocked over a shop's display of stuffed puffins (accidentally, naturally) but in no time at all it was time to walk back to the hotel to catch our bus to the airport. Naturally, we immediately got lost, and went on possibly the most convoluted trip ever, taking in their central motorway, what I'm sure was a red-light district, a park that looked like something out of Dangerous Minds and a car dealership. It took us almost three hours – with flat phones, no less – to get back to the hotel, twenty minutes before the bus departed. We did ask the one old man who didn't look like he'd knife us as soon as look at us for directions, but he spoke no English (quite right) and we spoke no Icelandic, though I reckon if I'd started choking on a Strepsil at that very second he might have made sense of it.

It was with a heavy heart that we boarded our bus back to the airport, after a minor panic after we were told that the front desk staff at the hotel hadn't actually organised our transfer. They sorted it out after much raising of eyebrows and strangling sounds. Naturally, we both immediately fell asleep on the bus, but well, it's only got one destination so you can't go too wrong. Did have a moment of despair when I spotted that there were almost 50 wee Scottish schoolchildren ahead of us in the queue to check-in, but actually, they were very well behaved and a credit to their school. I was disappointed, I had a perfect 140-character passive aggressive tweet all set ready to go to their school when landing in the UK. Bah. There's fuck all to do in the airport other than lose your passports and buy alcohol, although we did manage to cobble together two years' worth of annual salary between us which allowed us to buy a burger that, if needed, could have been used as a landing wheel for our approaching plane. Who knew moisture was optional?

The flight itself was uneventful, save for the captain coming on to say that if we were lucky, we'd see the Northern Lights through the window, which caused the wheezing behemoth in front of me to pitch her seat back pretty much into my lap. Apparently this afforded her a better view of the inky blackness and the engine lights, for she didn't shift an inch for the rest of the flight. No, honestly, what I really want to look at for the duration of my flight are your split-ends and cheap home hair-dye job, you inconsiderate, flaking sea-cow.

We landed smoothly, picked up our car and made our way through the night back to Newcastle. It was a lovely drive, punctuated only by a midnight stop at McDonalds for sustenance and a hurried crap about forty minutes later to dispatch aforementioned McDonalds into the murky brown yonder. Now, let us take a quick dirty diversion here. Those of a prudish disposition might want to alight for a couple of paragraphs and join us later.

Toilets, namely public toilets, I don't understand the sexual appeal. We stopped at some toilets in the middle of Fuck-All, Nowhere and every conceivable surface was covered in the type of graffiti that made even me blush, and hell, I have about as many sexual hang-ups as George Michael. But this toilet wasn't some plush outbuilding with comfortable ledges and a decent hand-drier for blowing the last drips off, no, this looked like something out of a Saw movie. There was more piss on the floor than there was in the sewer below, most of the lights were burnt out and three out of the four traps contained toilets that looked like someone had drawn an intricate map of the local A and B roads using faeces. Dirty doesn't begin to describe them! So who is willingly getting down on their knees in a place like that? It doesn't bear thinking about. For long. Brrr.

However, our practical reason for visiting these toilets couldn't be avoided and I risked death and urine burns to 'drop the kids off', as quickly and as delicately as I could. Whilst hovering above the pan like I was riding an invisible magic carpet, a peculiar bit of graffiti caught my eye – a bold (admittedly in very nice handwriting) statement declaring that a gloryhole could be found in the *ladies'* toilet. Now honestly, it takes a reasonably bold man to stick his knob through a hole in a toilet at the best of times, but to venture into the ladies' crapstation on the off-chance you're going to get a) a lady with teeth and b) who is up for a bit of action, instead of screaming loudly at your engorged willy suddenly appearing out of the wall whilst she reaches for a square of loo-roll to wipe her minnie-moo...well, those are pretty slim odds, surely? Brrr again!

Anyway, I once heard of a chap who had his knob sliced with a knife when he put it through a gloryhole, like the world's most budget circumcision, and another who had a cigarette put out on it. If I ever find myself in a lavatory and a knob that isn't my own suddenly appears, I'll be using it to hang the toilet roll on.

OK, prudish folk, come on back.

We made it home for around 3am, made a fuss out of our cats who, of course, totally ignored us and acted like we'd betrayed them in the worst possible way by daring to go away, and went straight to bed. Iceland done. Let's sum up.

Pros

- absolutely **beautiful** – now I know that almost goes without saying, but honestly, it's so alien and unusual and unlike anywhere we've been before that we'd recommend it just for that experience alone;

- so much to do – and even as two fat blokes, we never struggled with any of the activities, it's all very **accessible**

- tonnes of **history**, even if their museums are a smidge dry

- amazing **food**, especially all of their snack stations and tiny little places to eat

- the **Northern Lights**, I mean, come on

- not **rammed** full of either trashy British tourists or massive touring groups

Cons

- incredibly **expensive**, and it's not even easy to get around this – snacks and drinks are expensive, meals and nights out even more so – be prepared to spend

- if you're not a fan of **sitting** on buses to get to places, you'll struggle, but even then the buses are comfortable, Wi-Fi enabled and warm, so it's a hard one to 'con'

- the occasional **standoffishness**, but hell, you're going to get that anywhere

Go. We can't recommend it enough! If you don't love it, we'll be amazed!

We travelled with easyJet from Edinburgh to Reykjavik, landing early in the evening. We stayed at the Edinburgh Airport (Newbridge) Premier Inn the night before and then the Grand Hotel in Reykjavik. We organised all of our excursions directly with Grey Line Excursions or Reykjavik Excursions, including our airport transfers. All wonderful to deal with!

twochubbycubs on: snobbery

There was a heated discussion in our facebook group the other night about whether or not it was right for the NHS to fund access to places like Slimming World or Weight Watchers, or whether people should be expected to pay for themselves. For the most part people agreed that it was a marvellous idea and that a little bit paid out now might stop a lifetime of the NHS having to pay out for obesity related diseases. Seems sensible. Of course, if you're in a position to pay yourself, then you should, but if you're unfortunate enough to struggle to find the money for Slimming World (and let's be quite frank, although it might only "be a fiver", it's always a bit more – costs of getting there, bit of fruit for Slimmer of the Week, raffle prizes, magazines, books. Yeah, you don't need to buy into any of that, but let's be honest, there's plenty of ways to lose money so although it might only be a fiver, it's often a quite a bit more. Do we stop people going if they can't afford it? Say no, sorry, go home and cry into your Smart Price bread and Extra Value glass of rainwater? Of course we fucking don't, and it boils my piss that it was even suggested.

ANYWAY. The reason I bring this up is because Paul, quite rightly, vehemently defended the NHS (for they are marvellous) and pointed out quite saliently that we all claim from the NHS in some way, whether right now or in the future. It's there for all to use, and rightly so.

As part of his argument, he mentioned the fact he went to Cambridge University and, being from a poor working class background, was often made to feel inadequate by some of the folks there. Which is daft, because Paul is undeniably wonderful in every which way. He's even got a big knob for someone of his height, so you know, work with it. His argument was comprehensive and fair and surprisingly free of swearing and innuendo – I thought someone had swapped him out for someone else. One of the posters disagreeing with him kept having a pop, so he ignored her, only to wake up this morning to a private message (it's interesting, these folk never say what they want to say in front of others, only hidden away behind the shadows) from this woman who told him she couldn't "believe he went to Cambridge" because he was so "classless and uncouth". She "thanked God" that she never bumped into "someone like you". All this because Paul's an advocate for folk getting help when they need it as opposed to when they can afford it.

Naturally, he blocked her, despite me wanting to point out to her that clearly the Cambridge education of her son hadn't rubbed off on her based on her many spelling errors and nonsensical grammar. Disappointing. But honestly, how pathetic. I can't bear actual proper snobbery, especially when it's coming from someone who clearly has all the class of a fingerbang in a taxi-rank. There's something so undignified about someone in their late sixties scrabbling around on facebook trying to put others down based on class. It's like Jeremy Kyle but with Sanotagen. So your son went to Cambridge and you never saw anyone uncouth there? Pfft. I once 'went back' with a lad from Cambridge and he asked me to pee in his bum, the logistics of which I couldn't fathom, so stick that in your cigarette-holder and smoke it. I shan't name the lady and I don't want people to comment below adding their twopenneth, because sometimes it's easier just to let people's ignorance stand clear and undiluted.

The point to mentioning this? Well, just to lead to a reminder of what we are all about at twochubbycubs. We don't discriminate – we're awful about everyone, but in a teasing, gentle way. If you actually want help, join our page or our group and get asking and I'm fairly sure someone will be along to help, though don't ask for syn values otherwise you'll get a boot up your arse. We're all here for the same reason – we're fat and the smell of bacon follows us wherever we go. Our recipes are free (and I do think we could make a lot more money if we actually charged for them, but we don't) and hopefully there's something for everyone. Well, no, not everyone. If you're a needlessly haughty sort with hair like someone has run their finger around the inside of a plughole in the shower room of a men's prison, perhaps you should skip on by.

Bah.

Let us go somewhere nicer for a moment. I spent the afternoon volunteering at our local cat and dog shelter (Brysons) and had the pleasure of spending an hour with a tiny wee kitten called Spitfire.

He is a kitten and was absolutely terrified after spending many weeks by himself in the cold, he had a bloody nose from fighting, but now he's in the right place and will be loved and nursed. He was found after scratching at an office window to be let in from the cold. Oh, and when the RSPCA were called to pick up this stray cat, they told the caller to leave him outside and that there was nothing they could do. For a cat no bigger than my fist, stick-thin and shivering, with blood all over his face. Great work, "caring" animal charity. Brysons went to pick him up and are looking after him now, so all is well!

twochubbycubs on: my parking enemy

I seem to have acquired a new enemy. I say enemy, rather just someone who clearly doesn't like me and would cheerfully see me plummet to my death from the car-park like a slightly less camp Julie Martin from Neighbours. See, every day I park in the same spot on the same floor in the multi-storey near where I work. Not because I have to, just force of habit. Anyway, the last couple of weeks someone has got there before me, so I've started parking in another bay which has slightly better angles and less change of your car being smacked by some inconsiderate mouth-breather in a Saxo. Easy, no problems. However, it would seem that I've taken the space that someone else always used to park in. Oops. They aren't allocated, I hasten to add. The first time I spotted there was a problem was the other day when another car was driving right up my arse as I trundled up the floors in the multi-storey car park. My first thought was "goodness me, Keavy from B*witched seems to be in a frightful hurry" but all became clear when, as I pulled into "my" spot, she went absolutely apocalyptic in my rear-view mirror, effing and jeffing and waving her arms around like she was interpreting a Russian argument for the deaf. Naturally I did a wry chuckle to myself and parked up primly and professionally.

Since then, if I beat her to "her spot", I'm treated to the sight of her slamming her door, stalking across the car-park muttering and swearing to herself, before furiously click-clacking her way down the stairs. I'd understand if there was a shortage of spaces but it's literally me and her on this floor alone. I'm not driving a coach either, there's plenty of space even if she wanted to park right next to me. Her anger doesn't seem to be subsiding either. Probably didn't help that the other morning I cracked my window open a fraction and played 'Always Look On The Bright Side Of Life' as she stormed past, a vision of pure rage. I might borrow Paul's Smart car and park that in the bay instead, just so she can't see it until the last minute. That'll really piss on her chips. Mahaha. Listen, if I'm found in a pool of blood in the stairwell of the multi-storey in Newcastle with a Primark umbrella embedded in my skull, you'll know who did it.

I do wonder who else is filled with rage whenever they see my moon face appear on the horizon. Certainly there's a guy near where I work who must finish at the same time as I do. Whenever I see him, I can't help but smirk. Let me explain. A couple of years ago I was walking to my car when I spotted a man with singularly the worst haircut I've ever seen. It was exceptionally styled and colourful and would have looked lovely on a runway model but it was on a bloke who looks just like me but if I'd fallen on hard times. Imagine me with a peacock at full plume on my head. It was such an absurd juxtaposition that I laughed and had to cover it with a cough. He didn't see me, which is good because I'm not a total bastard and wouldn't like to think I caused any distress. Anyway, since then, without fail, whenever I see him I have to suppress a laugh purely because of instinct, so every time he sees me he must wonder what I'm chuckling at and/or if I have really bad wind pains. I know, I'm a terrible person, but it's become like blinking. Perhaps if he didn't purse his lips at me that might help. I wonder if there's a blog parallel to this one where he's writing about the fat gopper in his oversized coat who comes mincing out with a face that looks permanently like I'm about to come.

twochubbycubs on: council tax

I'm in a bit of a huff tonight, if I'm honest. Came home to find a big bill waiting for me on the doormat. Normally I never say no to bending down for a Big Bill but this one was our council tax and it's fucking £1700! What the hell for? They've turned off our street lights, driving on the roads feels like I'm playing Moon Patrol and they only pick up the bins when there is a full solar eclipse. There's more chance of me getting pregnant than getting a book that doesn't have Katie Price on the front cover out of our local library and if you fancy a stroll in the park, best get used to the dogshit and litter billowing around your feet like the shittiest version of the Crystal Dome. I don't know why they don't push all the dog-sausages into the fucking potholes in the road, at least that way I wouldn't get out of the car with my neck canted a forty-five-degree angle from being clattered off the roof of my car.

MOAN MOAN MOAN. But seriously, it would be a bloody welcome change if they said oh James, you work hard, here, enjoy your wage to do whatever you want with it, instead of grasping it out of my cold, cruel hands. I'm paying into a pension and being sensible by saving, but what's the use? So when I get to seventy the Government can take away my house and stick me in a care home? Fuck that. We've already decided that when we get to seventy, if we're both alive and capable of getting lob-ons, the house is getting sold and we're getting two lithe twenty year olds to rub our bunions and change our oxygen tanks. BAH.

I might start a go-fund-me accompanied by a picture of Paul looking sadly into middle-distance and footage of me looking through photo albums. Maybe.

twochubbycubs on: ten things I hate about you

I was in the bath earlier (what can I say, I thought I'd make an effort for work tomorrow and, after hours of hard gardening, my bollock-consommé was particularly strong) when I happened across a chapter in Bill Bryson's newest book where he listed ten of his irrational dislikes. First thought? The cheeky faced bearded bugger had clearly read my previous blog entry and nicked the idea. Second thought? As if a wonder like Bill Bryson would read my blog. I love Bill – my favourite author in the world. If I can get to 60 and be as witty and verbose as him, I'll be a happy, better-bearded man. My previous irrational dislikes can be found in the previous book but here's a few more...

spitting in public

Spitting should never happen. It's a vile process – unless you've ingested some kind of poison, there's no reason to blow great chunks of lungbutter out onto the street. You'll see people walking along spitting away merrily like they've got a mouthful of cat hair and it's all I can do not to reach across and set their face on fire. Apparently *I'm* the one in the wrong if I do that. Pfft. I'm tempted to add spitting in private onto the list but I can think of at least one situation where someone may prefer to spit rather than swallow. Amateurs. I gargle.

baby on board stickers

The most pointless, self-indulgent little sticker known to man, other than the picture of Alan Shearer grinning his big smug smile in the 1997 football sticker album. I can't bear Alan Shearer – I've met him, and he's a boring, self-aggrandising arse. Anyway, what's the point of these baby on board stickers? Do you think I was planning to drive onto your backseat and through your headrests until I saw your pink Comic Sans sticker of shite and decided against it? Some say it's for the fire brigade to know immediately in a crash that there's a baby somewhere in the crushed metal. I dare say that if an accident was so severe that the fire brigade couldn't spot your baby mewling away in the back then chances are no-one is walking away from it anyway.

people who say they're dyslexic when they're bloody well not

Dyslexic? Then of course you can make as many errors as you like, and anyone who judges you is a complete arse. People who can't be arsed to learn the difference between they're, their and there and then say 'BUT IM DYSLEXIC' when they're pulled up on it? Does my fucking nut in. Don't cheapen an illness by falsely using it to mask your own inadequacies. You turtle cant.

mothers using their pushchairs to stop traffic

Oddly specific one this. I drive to work down the same street every day, which coincides with when the parents are taking their adorable children to school. I say adorable children like one might say adorable terminal illness or adorable mass genocide. More often than not, some vacant-looking, red-eyed pyjama-clad monstrosity with more partners than teeth will, instead of crossing at the many safe crossing points, just push her pushchair into the road to try and cross. Nevermind teaching your kid how to cross the road safely, nevermind almost causing an accident because you're too selfish to cross in the right place, you just get out there. Bah!

self-appointed traffic wardens who wear cameras

This is a difficult one. I absolutely understand why cyclists and cars have those cameras which record the road in front of you – there's that many bell-ends on the road to justify it. But what makes me seethe is when you overtake a cyclist, leave plenty of room, indicate back in and they STILL tap their helmet and wag their fingers like I'm a dog who has shat on the carpet. You know that if you watch it back on YouTube later it'll be accompanied by someone's thin reedy voice reading out your registration and the sticky noise of someone masturbating furiously.

dings

I swear, everything in my house dings and dongs and bleeps at me. Put something on the fancy induction hob? It'll do a little chirrup. Our smoke alarm system occasionally decides to launch a test with a brash

American woman saying 'THIS IS JUST A TEST' – presumably a test to see how much blood can pour from my ears before I dismantle her. Our fridge beeps if we leave the door open for more than a second and it blares if the ice-dispenser gets too full or if the freezer is too full. The washing machine beeps each time it reaches a new stage in the cycle. My Wii U flashes when there's a new notification and my Mac beeps whenever someone leaves us a facebook comment, or an email, or every time Siri has a shite. TwoChubbyCubs Towers is beginning to look and sound like a NASA control room and it *vexes* me.

people who stir their hot drink like they're whisking eggs

There's no need! Just give it a couple of stirs with your spoon and sit the fuck down. It makes my teeth rattle and my blood boil when they go at it like they're trying to squeeze every last molecule of tea or take the finish off the cup, not least because I have decent Le Creuset cups and I don't want bloody scratches on them.

stupid comments

Look, 99.9% of comments we get via the blog and facebook are wonderful, funny or useful, but we get some proper humdingers too. No: we won't explain every facet of the plan to you, we're not paid and we're not consultants. Also, don't have a pop at us if your Tesco in Wolverhampton didn't have any 5% mince, it's not our ruddy fault. And if you're the lady with sand in her vag because I mentioned having to get up constantly in a cinema to let someone nip outside to the toilet and you took that as a full-scale assault on the incontinent, well, kiss my boobs. I knew the person I was getting up for and she's only verbally incontinent.

takeaway menus

Whenever we are on a diet, three things happen: Dominos have their 50% off week, Ben & Jerry's ice-cream goes to £2 a tub and we start getting a tsunami of takeaway leaflets through the door – all with the same dodgy photos of their food downloaded from google images, all with the same balloon fonts and all with the worst spelling mistakes. I like my nan (or rather I did, bless her, she's dead now) but the thought of a free hot and spicy nan with my korma puts me right off. These will be the same type of places where you get a) tins of pop rather than cans of coke and b) roughly fingered for a free kebab.

air-fresheners

I might have touched on this before with my many moans about scented bloody candles and their pointless bloody names (A Child's Fucking Wish, am I right?) but hell, it bears repeating. I'm yet to smell an air-freshener that doesn't make my nose crinkle. They're universally awful. Fair enough, if you spend decent money you can buy a decent candle with a reasonable smell (something like The White Company) but otherwise, open a bloody window. Those little hissy air-fresheners in public loos that smell ostensibly of pine? A load of bollocks! I'm not transported to a crisp and verdant forest with a tiny hiss, no, instead it smells like I've shit in a grass-clippings bin.

That's 10, I could go on. But let's call it a day.

twochubbycubs on: freebies

Plus, I don't know about you but we always seem to have three or four sweet potatoes rolling around in our drawers. It's like being haunted by a vegan – but how would you even go about telling whether a vegan is a ghost? God knows they're pale, wispy and whining in real-life. I'm **kidding**. Please don't write me letters, save your strength.

Things are still grim in Chubby Towers. Paul's been flirting with a cold for a good couple of weeks and now it has really got him in its snotty grip. He's currently lying on the sofa sniffing and snorting like Kerry Katona on giro day. He's coughing like a 200-a-day-smoker/his mother and I could toast marshmallows on the end of his nose. You know that bit in the movie Misery when Annie Wilkes gets walloped with an iron at the end of the movie? That's Paul. He's in a bad way. Now, traditionally, we'd rattle off a few jokes about man-flu but I've always thought that was reductionist and mean. He's just a soft arse. I'm sore because as a result of him snoring like an idling bus all night and keeping me awake and I'm tired of running around getting drinks and decongestants and nasal sprays and tissues – oh CHRIST the tissues, it's like I'm living in the bedroom of the type of blokes who get stung by online vigilantes – and I'm reaching the end of my goodwill. I'd make a shit nurse; I'm not going to lie. Anything more than applying a plaster and I'd be pressing a pillow into their face and turning off the alarm bells.

There was a brief shining glimmer of goodness in my day, however. I was given a free packet of crisps by someone in town today. Because I'm naturally cynical, I spent five minutes looking around for the hidden camera crew who would be recording me opening the packet only to get a face full of bees or something mean. Also, because I'm naturally morbidly obese and a greedy bastard, I spent another twenty-five minutes going around and around to the various people until I had seven free bags. I know, what a cad. Paul and I were once in the Metrocentre (the glitz! the glamour – it never ends because it never fucking begins) and there was a team of 12 people handing out bags of those Milky Way Magic Stars. We sharp calculated that if we split up we could grab 24 bags. Even better, once I had removed my glasses I could grab another twelve and better yet, when Paul put my glasses on, he was able to get another 12, even if he could see through time whilst doing so. Then, swap coats to repeat the whole affair, then go and sit in McDonalds for half an hour and go around again. In total we ended up with about 150 bags of Milky Way Magic Stars. This was back when we didn't drive so it meant an hour trip home on the bus with more chocolate than any fat bloke has a reason for having but we definitely won that day.

I can tell you now though – the allure of so much free chocolate is sharp lost after the 35th bag. We were eating those bloody stars for days and even now the sight of that four-eyed twat the Milky Bar kid fills me with absolute rage. I swear I was reclining in the bath when one of those damned stars floated out of my belly button.

Paul just chimed in from the sofa to add his best freebie story, so let me treat you to a wee bit more. Back when Paul was a nurse he, and a lot of his colleagues, were often treated to fun little freebies from drugs companies and other parasites. Mugs, laser pointers, chocolates and, somewhat inexplicably, a doorbell. Because nothing says 'best treatment for a prolapsed arsehole' like a doorbell. Anyway, he was super excited to be given a face towel roughly the same shape as a little pink pill. The gimmick being that you added water and the whole thing would rehydrate, unfurl and give you a charming, if somewhat moist, free towel to wipe your sweaty face with. So enchanted by this fabulously pointless gimmick that he saved this little towel-pill until he was at the gym and, with a proper flourish, rehydrated it in the changing room gym. Here's the thing: it was a great towel, but it's hard to look debonair and stylish when you're wiping a towel with VAGISIL imprinted across it in pink Mistral font. No wonder he doesn't bother with gyms now; the poor bugger is scarred.

twochubbycubs on: paul's shame

I make lots of mistakes. I'm sorry. I'll strip off and whip my back with a few Curly-Wurlys melted together. I'm like Jesus Christ but in elasticated Cotton Trader trousers.

I'm going to tell you a quick story about Paul which has been on my mind all day. I can't recall mentioning it on the blog when it happened but see, he's switched to a new employer and a new job and thus I feel we can get away with mentioning it without him getting into mischief. See, he used to work in a very serious area of social care and part of that meant attending very important, very serious meetings with doctors, the police, social workers, judges and lawyers all sat around a table. Due to the nature of what they were discussing it was mandatory for the meeting and everything that was said to be video-recorded, and this was done by several small cameras on the desk which would automatically pivot to whoever was talking. All terrifically serious and no jokes allowed.

Naturally, Paul managed to make an absolute tit of himself. See, he dropped his papers. That's fine, but Paul spends about 96% of his working time tucking his shirt back into his trousers so no-one sees the top of his arse. He'd forgotten to do that, meaning he had to awkwardly crouch down to get his papers rather than mooning all the very ashen-faced folk around the table. And, because he was tense and trying to bend awkwardly, he let loose with a fart that didn't so much echo around the room as fucking gallop around the table. That in itself wasn't so bad, but the whole moment of crushing embarrassment was punctuated by the sudden and accusatory whirr of all the cameras immediately spinning and pointing at the cause of the sound. His cheeks weren't red, they were slightly browned and smelling faintly of last night's Mongolian beef.

At this point, had everyone collapsed into giggles and chortles (though, more likely spluttering and choking, with people flinging themselves at the glass windows in the hope of sweet escape), the tension would have been relieved, but no. No, everyone shuffled their papers, cleared their throats and cracked on, leaving Paul to burn away merrily with shame and anguish. His boss did ask on the drive back to the office whether 'anyone had heard an unusual noise', bless, but everyone knew it was him. I blame myself – the beef was two days out of date.

Luckily, I've never had to endure such acute embarrassment, though I'm prone to making a tit of myself, it's always low-level stuff. For example, I can't make small-talk with male cashiers without it sounding like I'm leading them on or being plain weird. There's a young guy in our local Tesco who, bless his heart, could see both ends of a bus coming as it came round the corner. He's absolutely not my type. It doesn't stop me feeling I have to be 'nice' when he's helping me in the self-scan – last time I was there I asked who did his tattoos as they 'looked really nice', which instantly gave the impression I've been leering lasciviously at this bloke. He went pink, I went red and he forgot all about the security check and pushed my trolley through. Perhaps that's the key to shoplifting – as soon as you approach the Scan 'n' Shop bit just wink at the guy standing looking serious, paw at his arse and go 'OOOOH CUT ME OFF A SLICE OF THAT'. Or, don't.

I'm forever mis-spelling words in emails (signing off with kind retards, asking accunts to sort out expenses) to the point where I can't send an email without triple-checking things now, which is unfortunate when someone needs an answer straight away and I have to check to make sure I haven't slipped bumfucker into my 'next steps' paragraph. Oh, there was one time I managed to embarrass myself to the point where the air in my throat chokes me even now as I think about it – way back in high school my lovely form tutor sat us all down at the start of the year and told us she had some important news – her husband had hung himself over the summer holidays. Awful, of course, absolutely awful. But see, I just can't handle solemn silences, I get so anxious and stressed that it manifests itself into giggles and tics. Of course, I laughed, and I swear to God, I've never apologised to anyone more in my life since that moment. I remember masking it as a coughing fit but that just made it worse.

I'm not a complete bastard, please don't judge me. It's 100% involuntary and since that moment I've gone out of my way to remove myself from situations where people tell me sad news. Hell, I've only been to three funerals in my life and even at my nana's I almost burst out laughing because I imagined her hearing aid still whistling away in the coffin like a distant fax machine. My aunt and uncle died at the same time when I was a teenager and I was probably the only person in that church simultaneously crying and balling my fist into my mouth to stop the laughter – to be fair, they brought out the second coffin and set it down on a trestle table with very wobbly legs, giving me visions of the whole thing giving away and tumbling his corpse down the aisle. What can I say, I love a bit of slapstick.

twochubbycubs on: home technology

Today has me sat in the house waiting for our Sky engineer to come and fit us a new Sky Q box. Why this requires a) an engineer visit and b) me to take a day off work is an absolute mystery. I do have someone coming to finger my guttering at some point in the afternoon but really, when don't I? I semi-dilate when anyone with rough hands and a beard drives past the house. Paul sent me a text message ten minutes after leaving the house this morning to say "no need to suck the engineer off, we've already arranged a sizeable discount on the Ultra HD package", which I think is a bit below the belt. I mean, he's got a point – I'm a cheap bastard and I'd do full unprotected anal if it meant free fibre broadband for a year, but still. Give me some credit. Oh and speaking of Sky, it's lucky I checked the 'before we visit' letter which mentions the need to know our Wi-Fi password. Our Wi-Fi password, as it turns out, was **WELOVEBIGCOCKS8669!** – I've just changed it to something entirely more innocent – fancyafelchyouhunkybucketofspunk apparently didn't meet the security requirements. Who knew? I did toy with leaving it unchanged for a laugh but felt that it would look like a clumsy attempt at a come-on – long-time readers must recall that this is one of my fears with having workmen in the house, that every sentence sounds like I'm trying to set away some cheesy porn-style scenario. I'm such a clutz, I can barely pass over a cup of tea without putting my cock in it. Aaaah well. We'll see what time he turns up.

It's also a very sad day in our house. For years we've been saying we need to buy a Roomba to replace the old Roomba that broke and went beetling into our garage, never to return, when we moved house. But they start at £400, we've got a fancy Dyson Digital vacuum anyway AND we have a cleaner, so we couldn't really justify it. Until last Thursday night when we were pissed out of our nut on Waldhimbeergeist and lemonade (I don't know either: it was a random bottle of something from Lidl – could have been industrial bleach for all we knew, but it tasted nice and had a raspberry on the front so we rolled the dice and got smashed). It's amazing how alcohol changes your justification for spending money and as a result, we had a Roomba delivered by the good folks from Amazon on Saturday morning. How we gazed admiringly at it, knowing it would scoot about during the day time terrorising the cats and pulling the odd bit of hair and crushed cat treat from our carpet. We could finally relax with the gentle hum of the robotic whirring to sing us to sleep.

Nope.

Turns out Roombas can't function on black carpet. Our house, bar the kitchen, is either black carpet or black tile (don't worry, it goes tastefully with the Misty

Mountain grey on the walls: may I remind you we *are* homosexual) and as a result, the Roomba senses these black patches as 'cliffs', throws a bit of a strop, spins a bit and then beeps forlornly. Putting him down on the living room carpet must feel like, to him, being hurled into a black hole of no escape. We placed him into the kitchen for a laugh (our kitchen floor being black and white square tiles – our kitchen has an American diner theme, it's very fancy) and it was hilarious – I've never seen a robot actually have a fit but the poor fucker was jitterbugging and stuttering all over the place. I had to put a small pile of ground Diazepam down on the white tile just to calm him the fuck down. Anyway, back into the box and returned to Amazon with a naturally furious email about there being no mention of the Roomba's sense of existential dread.

Perhaps it's a good thing. Our house is too connected. One of my colleagues expressed some reservations about our 'House of Connected Things', citing concern about security and the ability for folks to hack our home. Really, I know it's more a pressing worry that I'm not going to turn up at work of a morning because I've been killed in my sleep by Amazon Alexa instructing a rogue Roomba to come and hoover all of the oxygen out of my lungs whilst I sleep. We buy our gadgets and nonsense because we don't have children to spoil and they're great, but I did think to myself as I walked into the house, said clearly "Alexa, please turn on the lights" only for her to turn one light on and start playing Bill

Bryson, how much time are we actually saving here? It's a novelty being able to turn our heating on from the sofa by telling Nest to 'turn the hallway down to 9 degrees' but again, it's no hardship at all to get up and turn the thermostat down. Actually, that bit is a lie – we get these things because we're bone-bloody-idle, so anything that minimises our movements is no bad thing.

I have discovered one excellent thing about Amazon Echo though – I can say "**Alexa, play The Archers**" whilst I'm having a crap and it'll start playing the latest episode through the house speakers. An episode of The Archers is just the right length to enjoy when you *have a shaggy brown dog scratching at the back door*. However, as we don't have a speaker in the bathroom, I have to "**Alexa: turn it up**" about eight times until it gets loud enough for me to satisfactorily hear it from the bathroom. The downside to this is that the Alexa gets so loud that once I've finished my business and moved back to the living room it is playing too loud to hear me shouting "**Alexa: shut the fuck up**" at it, meaning I get locked in an increasingly loud, shrill and vicious circle trying to make myself heard over the sound of POOR OLD HELEN ARCHER fussing about her joint bank account. I can't imagine, in the entire history of The Archers being on air, anyone ever seeming to react so violently to Rob being slow-clapped off the cricket team. My poor neighbours must think I have the most exciting time *paying my sewer-tax* with all the yelling and middle-class braying that goes on.

also: Not content with filling our house with buttons that automatically buy our shopping, we've invested in an Amazon Echo – essentially an always-listening little personal assistant (like Siri) who can automatically turn our heating up, turn our lights off, play music, that sort of forward-thinking thing. However, because it's voice-activated, my day has been spent listening to Paul bellow incoherently at the Echo: 'ALEXA: TELL ME A JOKE' was good, 'ALEXA: WHAT'S THE WEATHER LIKE' was even better, but 'ALEXA: Siri thinks you're a snotty slaaaaaag' yielded little worthwhile result and when I shouted 'ALEXA' and farted into the speaker, it just shut itself off.

I do like to imagine that somewhere deep underground there's a team of Evil Amazon Folk listening to our every move, because frankly, unless they like lots of shrieking over Forza Horizon, copious amounts of farting, ancient Janice Battersby impressions and arguments about who was the best Doctor Who, they're in for a disappointing time.

twochubbycubs on: if we were consultants...

Paul and I have been thinking about switching slimming world classes. Not because our current class has anything wrong with it, it's absolutely the best one in the area, but we've been going off and on for almost seven years. It's easy to fall into a rut and we're not staying to class anymore, so perhaps a new face and a new bank of folks to look at with my eye glaze over whilst they chunter on about 1/2lb here and there is exactly what we need. As I was mulling over this decision in the car on the way home, I started thinking about **my** perfect Slimming World class and what I'd do if I was a consultant.

Incidentally, we get so, so many people telling us they'd come to our class if we became consultants, but we offered our services to Slimming World way back when we were just starting out and didn't get a phone call in return. Which, frankly, was foolish – we've got plenty of disposable income and a very carefree approach to spending it. My house could have been more Hi-Fi bar than brick. But anyway. So here's how my dream class would go if I was a consultant. If you're a consultant, feel free to nick my ideas, but be sure to have a framed photo of us with a candle burning in front of it, like people do when someone's died in a car-crash.

For a start, let's not be tight with the venue. I'm sick of sitting on rock hard chairs in draughty church halls, getting piles and backache. Let's have the class in the back of the local pub, so people can pay lip service to losing weight and then get straight on the beers, wine and crackling, like EVERYONE WHO GOES TO FAT-CLASS does. The heating would be on but sensible – I've noticed classes are either so hot that you lose two pounds in sweat just sitting in your chair shallow-breathing or so fucking cold that you can open your third box of Hi-Fi bars with your diamond-level nipple.

I'd serve proper coffee and proper tea. There's no excuse for people to people to fork over £5 and then get hit with coffee so weak you can see the bottom of the cup through it, or tea that tastes like it was brewed up in 1957 and left to stand. Yes, it's a bit pricier, but let's class the joint up. I'd ban sweetener though because I'd get tired of people mooing at me about SINZ PLZ.

It would be mandatory for everyone to have the right change or a countdown when it came to paying. Let's be honest: we've all been in the queue, inwardly seething and wishing death on the poor bugger at the front of the queue fumbling around in the depths of their Michelle Cors handbag for 10p. Think of it like a bus: turn up, pay, bugger off to the seats. Weighing would be the same – it would be mandatory, punishable by death, to be ready to get on the scales. No holding up the queue whilst you take off your support knickers, bra, false-teeth, clit-ring, fanny-chandelier, built-up shoes and pleatherette belt. Get on, get weighed, ten seconds only of your fake surprise act or blustered explanations, then on your way to the naughty seats ready for class.

Now the most important bit: the chat. I have quite a booming voice when I want to so being heard wouldn't be a problem. I'd want the class to be full of laughter, fun and chatter, but if you're the rude arsehole who insists on chatting to your mate all the way through whilst people are shitting themselves from straining so hard to hear who is talking, Paul will nip outside and put your tyres down. We'd open with weight losses – but not the 56-minute-long affair of 'and Mary has lost 'arf a pound how have you done that Mary' (repeating the name a lot so it looks like you are invested in your members but haway, it's on your little screen).

Here's the cruel truth – this bit adds absolutely nowt unless it sparks a discussion about weight loss. The fact that Bob from Greggs has lost two pounds, his foot has turned less black and he's lost eight pounds overall in eighteen years means very little to most people unless you know them. No, we'd beetle about the room, giving out the stickers because let's be fair, everyone likes a sticker, congratulating people in groups (so all the 2lb losses would get named, then the 1lb losses, then the stayed the same) – much quicker and easier. Plus, you don't have to wrap your hands in gauze afterwards to stop the bleeding from clapping so fucking much. We're adults, not seals desperate for people to throw us a fish.

Then, 45 minutes or so of chat, decent recipe swapping and funny stories. Make it an hour where you'd actually want to contribute and make it more like conversation between friends, instead of 60 disparate chubbies all fretting and cringing until the moment their name is called. I'd want to hear people laughing more than hearing people sigh and yawn into their hands. More focus on eating – that's one thing I find so confusing about the groups – there's surprisingly little focus on good things to eat and ideas. I'd bring technology into it – have a decent sized TV in the background with recipes on it, changing every now and then. Naturally, being us, we'd slip the odd slide in of a giant bouncy cock for half a second, just long enough to think you've seen it before onto a risotto recipe. There'd be jokes and genuine admiration. Aaaah.

Slimmer of the Week wouldn't win a basket of fruit that's pretty much already turned into wine, no, the winner would get to take part in my game. I'd get my dad to build a massive wheel-of-fortune stand-up wheel with different segments and prizes – a free week, a box of Hi Fi bars, a tiny sliver for a free countdown, another for a big cuddle from the fattest person in the room, even the odd penalty to add a bit of risk – they have to put the chairs back at the end of the class, or come back to mine and cook us a delicious tea. Paul could mince on in a glittery dress like Debbie McGee's morbidly obese twin, we could make a proper spectacle of it. Much better than 'here's a bunch of black bananas, a sweet

103

'n' sour mugshot and some unidentified fruit with half a WHOOPS sticker on it.

Raffle would be for useful things that people can use to cook with – a decent pan, a set of scales, spoons. Every now and then we'd think fuck it and put a box of chocolates on there. Guarantee we'd have far more raffle tickets being bought then! As for contact during the week, none of the mushy stuff – texts saying 'Yeah, the chocolate might taste nice, but do you not fancy seeing your fadge again' or 'Try the mushy pea curry: you'll be shitting for England but you're sure to get that shiny star' or even just the plain old threatening 'Elnetta-MB has your details now. She knows where you live. DON'T EAT A PIE'. My facebook group would be full of rude jokes and recipe challenges and yeah, you'd still get stickers and certificates, but you'd also get arbitrary stickers like 'Can open a Mars bar without getting breathless' and 'managed to see the end of her toes'. Make it fun, make it entirely non-serious, make it good.

Aaaah a boy can dream, eh? I know the practicalities of money, time and corporate branding would put the kibosh on all of the above, but hell, we could give it a bloody good go before SW cracked the whip.

twochubbycubs on: birthdays

I'm not one of those folks who make a big fuss of their birthday either way – I have no time for people who go DON'T EVEN MENTION IT I'M TOO SHY or SAD or FEELING OLD. It's one day out of 365 (366 this year, pedantic) that you can get people making a slight disinterested fuss out of the fact it's been X amount of years since you came clattering out of a vagina. At the same time, the opposite annoys me too – if you shoehorn in the fact it's your birthday into every conversation, chances are I'll be hoping it's your last and looking temptingly at your back as you walk down a flight of stairs. I received some wonderful cards and presents and ate more than was entirely decent. Expect significant weight gains this week!

We spent bank holiday Monday geocaching, which if you're new to the blog and/or have anything resembling a social life you'll never have heard of. It's essentially dogging but with less sexual arousal and more digging around behind fence-posts looking for a Tupperware box filled with trinkets and sadness. People hide containers and clever contraptions all around the world in beautiful places (trust me, you've never seen a bus-shelter until you've run your hands over every conceivable surface trying to find a film canister) and you use GPS to find them. It's geeky as hell which is why it appeals to us. Actually, that's a fib, the fact that it's free of charge appeals to me more.

So that's what we did all day – drove to a pretty village, loaded up our cache maps and tottered around screaming and shrieking as we found each one. We're planning to hide our own, too, so if you're a geocacher and you want a challenge, keep an eye on the blog. I've made it all sound terrifically dull but really, there are some clever ideas. For example, one of the caches consisted of nothing more than a tube, sealed at the bottom, stuck to the back of a fence next to a brook in the middle of nowhere. No way of getting the hidden container out until you realise that you had to fill the tube with water so that the cache would float out. Ingenious! Luckily, I had just enough piss in me to fill the container though I'd had asparagus so I pity the next fucker to get it. Again, I'm kidding. We fashioned a scoop from an empty crisp packet, filled it with water from the stream and did it that way. Ingenious! Other caches included a container hidden on a well, another you had to fish out of a mysterious hole in the ground and a few containers hidden in the forest behind HMP Northumberland. Well, the joke almost writes itself, but... it's not the first time I've been on my knees in a forest being leered at by hard blokes whilst I desperately try and get my hands around a camouflaged package.

BOOM

In all we managed a new record of 43 caches and walked 11 miles, only stopping when Paul's blister became one with his shoe. The weather forecast said it was going to rain and be miserable, so you can imagine how much joy wearing a thick, long wool coat was when the sun stayed out all day. I looked like the most fabulous Dementor ever stalking around in the woods.

twochubbycubs on: Easter

Happy Easter, all – I've been forced to make a nice Easter recipe for chocolate cake filled pastel eggs, saying as I can barely hear my TV for the sound of fatties crying into their children's Easter Eggs and shallow-breathing around the empty Mini Egg packets. It's pretty to look at and I suppose it could be fun to make these with children, but not for me, as I dislike children. Snotty-nosed little poo-machines. Every day I run the risk of deliberately crashing my car into the central reservation when the 'child of the day' calls in on Radio 2 at half seven. They're always so achingly middle-class it enrages me. 'What are you doing today, little Randolph?' 'WELL **CHRASS UM** IT'S MY PICCOLO EXAM AT HALF SEVEN **UM** AND THEN I'M MAKING ARTISAN PARST-AARGH WITH THE HELP'. Pfft. At 11 I was too busy counting my pubic hair to worry about exams.

Pah. Sometimes I'd welcome the sweet caress of death.

Speaking of death, I got told off for being rude by a group of old ladies in Waitrose today for having the temerity to say 'excuse me please'. I know, shocking behaviour. I'm basically Harold Shipman but I murder with words. No, listen, I was making to leave when seemingly every elderly lady in a ten mile range of Ponteland Waitrose decided to meet and hold an impromptu W.I. meeting right in the store doors. Seriously, the automatic doors were stuttering back and forth whilst they gossiped and clucked in one giant lavender mass. I waited for a few moments, clearing my throat, tapping my foot, cocking my shotgun, but no. One old love looked me straight in the eyes (I assume, her cataract was haunting her vision) and then carried on chatting. Eventually I caved, collapsed forward into their huddled mass, sending copies of the Daily Mail flying and hips popping like popcorn in the microwave.

No, I said 'excuse me, please' and waited for the mass to disperse, which it didn't. It took me asking three times, in increasing pitch and volume, before they deigned to let me past, but not before some wizened old crone with lipstick bleeding into her almond-esque skin clutched my sleeve and told me to 'respect my elders'. Pfft. It was all I could do not to pick her up and post her into the charity token bank, hopefully into something ironic like Age Concern. Instead I smiled my most ingratiating smile and said 'terribly sorry Sir' and walked past. I assume she'll have sat bolt upright in her Medichair about ten minutes ago with a look of anger.

It didn't help that as I was leaving I was pounced on by some chap who felt it necessary to proper tell me off for apparently going the 'wrong way around the one-way system' which 'could lead to serious accidents'. Undoubtedly I was in the wrong, but in my defence I hadn't spotted the lettering on the road indicating it was one-way until I turned the corner and had it in front of me. I'll get a periscope fitted to the car just as soon as I can. He was needlessly officious about the whole thing despite my genuine apologies, banging on about those serious accidents. Serious accidents? If I had been going any more than 5mph I'd have been surprised – I was overtaken by a flock of grannies itching to get to the door for their meeting, for goodness sake. We weren't about to repeat the M4 motorway disaster. I wiped the flecks of his spittle off my coat and carried on, suitably chastised. I did notice that he wasn't doing jackshit about all the massive, perfectly spotless, ridiculously oversized Range Rovers parked up on the double yellows to the side of the store though. Wonder why.

Anyway, I couldn't have been in Waitrose for a more middle-class reason if I tried – I was after white eggs. Not boring old normal eggs, but white eggs, because they take the dye a lot easier for the recipe below. You can use normal eggs though, just leave them in the dye for a bit longer.

There's a myriad of 'Slimming World desserts' which are, without exception, disgusting. You can't make a good dessert because all the delicious tasting things are rammed in syns – caramel, sugar, flour, butter, cream, chocolate, toffee....no amount of stirring an Options into a friggin' bowl of fromage frais is going to fool your tastebuds into a food-orgasm, is it? Nearly all of the desserts seem to be the same – take more eggs than is decent, decant a jar of sweetener into it and then add something to give it a flavour, like a Rolo or some apple. That's not a cake. It tastes like a fart and looks like a scabby knee. It's no more a lemon drizzle cake than I am a successful heterosexual with fabulous flowing hair.

Now, don't get me wrong, I see why people **try** these things – because the idea of being able to eat cake and diet is a wonderful one, but personally, I think it's a con. I'd be amazed if any successful slimmer has managed to get to their ideal weight and **then** carried on making these eggy abominations. You're given 15 syns for a reason – to have the extra bits you fancy, to enjoy yourself and not feel like you're on a diet. Use them!

twochubbycubs on: a business trip to Glasgow I

Yes, last week then. See, I was sent up to Glasgow on a sort-of business trip to learn some new skills and socialise – both of which I'm terrible at. Had I been single I would have been up there so fast my shadow would have only appeared an hour later – Paul and I both love a Scotsman and between you and me (because who reads this, honestly) the biggest willy I've ever seen belonged to a Glaswegian. I didn't know what to do with it – I'm surprised he didn't pass out from lack of blood on the brain when he got an erection. It looked like a sausage casing stuffed with two cans of Carling Black Label. I didn't know whether to laugh, cry or smash a bottle of champagne off the side of it. But those days are behind me (though I still whistle like a keyhole in a haunted castle) and so I didn't have that to look forward to.

It also meant a whole week without Paul – I know. Before you're all sick in your mouth (although, think of the weight-loss) please understand that we haven't been apart for more than a week in the totality of our almost ten-year relationship. I was fretting at the thought of being unable to sleep without the smell of death being blown across my nostrils at five-minute intervals. I shivered at the thought of being able to occupy more than 10% of the bed without Paul's wandering hands, feet and knob poking and prodding me. There are nights I feel like a stress-ball. But hey, it had to be done, and it was with an aching heart and a threatening arsehole (we'd had easy peasy beef curry the night before, and whilst delicious, it was making a dramatic reappearance throughout the morning) that we schlepped off to pick up my hire car on Sunday.

I could see I was in for an easy time when I got to the desk and was assigned a car-rental-spokesperson who I wasn't entirely convinced wasn't dead. I've made more responsive omelettes. He didn't look up from his keyboard once – perhaps he was trying to find the 'wake the fuck up' key but if so, he failed miserably. He didn't check my insurance details, didn't check my payment details, didn't check my lyrics, nothing. I'd have had a more fruitful chat if I'd turned and had a discussion with the leaflet stand. I was going to ask him about fuel but I rather thought I'd need to fetch a defibrillator to just bring him back into some form of sentience, and well, my ankles were already hurting from having to concertina myself into Paul's tiny Smart car. He did perk up when he remembered he could sell me an upgrade, and, remembering the Ford Boredom we'd been given last time, I asked him what he could offer me. First a Skoda – no. Then a Fiat 500 – no. Then his trump card (honestly, his eyes nearly opened with the shock) – he had an Audi. Did I want an Audi? I leaned over the desk and tried to explain that I'd be unable to take an Audi because a) I know how to use indicators and b) I'm not a middle-aged, impotent, prematurely-balding twat, but he'd pretty much already signed the card for me and was back to looking like he was trying to remember to breathe in and out. Resigned (and a fair few pounds lighter) I went to pick up my car.

Well, I'm not going to lie. It was lovely. I wanted to hate it, really I did, but it drove well and was comfortable for a long drive. I still wouldn't buy one on sheer principle and I still think every single Audi driver — bar you and any of your charming family and friends, I'm sure — is a minge, but I can definitely see the appeal. I thought I'd do my best to be a decent Audi driver so I spent the first sixty miles or so driving gently and letting people out at junctions before a transformation took place and I was flooring it. You know how the Incredible Hulk turns green when he gets angry? I turned violet. In my defence I *was* stuck behind a little old dear doing 40mph on a single carriageway designed for 70mph and because I'm a nice guy deep down, I couldn't flash my lights, but by god was I raging. I had to stop at the next services just to have a McFlurry and calm myself down.

I drove on, loving every second of having the car to myself for a long drive. I could sing along to my music without any protestation from Paul and there was no Alanis Fucking Morrisette to contend with, which was lucky as I don't think my Budget Special Povvo Insurance would cover deliberately driving into the back of a petrol tanker. As I drove past Lockerbie the tyre pressure warning light came on. Horror! I pulled over, walked around the car kicking the tyres because I'd seen someone do it on the TV, then spent twenty minutes reading up on how to change a tyre. I have no clue. I know that I should have acquired this skill by now but really, I'm very much a pay-someone-else-to-do-it sort of guy (i.e. lazy). I didn't want some oily-handed mechanic to come and tut at me on the hard shoulder whilst I tried to make crass jokes about helping him with his tight nuts or jacking up. I waited a bit and kicked the tyres again and they seemed hard enough, so on I went.

You may recall I'm somewhat of a catastrophic thinker – well, this meant that I couldn't relax for the rest of the journey. That tiny light with the deflated tyre haunted me like the Telltale Heart, burning away at my retinas as I tried to think about anything else than my tyre exploding and sending me ricocheting into oncoming traffic. Imagine that – being found buckled into a shoebox cube of metal with the Audi rings imprinted on my forehead, with some coroner declaring me dead due to my lack of manliness. The last sixty or so miles into Glasgow were tenser than the last round of The Cube – I reckon there's still a fingernail wedged into the steering wheel. However, after navigating my way down to the Clyde (via the road system, as opposed to plummeting off the A74 in a fading shriek of ABBA Gold) I arrived at the hotel, the not-especially-salubrious Garden Inn Hilton. That's where we'll stop for now.

twochubbycubs on: a business trip to Glasgow II

There's not an awful amount to say — not because it wasn't useful (it was) or lovely (of course) but because my week consisted of me going to my temporary work, learning lots, coming back, eating lots, sleeping. Even I'd struggle to eke 1000 words out of that, but hey, that's never stopped me before! Some random thoughts then.

When I checked in I was offered a room with a view of the river — sounds great, right? I immediately snapped it up only to be told it cost an extra £25 a night for this view. I did enquire as to whether there was going to be a flotilla of rare boats I could gaze at or perhaps a Scottish take on the Oxford/Cambridge rowing, but no — which is a shame, as I love nothing more than watching cox thrusting away — it was just a letterbox window view of the Squinty Bridge. I'm ashamed to say I took it anyway despite the extra charge and actually managed to sweet-talk the charge off my bill later in the week.

Glasgow seems surprisingly amazed by the Squinty Bridge. I mean, it's nice, for a slightly-vagina shaped bit of metal, but I'll see your Squinty Bridge and, quite literally, raise you our Millennium Bridge.

Our bridge moves! I gazed out of the window for ages thinking that your bridge moved, but alas, it never did. Plus, I only spotted fifteen bodies floating down the river during the five days I was there — Taggart lies. Our bridge lifts up to allow ships to enter (it seems fitting for

Newcastle, actually: a giant, hard beast that opens up to allow easy access for seamen) and is ever so fancy.

The room itself was nothing to write home about, which was lucky because who wants to receive a letter stating 'bed clearly damaged by too many people rutting on it' and 'bathroom tiny but fine, who knew being able to shower and shit at the same time would be such a luxury'. Weirdly, there was no main light, meaning every moment before bed was spent turning off about 100 lamps and drawing the curtains against the glow of the lights outside. Just what you need before bed, a fucking bleep test. I missed Paul most of all when I was sleeping. I just can't get a relaxing night's sleep unless I'm sleeping with half an ear cocked for him finally being drowned by his own neck-fat. Ah well.

Is there a more fraught, tense feeling in life than having a white hire car and not taking out the damage insurance that covers scratches and dents? I swear I spent a good two hours a day gingerly driving my car a foot in various directions, terrified that if I parked next to another car their careless owner would come back and scrape their denim-clad arse all down the side of my car, leaving me with a ridiculous bill to pay. I've never felt such stress behind the wheel – I had to go for a colonoscopy just to calm down. There will be footage in some tedious collection somewhere of me trying to park perfectly within the lines of a bay in a perpetually empty car-park. Worse, I had to move my car at one point as I'd parked it directly under the Finnieston Crane and, being ever the worrier, I had visions of dead seagulls plummeting from on high and cracking the window. You know what makes this just the worst though? Anyone watching would automatically assume I was a braying arsehole who didn't want his precious Audi scratched – to be clear, it was all fuelled by me being a tight-arse.

Speaking of being a tight-arse, after one particularly taxing day, I made my way back to the hotel and stopped by their gaily-named little pantry for a snack. I snaffled a Crunchie and a can of coke and the lady behind the desk charged me £2.90. I was conflicted. As a fat bastard, I wanted the Crunchie. As a sarcastic sod, I wanted to ask whether she was confused and perhaps she thought I was asking her to accompany me up to chew the Crunchie and share the coke. As a Geordie I wanted to be outraged, bellow something about rip-off Britain and stot it off her noggin. Naturally, my elegant, fat, British side won out, and I took my Crunchie and coke and grumbled about it to myself all the way back to the room.

Weirdly, that's about the only things I have to say on the trip – as it was for business rather than pleasure there wasn't a lot of shenanigans to be had! I used Deliveroo for all of my evening meals. For those that 'div nat knaa', as it were, this is a service which picks up delicious food from local restaurants and cycles it round straight to your location. It's a great idea in principle and, judging by the sheer amount of hipsters who almost run me over every time I cross a street in Newcastle, seems to be doing well. My limit for each evening meal was £25 and I found a voucher for £10, meaning, because I like to get the value from these things, I ordered £35 every night. Mahaha. I know, it's shocking, but see it meant I could keep some for breakfast (though dolmades at 7am is a tough call) and stock up on drinks, so there was method in the madness. I did have to make a 'oh my other half is starving' crack every time the Deliveroo driver turned up to try and justify the huge bag of food he was bringing. He knew though. He knew.

twochubbycubs on: a very important message

Still with me, dear reader? I'd like to think you were keenly absorbing every word but haway, I know you better than that. I bet The Chase is on and you're half-heartedly wondering what that nice Bradley Walsh would be like in bed. I'd bet you'd take his final offer. Eh?

The reason for this little interlude is a tiny paragraph lifted direct from our blog.

It's been a very long day, livened up by a bit of life-saving. Not sure if that's over-egging the pudding (HOW MANI SYNS HUN) or not but for the first time in four years I got to use my first aid training for something other than a high-heel blister or a stapled finger. If you're looking for a fun read, have a read at my recount of my day at St John's Ambulance learning first aid from my previous book– though the box of faces will haunt you forever more. No, I had to step in to stop a colleague choking on her crisps. It was all very fortuitous because I just happened to be downstairs filling up my bottle with sparkling water (gotta add sparkle somehow, eh) when I saw a pizza being hurled across a table and a colleague looking wide-eyed and fearful. I almost shit myself. It's one thing sitting in a room full of factory workers being told what to do if someone pours industrial bleach up their nostril or sets their arse on fire, it's another thing kno wing you have to step in and do something. I remembered you're supposed to do five sharp blows between their shoulderblades and so, with a hearty 'THIS IS GOING TO HURT' I went into action and thankfully, on the five blow, out popped the crisp. I'm not going to fib: I think I was more relieved that I didn't have to do the Heimlich – I'd be the only person who'd need to stop after two er...thrusts (good god there's no other way of saying it) for a sit down and a puff on an oxygen tank. My colleague is fine – I apologised profusely for the fact she's probably got a huge hand mark on her back now but all was well. I went upstairs shaking like a shitting dog and I can assure you right now my catastrophic thinking went into overdrive: what if it hadn't worked? What if my first aid skills were no match for a shrapnel of smoky bacon crisp? It was all I could do to have a giant cookie and a cup of tea and then back to drafting documents.

It made me think though: if you don't know any first-aid, learn some. Seriously. St John's Ambulance provide training online and there's all manner of free videos on YouTube. Whilst I doubt what I've done could be classed as saving a life, you never know when **you** might need it.

twochubbycubs go to Cornwall: part one

Why Cornwall? Well, naturally, we were attracted to the endless walks, the wonderful surfing opportunity and the chance to lay on a beach and sizzle. Pfft, as if. Let's get this clear – the only surfing I did was via my iPad to find out when the local Tesco planned to shut off our clotted cream supply. No, we always tend to holiday out of England when we stay in the United Kingdom, but we thought to hell with it, let's try somewhere different.

And boy, was that a bloody struggle. Seriously – I've said it before, there is a massive market out there ready for milking for holiday cottages built for young, professional couples who don't have sticky-fingered kids, moulting dogs or an extended family travelling with them like fleas on a cat. We spent hours looking for places to rent for a week away and probably found about four cottages that matched what we were looking for. Everywhere else looked like the type of place you'd see on TV in a documentary about someone who got eaten by their cats or drowned in newspapers. Who has ever looked at a room and thought 'yes, this will do, but we must add more beige'? Eh? I want a cottage full of modern features, tasteful decoration, fun touches and unusual things. Not somewhere where I could see myself stumbling out into the garden to die of terminal boredom, face-down in a Chat magazine with taupe carpet fibres on my tea-stained jumper.

Now, Newcastle to Cornwall is a bloody long drive – just shy of 450 miles, fact fans. We could have flown, but it's Newcastle remember – the only flights available that weren't a vomit-express to Malaga didn't leave on the days we needed. Plus, I needed to work on our day of departure, so we decided to drive halfway after work and stop in a Premier Inn somewhere in Bumhole, Birmingham. I might have made that name up.

What a drive though – the glamour of the A1, the majesty of the M6. We elected to take my car rather than Paul's Smart car as we needed to take more than two lightly-folded t-shirts and a plimsoll, so his boot wouldn't have worked. Paul, having driven an automatic now for many months, gave me such a start as he lurched out, over-revving and kangarooing and generally being over savage with my clutch, but luckily we escaped certain death once he didn't have to slow down or be gentle. That's unfair – I'm just as bad driving his Smart car. But that's because I'm six foot of man pressed into a Quality Street tin sized car interior. It remains the only car I can simultaneously pop the bonnet with one knee and open the boot with the other. That'll be me banished from ever driving it again. Imagine my distress.

There is something about long car journeys at night that I love – and it's not that it usually ends up with me getting holes in the knees of my jeans in a layby somewhere, because that *simply isn't true*. No, it reminds me of my childhood, when holidays involved my parents shepherding my sister and I into a battered Ford Escort at 3am in the morning in order to get a good start driving up into Scotland to "beat the traffic", as though the A69 at Warwick Bridge was the equivalent of the roundabout at the Arc de Triomphe. Invariably it would be too cold to have the windows down so the first few hours of the drive would be spent coughing and spluttering whilst my parents hotboxed us to death via endless Lambert & Butlers. We'd get out for a desultory Olympic breakfast in a Little Chef on an industrial estate outside of Lockerbie with blue lips and a faint golden patina of nicotine. No wonder my sister and I always used to fight in the back of the car – my dad would barely have backed down the drive before punches were being thrown, ankles were being kicked and hair was being pulled – but see that was my sister all over, so I never hit her back.

Gosh, I might do a few blog posts about earlier holidays actually, I love reminiscing of times when I used to be a) skinny b) far less cynical and c) more easily impressed. Let's get back into the fast-lane though and talk about our current excursion.

I've mentioned on previous occasions how much I love stopping at service stations. I find them exciting! Everyone is going somewhere – normally to the cash machine to get £20 out to pay for two coffees and a side of abysmal customer service – and everyone has a tale. Travelling does something to my sphincter that invariably means I want to stop for a poo at every opportunity, so our short four-hour drive took about six hours in the end. Our stops ended up costing us £260 because I was so taken with a Deal or no Deal fruit machine that, when I came home, I ordered one for the games room. I've told Paul it'll help us save money and it will, not least because seeing Noel Edmonds face all lit-up in the corner of our games room will make me so nauseated I'll not want takeaway. We did have a hairy moment when we turned into Trowell Services at midnight and unpacked our brie and grape baguettes only to have a procession of chavs in their acne-carriages turn up and start doing spins in the car-park. It was Fast & Furious 9: Roaccutane Rush. Listen mate, you're not impressing anyone by sticking a 'RIP Paul Walker' sticker on your nana's haemorrhage-purple 02-plate Micra.

We left them to it, driving with a contemptuous sneer of our own which was somewhat diluted by the fact the Archers Omnibus theme-tune was playing through our car speakers as we glided past. At least it wasn't Yes Sir (I Can Boogie) which was the song of the holiday. Anyway, our moment of happiness turned into despair when, after a bit more driving, we were informed that the motorway was shut and that we had to find our way to the Premier Inn on our own steam. This was past midnight, remember, and I was tired – I hadn't managed to finish my baguette either. Paul took control and used a new app on his phone that acts as a sat-nav. Brilliant!

NOT brilliant. No, somehow, those last 25 miles seemed to take an eternity, taking us down all sorts of country roads, private lanes, farm tracks and tiny B-roads. I was cursing the whole time (remember, I don't trust Sat-Navs) but Paul was adamant we were going the right way. Because I wanted to listen to the end of Brain of Britain, I shut my hole, and carried on. It took us over an hour to reach our destination and it was only then Paul discovered he'd effectively selected the 'scenic' route option, avoiding major busy routes. My language was as blue as the bedspread was purple. Our Premier Inn receptionist booked us in, taking a moment to ask Paul 'who are you?' before realising that he was the 'Mrs' on my booking, and we sank into bed, top layer of skin burning and crisping nicely in the far-too-hot-bedroom. Ah, what a start.

twochubbycubs go to Cornwall: part two

Now, the last blog entry was bloody miserable, wasn't it? It all went a bit hello darkness, my old friend, did it not? Well come on, settle back in your chair and let me tell you some good things about Cornwall. It wasn't all bad, I promise. Look, we had a nice cottage. In fact, I even made a wee video of how it looks. Forgive the crap film style, but see this was originally just intended as a Whatsapp to a mate. Don't be mean.

It was charming – a small, hidden away little building nestled on a back lane in a small, charming village. It was decorated in that style that *normally* makes my eyes roll back into my brain but when I'm on holiday, I can overlook and admire. Lots of Orla Kiely, whose name still looks and sounds to me like a Countdown Conundrum, including a few feature walls clad in that distinctive colourful wallpaper which has the unique double effect of making me ooh and wince at the same time. A whoo, perhaps, only not so exuberant. The kitchen was well-appointed, which makes a bloody change, with lots of secret little gadgets that we enjoyed like a hidden plug socket that rose from the unit like a robot's knob and an extractor fan in the ceiling that opened up like a robot's arsehole. It really did! Don't get me wrong, I mean I've seen a bloody extractor fan before, but not a sphincter-edition that opens and shuts on command. Terribly exciting. The house was absolutely littered with the kind of living

127

magazines you'll often find in private hospitals – look at this table made from walnut and disdain, yours for only £16,000. I would love to be in a financial position where I could open one of those magazines and not pass out from sucking too much air in over my teeth. Actually, that's a fib, I could a billionaire and I'd still shop at IKEA, because all my shopping experiences should end in the consumption of a hot-dog.

Everything you needed was there, including a decent TV, a wine cooler, smart outdoor furnishings, fresh flowers, a little hamper welcoming us as guests, dressing gowns...ah yes, the dressing gowns. Obviously meant for people who eat wheatgrass for breakfast and think nothing of a twenty mile run before work, these barely managed to get around us. It was like trying to hide a sofa behind a tea-towel. We persevered though, and naturally this lead to embarrassment. See, we had received a text from either the owners or the people looking after the cottage to say they'd pop around in the morning. We forgot, of course, and set about on the first morning making a nice breakfast and a mess when someone knocked on the door. Paul, barely clad in his gown, answered the door, taking a moment to ensure the dressing gown met in the middle and covered him up.

It did – but, unbeknown to him, bless, he was so busy trying to cover his belly up and make small talk about fishing towns with the person at the door that he completely neglected to cover up his nether regions, meaning Little Paul was experiencing some Cornish air of his own. I was just out of sight frantically trying to mime 'COVER UP' to him but whenever he looked at me he assumed I mean cover up his belly, and he tightened his gown further at the top which meant the bottom opened up more. Paul, of course, has previous when it comes to flashing his willy – sometimes with my involvement as in Ireland, and sometimes completely on his own steam as in Corsica with the holiday rep. I'm beginning to feel he may have a problem – I reckon we shouldn't go back to New York, for instance, because he'll probably end up tripping over one of the live cameras and having a blisteringly highly-detailed, 80ft representation of his spam dagger projected across Times Square. Whoever was at the door had the good grace not to mention his accidental nudity and to their credit, we didn't hear them start retching until they had climbed back into their own car. Anyway, the police only kept him in for a few hours and then let him go. Kidding. Though they could have done me for handling swollen goods afterwards, kaboom-tish.

Speaking of nudity, the cottage also came with a very odd quirk – an outside bath in the yard. The yard itself wasn't overlooked and there was a large, wooden fence bordering you from the place next door, so there was no chance of anyone glancing over at me getting undressed and calling the police to report a runaway cow frolicking in the garden. I imagine that (and indeed, the write-up hints at it) when they designed the place they imagined lithe, hunky young couples sliding into the bath together under the stars and laughing tinkly at times past. No chance for Paul and I. If we had somehow managed to both get into the bath there wouldn't have been any room for so much as a cup of hot water and hell, no amount of Radox Muscle Relaxant would have got us out of there. Imagine two pickled eggs squashed together at the bottom of a jar and you have a faint idea. Paul's a complete jessie anyway when it comes to being cold so there was no chance of him joining me, though he did come to my aid when my tasteful piles of Love It, Take A Break, Hiya and Fuck Me No Way spilled out of reach across the decking. I don't know what it is about holidays that make me reach for these magazines, full as they are with medical woes, true crime and children's names that look like someone has had a half-hearted stab at spelling a normal name and added a hyphen and a 'Mae' onto it. I can't get enough. We took two books each to read – mine being a story about a man who travelled around Britain on a bus (I know how to live) and Paul brought along The Ragged Trousered Philanthropists. Again. That book has travelled the world with us to the point where I'm beginning to think I need to put Frank Owen on my bloody passport. I wouldn't care but it's quite a weighty book and takes up a lot of space in our suitcase, especially as it remains exactly there until it's time for the flight home again.

There is something a smidge unnerving about bathing outside, not least because whenever a light aircraft passed overhead it must have looked like the Hindenburg crash site. Worse was climbing out because, paranoia or no, there was a crunch of gravel on the other side of the fence. I can't imagine anyone was enjoying the sight of my hairy arse clad in Radox bubbles but hey, whatever floats your boat. Admittedly the gravel crunching was more likely to be subsistence or the ground shaking from me pouring out onto the decking, but I digress. There was also a log-burner which I can say, rather proudly, that I managed to light on the first go. Paul was giving it the whole 'put some more fuel on it' and 'throw more logs on it' like his knowledge of fire extends to anything other than clicking on his mother's gas fire. Pfft. I grew up with coal, damn it – if it has, at some point, stood upon this Earth, I can make it burn.

It did have an indoor bathroom, of course, we weren't having to shit in the yard, and this included a fancy double shower with a rainfall shower and one of those tiny little showers which people say is for washing your hair but I know that secretly it's for washing your minnie-Moo. Listen ladies, I know what goes on. The dials for the shower had no clue on them as to what made it go hot and what made it go cold, nor what shower they operated, so the half-awake morning shower became more like a scene from Saw as you dodged scalding jets on the back of your leg and an icy cascade from above. I half-expected a little doll on a tricycle to wheel around the corner, although if he was bringing me a fresh bar of coal-tar soap I'd be happy.

If we had only one complaint, it would be the bed. See, we're spoilt up here because we have an absolutely giant bed that we can tumble around in and lose each other in the heat of night, but this bed was your bog-standard, plain Jane affair. Comfortable yes, but Paul's both a snorer and a feeler (in that, if I'm not lying next to him, he'll be reaching out with whatever he can extend until he finds me) and, without space to escape, it made for a long, noisy, sleepless few nights. The pillows weren't the rock-hard type that we like (honestly, I reckon Paul would be more content if I had someone come and concrete a step onto the bed instead of pillows) and so we both managed to crick our necks. Me especially so, given I'm already carrying a weird neck injury at the moment. The upshot of this was that I couldn't turn my head right and Paul couldn't turn his head left, which made driving in Cornwall, with its labyrinthine roads and many, many junctions, a very fractious event. Many moments of calm and tranquillity in the Cornish countryside were ruined by the over-revving of my engine, me shouting at Paul to check my way rather than his way and him shouting at me saying he couldn't and then us both shouting at each other for confirmation and then finally shouting at some poor fart in the car in front for not pulling away sharp enough and thus forcing us to repeat the whole dance again. BAH.

That is the only complaint though. We had a remarkable stay and it's a place that, despite my crass and crude review, I can't recommend strongly enough. It was tastefully decorated, ideally situated, had everything you could need and, for once, it was made for couples rather than smelly children. We booked with www.uniquehomestays.com and the cottage was called Two Bare Feet. We'd go back in a heartbeat. Well, no, maybe if they moved it onto the Northumberland coast...

twochubbycubs go to Cornwall: Land's End

You can't go to Cornwall and not visit Land's End – it's like going to London and not seeing the Queen, or going to Southend and not getting roughly fingered under the pier by someone more hair gel than teeth. Oh I know, Southend is lovely and charming and really, what's a severe physical assault when you've got the glitz of the Rendezvous casino and the chance to spot a Subaru doing doughnuts in a McDonalds car park? I digress. I imagined Lands' End to be some quaint little village right on the tip of southern England, full of darling tea-shops and people laughing gaily.

Well, it fucking wasn't.

Excuse my swearing, but I've genuinely never been more disappointed with a place in my life. And I've been to Hartlepool. On a bus. What should have been a fairly tasteful and certainly interesting place to visit was nothing more than a tacky, ill-designed, grasping tourist trap, comprising of poorly thought out exhibitions and miserable staff. We had chortled our way down the A30 on a brisk, drizzly English day – all roads in Cornwall seem to go via the A30, I reckon I could drive it blindfolded now – and our hearts were lifted as the Sat Nav, inexplicably tuned to the voice of Colonel Sanders, told us that the exhibition centre was only half a mile away. I should have clocked there and then – an exhibition centre? Why? Let us look at the cliffs, the signpost and perhaps have a cup of tea and a moan about our knees. Exhibitions aren't needed – the beauty is exhibition itself. Nevermind. We indicated off into the almost empty car-park only to be waved down by someone who, a touch ironically, had a face like a wet weekend. He informed us that it was £5 for the privilege of parking our car into what looked like a plane crash site, all jagged and cratered. I try to crack a joke that 'I'm not bringing a coach in' but he wasn't having any of that, so we paid up and did the very British thing of sitting in the car bitching on about it.

£5 though. Yes, it's not a great amount of money in the grand scheme of things, but it's grasping. Why a fiver? Am I going to tear up five pounds' worth of tarmac primly parking my DS3? Was he going to bring it around for me when we left? There's simply no need for it, especially out of season. Still twisting our faces, we stole a glance at the leaflet, which promised 'something to do for every member of the family'. Hmph.

I just want you to know that at this point I had an absolutely killer joke lined up but the other half censored it because he said 'think of the complaints' – spoilsport. But see we do have limits.

Our first stop was to the giant tat shop, which was full of all the lovely things only people in their nineties buy for other people in their nineties that they don't like – fudge that predates decimalisation, clothes you wouldn't wear for a bet and all sorts of lead-based paperweights, pencils and cough sweets. I can't imagine a single soul in their life has desired an ashtray showing people they once went to the absolute arse-end of the country they're smoking in, but hell, here they were, and cheap at only half your dignity. We sniffed the scented candles with all their wank names: "Cornwall Wash", "Grasping Bastards" and "Fuck Me, A Fiver?!" all leaving a sour taste in our mouths. The one item I quite fancied, a small slab of designer (!?) chocolate, caught my eye, until I realised it would be cheaper to buy Hotel Chocolat in Newcastle and have someone walk it down to the Cornwall cottage. We did end up parting with coins though – everywhere we go we always get some item of pure unadulterated tat for the games room – and so a lovingly, hand-painted snowglobe was bought, depicting what looks like Dachau in the midst of a wailing snowstorm, but is ostensibly a tiny representation of the visitor centre. Incidentally, Cornwall is the least likely place to get snow in the entire United Kingdom, so it only seemed appropriate that they'd have a huge display of snowglobes. Perhaps it was tiny fivers billowing about under the glass. Again, and there's going to be a theme here, sorry, but we were served by someone who had all the personality and warmth of an unapologetic fart. She served us like we were inconveniencing her terribly, despite us and a gaggle of equally depressed looking Chinese tourists being the only people in her shop, and she slapped down our produce and money like they were on fire. I've never heard have a good day said with such venom. We pressed on.

They describe the opportunity to 'feel like a giant by visiting our miniature village'. I love stuff like this, it's such a British thing to do, but once we'd lumbered over there, it was shut for repairs. I looked carefully and didn't see any 1/16th sized cement mixers going about their business or Subbuteo-sized men in hi-viz jackets standing around scratching their arse. Ah well, there's other stuff to do, something for everyone remember? We looked at the leaflet and saw we could choose between an 'Aardman exhibition' (I'm sure I went to something along those lines in Berlin) or 'Arthur's Quest'. Well, nothing says welcome to Cornwall like nosing around claymation and oohing over a bloody animation studio based in er, Bristol. Right. We thought we'd give it a go, not least because it was indoors and it was getting a mite cold so close to the sea, but er, it was shut. Wahey – that fiver's worth of parking seemed even more reasonable at this point. Being plucky, cheerful Geordies, we sucked up our disappointment and decided to try Arthur's Quest, which was an interactive maze narrated by Brian Blessed. Even if it was appalling, the fact that Brian was going to be shouting orders at you would make it hilarious. The man has a gift – he could sit me down and tell me my spine was turning to dust and my penis was about to fall off and I'd still walk out of the surgery slapping my knees and guffawing.

But, it was closed. Three for three of pure disappointment. That left buying a Cornish pasty at the little café but frankly, Paul was beginning to have chest pains through too much pastry so we sacked that off and decided to walk, slowly, to get a picture of the famous sign which points to various destinations around the world – New York 3147 miles, John O'Groats 874 miles, decent tourist attractions anywhere but here. Here's another cherry on top of this bun of disappointment. You're expected to pay £9.95 to get your photo taken by the sign and it's actually chained off so anyone with the temerity to think this is a bloody rip-off can't just hop over and take a photo. There's a passive-aggressive sign saying it's someone's family business and to respect that. The man in the little booth glared at us as we took a picture regardless. I would have cheerfully have paid a couple of quid or stuck a smaller note into a charity box but a tenner? For a photo? Haway. It's possibly the most famous sign in Britain, let people take a photo with it and then they'll go spend the rest of their money in the eateries and shops around (assuming they're bloody open) and everyone is a winner! This outrageous nickel-and-diming, prevalent all throughout Cornwall, did my absolute nut in. It's free to have a photo taken at the other end up at John O'Groats, and I can't imagine you need to pay to park either.

You know when you think a place couldn't get any worse? It managed it – the telescopes to look out to sea were more expense and only sought to bring the fog and mist closer to us. There was a wee lighthouse to look at but I could have had the same magnification effect by moving my glasses an inch down my nose. Paul was inexplicably wearing his sunglasses despite me referring to him as Homocop all day. There was a little bird hide to sit for a bit to see the kittiwakes, but naturally, that was closed too. That especially disappointed me because I was at least hoping for a magnificent shag at this point, given there was no-one around. Bah! We mooched on for a bit more and decided to try and salvage the hour by having a cup of tea in the First & Last House a bit up the hill. I presume that's been renamed from 'The Last Place in England' because they were sick of hearing people saying they'd never drink there again if it were the last place in England. We asked for two cups of tea and were handed two paper cups of hot water with a teabag hanging in it. For not a kick-off-the-arse-of £4. Something which I reckon would cost at maximum 5p to make. Even the milk was in those awful little sealed cups you get on aeroplanes, that jettison their contents all over your trousers if you so much as blink at them. And, yes, the woman serving us was hostile and unpleasant and had a face like a grieving cod.

At this point we'd spent £16.70 for the opportunity to make our own tea, park in a crater and look at some 'closed' signs. I was spitting. I'm not a tight-arse when it comes to money, far from it, but there's got to be a line. I'll happily put money into a charity pot or buy a magazine or wince my way through an overpriced ice-cream but charging people to park up and then not telling them most of the exhibitions are closed, or to take a photo of a landmark? Ridiculous, and honestly, it's very much a southern thing. That isn't some parochial Geordie tub-thumping either, but take for example our Angel of the North – you turn up to this massive piece of artwork, park for nowt, can walk all over it, climb on the bugger, hell someone even put a giant Newcastle shirt on it once, and it costs not a penny. There's occasionally an ice-cream man there peddling 99s but that's about it. If Anthony Gormley had had a fit of the vapours and plopped his pin in Newquay instead of Newcastle, you'd have the Angel boxed off from sight unless you paid a tenner, someone selling pasties the size and price of a small family car between her legs and an inexplicable (and inevitably closed) exhibition all about something local and relevant like ooh...geisha girls, for an extra forty quid. Bah.

I'll say one good thing: the cliffs were pretty. But then so are the cliffs at the Ring of Kerry and I didn't have my pockets patted down there either.

I've never driven away from a place so quickly and angrily as I did that afternoon. The sound of gravel and soil churning under my tyres was almost drowned out by the sound of my teeth gnashing. If I can take one comfort from all of this is that I managed to at least use £5 worth of toilet paper dropping off a tod of barely digested pasty in the netty before I went. Take that, you grasping bastards!

twochubbycubs go to Cornwall: part four

The last three entries of our Cornwall trip didn't exactly make the heart sing with joy, did they? Fair warning, it doesn't get much better. I don't know what it was about Cornwall that disappointed me - it's beautiful (in places) and I'm sure there's lots to see and do if you're not a curmudgeonly fatty whose sole exercise is leaning over to fart - but perhaps I'm spoiled. I live in what I reckon is the most beautiful county in England - Northumberland - and eye-watering beauty is never more than a twenty-minute drive away. Anyway, hush. It's been so long since we went away that we'll have to forgo a chronological narrative, so just assume that wherever there is a full-stop, it's where Paul and I stopped the car to eat a pasty.

The Eden Project

Sitting in our cottage in Perranporth, with the unseasonable grey skies blowing around overhead, we decided to head for the Eden Project, a thirty or so minute drive away via relatively easy roads, according to our sassy in-car Sat-Nav. Nope. You may recall that I was stricken with a poor neck which meant I couldn't look right and Paul was equally laid-out with a sore back that meant he couldn't look left, so you can imagine how much fun driving a car was. Every junction was one step closer to divorce. Things became so tense that I actually just started pulling out of junctions blindly in the hope that a clotted cream tanker would crash into the side of the car, putting us both out of our misery. We'd die the way we lived: sitting down and covered in fat.

The sat-nav did indeed take us the most direct route but for some reason, confined us almost exclusively to single-track roads. I reckon if you counted up the miles we did in reverse it would actually work out that we never left the cottage in the first place. Why does every road in Cornwall need to be framed by an impenetrable hedge or crumbling wall? At one point we were stuck between a car coming towards us, eight walkers in rustling (is there any other kind) all-weather-ware, two cyclists and a lorry behind us tooting his horn. It was like playing Screwball Scramble, but in a DS3 littered with crumbs and sheer, blinding rage.

We arrived, filling the valley with swearing and Cher, and parked up in the lime car-park. Cheek, I'm a gay man, put me in the plantain park and I'll be sure to back up correctly. We did think about waiting for the courtesy bus but we could see the entrance only a moment's walk away and thought better of it. That's a fib actually, there was a coach full of old folk gamely walking down the hill and putting us to shame so we couldn't. Buggers.

Getting into the Eden Project cost us £50 between us. That, right there, tells you everything you need to know about it. Yes, it's lovely and pleasant and the work they do is great, but £50? Kiss my arse. They temper this by allowing you to visit all year long but given that most of their visitors are tourists, that's a bit of a pointless endeavour – it's not like I could turn to Paul on a windy Sunday and ask if he fancied a nose round the gift-shop at Eden, and could he prepare the car for the 800-mile round trip. Pfft. I appreciate these places have to make money because gosh, who else is going to pay for all the wank, but haway.

You could have put what we both knew about the Eden Project before we visited on the back of a seed packet. Paul had a vague recollection that it was used in Die Another Day and I automatically assumed that those giant plastic zits were full of bees like in The X-Files movie, but we were both wrong. No, The Eden Project is a very worthwhile endeavour by lots of horticulturists (my favourite horticulturist? Brian Sewell – boom boom) to get as many tourists as possible in one place.

How we admired the many different ways that people could inconvenience us – one particularly (and quite literally) pushy mother gently nudged me out of the way whilst I was reading an enthralling information board on bamboo. She wanted to take a picture of her child, but I hazarded a guess that had I picked up said child and pitched her into the wilderness that I would have been asked to leave, and damn it, I wanted my £25 worth.

We wandered around the herb garden, we idled around

the flower section, we sweated our tits off in the rainforest section. It was all very interesting – we're not complete philistines, you understand – but the sheer amount of people similarly feigning interest in a sugarbush was hard to take. We climbed various stairs and gantries to get a picture of the waterfall only to find such a task impossible due to the sea of giant lenses and Mumsnetters that filled every conceivable space. Deflated, both from disappointment and the sweat wicking away from our body, we left the biomes and staggered outside, where a fine mist (either rain or aerated sweat) greeted us. That, at least, was pleasant.

Now, look here. We're just as capable of enjoying a garden centre as the best of them. You'll often find us at Heighley Gate on a Sunday afternoon fingering the dahlias or cooing over the roses. We've had lengthy and earnest conversations about the merits of various composts: I prefer to buy in, Paul's rustic and would spread his own if I let him shit in the garden. But something about The Eden Project left us both cold. Ho-hum.

We stopped for something to eat, thinking we could at least salvage some of the entrance fee by having something delightful in the onsite restaurants, but even these were overpriced and understaffed. Everywhere was noise: children screaming, old people clacking their teeth, parents sighing and braying. The food was what you'd expect from a place like this plus a 20% tedium surcharge. We went outside where, thanks to the rain, we were relatively alone. We ordered a small pasty and a coke (I say coke, I'm sure at least three varieties of dandelion were pressed into it along with a shock of hipster beard hair) and sat down in the drizzle. The pasty was drier than a popcorn fart and the coke was flat. Ho-hum, again.

We made to make our way back to the lime car-park and spotted that this would involve a walk at a level significantly more than horizontal. Panic set in until we spotted that a little tractor with a trailer on the back was trundling around picking up visitors. We hastened over and climbed aboard with barely enough time to wipe the pastry crumbs away from my shirt (I was worried that they'd burst into flames if they rubbed together given how fucking dry the thing was). We were joined in the carriage by another couple – a cheery man with the strongest Geordie accent I've ever heard (and bear in mind my dad's accent is so strong that Paul didn't understand a word of it for six months, becoming the only person in existence to form a familial relationship on nothing more than polite nods and 'ee-I-knows') and a woman on an oxygen tank.

We had spotted them earlier gamely making their way around the biomes and they spent a good five minutes chatting with us, which was lovely. At one point she took off her oxygen mask and told us they were only getting the tractor because she couldn't manage hills with her failing lungs and we felt terrible: not just for her, but also because we were clearly only getting the tractor because our fat ankles were bowing under the weight of four days of constant and committed pasty consumption. We bid them goodbye (well, I did, Paul was struggling to understand – to him it probably sounded like me and the other gentlemen were arguing in Icelandic) and made our way back to the car.

Just like Land's End, I drove out of the car park in an absolute fury. The whole exercise just annoys me, you know. People say to holiday in the UK but every god-damn tourist attraction is out to extract just as much money as they can get away with short of employing urchins to root through your pockets for change whilst you go for a piss. I appreciate that places need money to stay afloat but for goodness sake, calm the fuck down.

We took our time driving back to the cottage and decided to stop at a charming little pub that we'd spotted on the way to Eden. It was in a fantastic location – beer garden looking out over lush green fields with a bit of twinkling sea just off on the horizon. The weather had lightened up and, after some energetic singing and maybe, just maybe, a cheer-up-for-fuck's-sake-blowjob from Paul, all was well. We fair cantered (Paul more so than me – I had to do that discreet unsticking of James Junior from my leg that all men know) out of the car hoping we'd at least get some ale (just a half for me) and food. What could go wrong?

YET AGAIN: EVERYTHING. You know in comedy sketches they occasionally do a joke where a stranger walks into a bar and the whole place falls silent? That's exactly what happened to us. It was like someone turned off my hearing as soon as we stepped over the threshold. Admittedly there were only a few chaps in there at 3pm in the afternoon but they all looked at us silently and furiously. If it hadn't been for the disembodied electronic voice of Noel Edmonds shrieking at me to hold my nudges blaring out of the fruit machine I would have sworn I had gone deaf. Paul pushed me from behind (lucky me!) and we made our way to the bar.

The bar man had one of those faces that told me he'd last smiled in 1977, perhaps when a barn-fire had killed his more handsome brother. There was no hello, how are you, what would you like – just an impassive stare like I was some unwelcome intruder on this otherwise jumping social vista. It felt like I was trying to order from a grazing cow. I asked for two drinks with equal solemnity, paid for them and moved away, all in the continued silence of the bar. We sat outside and had no sooner taken our first pull from the all-head-no-beer drinks when Mr Chatty came outside and started moving tables around, ostensibly because they were expecting a wedding party. I decided against asking if he was doing the best man's speech as I didn't fancy driving home with a pint glass sticking out of my face. I haven't felt as unwelcome in a drinking establishment since I got caught giving my then-boyfriend a blowjob in a Yates Wine Lodge.

Listen, I know, I'm ashamed of that too. I mean come on, a Yates Wine Lodge? What was I thinking?

We didn't bother finishing our drinks. We didn't bother looking at the food menu (I presumed that the food would be served with the same kind of panache as the witty raillery from the barman). No, yet again, we drove furiously out of the car park and went back to the cottage, where actually, we spent a very pleasant night getting drunk and smoking cigars the size of shot-putters' arms in the garden. I only hope that some of that thick smoke made its way across the valley and right up the nostrils of that miserable arse of a barman. I hope his sinuses throbbed and ached and the wedding ended in disaster.

Pfft: Cornwall. You're really on a roll...

twochubbycubs go to Cornwall: part five

I wish I could pretend things improved with Cornwall, but they didn't. Disappointment, rudeness and expense lurked around every corner. Don't get me wrong, there were some charming people and pleasant vistas, absolutely, but it didn't compensate for my growing sense of rage. This is evidenced by the fact that my notebook, where I usually write down my thoughts of the day and which in turn gets turned into these blog entries, consists of page after page of angry faces and lots of instances of the word 'bah'. Because of this, I'm going to break with tradition and just do a summary post of all the other scraps of our Cornwall trip that I can't bring myself to put into flowing narrative.

Padstow

We love Rick Stein – he's a cheeky-faced cooking wonder and we watch everything he's in whenever he's on the telly. I could listen to him describing Russian phone-box repair and still feel a quiver of excitement. It's not some weird daddy-fetish, he's just wonderful. With that in mind, Padstow seemed like an obvious place to spend a fresh Spring morning.

Nope. First of all, I've never seen so many Audis, BMWs and Mercedes cars in one place. Secondly, same sentence again but replace cars with braying Jigsaw-wearing idiots. We parked up – eventually – took a stroll around the quaint ten-a-penny tea-shops, the lovely seen-it-all-before craft shops and the 'oh I get it, it's Seahouses but for people with a buy-to-let portfolio' restaurants. It left me cold. I don't think I have an inferiority complex – I'm not worthy of one – but the sense of snootiness and unbridled tra-la-laing wasn't for me.

We decided that, as we didn't stand a chance of a walk-in appointment at any of his fabulous restaurants, we'd treat ourselves to fish and chips from Rick Stein's fish and chip shop. Naturally, it was all very to-do, but fair play, it was delicious. We ate them on the harbour and it was only their deliciousness that saved me from pitching forward into the sea to end my misery. Though, just saying, I can get a pizza, kebab wrap, large chips, can of pop (oh how I hate that), salad, curry sauce AND pot of pink up here for the same price I paid for one fish and chips down there. That said, Rick's chips didn't come with a side hockle of phlegm like the ones round here do.

We left, disappointed.

Newquay

...and I thought Padstow has bad. Sweet Jesus. I'm sure Newquay is fabulous in the summer when you can get a tan to go with your stab wounds but in the pissing rain on a cold afternoon, good heavens no. I've seen grim working towns – I went through Sunderland once on the train – but this takes the biscuit. If you're from

Newquay and someone is reading this to you please don't get yourself in a fuss (think of your invariably high blood pressure); I'm sure the bit where you live is lovely and I'm just being a horrendous snob.

We should have known not to trouble ourselves with Newquay at all when we parked up only to have someone offer to look after our car 'for a reasonable fee'. I was tempted to enquire what this service would get me and what the possible repercussions of failing to take it up where but his yellow tooth frightened me and so we moved on. We found another car park a little further down and set out for adventure.

We found none. We walked to the beach only to be met with sea fret and the smell of fish. I can absolutely see why it would be just so in the summer, however, so please don't think it's all bad. We climbed to what I assumed was the main street only to be met with what is increasingly becoming a sad, common sight in the United Kingdom – a row of bookmakers, discount stores and charity shops. I would have been made up if I had wanted to bet on a horse and buy myself a cardigan someone had died in back in 1977. There was a shop nestled at the end called Fat Willy's which did tickle me (they often do), but it sold surf supplies and there isn't enough lycra in the world to make me look good on a surfboard.

We decided to try our luck in the bright lights and glitz of the amusement arcade next door. I've looked it up on

Google Street View and it doesn't seem to have a name. I presume that's because they don't want people on the internet revealing what a massive bloody swizz it is. My nana had more grip in her arthritic fingers than the bloody claw machines in here. I spent four pounds trying to win a Luigi plushie only to give up when I realised I'd have more chance winning the fucking thing if the machine wasn't switched on. I'm all for a competitive edge but Christ, give us the faintest glimmer of hope, eh?

Things turned nastier still when two girls, both seemingly sharing the same set of teeth, started following us around making eyes at our pocketful of jingling change. You know when you get that feeling that something isn't right and you're either about to end up on The Real Hustle or Silent Witness? That was one of those moments. Paul nudged in a set of cherries and I could see sheer avariciousness in their eyes. I clutched my murse theatrically to my side and we made a quick escape.

I know it's a weird thing to get vexed about but these places are for children, surely? Why not let them have some fun and win a toy without prising £20 out of their parents' wallet? Why must every other coin be glued down on the coin-pusher or fruit machine rigged to pay out on the twelfth of never? Another tiny example of grasping UK. Pfft.

We spent another forty minutes looking around the

shops before both deciding that we'd given it a chance and were justified in going home, despite paying for four hours of parking. Oh, and as a final point, if you were the woman serving us in the little pasty shop on the corner, a bloody smile goes a long way. I felt as though I'd made a mortal enemy for having the check to order two lamb and mint pasties. You know when someone gives you a look of hatred that chills you to the core? That's what we got as thanks for our custom (and before anyone says it, I'm always unfailingly polite when I order, no matter how poor my afternoon is going). Brilliant. I wouldn't have minded so much but even the bloody pasties were awful – I've had morning farts with more taste to them.

We left, disappointed.

The Lost Gardens of Heligan

We kept seeing signs for this place as we beetled about and knew nothing about it. We didn't bother to research and when, on the fourth day, I loudly exclaimed that we should go to Heligan, Paul simply replied 'What, Newquay?' – kaboomtish.

Once we've stitched up our sides and located the Lost Gardens of Heligan in the Sat-Nav (so they're not *that* lost, just saying) we were on our way, and it felt like no time at all until we were pulling up aside a Saga coach tour. It was fortunate that these elderly day-trippers were so slight as it made pushing them out of the way of the entrance all the more easier.

Oh I'm kidding, before anyone rings Age UK. They were still stumbling off the bus by the time Paul and I had completed a full lap of the grounds and got back in the car.

The Lost Gardens of Heligan are, according to the sweaty nerds at Wikipedia, one of the most popular botanical gardens in the UK. They were bought by a fancy sort back in the 16th century and immediately divided into lots of lovely sections, such as a 'jungle' and a rhododendron garden. The moment I spotted that on a sign I burst into 'I Beg Your Pardon, I Never Promised You A Rose Garden' until Paul saw fit to stick twigs in his ears to stop me. Poor sport. Anyway, the gardens fell into disrepair until they were restored in the early twentieth centuries, and now, here in modern times, they're only a reasonable entrance charge away.

Now let me tell you this: I have been miserable throughout these Cornish entries. Nothing has managed to make my heart soar or my eyes sparkle. There's barely been a moment where I haven't been thinking longingly about the five holiday days I'd used up at work to take this trip. But these gardens were *amazing*.

I'm not exactly sure what pleased me so much – it was just a garden, after all, albeit a massive one split over many acres – but it was terrific. For a start, it didn't cost the Earth. I'd become so accustomed to handing over wads of notes that it was a pleasant surprise to be told it was a very reasonable £13.50. Then there was so much to see and do – everything clearly laid out and mapped in the little handbook they give you. We spent hours just drifting from scene to scene – we had literally stopped to smell the roses and it worked a treat with cheering us up.

It helped that we had the place mostly to ourselves, save for the odd walking group and gaggle of tourists trampling in the flowers. This meant we had time to read the excellent information boards and talk to the staff, who I'm sure would have rather we left them be so they could crack on with the gardening. I can prove that we at least absorbed one fact: Heligan remains the only place in the UK that grows pineapples – albeit very small ones – in horse poo. Fascinating stuff! Along similar lines, Lands' End in Cornwall is the only place in the UK where you can spend over £20 and get absolutely fuck all back for your money. What a time to be alive!

We took ourselves down to the animal area and sat for a good half hour watching birds from the little lookout they've installed then wandered gingerly down the very steep slope to the ponds. We spotted that somewhere amidst all the flowers and trees there was a rope bridge and so we spent a good twenty minutes hunting that out, managing to miss it twice despite it being signposted.

Well, goodness me. Didn't we look a sight. I'm sure folks far more light-footed than me could trip over this bridge with dainty steps but when we both lumbered on the metal shrieked and the rope audibly stretched. I couldn't relax, waiting as I was for a loud TWAAAANG sending us plummeting to the pond below. I say plummeting, we were six foot in the air, but come on, dramatic licence. As the bridge had sagged quite considerably under us it became quite a chore to pull ourselves up to the other side, a situation not helped by some red-faced little urchin crying out that he wanted a go. This was tough. Luckily, Cornwall Fire and Rescue came to our aid only forty minutes later.

Nah I'm kidding, we made it across, but we were bloody knackered. Of course, we'd also forgotten that the steep slopes coming down which once seemed to fun and hilarious to slide down would become an awful slog going back up. We took our time but it was with a shameful amount of huffing and puffing that we had to stop twice on the way up. To cap off our embarrassment, we were overtaken by a woman pushing herself along in an off-road wheelchair up the hill. I felt so ashamed.

We finished our afternoon by having a mince around the forest, where lots of giant curiosities were hidden. I came across a large hand deep in the undergrowth, which wouldn't be the first time. Paul was taken by surprise by an erection poking out of the bush, which wouldn't be the first time either. It really was wonderful and it was with a big genuine smile that I declined the offer of annual membership as we left. Perhaps if you dug it up and put it somewhere south of Hexham, I'd consider it.

We did stop by the farm shop with an eye to buying a range of meats and cheeses but the prices of everything in there sharp put paid to that idea. Listen, I'm not averse to slapping down the cash for good food, but these prices were little more than a tourist trap. I asked for the price of a small wedge of Little Stinky only to be told it was more than a tenner. I leant over and whispered confidentially that 'I only want to buy the cheese, not rent the cow' but her stern, weathered face was having none of my japery.

We left, disappointed.

But only at the farm shop – the actual gardens themselves were an absolute treat and I can wholeheartedly and without reservation recommend a trip.

Honourable mentions:

Mevagissey Model Railway – we loved this. It was like falling into Roy Cropper's wet dream. There was more than a hint of foist about the place but the owner was knowledgeable and welcoming and it was very much a 'British' piece of entertainment. Well worth a visit, although I wouldn't pencil out a whole afternoon for it.

Lappa Valley Railway – we turned up, decreed it far too expensive (although looking right now on the website it seems a lot cheaper, so best not write it off in case I was just having a mild aneurysm or something) and cleared off. I do still get a tickle from the fact they have an event called a 'Steam and Cream' for the over sixties. I thought most trainspotters just jizzed straight into the same quilt they've had since they were 14?

The Chapel Porth Hedgehog – I can forgive the National Trust for charging me to visit a beach when I'm presented with an ice-cream like the Chapel Forth Hedgehog. For those wot div not knaa this is Cornish ice-cream which is then smothered in clotted cream and them dipped in honey-roasted hazelnuts. It's served with a warm smile and fifteen minutes of CPR. Bloody amazing. Beach was nice too.

Overall

If you're reading this entry and feeling apocalyptic that I've dismissed Cornwall as an awful place full of chintz and nonsense and bloody rude people, please, take a moment. There's no need to be so quick to anger. Holidays are unique to everyone and I just didn't 'feel' Cornwall. I can see its many merits mind – I like the fact that the air feels crisp, for one. The views are wonderful but as I've previously touched upon, I live in what I believe to be the most beautiful county in all of the

United Kingdom – Northumberland. I have beauty on my doorstep.

Remember, opinions are like arseholes – everyone has one. It's just unfortunate that I've made a hobby out of talking out of mine.

twochubbycubs on: speeding

A friend of mine received a speeding ticket over the weekend and it made me think of the speed awareness course I went on. I've touched on it before but I recently found my hand-written diary and the notes I put down put some putting together – I essentially scribbled 'whistler, bald, Posh Spice, 80s' on the back of my 'naughty boy admission' card and frankly, that deserves fleshing out. That's how I remember things, by the way – I'm forever jotting down nonsense on the back of things and then putting them away somewhere to get lost forever – if I ever die suddenly and they can't find Paul, they're going to be really confused when they open my desk drawer and a load of ASDA receipts with 'cock, gingivitis, farting am-i-right and spiraliser' on the back come tumbling out.

I was made to go on a speed awareness course after committing the heinous crime of doing 55mph in a 50mph zone at 6am on a motorway. I know what you're thinking, it's amazing that I didn't kill anyone. To be fair, it was probably more to do with me caterwauling and screeching away to Smooth FM than anything else, probably knocked a sleeping policeman out of his slumber. The last time that happened was Raoul Moat and look how that ended up – that could have been me crouched all roided-up in a ditch in Rothbury, shouting at the police helicopter until I decided it was time to clean my ears with a sawn-off shotgun. But hey, a crime is a crime and I was speeding so it's a fair cop, guv. I received a letter calling me a tinker in the post and was offered a speed awareness course or points on my licence.

Naturally, I chose that, and I was ordered to attend a course in a Holiday Inn near my home. A Holiday Inn, I might add, that's slap-bang in the middle of a gay cruising ground, because who doesn't like looking out over two carpet salesman furiously frotting away whilst they learn about road-signs? Incidentally, you know why they call it a Holiday Inn? It's actually short for 'Fuck me, I'd rather Holiday Inn anywhere but this shithole'. At least the one at Seaton Burn is. With a heavy heart, I turned up in the morning and was made to sit around a table with various men, all at various degrees of baldness (in my ideal world I would have stood up and rearranged them like matryoshka dolls) and each one, to an absolute fault, with appalling coffee-breath. I didn't feel I knew them well enough to offer up chewing up or a hydrochloric rinse either, so I was stuck crinkling my nose all morning.

One guy was late, bursting in through the door 20 minutes after the course had started and we'd all done our introductions ("Hi, I'm James, I was speeding because I was too engrossed in the harmonies on Boyz II Men's End of the Road, ironic, am I right?") and explained that he had been stuck in traffic. I made a gag – my one and only of the day – that he should have put his foot down, but that was met with a few people sucking air over their teeth and the guy leading the class looking at me like I'd wiped out a bus full of children. His very next sentence was that 'we needed to show we had the right attitude or we would fail the course' and it wasn't so much pointed as me as lubed up and rammed up my arse. I bit my bottom lip and tried to look as solemn as possible.

You know what though, despite my reservations that we were going to get shouted at by someone with bad teeth and glasses as thick as my wrists, it was actually really interesting. I'm not going to lie and say the day passed in a blur like a visit to Disneyworld, but I didn't die of terminal boredom, not least because of the instructor's tendency to add horrific detail into the most innocent of sentences. I'd be slumbering my way through a bit about junctions when he'd casually mention that he'd found a decapitated head once in a layby and shock us all back in the room.

We paused for coffee at about 11. I say coffee, it was some brown water that was dispensed sputtering from a machine first used in the Sufi monasteries in Yemen back in the sixteenth century. I can't make small talk, not least with people whose only common denominator was that they were heavy on the accelerator, so we all sat in silence looking at our phones, a pointless endeavour as they didn't give us the Wi-Fi password and the mobile reception couldn't get through the asbestos. Anyway, it didn't feel right to check into Facebook on a speed awareness course, not least because I didn't want my mother finding out and ringing with an earbashing. I'm 31, by the way.

Perhaps the most unusual part of the day was the little video where we learned all about stopping distances. All very sobering and factual – I've never looked so intently at a chart full of numbers since my doctor weighed me and told me it would be kinder just to push me into the sea and have done. No, what made this unique was the fact they used a cardboard cut-out of Posh Spice as the target for the speeding car. Even now as I speed merrily along the motorway the sight of Posh Spice bouncing off the bumper of a Nissan Sunny and crumpling under the tyres will creep into my thoughts and make me slow down. Maybe that was their plan all along!

Anyway, after we all promised to be good and signed a form saying how naughty we were, we were released back to the car-park. There's a bit in the Simpsons where they all leave the road-rage camp at the same time and everyone is unfailingly polite. Don't worry, it was the same for us, which made me screeching past the waiting Audis much easier. I'm kidding, I spent so much time waving people out that my wrist sounds like a cement mixer.

twochubbycubs on: children

I can't bear this time of year – I've had six weeks of being able to roll out of bed at 8.00am, have enough time for a good scratch of my balls and a morning poo, a warm shower and a hot coffee, then to make my merry way to work with no pressure or stress. Now the kids are back it means the roads are full of red-faced parents erratically driving cars the size of a combine harvester, swerving over the road as they simultaneously do their kid's homework, feed them porridge and tan their backsides for being cheeky. Everywhere suddenly becomes super busy and I can't even relax on Facebook as my feed is full of children in uniform standing in front of doorways showing off their uneven teeth and inappropriate-for-school-haircuts. Listen, I know you think your children are adorable and they undoubtedly are, but I'll never find out why DENTISTS HATE THIS SOUTH SHIELDS WOMAN AND HER $20 TOOTH-WHITENING TRICK if all I can see is little Letitia and Amyl writ large and toothy on my iPad.

Caveat time: your children are fine. When I'm talking about annoying children, I obviously mean the offspring of everyone else.

One good thing that comes out of this return to school

period, however, is the inevitable deluge of moon-faced parents doing a sad-face to camera in the local papers because the school sent home their little darlings for not observing the uniform rules. I've already seen one where the kid has hair like a pineapple and his mother is mooing about human rights, as though King John himself demanded a clause in the Magna Carta to cover dressing like an insufferable arse. I'm not a complete monster: I think sending kids home or putting them in isolation because they have grey trousers instead of black is ridiculous and often the sign of a power-mad tosser in charge, but when you've got teenagers walking around in skirts so short you can lip-read and boys with hair that looks as though it's been cut underwater with a power-sander for a bet, you have to draw a line.

And that line should be 30cm off the ground in a light charcoal, thank you very much.

Perhaps these parents are the same folk who think going shopping in pyjamas is the correct and adult thing to do. Let me tell you now: it isn't. You sleep in those clothes. You sweat in those clothes. Knowing at least half of the readers of this blog, you probably scratch your minnie until your lips turn blue in that outfit. I don't want that sweaty terry-towelling number brushing over my vine tomatoes, thank you. I'm not demanding a return to top-hat-and-tails or anything, just a modicum of common decency. The sight of someone accidentally flashing their growler at me

166

whilst they bend down to pick up the Daily Sport is not a risk I should have to take. It's bad enough I see so many tops of arses peeking out over jeans without belts – not because I find the arse an especially ugly thing (hell, I dare say I've seen enough of them from enough bewildering angles to draw you a topographic map of the average English anus) but because I yearn to drop a pencil down the crack – or, if they're especially zaftig, a fire extinguisher.

twochubbycubs on: Boundary Mills

We bought our cat a Dreamies mouse the other day and since then, all we've heard is the click-clack of the blasted thing in the kitchen where the cat is bouncing it off the walls. We took it away this morning because the sound was proving distracting whilst I was, how to put this delicately... *checking Paul's oil*. The cat has taken great umbrage and taken to dying at random opportunities all round the house – he came into the bathroom and collapsed (much like I do after Paul has been there), he died again on the television stand and then he chose to die once more in front of our lovely see-through toaster. You know, I don't know where he gets this dramatic side from. Don't worry though – he immediately springs back to life if he hears Paul straining to take the lid off the dry cat food box.

Hasn't it been a lovely bank holiday? We had my family over for a BBQ yesterday. I didn't think my mother would catch but once we'd applied enough petrol, she was away (must have caught up with all the Jim Beam in her blood) Boom. No, despite both Paul and I absolutely hating having anyone in our house aside from ourselves – and even then that's sometimes more a chore than you'd expect – we gamely invited everyone over for food and drinks. With everyone arriving at 4, we realised at 2.30 that we had a) no meat b) no normal alcohol and c) no charcoal. No chance, you might think, but Paul leapt into his Smart car, broke both axles, gingerly got into my car and sped off to ASDA. £90 later, he returned. I mean for goodness sake, we have a freezer full of meat, a bookcase full of liquor and all manner of nonsense we could have burnt, but with nothing defrosted and no alcohol that you don't ordinarily stick a sprinkler and paper umbrella in, we had no choice.

It was lovely, though. My nephew in particular was in good form, not least because he's stopped bursting into racking sobs whenever he sees my face. We went through almost two years of bawling, screaming, red-faced anger before he finally mellowed. Now he's always laughing and chortling and although I still can't get past my phobia of being near children because they're a) so fragile and b) so loud, it was pleasant enough to see him (and all). In the one minute that I allowed him to sit next to me on the outside table he immediately tumbled backwards onto the brick patio and was saved from his brain being turned to scrambled egg only by the quick reactions of my sister's charming friend. Oops! Anyway, such a roaring success was it (no-one had the merry shites from undercooked meat, no family arguments erupted and no emergency services were called) that we've all agreed we must meet up and be eat together more often, which means I'll see them again in 2017 and that's that. Similarly, we've decided to go down to see Paul's parents next week, which I'm incredibly enthusiastic about.

One thing I strongly dislike about where I live is that you can't do anything in our garden without people passing by and nebbing in, invariably adding some witty comment or rejoinder, because yes, I really give a toss what the man in the nicotine slacks has to say about how I cook my meat. We have one couple opposite us who are just wonderful but there's a few 'chores' around. If I'm washing my car, they'll nip across and go 'when you doing mine oh ho ho' and start slapping their knees, amazed by their own wit. I smile politely, but oh how I wish I could reply 'after I've done yer dad'. I know they're being nice to our face but the same guy told another neighbour of ours that when 'the puffs move in, the house prices will fall', so he can fuck the fuck off. Twat.

We had a quieter day today, doing very little other than picking tomatoes, tidying up and breaking up the day with a visit to Boundary Mills. For those lucky enough not to know, Boundary Mills is a giant shop up near the coast that is advertised regularly on the TV up here with some loud nonsense and lots of smiling people milling about. I've managed to avoid it for thirty years but see, a friend from work recommended it so highly that I thought, why not.

Well, here's why not. It was what you'd get if you combined the waiting room at Dignitas with a village jumble sale. I've never seen so much tat and nonsense under one roof. What stressed me out more than anything was the total lack of a coherent theme – a Yankee Candle section sits next to a cookery book stand which sits next to towels which sits next to reduced skirts with a display of shortbread balanced on the top. Why? Who has ever clutched their heart in anguish and bemoaned the fact they can't buy their scented candles, valance sheets and tin openers under one roof? Paul took a cursory glance at the Yankee Candle section and informed me that they didn't have anything he didn't already have in a drawer at home. We pushed on at the speed of a melting ice-cap thanks to the bundles of tiny old ladies milling about sucking their teeth and complaining, then made hastily for the exit. I've never been so relieved to see Paul's matchbox excuse of a car.

I understand from their website that they actually organise bus tours for the old folk to come and have a day out – I don't know how they dare, to be honest – they're already close to the grave and the tedium would surely push them over. Well, honestly. It would be quicker and kinder to seal the doors, put a brick on the accelerator and let the bus drive into the sea.

twochubbycubs on: an accidental sphincter

Here's the thing about my husband — I love him very much, but he can be an absolute liability. He's managed to get me temporarily banned from interacting on Facebook, which is vexing because there's a child out there awaiting a heart transplant and if the doctor gets 1,000,000 likes, they're going to operate on him, and without me as the millionth like, I guess it's into the soil for poor wee Jimmy Fictional. Let me explain how. On a Sunday, we set aside an hour or so to schedule some links to our older posts via our Facebook page, which has just shy of 85,000 people on it. It's simple enough — write a bit of blurb, post the photo, add the link and then diarise it so it gets posted automatically on a set time and date. We forgot to do it this week, so we've had to do them the night before in a bit of a rush. Paul was given the task of doing Friday's posts and in his haste to get them done before the chips were cooked, he managed to not like to a tasteful picture of our lovely steak with hasselback potatoes, but to a three second film of a sphincter dilating in and out.

Not his own, I hasten to add, but one that he'd found on the Internet to whatsapp to his nursing friends for a joke. Thankfully, it's a lovely clean balloon-knot as opposed to some pebble-dashed wormhole, so it's not all bad, but when I reposted the tale in our group, I got automatically banned for 24 hours for sheer filth. Aaaah man. So: if you're a fan of ours and you love our

Facebook page and happened to witness a giant arsehole instead of a steak dinner, I can only apologise. And laugh. Oh my how I laughed – when I spotted the mistake at work, I had to leave my desk and go sit in the gents for fifteen minutes with my fist in my mouth trying not to laugh out loud. Good times.

Anyway, some exciting news. The cat is much better and has stopped licking away at his bellend like it was made out of Kitekat. Definitely worth the expense just to say him back to his normal self of punching the other cat about and showing us his anus.

I spotted, somehow, that Big Brother finished last night, and I'm just amazed it is still going. How? Whenever I catch it it's full of self-aware knackers mooing and braying and playing up to the cameras. Lots of bronzed folks walking around in undeserved vests showing arms that couldn't snap a wet cigarette and tattoos that mean nothing and look awful. By far the worst, for me, is our lovely local representative Marnie, who got her gash out on telly, sucked someone off and swore like a trooper. Listen, we're not all like that. I mean, I don't even have a gash. But Big Brother is ruined now, yet it used to be genuinely interesting TV.

I remember where I was when the original series went big and everyone started to watch it – on the Isle of Arran with the world's most boring family in the world's most boring cottage with the world's most boring set of activities to do. You know the type – lots of corduroy

173

trousers, thick sex-offender glasses and rustling rain-wear. At no time, either before or since, have I ever been closer to dashing my head against the rocks on the beach just to liven things up.

The deal was that my family took my then best friend on holiday with us to Portugal and I'd then get to join his family on their holiday. My family's holiday was full of food, fun and sunshine (although he elected to stay inside the apartment and watch Sky News), his family's holiday was lots of earnest discussions over turnip dinners and early nights. Not the good type of early nights where you might get your end away, no, the type of early night where the only excitement comes hoping you'll die in your sleep. Seven nights I spent on that island surrounded by four people who couldn't entertain a thought, nevermind a guest. They wouldn't allow us to have the television on because "we were on holiday" so the only outlet I had, after I'd walked around so much my feet were one with my shoes, was copies of The Sun that I bought in Blackwaterfoot, and all of the salacious Big Brother stories they carried.

Listen, it was very much a last resort, buying The Sun, but that's what got me into Big Brother and prevented me from becoming so depressed I'd have my own Livejournal and emo haircut. Paul and I went back to Arran as a couple a few years ago and it was a marvellous place, not the grey cesspit I remembered it as with my jaundiced eyes, so it just shows that it's definitely the person you're with that makes a place. *Actually*, I've got my notes from our Arran trip way back when, so if I can be arsed, I'll turn them into a blog entry.

twochubbycubs on: anxiety, revisited

I spotted something interesting in the papers today (ok ok, I'm sorry, it was on the Sidebar of Shame on the Daily Mail – I'm mortified enough to be viewing it at work on my lunch computer that I cover most of it with some fisting porn in case anyone gets the wrong idea). Chiselled, Australian hunk Chris Hemsworth was wearing a t-shirt with 'it's not weak to speak', which links to a mental health charity in Australia who are trying to get across the message that people shouldn't feel ashamed about suffering from a mental illness.

He's spot on, and I'm not just saying that because he could cheerfully sit on my face and pedal my ears. I've written about my anxiety before and I describe it as a slow rollercoaster – it's always going to be there in the background, but most of the time I'm on an 'up' and don't really notice it – or at least, I can take control of it. My anxiety manifests itself through health anxiety – I don't have panic attacks (much) or depression, but I fall into the trap of analysing every little quirk of my body and thinking it is something sinister.

Well, unfortunately, I'm in a pretty big dip at the moment. It all started a couple of weeks ago when my left hand started going intermittently numb and tingly, something as innocuous as that. I'd been feeling great for over a year so this came as a bit of a surprise. I reassured myself that it was nothing to be concerned about and that worked for a fair while, but the fact that it comes and goes troubles me. Here's how my mind works:

rational mind: I sleep on my arm a lot, I've been having problems with my neck, it'll be a pinched nerve, the fact that it comes and goes is a good sign, I can still grip, I hold my iPad up in bed for an hour each morning using my hand so it's no wonder it's struggling a little

irrational mind: muscle weakness and tingliness is a sign of MS (which is my big fear), it's definitely happening, can't be anything else.

PLEASE: I don't want any comments confirming my irrational thoughts, no tips to go see a neurologist – nothing. Feel free to comment if you sometimes get a tingly hand and you know it's because you've pinched a nerve or something!

What then happens is a constant struggle between being rational (95% of the time) and 5% being irrational. Because I'm distracted by thoughts of something scary, I become hyper-aware of everything. How I speak – if I stumble over my words, it's because my brain is turning to cheese. If my knees hurt (which given my weight is no bloody surprise) it's because my muscles are atrophying. Because I'm up a height, I don't sleep too well at night, which in turns means I'm knackered during the day – and then I worry because I have no energy, I keep forgetting things and my vision goes blurry – all of which happen when people get tired, but all of which add to my worries.

It's exhausting. I've beaten it before; I'll beat it again. It's just a quirk of my body. I'm at the doctors on Wednesday and I'll mention all of the above on the off-chance it is something to be worried about, but it'll be nothing, I'm sure. I end up feeling guilty because it's almost like I'm making a mockery of those with genuine concerns, but see, this is a genuine concern to me.

But here's why I'm mentioning it – I'm lucky, because I've got Paul, family and friends to talk to. Although I'm pretty good at dealing with this stuff myself, Paul's always there to reassure me that I'm shaky because I've had two tubs of Ben and Jerry's, not because I've got Parkinsons, or that I don't have dementia because I'm able to tell him the room number from our trip to New York. It helps so much to be honest. If you're out there and feeling blue, find someone to talk to, even if it's just yourself in the mirror. If you're feeling fine, take a moment to speak to someone who you're worried about, or listen to people if they're trying to tell you they're not right. It's the small gestures that make a difference to people's lives.

As for me, don't worry. I'll be fine. I'll come right back around and crack on. Sorry to be a downer!

twochubbycubs on: hired help

Firstly, thank you to all and everyone for the reassuring words in response to my last post about health anxiety. I'm just having a wobble; all will be well. Always darkest before the dawn and all that shite. I did see the doctor today who mentioned carpal tunnel syndrome and gave me a few exercises to try with my wrist. Now that sounds filthy, but I can assure you it's all non-erotic and safe. I don't pay for private healthcare, after all. He did ask what I thought may have caused it and I tried to explain that there is quite the collection of Audi drivers around where I work, and frankly, given the amount of wanker-signs I do in my mirror it's not surprising my wrists sound like a popcorn machine.

He told me not to worry about my fogginess and had a bit of a feel of my stomach. He had the good grace not to ask for the block and tackle be brought in. I hate taking my shirt off at the doctors (almost as much as I used to hate taking my underwear off in church) because, although my doctor is wonderful, kind and non-judgemental, I'm embarrassed that he has to see how much I've ruined my beautiful body by filling it with gravy and chips for a solid ten years. At least I get a brownie point when he asks if I smoke and I get to say *only after sex*, because then he remembers I'm married and therefore that means two cigarettes a year. I certainly can't claim I'm tee-total anymore, given we've now got a giant bookshelf full of hard liquor.

Liquor? I barely knew her!

Paul dealt with the man who came to test our boiler. This is possibly the most terrifying thing for me – we've touched upon my hatred of having anyone in my house who isn't delivering food and boiler men are no exception. See, to get into our loft (we're a bungalow) you climb through a hatch in the ceiling via a strong metal ladder that comes down automatically. Yes, that *is* the most pointless sentence I've ever managed to write – you're hardly going to trampoline into the fucker, are you? When Paul steps on this ladder, it doesn't so much strain as shriek.

I've watched enough Air Crash Investigation to know what metal fatigue is and this ladder is absolutely fucking knackered. I try to ask Paul to make sure the ladder is locked before we have anyone climb up so it doesn't snap down but he ignores me on the basis I'm being irrational. Of course I'm irrational – you're talking to someone who diagnosed himself with a brain tumour because his ears were warm, for goodness sake. I have visions of some gruff type climbing the ladder only for it to plunge down on his hands and cleave his fingers right off. Paul always looks at me non-plussed as I try to demonstrate why this is a bad thing by thumping my palm on a piano or clumsily trying to pick up a pen with a balled fist. Jeez. As it happens, the guy went up the ladder like a rat up a drainpipe, banged around a bit, confirmed that our boiler wasn't killing us and beat a hasty retreat.

He's probably been warned by either the last guy who went up into the loft only to be confronted with a big old box of free condoms that well, we don't have much use for, or the alarm guy who couldn't help but notice the douching bulb that was unfortunately sat on top of the alarm box. Meh. I hope we're not getting a reputation – although actually, I did put 'If you're quick, I might nosh you off Paul xxx' on our Just-Eat order last night knowing that Paul would have to get the door when the delivery man came. That was my revenge for Paul writing 'I <3 COCK' on the back of my car and letting me drive it around for a week. Do you know, I wasn't so angry with that as the fact I didn't get **one** beep'n'leer from passing lorry drivers.

We also arranged for new cleaners, too. Which I know sounds terribly froufrou but hey, got to spend the huge advertising spoils somehow. Our last cleaner was great at cleaning but ridiculously expensive (only because she came from Sunderland, so we had to pay danger money) and used to leave the TV tuned to MTV Clubland at full volume, which was a fright when we came home from a hard day's graft. Nothing says *...aaaand relax* like some harpie more herpes than woman screaming 'BUY CLUBLAAAAAND EIIIIIGHTY-SIIIIIX NAAAAAAAW' over some sped-up Faithless.

We did manage to cause instant intrigue by telling them they must never enter our bedroom. I know, suspicious, but I don't want anyone seeing our black sheets and thinking they're a Jackson Pollock homage. I know they'll have seen it all before but still. They start on Friday and seem like lovely people, so fingers crossed.

Finally, we fixed our cat. He's been licking away at his knob all summer. I know what you're thinking, we'd all do it if we were able, but I reckon he'd probably scratch your face if you tried. We had him checked to make sure he could urinate properly (he can, and evidenced the fact by having a long, luxurious piss on the vet's table when she squeezed him) and all was fine. But still he persists. It seems I can't go outside without seeing him sitting on the path in front of the neighbours licking away at himself with his bumhole on show. They must think our lifestyle is catching. One of our neighbours absolutely hates our cats – he's taken to staring furiously at the cats whilst they pad about in our garden. I'm not sure who he thinks he is scaring, but honestly, even a cat wouldn't be intimidated by a man who looks like he bought all of the clothes he'll ever need in one trip to Woolworths in the seventies. He's the same man who once came pounding on our door inviting us to look at the shit one of our cats had apparently done in his flower-bed – notably how large it was. I wasn't sure if he was expecting us to stick a 1st prize rosette on it or something. We just let him go red in the face.

Anyway, turns out our cat is allergic to fleas. He doesn't

have fleas, which is lucky, but every time he fights with another cat who has been in contact with fleas it makes his skin itchy then he bites away at it, hence the sore bit around his knob. Our vet, a very jolly woman who looked like a farmer's wife from a James Herriott novel, and had bigger hands than I did, manhandled poor Bowser this way and that and then gave him an injection. He already seems much happier. I was less happy when I was presented with the bill – £49! For one injection. I mean, he's worth it, don't get me wrong, but what the hell did she inject him with? Saffron via a diamond syringe? He's fully insured but that's too little to claim, meaning we'll just need to soak it up. Things between us and the cat were tense on the car-ride home, with Paul barely slowing the Smart car down as we passed over the speed-bump into the street and the cat sulking all the way home.

It's a relief to know that I might not be woken up by looking directly into Bowser's balloon-knot tomorrow morning, though.

Right, let's get this wrapped up. Great British Bake-Off is on soon and I need to prepare myself for an hour of looking furiously at things I'll never have and idly wondering whether Mary Berry ever climbed our loft ladder.

twochubbycubs on: getting paul up

Albert Einstein once said that the definition of insanity is doing the same thing over and over again and expecting different results. I might have changed his wording a little, but damn it, this is my blog not his. He's absolutely right, though. I'll give you an example – I have many, many cake and cooking tins from the halcyon days way back when I used to bake all the time and delight my friends and co-workers with biscuits, cakes and goodies. Now all they get is barely disguised contempt and secretive farts into my office chair. One of these tins is a fancy Lakeland square tin with one of those bottoms that you push up (same as Paul) to release the cake. Great idea. Has it ever worked? Has it balls.

Does that stop me trying it? Of course not. No, every time a recipe requires something square, out it comes. I spend a few minutes looking owlishly at it, demanding that it doesn't leak, then proceed with the recipe. This time it was for a fancy quiche – lots of cheese, egg whites, decent ham. I spent an age cutting up the onion, sweating them down, making everything just right. Popped the mixture into this non-leak square tin, placed the tin in the oven, turned my back for one moment to set Just a Minute away on the iPad and turned around to see all the beaten egg dripping out of the oven. My kitchen floor looked like the gusset of a £5 prostitute's knickers. It would have been more effective had I left the removable bottom off.

Well I was furious. I'd given this fucking tin enough chances. Yes, I could line it, but it was sold to me on the basis I didn't need to line the fucker and I'm not going to be dictated to by Lakeland. I salvaged the contents of the quiche into a Pyrex dish, covered it with egg-white and took the scalding hot square tin outside, where I set about it with a sledgehammer. Do I feel better? Yes, I do, and I'm all set if I ever want to make a rhombus-shaped Christmas cake.

Anyway, that's the only wrinkle in an otherwise lovely, quiet weekend. You know we aren't ones for doing anything that requires more movement than entirely necessary, and that was certainly the case on Saturday, when we literally moved from the bed to the settee and back to the bed. We make no apologies; we have busy working weeks. But last night Paul turned to me and said, through a fine mist of pastry crumbs and spittle, that I was to wake him up early in the morning and not let him sleep in late. Pffft. Let me explain how weekend mornings work in our house.

I wake up about 8.30am, always have. I'm not one for sleeping all day – once my eyes open, I'm awake and that's the end of it, thank you. Knowing he is tired, I'll generally stay in bed until half nine so Paul has something to lie against and act as ballast to stop him tipping onto his front and drowning in his chin-fat. I'm like one of those tyres you see strapped onto the side of piers for the ferry to rub against. He'll murmur incoherent nonsense in my ear, put a clammy hand around my belly and fart those indescribably foul morning farts in my general direction all the while. I don't know what his body does to food overnight but I swear you could power a small city on the strength of his morning flatus. He chuckles away to himself whilst he lets them out, which I do find endearing as I'm clawing at my throat trying to find oxygen.

At around half nine, I get bored with looking at Reddit, not masturbating and spending our money and decide to wake Paul up. This is a complicated process. First I'll start by cuddling in so he gets far too hot, but then he just moves away or lets out a warning fart, making me retreat. The next step is to start shaking the bed by jiggling on the spot, but that does nothing other than occasionally illicit a cry from him to 'STOP WANKING'. Plus, our bed is so ridiculously oversized that by the time the tremors eventually hit him, it's usually night-time again.

With the shaking of the bed bearing no fruit, I turn to shaking him directly, starting off with the buttocks, moving up to the stomach and then, if that doesn't work, his shoulders. This normally does the trick and after he's wiped the sleep from his eyes and tried his luck with Little Paul (not happening, matey, not without a shower and caustic acid) he reassures me that he's going to get out of bed as soon as he's 'done his stretches' and could I make him a coffee? I'm happy with this – I'll mince, invariably stark-bollock-naked, into the kitchen, make him a coffee and return only to find him fast asleep and pulling that face that reminds me awfully of what I imagine his mother looks like when she hasn't had the formaldehyde in her tank topped up. At this point I generally take a huff and set about cleaning the kitchen instead, which really only punishes me instead of him. At 11 I'll go in, flap the duvet, wake him up and tell him to get up. At 11.30 I normally go in and take the duvet away altogether, which only results in him sleep-farting more in an effort to heat the room.

Noon means the nuclear option. I've touched on this before, but we've got speakers in each room of the house that can be controlled centrally via the iPad. These ones, if you please. They're useful for cleaning – a bit of Dolly in the bathroom, some Radio 4 in the kitchen. Great stuff. At noon, I choose the worst song I can possibly find, turn the volume up to 100 so the bass shakes your fillings out, sneak in and muffle it a little with a towel so I don't deafen the fucker, then on goes something genuinely frightening: We Want The Same Thing by Belinda Carlisle has a very loud intro, for example. There's been Minnie Riperton singing Loving You, too, but that starts out slowly. This morning was Magic Dance from Labyrinth, which worked, but only because he was laughing so much.

I called him Hoggle, he called me DCI Vera Stanhope. Paul was awake and all was right with the world again.

Seriously though, what does fuck me off just a smidge (if you're reading this, my little clartyarse) is that he'll invariably turn to me fifteen minutes after getting up and say 'you really need to start waking me up earlier'. How we both laugh as I imagine waking him up with petrol and matches.

twochubbycubs on: landlords and tenants

Why do people write on their own walls? Hear me out. Chunkles and I were watching Britain's Benefit Tenants yesterday, laughing at the poor in-between handfuls of caviar and swigs of champagne. Not quite – we had been watching something on Channel 4, the remote fell out of reach and we couldn't be arsed to switch over. It was illuminating. I'm not going to get into the whole 'landlords are bad' / 'tenants are scum' because obviously there's good and bad on all sides, but it did make me think, not least whether there a direct correlation between neon pink walls and jet black teeth.

What troubles me is the state of some of the houses. Look, I can be as slobby as the next person, but unless you're unwell, there's very little reason for your house to be so *unclean*. You see the same old tropes – the writing of names on the wall (why? WHY? It's not even graffiti on an outside wall, just shit scribbling and the inevitable weed leaf on the living room wall), dried up dog poo in the kitchen and, in the garden, a broken Fisher Price slide that someone stepped through back in 2005 and two dogs so inbred and vicious that they're fighting their own feet.

Now, I know, I've always been lucky in that, so far, I've always been gainfully employed and in reasonable health, so until I moved into the house I own, I always paid my rent. I do wonder if I was a mug for doing so, though, given it seems to be a-ok for someone to rent a house, smash it up and then move on to be rehoused. It's why we don't buy our own property to rent out – I'd be fucking livid if someone decided it was an appropriate reaction to kick their foot through my internal walls. Oh and plus, if we were landlords, I know we'd be the type you see on Crimewatch rubbing our thighs and suggesting 'we come to other arrangements' if the tenant so much as called in to report a leaky tap.

twochubbycubs on: James' day out

I had a half day off work today. Now, that might not sound very exciting – a Tuesday afternoon all to myself – but it was glorious. I love Paul to bits (even if he cuddled into me the other night, whispered 'who has a sexy arse...' and then followed it up with 'not yours, your arse smells like death') but see a day where I can do my own thing and trot about is never a bad time. I decided, possibly against my better judgement, to go for a walk in the woods again – this time to a place called Plankey Mill. The weather decided to play ball, my morning's work wasn't too strenuous and, with all of the impulsiveness of someone who says he is trying to save money but finds the whole affair rather boring, I bought two annual passes for me and Chubs McGee for the National Trust so that I wouldn't have to pay £2 for parking. Makes sense, right?

I did, somewhat mischievously, put myself down as a doctor (I have health anxiety, I spend all day diagnosing myself with various illnesses, so it sort of works) and Paul does as a 'Rear Admiral'. Well, he's certainly swabbed more than his fair share of poop decks, the filthy swine.

Plankey Mill is a charming walk along the River Allen and we used to go there a lot as children, possibly because it was free, possibly because my parents were hoping we'd fall in and be swept away to pastures new so they could jet off to Ayia Napa and open an English Breakfasts bar called Sticky Fingers. I remember it fondly through nicotine-tinted glasses and thought it would be the perfect place to spend an afternoon. I remember reading that most of the path had been swept away in 2014 but thought that the National Trust must have sorted it by now, given they had Rear Admirals in their ranks.

I was right, but only sort of. I turned off the A69 just outside of Hexham after spending a good ten minutes shouting animatedly at the back of a caravan, who I can assure you was in absolutely no rush at all, thank you very much. When I eventually managed to overtake I snuck a glance at the driver and yep, easily 125 years old, driving with that eyes-on-the-road-fixed-lips-no-nonsense expression that they always have. I like to think he pulled over later and felt guilty about holding up the traffic, or, even better, drove into a tree in an explosion of MDF and travel kettle shrapnel. Either or.

The first problem arose when, after lulling me into a false sense of security with one bold road sign, the directions to Plankey Mill suddenly stopped, and I found myself hurtling along single-file tracks with only sheep nodding at me as company. After farting about for a good twenty minutes I decided, somewhat reasonably I might add, that it was unlikely that a river walk would take place at the very top of a hill, and so spun the car around and down an unmarked path. After half a mile or so of uncertainty, a tiny sign that I assume Emperor Hadrian put up as a side-project appeared and I knew I was on the right path. Sadly, there was someone else on my path, an Audi coming in my direction. Single file, remember.

Now, because this is going to make me sound like an arsehole, let me preface the next bit with a simple fact: she drove past TWO passing places and then up the hill AFTER she saw me. I had nowhere to pull over.

So there she was, in her spotless white Audi, nasty cheap sunglasses making her look like a bee, all but demanding I reverse my car back up the twisty turny hill. Well, no, that's not happening. I stood my ground. So did she. Mexican stand-off style. Eventually she folded like a cheap suit and began the laborious process of reversing down the twists and turns, only she did such a piss-poor job of it she ended up in the muddy verge twice AND she had to go back to the first passing point she passed as in the time it had taken her to realise that an Audi doesn't mean she's Queen of the Road (my title), another car had pulled in behind her.

I make no apologies for it, I really don't. I gave her a sickly little wave and a tinkly 'thanks EVER so much' as I drove past her and she looked absolutely furious. You can imagine just how much distress that gave me. I carried down the track and eventually ended up where I remember we used to park way back when, in a little field by the river.

Only now – of course – the farmer had decided that he really ought to squeeze a few pennies from everyone and had put a gate on the road, only accessible by the payment of £2 into the honesty box. I know, it's £2, but come on. This is what I hate about Britain – if there's a chance to shake some money out of your pockets, by god people will find it. Already grumbling, I parked up amongst discarded disposable BBQs, empty bottles and other such nonsense. It was a mess and a bloody shame. Nevertheless, I decided to crack on and make the best of it, knowing that the beauty of the countryside would soon envelop me. I fair pranced over the wee bridge crossing the river (though I was surprised not to find the farmer at the other end asking me for £3 towards the wear and tear I'd placed on the steel cabling) and happened across another sign. Perhaps it would warn me of poisonous plants or a diversion or something else equally as arresting.

No, the bloody path was closed. The 2014 landslide had taken away a good chunk of the path and it just wasn't safe. I did ponder as to whether they were planning on waiting for another flood to see if a replacement bridge would be washed down the river but the thought provided little comfort. The sign did helpfully point out that there was another path back over the river that would take me to roughly where I wanted to be – all I had to do was to follow the path marked in brown. Listen, I've been following 'the brown path' all my life, mate, and even the thought of an extra mile didn't deter me.

The fucking cliffs did, though. Brown path my arse! I crossed the river, searched high and low for the start of the brown path (clearly marked it said – with what, a sheer rock face?) and could I buggery find it? There was no path. Of course not. Perhaps if I'd thought ahead to bring my crampons (in fact, I would need to have thought even further ahead than that, as I'd need to learn what a fucking crampon is first) I could have deftly made my way along like a morbidly obese Spiderman, but no. Hmm.

On the verge of giving up, I spotted one more public footpath heading in the opposite direction and made for it, only to find the very first field was full of cows. I hate cows. They trouble me. Yeah, they're happy enough eating all day and shitting everywhere, but so is Paul, and I don't have the risk of being turned into a lumpy paste on the floor by him. You can't trust a cow, especially when they're hot and skittish.

I threw up my hands in a camp display of annoyance, stomped back to the car and sulked for five minutes. All I wanted to do was to walk: how rare to hear someone of my bulk say that. But no! Plus, I'd wasted two fucking pound to park my car, read a sign and be disappointed from quite literally every direction. I spun the car round, made for the gate, waited for someone with a face like a charity shop handbag to fumble the catch and open the gate for me, and sped off.

Luckily, my day was saved a mere mile or two later, when I spotted the actual car park I should have parked in, Staward Gorge. Oops. Clearly I was too busy singing along to something shite on the radio as I had managed to drive past it twice on my way in. Bah! It was quiet, though, and after sticking my temporary Rear Admiral badge in the window, I left the car and headed up into the forest, and it was wonderful. Very hilly in places, yes, and my ankles were protesting almost as soon as I got out of the car, but I walked for an hour or so in one direction before returning to the car, only passing a couple of old folk and a committed hiker on the way.

Can I quickly mention those hikers who go out for a quick walk in the country and yet dress up like they're trekking the Hindu Kush? I can understand a trekking pole if you're a little unsteady, but I passed one guy who looked, from a distance, like he was being fucked from behind by a wardrobe clad in rustling, luminous polyester. That can't be comfortable. I'd understand if he was walking Hadrian's Wall or similar, but it's a 5-mile loop and frankly, if I can shift my colossal bulk around it without too much bother in my work shoes and Tesco Finest work trousers, so can he. I was tempted to ask if he was selling pegs when he walked past but frankly, he had a crazy look in his eye and I didn't want to be found two months on face-down in the bushes with a telescopic peg hammer wedged in my arse.

I do recommend the walk, though – I can't tell you how much I love living in Northumberland. The place is awash with beautiful, hidden idylls like this. Yes, you'll break a sweat, but the feeling of reaching the top, being brought back to life with a National Trust defibrillator and then taking in the views of the rolling fields, shaded forest and little swirling river below, well, nothing beats it. I made my way back, cheer restored. One thing to note: I decided to go for a piss before the drive back only to find a big warning sign on the door from the National Trust telling me 'HONEY BEES ARE NESTING IN THE ROOF – PLEASE USE CAUTION'. Caution? Nevermind fucking caution, use fucking napalm!

I jest, I'm all for bees, my garden is full of bee-friendly flowers, but Christ almighty, there's a time and a place and it's not when I've got my cock out, I can assure you. I did think about chancing it, reasoning that if the danger was that high they'd shut the loo – but when I creaked open the door and heard the very loud, very threatening buzzing, I minced right back to the car, the need to urinate completely gone. All down my leg. No, not quite, but goodness me – who needs that type of threat when they're having a piss? They might as well have put 'Shit carefully, folks, as we've rigged one of the toilet seats with plastic explosives and a depth charge'. I haven't heard such terrifying buzzing since I lived with Mary and I accidentally turned on what I thought was her thermos flask but turned out to be her robocock. I'm surprised she didn't chip her teeth, the dirty bitch.

I decided to cap the day off with a visit to Brockbrushes (our local pick your own fruit affair), but after parking up and negotiating – in turn – the sausage shop, the ice-cream parlour, the garden furniture stand, the farm shop, the coffee shop, the herb garden, the bouncy castle, the second bouncy castle, the cheese stand and then finally, FINALLY, the bloody place where you get the baskets to go pick your own, I was told that they had no fruit. No raspberries to pick, no blackcurrants, no redcurrants, no nothing. Strawberries were 'very limited', apparently. I did ask the guy behind the counter if there was anything I could pick in the hope he'd at least have a sense of humour and suggest 'your arse' (like I would have) but he just shook his head grimly. This annoys me – picking your own fruit is literally the point of a pick-your-own-fruit farm. If they have no fruit, fair enough, but then put a bloody sign up on your fancy smiling strawberry sign by the side of the A1. Don't waste my time. I took a huff and walked back to the car, stopping only to admire some farm-made cheese before realising I only have £270 in my wallet and thus, couldn't afford it. I came home.

Now, that probably all sounds like I had a rotten day, but listen, I thrive on any excuse to have a moan and a whinge. I'm never happier then when I have something to kvetch silently to myself about. It's just a shame for you guys that this is my outlet for it and you're treated to 2000 words on what amounts to me driving to a river, walking a couple of miles and not buying strawberries. But you love it, you know you do.

twochubbycubs on: a walk in the woods

I nearly died yesterday. OK so yes, I'm prone to melodrama and perhaps I wasn't as close to death as that dramatic opening sentence suggests, but honestly. See, Paul told me he had to go into work and move his desk around – presumably pulling it further away from the wall so he can get his gunt behind it – and that left me with an afternoon to fill. What were my options? Stay at home watching the Olympics and masturbating? Not likely, it was diving. I'm not a fan. Paul and I can cheerfully watch the weight-lifting as men built like bridge pillars come out and hurl weights around – part of us is watching because they're hot, part of us is scare-watching in case someone has an anal prolapse and everything comes pouring out like someone stepped on a sausage roll. There's some things you don't need to see in 65" ultra HD, I can assure you.

So, given it was a nice day and I'm a lazy, lazy man, I thought it would be a good idea to take myself out for a walk. Growing up I was forever out walking about – it's how I lost so much weight in my late teens – and I've fallen out of step (boom boom) with that since meeting Paul and learning how to drive. Paul is wonderful but he'd take the car to go to the bathroom for a piss if he could. Actually, he probably *could* do that now he has a car that Polly Pocket herself could drive. I used to adore tramping about in the woods with nothing but my bottle of tapwater, knock-off Rockports (Rickparts by

George at ASDA) and a crappy little MP3 player that a friend gave me that I loaded up with downloaded episodes of I'm Sorry I Haven't a Clue. No regrets! With that joyous image of young me in my mind, I asked Paul to drop me off at the nearby Plessey Woods and to pick up me up three hours later when I called him with my location.

Well, honestly. I knew from about three minutes in that I'd made a mistake. Firstly, I was wearing Paul's trainers meaning every step pinched my feet and chewed my skin. I could feel the ghost of his pitted keratolysis haunting my toes. Second, the very moment I stepped out of his car my phone immediately lost signal. I don't know if the trees of Plessey Woods are lined with lead but I didn't get a signal again until an hour later. Nevermind, we made do before and we'll do so again – I had downloaded a week's worth of The Archers and three Food Programme episodes on the iPlayer before I set off so it wasn't too bad.

You know what ruins public beauty spots? The public. I'd forgotten for a moment that I lived in the North East of England and that Geordie law dictates that as soon as a beam of sunlight hits the end of a Lambert and Butler, shirts must come off, disposable BBQs must be bought, lit and covered in 46% mince burgers and children must be encouraged to run around screaming with full nappies and empty minds. I'm so curmudgeonly these days, I know, but wouldn't it be a treat to go somewhere and not experience a cacophony of kids blaring and parents bellowing and mooing at them? I put my headphones on and waddled down to the river like an angry buffalo.

Once in the forest though, it was wonderful. Always is. Most of the families stayed within a 200 metre of the ice-cream truck lest their children went more than five minutes without a Costco Calippo smeared across their face, so within no time at all I had the place to myself. I followed the river, marvelling at untouched beauty of it all, enjoying the silence. There was a brief startling moment when I happened across a tiny notice warning of a wasp nest up ahead – no actual instruction on where it was or what to do. I plodded on, knowing that if I did stumble into a wasp nest, that would be it for me. No chance of running away thanks to my bulk. They'd find my bloated, wasp-filled corpse floating down the river with my face frozen forever in a 'COME AT ME, YOU FUCKING SHIT-BEES' snarl.

Didn't happen though, thankfully. No wasps and no other drama for a good two miles or so until I popped up on the side of the A1, sweating and confused and tired. Oh! One thing – let me explain an irrational fear of mine. See, alone in the woods, I only came across (bad choice of words given what is coming) another walker, a sole female walking towards me through the thick trees. I always instantly worry in a situation like this that the lass is going to see a red-faced, angry looking shaven-headed man blundering towards her and immediately reach for her pepper spray. I'm a kind, gentle soul but even I sometimes shit myself when I see my ugly mug in the mirror when I get up in the night for a piss.

So, what do I do? I can't grin inanely at her from a distance because I have the type of grin that says 'it's going to hurt you more than it hurts me'. I can't shout a cheery hello because then I'd just look insane. I don't want her thinking I'm a threat in this crazy frightening world so the only thing I can really do is camp it up and make it clear that, how can I put this delicately, *I take it up the Glitter*. Thus, hand out like I'm clutching an invisible rail, dainty point feet as I gambol lightly over the rocks on the path, tra-la-laing along to the Archers omnibus theme tune. If I'd had my drill kit I could have set myself up behind a gloryhole in a nearby oak for good measure but there was no time, and she passed by unfazed, with a loud hiyaaaaaa from me. I do worry too much, don't I?

After emerging onto the side of the A1 and spending ten minutes trying to cross it whilst half of the United Kingdom sped past at 100mph, I decided to send Paul a text to let him know I hadn't a) fallen in a river or b) been raped and left for dead by some forest-dweller. His reply was 'shall I get us a McFlurry before I pick you up'. Soothing. I told him I'd press on because I was enjoying myself and I'd call him when I was ready, spotting a barely visible public footbath through the Blagdon Estate, I minced onwards.

THAT's where things turned deadly. Or at least, mildly inconvenient. I got lost. I so rarely get lost, I'm excellent with direction and hell, I know the area like the back of my hand, but I don't know if I stumbled in the wrong direction trying to avoid cows or was distracted by something shiny on the horizon, but I completely lost my bearings. No mobile signal. Mild panic set in. Every field looked the same. The tracks were endless. I only had a little bit of water left and the day was hot. Clearly, the situation was grave, and given how prone I am to catastrophic thinking, I knew this was it. I stumbled bravely on for another couple of miles or two, trying to distract myself with The Archers but only making myself angrier because of silly Helen, until, finally, rising from the trees like the most middle-class mirage ever, the Northumberland Cheese Company. Phew.

Naturally, it was shut. I was gutted. Nothing quenches a raging thirst like a nettle and elderflower pressé and a truckle of expensive cheese. Salvation came in the form of FINALLY getting a signal on my mobile and I called Paul, who immediately dispatched himself to come to my aid. Took him forty fucking minutes. He wins a MASSIVE gold star for effort for playing Nearer My God To Thee through his car-speakers as he came hurtling over the horizon. Clearly at this point I was close to death, and imagine the indignity of such a froufrou death as collapsing outside a cheese farm from heatstroke with only Sheila Dillon twittering on about strawberries to comfort me into the blackness. PAH. Paul bundled me into the Smart car (the fat equivalent of trying to stuff a telephone directory into an A5 envelope), pressed a McFlurry into my hand and sensitively pointed out that I was a little red in the cheeks. I'll say: I walked, accordingly to my Fitbit, almost 8 miles in the blazing sun.

I'm paying for it today mind – my ankles hurt, my skin feels a bit tight and my chest hurts, presumably from my lungs having to do anything other than filter out shards of Smarties and chips. I, thankfully, don't seem to have burnt myself though. I did have a moment of panic this morning when I woke up and felt my skin peeling from my face, only to find when I went to the bathroom that it was something else entirely – the happy by-product of a successful, loving marriage that had somehow splattered a little off-course and been missed in the after sex clean-up. It's great for the skin, by the way, though I can't see Montagne Jeunesse releasing a fuckmuck edition.

twochubbycubs go to New York: part one

Book edit: we actually visited New York at the start of the year, but I thought it would be nicer to spread out the travel tales! Hence the snow references. So crack on.

Before we get started on the actual travels, the exciting part – this was a complete surprise for Paul. We weren't planning on taking any holidays after Corsica and Iceland being so close together, but I was driving home from a first-aid course when an advert for Expedia came on espousing cheap deals to New York. I drove on for another mile or so mulling it over, pulled into a layby, booked the time off work and emailed Paul's lovely boss to get clearance. I left the small detail of actually booking the holiday until a few days after. I've mentioned before how easily led I am by advertising – thank fuck an advert didn't come on for haemorrhoid cream else I'd have squatting down in a bus-stop feverishly applying Preparation H to my bumhole in the manner of a man spreading butter on a crumpet. Having managed to secure the time off for the both of us and after many, many "trips to ASDA" for poor Paul to get him out of the house so I could use the computer, I found a really decent deal with British Airways staying in a nice central hotel for six nights. Booked it there and then. Paul then had to endure ten days of me looking at him excitedly and dropping 'a big secret' that he probably thought he was getting divorce papers in the post. As if! I'm saving the divorce papers for when he's paid off his half of the car.

That's clearly a joke – I'd never divorce a man so perfectly squashy and who turns the shower on for me every morning so I don't have to stand for a moment in a chilly bathroom. You might think he gets the shitty end of the stick (depends how careful he's been with the old douche-bulb I guess) but read the above paragraph and think again!

Going to America always necessitates a full-on panic about travel insurance for me – I don't want to fall ill in America, find out my travel insurance is void because I didn't inform them someone once hurt my feelings in 1996 and then bankrupt my friends and family as they try and pay for my hospital treatment in a country which, for god knows why, doesn't have decent free healthcare. Listen, I know my family, they'd just send someone out on an economy flight to fill my drip-bag with Cillit Bang and stop my heart. Fuckers. I spent a good hour on the phone to a very helpful lady at Coverwise who went through my various worries – do I declare heart palpitations four years ago? Yes. Do I declare obesity? Only if I need help getting in and out of bed – not quite there yet. My hair is thinning and I look like Steve McDonald drawn Castaway-style on a beach ball – apparently I don't need to declare that. She then proceeded to take my payment but accidentally deleted all the details we had just decided upon, so we had to do it all again. Great times.

The night before the holiday I told him we were going away somewhere mysterious and to pack a suitcase. Naturally, Paul, being a keen and conscientious worker, immediately started fretting about meetings and out of office nonsense, until I told him it was all fine and that I'd been masterminding this scheme right from the off, like an evil Judith Chalmers. All he had to do was pack some clothes, find his passport (I told him we'd need it for car hire within the UK so he didn't twig we were going abroad) and get to bed, as we had an early train in the morning. He sensibly did the right thing, although we did have a minor panic when we realised that I need a new passport very soon – thankfully, we were just within the limits for USA travel. I'll be sad to see that passport go – it's about the only ID I have where the picture doesn't look like it should have a caption underneath saying '...jailed for eighteen months for public indecency'. Doubtless when I get a new passport I'll be back to looking like a sandblasted puffer-fish. I'll definitely need to get my hair cut before that day comes – the last time I want happening is someone at easyJet saying 'Aaah Mr Trump, we've been expecting you'.

Off to the train station at ridiculous-o-clock then. This necessitated a taxi drive with the world's most vocal taxi driver, who had an opinion on everything from my suitcase ("not very butch" – fuck off mate, if anyone can make a four-wheeled suitcase work, it's me) to Uber.

Uber, he took pains to tell me, was a danger because "anyone can drive them, they're not vetted" (which was rich, as he looked like the type of man for whom Incognito Mode was the default status on his browser) and that "their cars aren't checked, they could be death-traps". This one really struck a chord with Paul, who texted me to point out that the driver's rear-view mirror was gaffer taped to the roof of the car. I pleaded with him not to say anything lest we got bundled out at high speed on the Seaton Burn roundabout. Instead, we just spent the journey nodding politely and making 'hmm' and 'mmm' noises until, after seemingly taking us via Darlington, we arrived at the station and boarded our train.

What to say about the train journey that I haven't covered before? It was entirely uneventful. I was given a cup of tea that had cleaning products in (thank god for the travel insurance!) but luckily, I spotted, or rather smelled, the problem before it had a chance to burn through my throat and cascade down my chest, ruining my nice shirt. The train had to take a long diversion at some point and the trip ended up taking five hours, but it was quiet, comfortable and, with it being first class, we had more biscuits than is possibly decent. It does vex me a little that they take the meal service off in first class during the weekends – frankly my train journey isn't complete unless I'm eating something microwaved and slopped on a plate. Paul got up to go for a poo at some point and disappeared for twenty minutes.

Naturally, I was so concerned it was all I could do to put down my iPad, pause the YouTube of the Crystal Maze that I was watching, and glance down the corridor. Had he alighted at a passing station, tired of looking at my angry face across the table from him? Had my still-awake-but-really-comfy-snoring angered him so? No. Turned out, being a wonderful husband, he'd walked/stumbled to the other end of the train, bought us two double gin and tonics each and a grilled cheese sandwich. As delighted as I was with the nourishment and booze, I couldn't mask the alarm in my eyes, but he reassured me that it had only cost around £780.45 for this little treat. Good old Virgin!

On the train I told Paul we were going to Heathrow, so he knew at that point we were off abroad. We transferred onto the Heathrow Express, arrived in plenty of good time to nip into the terminal, buy some wine gums and play on the fruities before climbing inside those automatic toilets that whisk you around to various parts of Heathrow. Our destination? Why, the wonderful Thistle Hotel of course, which you may remember we weren't particularly overtaken with joy with last time (by the way, that links to one of our favourite recipes, too)? Listen, it's convenient and Paul loves that POD system, so that's why we chose it. Naturally, our room was the size of a small shoebox and I had to spin around in the shower to get wet, but eh, it's a bed. We had a Dominos and watched Vera. Vera is very much a guilty pleasure for us, although I can't tell you what it looks like because I spend most of the time wincing against her attempt at a Geordie accent. Very few people in Newcastle actually substitute 'pet' where a full stop would normally go, but by god she does it. They were filming around where we live a few weeks ago so I fully expect a shot of her solving crime whilst my filthy car drives past in the background with me squinting to see what's going on. I should have shouted 'HERE MAN VERAH PET HAS THERE BIN A MOORDA PET HAS SOMEWURN HAD THEIR HEED CAVED IN EH'. Authentic!

I revealed to Paul that we were off to New York as we approached the ticket desk in the morning (well, it would have been tricky when she asked where we were going and he said he didn't know his final destination) and of course, he was delighted. As we were in Terminal 5 it felt altogether too busy and crowded for a 'thank you' bit of bum-fun, so we just settled for oral instead. I'm kidding, we're not that raunchy. It was a handjob. OK enough. We were given our tickets and the old problem of finding something to do early in the morning at Terminal 5 reared its head. We settled for an expensive, tasteless breakfast, a good poo and an hour of aimlessly wandering around smelling aftershave I wouldn't use to clean a litter-box and avoiding a rather excitable woman who was determined we 'sample her Baileys'. I noted with relief that we weren't flying on a Dreamliner, which I was absolutely sure was the plane that had come up when I'd checked. I texted a friend to explain that I wouldn't be making an unscheduled, on-fire stop in the Shetlands and boarded.

The flight was lovely. Smooth with no turbulence, aside from a moment of panic on my side as we were taking off and it felt as though the plane was struggling. It wasn't, of course, but naturally my anxiety around taking off qualifies me as a fully-trained aeroplane pilot and I felt I had to tell Paul we were clearly going to crash. We've only flown British Airways once before and the last time was ruined by having a stewardess whose only regret in life was not being born into the Schutzstaffel, but the crew were amazing on this flight. Seats were comfortable, drinks were plentiful to the point I had seven miniature bottles of gin sitting on my table, and when they were taken away, the big bear steward, clearly feeling the rainbow connection, bought us four more. We dozed and watched movies (I watched Spectre, Paul watched bloody Ghost) and, aside from a moment where the inconsiderate oaf behind us decided to use the back of my chair and my hair to hoist himself up, it was lovely. He apologised, though I think my surprised shriek probably put me on a watch-list somewhere. We landed in JFK.

American security though, jeez. I've done it plenty of times to know that you don't crack jokes and that they aren't exactly forthcoming with the charm, but this was a whole new level. When he asked me to put out my fingers for scanning I honestly expected him to rap me on the knuckles with a wooden ruler. I'm here to spend money in your wonderful country, please don't greet me like I've shit in your dinner. Don't get me wrong, I'm not expecting an elaborate song and dance routine or a free cake with every stamp of my passport, but haway. Of course, by writing this, I'm sure I'll immediately be put on a list that means the second I land in the USA I'll be greeted by someone shining a light in my face and sticking a gloved finger up my bum. Listen, all I ask is that you tweak my nipples a bit first, get me going.

That's us, then, on American soil. I'll continue with the next part sometime soon!

twochubbycubs go to New York: part two

After landing at JFK and undergoing the most intimidating entry interview I've ever faced (normally I'm not asked many questions prior to anyone admitting me entry, rather just a plea to be gentle and to call them after) (pfft!) (or rather whoooooooo....) (work that out) (jeez, this is a lot of bracketed thoughts), we were on our way. We decided that, rather than paying a billion dollars for a taxi to our hotel, we'd be savvy and streetwise and take the subway, not least because the subway is famous and exciting. I say exciting, there was a TV playing in the station whose main headline was 'SEVENTH SLEEPING SOUL SLASHED IN SUBWAY'. Now, I'm all for alliteration and sharp headlines, but knife attacks aren't usually an enticement to travel. Nevertheless, we ploughed on, trying to figure out what ticket we needed to buy for the week to get us from JFK and then afford us travel throughout the network all week. God knows what we bought – I was hustled into buying something in a newsagent by a strident sounding lady who was more weave than woman. The tickets worked in the barrier (after much 'PUT IT THAT WAY, YOU'VE GOT IT THE WRONG WAY, NO YOU NEED IT PARALLEL TO THE Y-AXIS, YOU STUPID POMMIE ASSHOLE!) and we were on our way. Hooray! At the risk of sounding like a hipster twat, I like to take the subway rather than taxis because I feel it adds to the experience.

Sadly, I was stabbed in the lung and spent the rest of the holiday in an American hospital being shook from my ankles until the coins fell out of my pocket.

I jest. After a couple of transfers and a brief interlude to watch a genuinely crazy man shouting and bawling into a litter-bin, we arrived at 34th Street – Penn Station. I don't know what had caused the shouting man such ire but by God that bin had infuriated him. I find it remarkable that Paul and I can find our way around any foreign subway system given all we have to practice on up here is the Tyne and Wear Metro, which consists entirely of two lines and spends more time being apologised for than actually going anywhere. I used it briefly for about two months but eventually made it to my destination. Anyway, I digress. We climbed a set of stairs, exited the station and goodness me, what a shock. Everything is so *tall*. That may seem ridiculous to you, I don't know, but I hadn't realised almost every building in the streets would be so many storeys – it creates the illusion of feeling a bit bunkered down – but not claustrophobic. I was expecting the streets to be busy, and they were, but I never felt as though I was in the way – which when you consider that combined Paul and I take up as much room as a modern housing development, is quite something.

Our hotel, the Wyndham New Yorker, was over the road, and we hastened across, taking care to observe the flashing white man (who wouldn't?) to permitted us to cross. Given my experience with the officers upon entry I didn't fancy getting banged up for jaywalking, though it didn't stop anyone else. The crossing was absolutely filled with cars coming from all directions, pedestrians, suitcases, people asking for money and a horse. Not people asking for a horse, rather, just a horse. Naturally. We had picked the New Yorker on a whim – it looked pleasant enough and the location was perfect, but that was the limit of our research. Well, it was delightful. It's an art-deco hotel, opened in 1930 and not modernised too much – the lifts are grand, the lobby massive, the staff all well-to-do and pleasant and the plumbing clearly hasn't been touched since the first brick was put down. I'll touch on that in a moment. We checked in and were directed to our room on the 27th floor. I was sure that meant a penthouse or a decent suite but that was soon dispelled when we got into the lift and realised there were 43 floors. Boooo! We had sent ahead and mentioned it was our anniversary and I'd gone so far to book the room as Professor J Surname rather than plain old Mr, but nope. Ah well. Our room was perfunctory – pleasant, but nothing you'd write home about. You'd have a hard job given there was no writing desk or pens. The TV was small and the bed was so lumpy that I had to check we weren't lying on top of the previous guests, but it was clean and warm and had an excellent view. We bravely set about emptying our suitcases into the tiny wardrobe (with four coat-hangers – we had to call down for more, I felt so stereotypical) and then immediately shoving everything we could possibly lift into the suitcase. It's just the done thing to do.

I wish I could tell you that we spent the evening out in the glitz and glamour of New York, but, somewhat jet-lagged, we opted to stay in the room watching Wheel of Fortune and eating Jolly Ranchers. We both feel asleep almost immediately and didn't wake again until 6am the next morning, where I was alarmed to find a half-sucked blue raspberry Jolly Rancher had tumbled out of my sleep-open mouth and into my hair. I'm a classy guy.

So, at 6am in the city that never sleeps, where do you go? I'm ashamed to say we spent a lot of our holiday time doing the really obvious sites, but listen, you can't go to New York and not take in the obvious. To that end, this whole trip report will be a series of ticks off the list. We started the day right by nipping into the Tick Tock Diner right next to the hotel for a breakfast – I showed British restraint, having only three eggs, corned beef hash, sausages, bacon (it's not bloody bacon, it looks like grilled hangnails, but nevermind) and toast on the side. My eggs came covered in cheese which should tell you everything you need to know about breakfasting in New York. It was AMAZING. Paul had pancakes – great big lumps of dough and syrup which he seemed remarkably content with. His eyes glazed over, but I reckon that could have been the maple syrup pushing through from the back like shampoo on a sponge. We finished our meal, paid the bill with a slight grimace (I had forgotten it was obligatory to tip over in America – I nearly always do anyway, even in England, but I do so hate how I'm *forced* to tip) and we were on our way.

First stop – the Statue of Liberty, which immediately set Paul off going '**I THINKA CAN SEE THE STACHOO OF LIBERTAAY AL-A-READY**' like that tiny Italian man from Titanic. There were a *lot* of Titanic quotes on this day. A good friend of mine had recommended I book everything well in advance, so we had tickets booked for Statue Cruises which set off from Battery Park. Once on the island we had a choice of going up to her crown, just into the general minge level or walking around the outside. We had opted for the minge option (I think they call it Pedestal Level) and were very much looking forward to it, so much so that we arrived an hour early. Oops. I entertained myself by going for a poo in the park toilets, which is always a terrifying experience in America as they like to leave a giant gap down the side of the doors plus make the door itself the size of a postage stamp. This is just awful – you end up desperately trying not to make any eye-contact with passing folks as you're busy pushing brown. I get that it's to stop cottaging and drug-taking but come on, people like a bit of privacy whilst they poop.

After a poo each and a good cup of coffee, we noticed our boat was coming in and so made our way through the security check, removing our belt for what would be the first of many, many times throughout this holiday, and dealing with customer service people who hated their jobs and everyone involved in it. I wear this necklace:

and the charming woman on security held it up for everyone to look at and asked me 'it's meaning'. I almost said OOHO IT'S A BIT OF VIV WESTWOOD LOVE' but didn't. I wear it because I like it, and it's quite literally the only piece of designer anything I own. I'm too fat for designer clothes and too poor for designer furniture, so I can only have nice jewellery and shoes. And I buy my shoes from the same place I buy my toilet roll, so, you know. I wasn't expecting to have to justify it to someone who had clearly only just remembered to have a shave that morning. She waved us through. Paul never gets any bother with security and he's got half a bloody Meccano set keeping his arm together since he gashed it open on a discarded shopping trolley half-submerged in a ditch in Peterborough, or as they like to call it, a 'child's play area'. Our boat docked and about ten thousand people appeared from nowhere to disembark, pitching the boat at a perilous angle where I genuinely thought it was going over. Of course it wasn't, but what's life without melodrama. We boarded, seemingly with the entirety of China's under 35's, and were on our way in no time at all.

The cruise, such as it is, takes fifteen minutes, which afforded Paul enough time to discover a snack shop and buy us a cup of coffee that had seemingly come fresh from the sun. My lips blistered just taking the lid off the cup. Let me save you some money – if you're going to New York, unless you're massively fussed about seeing the statue up close and finding out more about it in the museum, you don't need to visit the old bird. Take the Staten Island ferry and see it from the water – it'll cost you next to nothing and you won't have to indulge in a scrum to get on and off the boat. We love a good nosey around a museum though so we were champion, cooing and oohing our way around various cases and replicas of her giant toes. She certainly didn't have a problem with an ingrown toenail – oh how I envied her. If you're squeamish, skip the next paragraph.

I remember once holidaying in France with an ingrown toenail so bad that my toe actually exploded in my trainer on a hot day, showering my sock with pus and a dead nail. The relief I felt though – no sex has ever come close to that feeling. Not quite grossed out enough? I used to let the family dog clean my toe because I was told a dog's tongue has antiseptic qualities and he seemed to enjoy it! Eee, that'll be me straight to hell now. Still, he did a great job until he died of advanced sepsis two months later.

I know, gross right? I'm so sorry. Poor Oscar.

We bought a tiny replica of the statue, took a few upskirt pictures of the old bird and then fannied about with the telescopes for a bit. It was a lovely day – warm but spring-like and fresh, perfect for the massive wool coat I was wearing. At least I had my magma-esque coffee to cool me off. Then, back onto the boat for a short hop over to Ellis Island, an optional freebie excursion where you can see the famous Immigrant Inspection Station and the housing and suchlike. It was all very interesting indeed but at this point our crippling obesity was beginning to play havoc with our ankles and we needed a good old fashioned sit-down, so we went into the little restaurant and seemingly emptied my wallet in exchange for two club sandwiches the size of my arm. We sat down and immediately regretted it as we had a talker immediately to our left, an octogenarian with a lot to say. We couldn't ignore him because he seemed lonely. 'So where you guys from' was his opening gambit, and when I replied with 'Newcastle, England' he took such a gasp of air that I almost gave him his last rites, thinking perhaps an errant crisp had lodged in his windpipe. No, it was just genuine surprise which didn't subside when I explained it really wasn't that far and we didn't row across the Atlantic. He then kept us at the table for a good half hour, clutching my arm every time we made to leave. To be fair, he was actually very interesting and my ability to make small-talk never failed me, so the time flew by, but we did miss our boat back, meaning we had to spend another hour on the tiny island, trying to keep out of view of this old chap. I felt like I was sneaking into America myself.

After Ellis Island we got the boat back over to Battery Park and decided to take a walk over to where the Twin Towers used to be and where the new One World Trade Centre tower now stood. Let me say this – although it is easier to walk to places in New York rather than fannying about on their labyrinthine subway system, make sure you gauge the distances before you set off. We ended up with feet like corned beef by the end of the holiday. It's more interesting though, seeing a city on foot. That's what I told Paul as he poured blood out of his shoes.

Nothing can be said on the Twin Towers disaster that hasn't already been said, but I'll add my own thoughts. It's always been something abstract – images on the TV or in the papers – and whilst utterly horrific and downright barbaric, I've never been able to actually get my head around it. Standing there then in the shadow of the new tower, with the two massive memorial pools in front of us, it actually hit home. Imagining not one but two of these towers falling into the street and the absolute mayhem and terror that would bring, well, we both actually got emotional. You need to understand – the only time I think I've seen Paul cry was when I hid his selection box at Christmas or when I clipped a peg onto his bumhair and accidentally nicked his sphincter. You stand at the bottom of this tower and look up and you can't see the top. Imagine that the other way around and knowing you had to jump down to your death or burn. Horrendous.

We entered the new tower and boarded the lift up to the 102nd floor which was an experience all in itself – 102 floors in less than 60 seconds, with the lifts being made from a 360 degree set of TV screens which model New York in front of you. I've done a shit job of explaining that, so take a second right now to look on YouTube.

It's OK, I'll wait.

Come on now, that was something special. After leaving the lift, you're taken to a row of cardboard cut-outs of skyscrapers in a darkened room, upon which a cheesy video about New York was projected. Naturally, being a cynic, I was about to moan to Paul that we'd paid $100 to watch a movie when suddenly everything in front of us rose out of view and was replaced with floor to ceiling glass windows, affording us the most incredible view. My flabber could not have been more gasted. It's initially very disorientating as you forget you're so high up until New York is revealed before you like a magician's trick, but it's genuinely wonderful. We spent an age walking around taking pictures that we'll never look at again, like everyone else, before nipping up to the bar for a cocktail.

Are you sitting down? Our two cocktails cost $58. Yes, you could get a glass of tap water but fuck it, we were on holiday and it was money well-spent, although such very strong alcohol combined with the natural swaying of the building leads to a slightly unsettling experience.

The lift down was as fun as the lift going up and let me tell you, we were genuinely impressed with the whole experience. There was no gung-ho over-the-top patriotism like we expected, we weren't forced to pay extra for stuff time and time again, and the views made it completely worthwhile. I'd recommend this in a heartbeat. We spent half an hour looking around the memorial pools and that's another thing that seems odd — it's so quiet. No-one is shouting or running around, just quietly paying respects. Roses are left pushed into people's names that have been etched into the shiny black marble that surrounds the pools. It's tasteful and thought-provoking. Not so much for a couple of very prissy knobheads who decided to treat the experience like a fashion show, lying across the memorials, draping their scarves on one another, squealing and clapping and generally being obnoxious dicks (and hell, that's my job on holiday, surely?). We ruined a good number of their photographs as a petty revenge, walking behind them and into shot with stupid expressions on our faces, until I tired of the game and whispered loudly as we walked past that 'they should show some fucking respect and stop being selfish boys'. I may not have used the word boys. I might have said something that rhymed with punts. The photographer of the two went squealing over to the other and they stalked off in a huff. Way man. A bit of respect, that's all.

twochubbycubs go to New York: part three

Firstly, I almost died today. Perhaps a slight exaggeration but I was busy eating my 28g³ of bran-flakes as per Mags' orders and watching a particularly loud Jeremy Kyle when an errant bran flake shot down my wind-pipe and got stuck there. I immediately started spluttering and choking but Paul just looked at me with a 'Oh I know, and look at their yellow teeth' face, no help at all. It took almost thirty seconds of trying to dislodge this bran flake before it finally shot out and landed with a splat in his bowl of cereal – that'll teach the unobservant fucker. My whole life flashed before my eyes – far more sitting in front of a computer trying to come up with fresh gags about fellatio for my liking – and let's be honest, thirty seconds is a long time for a fat bloke to hold his breath, let alone one who smoked twenty a day for three years. Hell, it's hard enough for me to not eat for thirty seconds, nevermind breathe. Plus, imagine having bran as your cause of death? You quite literally could not have a more boring reason for expiration, unless you were mumbled to death by someone with dried egg on his shirt.

Speaking of boring farts with dried egg on their shirts, we got a rather arsey message from someone "in charge" of a geocache that we visited last weekend, stating that because he couldn't see that we had signed the log, he would delete our find. Well, you can imagine the devastation that caused in our household, can't you? It was like when Princess Di died, only I hadn't accordioned my car into a Parisian tunnel. His message was so infuriatingly terse and snippy that it got my back up something rotten. Why would anyone lie about something so insignificant about finding a tiny container hidden in some nettles by the side of the A696? Goodness me. I explained that our pencil had broken and he went "away to consider the options". I like to think he tossed and turned all night with his little GPS unit calling to him like The Tell-Tale Heart. I genuinely don't think I'll ever come across in my lifetime someone imbued with such a misguided amount of self-importance in relation to the tiny amount of power they've been granted. Honestly.

Anyway, it's been a while since we revisited New York, hasn't it? Why don't we take a trip and chortle our way through another day of our holiday in The Big Apple. I hope I don't get an email from you lot asking for proof that I actually visited New York, but if I do, I can show you a blurry photo of Paul's arse-cheeks as he took a piss in Central Park.

I can tell you one thing right from the off about New York – there's hardly any fat people. It's the most confusing thing. I was basing my expectations on Florida, admittedly, where if there had been an earthquake I reckon 80% of the occupants in Disneyworld would have crashed together to form one amorphous blob (imagine a lava-lamp falling over), perhaps with eight or so of those mobility scooters whirring away underneath. It's genuinely the only time in my life I've ever felt skinny. I was expecting New York to be the same, but no, as we are in the UK, Paul and I remained the fattest of them all. Eh, who cares right? As long as our ankles don't give out from under us, we're good to go.

We started with breakfast, naturally, which I'm sure involved half a pig and some Smuckers, which I still think sounds like something your bumhole does when you're got the skitters: "oooh, Elsie, put an Andrex in the freezer, my hoop is smuckering" or something. Our first destination was Times Square and after getting lost several times and ending up in the same K-Mart – twice – we finally found our way there. I'm not sure what we were expecting – yes, lots of big screens and people bustling about...but it really is just a meeting of streets. Am I missing something? Seeing an eight-storeys-high Gordon Ramsay advertising Hell's Kitchen in ultra-HD will haunt me until my dying day – I swear I could almost hear the wind whistling through his digital forehead wrinkles. It's how I go to sleep now, counting the pores on his nose in my mind's eye.

We did spot an interactive screen by L'Oréal, which implored couples to stand on a spot and wait until one of the giant screens was filled with a live stream of them, then you were to pose kissing or cuddling and SHOW NEW YORK LOVE. Now, obviously, there was someone out of sight deciding which couple gets projected onto the massive screens, and when it was Paul and I standing there...well...they didn't put on the big screen. Sob! Was it because we're fat? Was it because we're shirtlifters? Who knows. Paul was all for heading straight off and letting the beautiful people have their moment in the digital sun, but not me. Oh no. I stood there with Paul by my side for a good ten minutes until we were eventually projected to all of New York – we kissed, but sadly the photo was taken at such an angle that it looks like I'm gnawing on Paul's head and he's trying not to Smucker in his trousers. Nevermind, we still got our moment.

We spotted that a nearby museum was hosting an exhibition by Gunther von Hagens, the German anatomist who travels around with those stripped back skeletons and bodies that show the various muscles and whatnot. Hard to describe but hopefully you know what I mean. Fair warning, there's a pretty grim picture coming up, so if you're a sensitive Betty get scrolling! We've always wanted to see his 'show' but forever missed it, so this time we were at the front of the queue. Is it wrong to show such a fevered desire to see bodies and bones? It was like our arrival at the Icelandic Knob Museum all over again!

It was brilliant – all very scientific and tasteful and interesting, although let's be honest everyone there was gagging to see how funny the knobs looked hanging down and stripped of skin – like weisswurst, since you ask. Around every corner was something of note – the tiny bones of a premature baby, the nervous system all laid out like a colossal piece of broccoli, four naked men sitting around playing cards with their bollocks hanging down like tiny church bells. As you'd expect, Paul and I tutted at the giggling school party who were shrieking into their sleeves and nudging each other at the sight of a lady's vagina (well it wasn't going to be a bloke's vagina, after all) all laid bare like a broken oyster, then we proceeded to stifle our own giggles at the 'sperm and egg' portion of the show. I'm a man who loves his puns see, and it was all I could do to hold back from '…and THIS is what it's come to' or suchlike. Museum fatigue set in for me before Paul, meaning my eyes had glazed over to the point where, had I not moved for a minute more, I could have passed as part of the exhibition.

Exhibition over, we decided we both needed to say goodbye to our breakfasts, which led to the next awkward toilet encounter. Remember in my last post I complained about the fact that American toilets have that weird gap under the door and a huge crack (especially when I'm in it) between the door and the wall of the cubicle next to it, meaning every hastily taken shit is a lesson in trying desperately not to meet someone's eye as you crimp off a loaf? Well, no sooner had we both settled down (in adjacent cubicles, we're not *that* close) and preparing to drop anchor when in walks a janitor who proceeds to start mopping the floor. Fair enough, in the UK someone would have knocked on the door, waited outside and given you a filthy look as you leave and they walk into your arse-cloud, but no, this cheeky chappie starts whistling merrily and going about his business. That wouldn't have been so bad if he hadn't then stuck his grimy mop under the friggin' toilet door and sloshed it over our shoes. NOTHING makes the shutters close quicker than something like that happening, and Paul immediately WhatsApped me to say 'he couldn't go' and that 'we should leave'. The janitor gave us a proper smirk as we left too. He totally knew what he was doing.

As soon as we left the Body Works museum I immediately got a nosebleed. Smashing! I have a really fragile nose and go through spells of heavy but entirely non-serious nosebleeds, and boom, here we were. Well goodness me, you've never seen so many tourists swerve out of someone's way then that day, in the rain, when I came shuffling towards them with a face full of blood. N0-one offered to help, of course, so Paul dashed as fast as his swollen feet allowed him into Walgreens, where a security guard, after a LOT of persuasion, tore me off a piece of fucking parcel paper to wipe my face with. I'd have been more bloody comfortable wiping my face with a square of 1200 grit sandpaper. I muttered my thanks and sent Paul back in to try and find some tissues, only for him to disappear for ten minutes and reappear having been forced a packet of $8 aloe-fucking-vera face-wipes. Luckily, my inbuilt Geordie tight-arse came out and the outrage at having to pay so much to stop myself passing out distracted my brain from pouring my life out of my nose and we were soon sorted. I left a charming puddle of blood around the back of a donut shop, which I like to think will have confused the police for a few hours at least.

I can't help but feel that had the janitor at the Body Works exhibition allowed me to have a dump, the pressure in my body would have settled and there would have been no nosebleed. I should have nipped back and dripped all over his urinals.

So, unexpected epistaxis aside, we made our way to M&M World, where we treated ourselves to a few bits of tat and quite possibly the most awkward photo we've ever had taken. I'm not posting it. A tiny lady in a massive red M&M costume came tottering out of a door to entertain the waiting children when we asked if we could have a photo. Well, I've never seen a costumed figure with a six-foot-wide smile manage to look so dejected and uncomfortable but by God, the photo doesn't lie. It doesn't help that Paul, in his effort to get his hands around her to make it look like he's hugging the 'giant M&M', just looks like he's trying to fingerbang her through the felt. I bet we're on a Tumblr blog somewhere with someone screaming TRIGGERED. We made a sharp exit, stopping only to buy a glass 'Big

Apple' with chocolate M&Ms inside, which I am genuinely proud to tell you we still have and haven't smashed open in a fit of hunger. It's only the thought of swallowing glass that puts me off mind, rather than any sense of decency.

For reasons still unknown to both of us, we decided to visit Ripley's Believe It Or Not (well, it was chucking it down and we didn't want to walk far). The first believe it or not came when she charged us $65 for entry. I told her that, actually, I didn't believe it (ho ho) but clearly she had suffered a long, miserable life of gags like that and fixed me with a stare that nearly set my nose away again. These places are what you make of them. Go in expecting a load of frippery and nonsense and you'll thoroughly enjoy yourself. Where else can you put your head down amongst thousands of skittering cockroaches (aside from a Travelodge bed) or 'enjoy' medieval, ancient equipment designed to torture and maim (aside from a Travelodge bed)? We had a whale of a time until the bit at the end where you reach a 'dizziness machine' and have to walk along a platform whilst a curtain of paint-splattered material rotates wildly around you. Yikes. I get dizzy unscrewing the lid off a bottle of Coke, let alone having to endure a simulator of what it must be like to be Paul Gascoigne. I closed my eyes, walked through, straight into Paul who was taking a picture and sent him tumbling. Calamity Anne strikes again.

Once Paul's concussion had wore off, we wandered down to Grand Central Station, where, like the boring old farts that we are, we elected to take an audio tour. Well, what a revelation! Aside from having to wear headphones last used to guide Apollo 13 back to Earth, that is. The tour took us all around the various nooks and crannies of the station and was absolutely worth doing. There's nothing much funny that you can write about an audio tour of a train station so let me just strongly recommend it and move on. We bought a set of metal subway signs to go above all the bedroom doors in our hallway – well, the 'Next customer please' sign was getting a little faded and the bulb in the red light had gone. We stopped at Starbucks (which wasn't hard, given how many Starbucks stores there were – I half-expected to be offered a venti mocha frappucino when I went for a piss in the night. I was restrained, I have a peach iced tea, but Paul went all out for a drink that looked like someone had emptied a sheep dip into a bucket and topped it with enough whipped cream and syrup to make Mags' buttocks clench in horror. The barista *cough* managed to misspell Paul as Pawl but it's OK, we were able to identify his drink due to them having to move chairs and tables out of the way to bring it through.

Now I wish I could tell you we spent the rest of the day flitting from each wonderful thing to the next, but we actually did something terrible – we found a bar that served all sorts of wonderful beers and spent the rest of the day and most of the evening in there getting absolutely sozzled. We only popped in for one. Flight 151 in Chelsea, if you're curious. It was brilliant – I'm a large fan of this 'beer flight' idea where you get several small beers to try on a fancy ladder. I was such a fan that I had four flights and Paul had to stop me when I made to put Conchita Wurst on the jukebox.

We spotted that they served 'British' beers and ordered a Newcastle Brown Ale and a Guinness each. Both seemed fine but Paul immediately made sure that we couldn't possibly go back to that bar by checking in on Facebook on their page and saying 'Wonderful bar but can't pour a Guinness'. Once I spotted what he'd done, I shooed us out of the door. He's very skilled and making friends and influencing people.

Can we talk for a moment about tipping? I find it hilariously awkward and even more so in a bar. We were sitting at the bar and every round of drinks, I was leaving two or three dollars on the bar when they passed me the change. I did try to give him a tip directly but he waved it away – odd – so the dollars just sat in the beer foam crinkling up. He eventually swept them up with a flourish and a thank you but did I miss something? I tried telling him to keep a couple of dollars back from my change but that got ignored...ah it's so stressful. I know why people tip in America (wages for waiting staff and bar-folk are abysmal) but as a Brit, don't put me in such a socially awkward situation! Take as much money as you like, just don't make me cringe with the awkwardness of what to bloody do with the tip!

We staggered back a fair distance to our hotel, stopping only to stumble through the doors of a closed post office in the vain hope of finding a lavatory (nope) and fell asleep in our clothes. Classy 'til the end.

twochubbycubs go to New York: part four

One of the things you apparently must do when in Central Park is a trip on a horse-pulled carriage. A quick look on tripadvisor would tell you that it's simply a quick way to have your wallet emptied by toothless crones running scams but hell, we like to live life on the edge and anyway, any activity that meant we were moving without having to use our feet was good enough for me because at this point in our holiday the bottom of my feet looked like something unpleasant that had been run over. Pouring blood out of your shoe isn't a great look.

We wandered around a bit trying to catch the eye of one of the swarthy looking gentleman in charge of the horses but to no avail, meaning we eventually had to go up and ask for a romantic half hour trip. Well, Paul did, I didn't want to be witness to seeing how much money had to change hands. No, I was busy watching the horse who, upon seeing me and Paul shuffling towards it, looked absolutely terrified by the thought of having to pull us two lardarses. I suppose it's the equivalent of me nipping outside and pulling a bus with the hairs on my arse. We climbed aboard. The horse immediately filled his nappy which I think was possibly a protest, but it really did set the scene.

Luckily, our driver's grasp on the English language didn't extend further than telling us the price and shouting at his horse meaning we were free to enjoy ourselves without making painful small-talk but actually, the whole thing felt awful. He kept yelling at the horse, seemingly for going too slow, which felt rather cruel given the poor bugger was pulling the equivalent of a Skoda Octavia behind it, then when he wasn't shouting at the horse he was bellowing incoherently into his mobile. Perhaps he had another horse on the line. Either way, between the dirty carriage, world's angriest jockey and poor, frightened horse, it was awful. About as relaxing as trying to solve a Rubik's cube whilst someone sets your trousers on fire.

After about ten minutes of this we motioned that we would like to disembark and cut our 45-minute trip short. Of course, he was furious, but hey, at least it gave him a chance to shout at us rather than the horse. I like to think that made us equal, my equine friend. He stuck his hand out for a tip *after* arguing with us for five minutes and I had to really resist the urge to give him a high-five and tell him to fuck off. It was a tempting thought but I didn't fancy Paul having to scrape half of my face from the tarmac path afterwards. We bustled away and he shot off with the horse, shouting and ranting until he was nothing more than a speck on the horizon. Even now, when I shut my eyes, I can hear *"estúpido caballo de mierda"* over and over...

Well, that left us in rather a pickle. We'd planned a nice easy jaunt around Central Park, letting the mane take the strain (boom boom), but now we were in the middle of nowhere somewhere near the top of the park with the horrifying thought that we'd need to explore under our own locomotion. But, you know what, that's exactly what we did – and it was terrific.

We spent a good few hours just walking slowly through the park – taking little side paths, exploring nooks and crannies, unusually, not dogging – it was lovely.

At one point we decided to cut out of the park to grab a coffee from Starbucks (don't worry, there's one every four buildings so you're generally OK). We sat and read the papers and people-watched. I declared, as I always do on holiday no matter where we are, that we should really sell our house in England and move here. I could be a writer with a tiny balcony on which to type my stories and Paul could go and serve beer somewhere where his fatness would be appreciated and welcomed, like a leather fetish bar. We could tell fabulous tales of our metropolitan life, start a food blog, eschew Slimming World and all the pointless rules about not eating avocados...basically, live the dream. We'd get to 55 years old and, having made a pretty penny selling stories and blowjobs, we could jack it all in, mortgage our property and open a little cigar bar in the gay district and call it 'Big Brown Butts'. We'd laugh uproariously and drink beer and develop a decent salt-and-pepper beard before one of us died from emphysema and the other was reduced to giving handjobs on the subway to make money. Oh my.

Paul immediately burst my bubble by waving the property section of the free paper in front of me where an apartment about the size of our bathroom cost more than our entire house. I might add: we own the most expensive house on our street – it's no wonder all the other neighbours look furiously at us as we skip mortgage-free to our cars in the morning. That put paid to our dreams and, a little deflated (I mean come on, Big Brown Butts is an amazing name for a gay cigar bar, yes?), we made our way back to Central Park, giant waste-paper-bin-sized coffees in our hands.

As we re-entered the park we noticed a terrific fuss at one of the entrances and a lot of shrieking. Turns out it was a gay wedding and they were pulling up at the gate to have some pictures taken. Aww. We've come a long way, baby. The gay man in me (Paul, usually) felt a bit of pride that it was all so accepted and lovely, but then also, the gay man in me winced a little at their completely white suits. We're talking Gareth Gates in the video for Unchained Melody, here, only without his Jordan-torn foreskin* dripping down his leg. Listen, that wouldn't have been so bad (and I'm far from a dedicated follower of fashion in my ASDA shoes and Bet Lynch coat) but they'd overdone the fake-tan to an especially luminous degree. Their long white bodies topped with a bright orange face gave them the odd appearance of looking like cigarettes from a distance.

Now, there's an obvious joke there, but I'll be the better man and not make it.

* Can anyone else remember that? Jordan claimed to have shagged him so hard that his tight foreskin ripped in two. How the fuck have I remembered that? No wonder the poor bugger had a stutter – it was probably fear of round two with that tangerine tart.

We stayed back for a bit whilst they fussed about posing before we both got bored and, realising that there was no way of getting past without interrupting their photo, we walked back up a bit to another entrance so that we could walk back down behind them. See, we can be considerate, especially when fellow chutney-ferrets are involved. We did rather think that once we got back to where they were they'd be finished and we could walk on by, but no, when we got there they were releasing doves. I wanted to stick about in case they wheeled out Elton bloody John (although, given his predilection for olive oil, they could have just slid him down the street) but the day was drawing to a close and we really had to get going. As a result, we should probably apologise to our orange friends who have a set of wedding photos with Paul and I bustling away behind them in our discount coats and me with Frappuccino froth in my 'tache.

We wandered for ages more – just taking our time, enjoying the crisp, Winter air and the magic of being in Central Park when it was a bit snowy and cold, looking desperately around for the bird lady from Home Alone 2 (though on reflection that was fruitless, as she was at home in Peterborough dropping cigarette ash into Paul's brother's dinner) and just having a nice time together. It was all very romantic. Paul was clearly swept up in the romance as he allowed me to buy some food from a street vendor – I wish I hadn't bothered. They were selling those giant doughy pretzels that I loved so much in Orlando – the ones where when you bite into them you're rewarded with cheesy goodness and warmth. Pfft. I could have given myself a full body shave with this one it was that dry and tough. I almost went back and bought another so that I could fashion a pair of snow shoes out of them but didn't want to hand over any more to the grasping charlatan behind the cart.

Eventually, as dusk gave way to night, we found ourselves at the giant ice-rink. We had no intention of strapping blades to our already swollen, sore feet – that would just be ridiculous. Naturally, we ended up doing exactly that ten minutes later after a lot of 'it would be silly not to' and 'I'm sure it'll be fine'. It was, for me – I can ice-skate, despite it looking like a wardrobe is thundering around the rink – but Paul has all the co-ordination you'd expect from someone who is twice the weight he should be and has eyes that move entirely independently of each other. It was like that poor horse from earlier had strapped on a pair of blades. Like Bambi, but with something terrifying pressing on his brain stem. We couldn't skate for long – our ankles were bending as though made from playdoh – but it was a good laugh. Paul did almost take some poor child's fingertips off when he skated perilously close to her fallen body but luckily, all was well. We decided to stop before we injured someone irreversibly and, after spending about fifteen minutes trying to take off the skates without everyone hearing our rasping, heavy, exhausted breathing, we were back on our way.

Thankfully, without realising it, we'd walked almost to where we started and were able to get an Uber straight back to the hotel. I say straight back but the journey took almost fifty minutes thanks to traffic and tourists. Tchoh. Tourists. Our Uber driver, unusually, wasn't a frightening ranting racist but instead a perfectly erudite young man who displayed excellent taste by telling us he wanted to move to Scotland and live on an island. We traded stories and the time flew by. We tipped generously, staggered to our room and put our heads down for a quick nap before going back out.

Nope, in what is becoming a running theme for our holidays, we knacker ourselves out so much during the day that we fall asleep early evening and sleep right through. I woke up at about 11 and tried to shake Paul awake so we could go out and get some scran in the city that never sleeps, but he just grumbled something uncouth at me, farted heartily, then went straight back to sleep. After a moment's furious sulking, I did exactly the same. Night night.

twochubbycubs go to New York: part five

We decided to break with looking around the busy city and to take a nice walk along what is known as The High Line – a disused railway line that runs for a mile or so around Manhattan and affords lovely views of the Hudson and various arty-farty establishments to poke about it. We didn't really have much of an excuse, it was only a ten-minute walk away from the hotel and boy did we need some 'fresh air'. New York is amazing but you don't realise how built-up it is until you look at your partner and he's milk-white from lack of sunlight.

It was charming. I hate to use that word because it's what pretentious knobheads use to describe tiny coffee places where they serve the coffee in a flat cap but I mean it. We went early enough so that it wasn't completely awash with hipsters and pretty much had the place to ourselves, save for a few joggers. I was pleased to see that the 'I'm about to cum' face that British folk adopt when they run seems to have made it over the pond. Seriously, why pull that face? Running isn't that exciting. At least, I can't remember it being so – admittedly the last time I ran was back in 1997.

The High Line is full of little activities and things to do. We happened across a tiny park with stepping stones and tunnels to climb through, which then allowed you to pop your head up through the path to frighten passer-by's. Great fun, until you realise that the tunnels probably weren't designed to accommodate some twenty-stone Geordie with a fat arse and cheap jeans trying to turn around in there – it was like trying to turn a sofa around in a lift. I managed to get in alright but every time I moved backwards my coat scrunched up on top of me, stopping progress. It was only after my plaintive cries reached my dear husband – and in turn, once he had stopped laughing and taking pictures of my jammed arse – that he reached into the tunnel and pulled my coat free, allowing me to scuttle back out.

Later, Paul spotted a statue with the instruction 'kiss to receive water'. Naturally, being Paul, he bent down and mimed performing cunnilingus on it so that I had a classy photo to put in the album. He was tutted at by someone who was more beard than man but hey, we have fun. We stopped at the end for a bagel and coffee and discussed where to go next, before deciding on the 9/11 Memorial Museum. Because we're fat, we got a taxi. I've never heard my own feet say 'phew'.

We arrived at the 9/11 Memorial Museum and were glad that the snaking queues we had witnessed a day or two before had dissipated and that actually, it wasn't too busy.

It's funny. We've all seen the footage on the TV or in print but until you're there, it's truly impossible to put it into perspective. To imagine the size of the buildings, the sheer amount of people caught up in it, the absolute terror that must have ensued. The museum itself was surprisingly sombre and tasteful – I admit I'd expect a certain amount of 'America is Great' bombast, but there was none. Just recollections, pieces of the building, subdued reconstructions and hushed tones.

One beautiful piece is a wall of almost 3,000 pieces of fabric paper painted in different shades of blue – it's a tremendous sight with a sobering quote in the middle: 'No Day Shall Erase You From The Memory Of Time'. Very true. Behind the wall is a room full of the unidentified remains of people caught up in the attacks, where they will lie forever until they are positively identified and taken by families, something which made even granite-faced me dab at my eyes. I'd encourage anyone visiting New York to have a look – it makes for a depressing hour but some things should never be forgotten. We moved on, and, because I want to change back to our normal tone of writing, let me draw a line under this.

....

Fancy! Next on our list was the Grand Central train station. You'll have seen it before in so many movies – it's a fabulous, colossal train station full of period detail and busy people. You may remember seeing it in such famous Lindsay Lohan movies such as 'Just My Luck', or infamous Lindsay Lohan movies such as 'Yes, I'll Let You Eight Guys Ride Me Like A Train for some meth'.

We decided to take a headphones audio tour of the

station and do you know, it was one of the best things we did in New York. I know that sounds ridiculous but it was just the right mix of getting in people's way, hearing interesting facts and having sights that you would never have known to look at pointed out to you. Case in point: the ceiling of the main concourse. Who ever looks up when they enter a train station? You should here – it's a gorgeous astronomy map with glowing stars. That's fascinating in and of itself, but see the ceiling was almost hidden from view by years of tobacco smoke and pollution. It took twelve years to clean it and restore it to its natural beauty, with one tiny square left to show the difference.

I made a mental note to contact Paul's mother on my return to see if she wanted to hire the same cleaners to try and get the fifty-eight years of Samson roll-up smoke peeled from her ceiling (it'd be like using a spatula to clean the grill pan), but then promptly forgot about it when our audio tour guided us to the whispering walls.

Seriously, what fun. Under the main concourse is a dining area and part of that, near the Oyster bar, is the Whispering Wall. Due to the way the tunnel is built, sound whispered in one corner of the giant room travels all along the arch and can be heard a good ten metres away across the room. It's a bloody weird effect.

Naturally, I stood in one corner and sent Paul to where I thought the whisper could be heard across the tunnel. Well, look, I can only apologise to the little Chinese lady who was very startled to have the ghost of a Geordie whisper the word c*nt in her ear from apparently nowhere. Turns out Paul was standing in the wrong place. In my defence, it was hilarious. We sharp moved on.

By some amazing coincidence our audio tour ended with us being taken into the gift-shop. Fancy! We were taken by all the lovely cartographic items and ended up buying six metal subway signs to sit above the doors of our house. Which, yes, sounds shit, but trust me when I say it looks good. It adds that New York sophistication to stumbling to the shitter to drop the kids off at night, trust me.

Next on the list of things to do was lunch, and, I'm ashamed to say this, we ate in a TGI Fridays. All those wonderful places and we ended up somewhere where a chav takes a hot-date in the hope of getting his fingers dipped. In our defence, it was the one in Times Square and we only went there because at this point, our feet were more blood than shoe, but it was grim. Because they don't have to try, they absolutely didn't. The food was bland, the drinks were sickly sweet and the waiter so full of false bonhomie that I could have asked for a blowjob instead of a dessert menu and he'd have sunk to his knees just to see me smile. His name tag was 'Will!', which I imagine took immense willpower (pun intended) not to put eight exclamations after.

We did leave a substantial tip though – the place was

awash with British families taking a break between smacking their children and complaining to eat something similar to the Iceland muck they have at home. Past experience tells me that they won't leave a tip because 'it's not right, we don't have to do it, blah blah' and frankly, that's just shitty. Our lunch might have been shite but see, that wasn't the fault of Smilin' Will.

After lunch we waddled over to the Rockefeller Centre. You'll know this place, too – it's where they put the massive Christmas tree and ice-rink every year. We had paid for a day and night pass, which allows you to see the views during the day and then return later to see the same view but in inky blackness.

It was wonderful – there's only so many times I can write about going up a tall building and making it faintly interesting for you, dear reader, so just let me say that being able to sit on a bench 70 floors in the air in the winter, looking out over New York, was just lovely. We had a romantic moment (which makes it sound like I noshed Paul off, but no, we just had a cuddle) and stayed up there a while.

As we left we were shepherded through a room of interactive lights – if you stood on the floor, certain ceiling lights would come on and your movement would be tracked. I suppose this is modern art. Paul exclaimed that it was 'just like I'm in a video game' and my reply of 'Yes: FATRIS' was a little louder than I had anticipated, leading to lots of shared guffaws amongst everyone. I do worry that I come across as such an arse to poor, put-upon Paul, but listen, he gives as good as he gets, don't you worry.

Having satisfied ourselves of the view and done about as much marvelling as one can do before your face caves in through smiling, we made our way back through the building and back out onto the streets. After a little idle wandering we spotted a nearby church, and, never missing the opportunity to sit down and let my chafing thighs cool, we went in. If memory serves me right, it was St Mary the Virgin's church and it was utterly beautiful.

Unusually, we didn't burst into flames the second we stepped over the threshold and nor were we cast out for being sodomites. Religion, am I right? The church was gorgeous – beautiful stained glass windows, comfortable pews, perfectly ornate detailing, just lovely. It was heart-warming to know that the donations and money raised was going straight into keeping this prime piece of real-estate looking pretty so that all the homeless folk outside could at least have somewhere charming to rest their heads between starving and freezing to death. Hmm.

We sat in the pews for more time than is entirely decent, trying to discreetly rub our throbbing feet and not shallow-breathe on the necks of the people in front, who were bowed in prayer. I'm not a religious person but even I said a quick prayer for one of those feet-spas that all mums had in the Nineties that bubbled a bit of Radoxy-water around their hairy toes.

The serenity of the moment was shattered somewhat by the sound of a clearly mentally-ill woman bursting through the doors, running down the aisle screaming and then falling on the floor. She was treated with all the compassion and understanding you might expect from the Church – pinned to the floor by the security guard's knee, shouted at by some hurly-burly prick clutching a bible and then unceremoniously picked up and thrown back out into the street like a piece of rubbish. It was all very inelegant, though it did cause enough of a distraction for me to break wind, which, with my cheeks firmly pressed against the wood of the pew, sounded like a little helicopter landing. Sweet relief! Air befouled, we moved on.

Unfortunately, my notes for the day end here, which leads me to think we just went and got progressively more drunk during the rest of the day and then stumbled back to the hotel at some indecent hour. I have a faint recollection of being in a late-night pharmacy buying Doritos and spinach dip. Hey, we know how to party! We definitely ticked off the 'buy a slice of New York pizza' activity though, and I know this because there's a photo on my phone of Paul fast asleep with a chunk of crust sticking out of his gob. We're a classy pair, you know.

twochubbycubs go to New York: part six

At SOME point during this holiday we visited the Empire State Building – but can I balls remember what day it was. As a result, I'm just going to squeeze it in right here, on the last day we were there.

We woke with a start at around 6am – it's true, you know, New York is truly the city that never sleeps. We know this because there was a mad person shouting obscenities down on the streets below. Nothing rouses me from slumber quicker than someone with spittle on his lips shouting about the coming apocalypse and the risen Jesus. It was the last day so we showered glumly, packed our things sadly and exchanged blowjobs with a downturned mouth. It's difficult to be enthusiastic on the last day. We left our luggage with the charming staff in the lobby and made our way out.

Well, it was certainly bright. Turned out that the city had received a fair dumping of snow overnight and the streets were white and pretty. I fretted momentarily that we would be trapped in New York (oh no, imagine my devastation) but found that this thought was giving me far too much joy for so early in the morning. We could see the Empire State Building way off in the distance so decided to head there, walking the three miles or so slowly to prevent any accidental slips or falls. We were in the most litigious country in the world, after all. We stopped for a quick breakfast in a tiny corner deli – I had a sandwich the size of a church draught excluder, Paul had a slice of cheesecake. Of course!

The Empire State Building was astonishing, though. The lady dishing out the tickets warned us that we would be unable to see anything much due to the heavy cloud but we waved her worries aside – we at least had to tick it off the list. I'm so glad we did. It's an absolutely gorgeous building, both inside and out, done out as it is in the fabulous art-deco style of the time. We had the tourist part of the building to ourselves, most likely due to the early morning and the winter weather, and we were able to wander about and take our time.

Proof that we enjoyed the tour was the fact we took on board two facts about the Empire State Building: two separate people have attempted to commit suicide by jumping from the observation deck only to be blown back into the building on the way down. I'd certainly feel like I was born again in that situation: imagine expecting to be a thin red jam on the pavement only to find yourself safe and sound with only ruffled hair to account for your troubles. Along similar lines, the world record for the longest **survived** elevator fall took place here, when rescuers saving poor Betty Lou Oliver from a plane hitting the building managed to miss the fact that the elevator carriage she was riding in had weakened considerably. Just as they reached for her the cables holding the lift snapped and she, and the lift, fell 79 stories. She survived with serious injuries but fuck me ragged, I had my heart in my mouth on the Tower of

Terror ride at Disneyworld, I can't imagine doing that for 79 floors! Blimey.

The kiosk lady was right, by the way – we couldn't see very much. But the feeling of standing on the 102nd floor in the middle of a snowstorm was incredible. I felt like I was in a chewing gum advert. However, a minute standing outside had sent my bollocks retreating somewhere behind my lungs so we sharp made our way back in and into the gift shop, where we bought all manner of tat and nonsense.

Knowing our flight wasn't until the evening we decided to spend the rest of the day just walking about to see where we ended up. Oddly enough, after much random mincing and stopping for coffee, we found ourselves down on Pier 86 at the Intrepid Sea, Air & Space Museum, a museum devoted to well, air, sea and space. We had time to kill and ankles like jelly, so why not? They have a decommissioned aircraft carrier to nose about, and well, I haven't had a chance to visit an old wreck full of seamen since the last time I visited Paul's mother. Ouch.

As seems to be the way with attractions in New York, there was a bewildering array of entrance tickets to be had – some with simulations included, some with access to the space shuttle, some with a frisky handjob by a passing sailor. We chose the standard admission and were immediately told to decide which simulator we fancied. We elected to have a trip on the exciting G-

Force Encounter, half-thinking it might be one of those centrifuge things where they spin you around and you're left with the arresting sight of double chin snaking its merry way up over your face.

Well, it certainly wasn't that. We were 'boarded' by an indifferent Kenan and Kel and told to strap ourselves in. Sounds exciting! Well, let me tell you this: I've felt more G-Force getting out of my computer chair when the takeaway man knocks on the door. The perils of war-time flight were bought to life via the medium of Windows 95's very best graphics. The simulator creaked this way and that and there was an awful lot of hissing – we probably broke a hydraulics pipe somewhere – but that was it. Thrill ride? I had more excitement reading the opening hours.

That was the only downside, though. The rest of the exhibition was great. We spent a good hour or so wandering around the aircraft carrier, getting a taste of what it must be like spending all that time locked away with nothing but other men to keep you company. We both signed up for the US Navy as we left.

Not just content with letting us explore the poop deck, the museum also had all manner of aeroplanes and helicopters to look at. I have to confess: this struggled to hold my attention. I mean, they looked great and all, but a plane sitting on the ground is still a plane sitting on the ground, you know? We did spot that they had a Concorde parked down by the water so we bustled over to it. I've been in Concorde before, though not for a flight (sadly) and the bloody thing is tiny. You're fair jammed in with the rich and famous and I imagine it's like crossing the ocean in a cigar tube. Of course, you get no sense of this lack of space as you're not allowed to board the Concorde at the Intrepid, which is a pretty poor show.

I do wish they'd bring back Concorde, however. Imagine flying from London to New York in three and a half hours, as opposed to double that with BA's current fleet. I'd barely have enough time for the blood around my swollen ankles to clot before we landed. Paul's dad has been on Concorde, and, having met Paul's mother, I can absolutely understand the need for supersonic flight. That's two jibes in one article, I am awful.

Next on the list was a trip into a submarine – one which was hilariously named 'Growler'. This meant that Paul had to endure about twenty minutes of me saying 'I've never seen a Growler this big' and 'do you reckon I'll be able to fit in the Growler, it looks tight' and 'I hope the Growler doesn't smell of fish and damp from being underwater'. I only stopped when blood started trickling from his ears. We joined an orderly queue of prim, exceptionally thin people who were all shepherded aboard before us. This meant that we were now at the front of the queue with people behind us which immediately gave me the heebie-jeebies.

Why? Because what if we didn't fit through the

absolutely tiny doors onboard? There were warning signs everywhere. All I could imagine is my arse acting like a giant plug and everyone behind being slowly starved of oxygen. As it happens it was an incredibly tight fit but I managed fine – it was actually Paul, with his tiny coffee-table legs, that struggled, given you had to lift your legs really quite high to climb through. At one point I nearly cried 'abandon ship' and made for the exit but it all came good in the end. I bet though – in fact, I absolutely guarantee – that our denim-clad arses are on at least eight Japanese iCloud accounts as we speak.

We wrapped up our visit with a trip around their space centre, which held the space shuttle Enterprise and lots of bright and interesting information boards. I've been to NASA in Orlando so seeing the shuttle wasn't so amazing, but I'll say this: when you see it up close you realise exactly how much fun it must be being in space. Honestly, I'd never get tired of shooting various liquids around in zero gravity – after twenty-four hours the live feed to the inside of my space-shuttle would look like a badly tuned TV channel.

I tried to buy a helmet from the gift shop but yet again, my elephantine head defeated me. We have a photo of me wearing their biggest hat and it only just gets over my ears. I'd love a hat, I truly word. Ah well.

Seeing that we'd need to get a move on and head back to the hotel, we wandered up the streets, retracing our steps from the morning. We were side-tracked for another hour or so by a stop at a beer bar (The House of Brews, firmly recommended) where we managed to put away several pints of various beers together with a plate of nachos that was positively indecent. I love American nachos – they do it properly, with loads of chilli, cheese, sauces and spice. What do we get? A microwaved packet of Doritos with a Cheesestring melted over the top. Bah. We spotted a dartboard and, perhaps fuelled by that rare beast testosterone, had ourselves a little tournament. Naturally, I won, but then I've always been accomplished at finishing myself off with a double-top.

We made it back to our hotel, had a very strong coffee to stop our eyes swimming, and picked up our luggage. With a heavy, cheese-stuffed heart, we were bidding goodbye to New York.

twochubbycubs go to New York: part seven

We decided that it was imperative we be at the airport in good time lest we be late and miss our flight — I mean, can you imagine being stranded in New York? I'd feel like little Kevin McAllister, only without the shenanigans and inappropriate touching. As such, rather than clart about with the trains, we hailed a taxi Our taxi driver was colourful with his language, going to great lengths to tell us what's wrong with most Brits (we don't tip, we're too hoity-toity, Paul's too fat, that sort of thing) and speeding through the streets like he'd stole the car. When it came to paying the fare I made a gag about asking Paul if he had twenty cents so we could give the exact fare and I swear to God, I thought the driver was going to shoot my face through the back of my head. I don't like to exaggerate but I've never seen such ire in a man's eyes — and I've gone in dry on more than one occasion. Just saying.

Naturally, with Speedy McMoodytits at the wheel, we arrived at the airport thirty minutes before check-in even opened, meaning we had to sit around forlornly by the front doors with our suitcases. It's about the only time I miss smoking, at airports — it gives you something to do between getting fingered by some terse security attendant and spending the rest of your 'foreign money' on expensive tat for work colleagues. Do you know, I don't think I've successfully managed to pass through an airport without buying a giant Toblerone since I was eighteen and got my first job? There's always sarky remarks about originality but hey, at least it wasn't a giant bag of wax fruit sweets that every other fucker brings back from their holiday.

I remember the first time Paul and I flew long-haul together (to Orlando, the tales of which you can find in our honeymoon book, which I've told is attractively priced on Amazon and available at the touch of a button on the very device you're reading this on now). We were committed smokers at that point and the thought of nine hours in the air filled us with terror and dread. We spent almost an hour mainlining fags outside of Manchester Airport then, once we had landed, it was literally the only thing we could think of. Fuck Mickey Mouse I cried, we've got emphysema to nurture. Naturally, Paul had lost the lighter and we spent a tense fifteen minutes trying to buy matches before some kind soul wheezed to our aid. It's embarrassing, looking back.

Anyway, without smoking to pass the minutes, we occupied ourselves by streamlining our hand luggage and eating the bags of sweets I'd bought for my parents. It's what they would have wanted. Finally time moved forward just enough for us to be granted permission to check in. The guy behind the counter was another grumpy sort who spent more time than I thought was decent fannying about with my passport. I resisted the urge to touch his hands and say 'I know, such beauty can't truly exist' but again, I value my ability to breathe unaided.

What followed was the longest three hours of my life. Is there a more surprisingly awful, boring airport than JFK? I assumed that, being an exit hub, it would be full of vibrant shops and classy eateries for the carefree tourist to spend their money in. Nope. We had a Starbucks and watched the planes for a bit. Then we had a McDonalds and watched the planes for a bit. I enjoyed twenty-five minutes of furiously looking at my iPad whilst it failed to connect to the public Wi-Fi. We both went for a shite just to pass the time but found ourselves unable to commit the dirty deed because yet again the toilets only had a metal postage stamp for a door. I hate making eye-contact with anyone, let alone when I'm trying to birth an otter. Bah!

After looking around the duty free shop for the fourth time (why? Perhaps we thought there was an undiscovered wing to explore just behind the Smirnoff stand? Or that they rotated the stock on an hourly basis?) we succumbed and bought some aftershave: Paul some cloying Issey Miyake stuff, me some classy Tom Ford. I've come a long way since spraying my Mum's bottle of Mum under my boobs before PE, I can tell you.

Finally, it was time to board. As usual, four hundred people leapt up at once as though fearful the plane might accidentally nip away before they'd had a chance to fuss about with the safety cards and put their duty free in the overhead bins. We hung back – we're too fat to move safely in crowds – one of us trips and we're taking people out on the way down. When we eventually made it to the final beep-beep check of the tickets and passport, a very stern lady with ice-blonde hair and a face that had never known joy told us to stand to one side.

They then took our passports and tickets away from us whilst people walked past tutting at us as though we were terrorists. I mean, fair enough I hadn't shaved, but I wasn't a complete disaster. For almost five minutes we waited whilst they let other people past. My arsehole was nipping so much I was surprised the two kilos of coke stuck up there didn't fall out. Paul remained calm – as usual – I could hurl a burning pan of hot oil into his ear and he'd still yawn and look impassive, though he might feel a bit sad that he wasn't getting chips.

Finally, we were given new tickets and told we had been moved from our original seats. We're not fussy so didn't say much and rejoined the queue. It was only on boarding that we were told we'd been upgraded. Hooray! Premium Economy is the lowest class we'll fly because we're fat and snotty (just kidding: it really is just because we're fat) so anything higher was always going to be great. A genuinely lovely end to a fantastic holiday.

Quick thoughts? It was great being able to lie down properly on an overnight flight, although I didn't like not being right next to Paul – I find it hard to sleep unless some of his fat isn't rolling over me and the sound of him choking on his own neck is lullabying me to the land of nod. Having my own 'pod' was a novelty though – I spent a good forty minutes pressing every switch, turning on every light, opening every little drawer (a drawer to put my shoes in: how clever!) and carefully secreting every freebie into my bag. It was only when the Captain announced that someone was draining the power from the engines that I stopped whirring my chair and charging my iPod.

The stewardesses came around shortly after take-off and asked everyone if they would like anything to eat. Paul, much to my horror, said he was full and only wanted a vodka. I was foaming. Everyone knows you need to make the most of this type of situation, even if it makes you look like a grasping harlot. I ordered a gin and tonic and a full meal (despite having already had a three course meal in the airport – ah well, I had plenty of time to sleep it off).

Here's the thing – this is why I can't have nice things. I was served a wonderful array of dishes but to me, they were nothing special and the portion sizes were tiny. I appreciate this is just me being a big fat pig but it seems the more you pay for food, the less you get. Don't get me wrong, I put it all away in record time and did a celebratory burp into my pillow for good measure, but I don't like being served a big white plate with a shaving of radish on it and a flea-bite of cheese. I could have breathed my dinner into my lungs. I did make Paul watch me eat a delicious chocolate melting pudding, though – I stared right in his eyes and smacked my lips. That'll teach him.

The night flight passed smoothly, soothed as I was by the sounds of my fellow fliers sleeping soundly and farting long into the night. Paul woke up at one point thinking the landing gear was coming down until I explained it was merely the mechanics of my chair adjusting under my bulk.

I was disappointed by the toilets – I wasn't expecting someone to come in and wipe my taint but really, it's not very upper class to be standing in someone else's piss whilst you slap on the Elemis eye-cream. I know that on Emirates' A380 you can actually have a hot shower whilst you fly. I can't conceive of something I'd rather do less at 38,000ft – I know that as soon as I undressed and climbed into the shower we'd hit extreme turbulence and I'd end up shooting out of the bathroom with suds in my hair and my cock a-flapping whilst everyone screamed around me. It's what happens when I get changed at the gym, why should it be any different in the sky?

We landed in good time and, unusually, were through security in no time at all. We did the usual things –

updated Facebook to show off our fancy flying, texted my mother to tell her that I hadn't made an unscheduled stop into the sea and that she could cancel the hearse, then made our way through grey London for our Virgin train back home. As you'd expect with a train journey, it was entirely uneventful, and we were home in no time for a good sleep.

That's that! New York – done. It's somewhere we've always wanted to go and it was made all the sweeter by Paul not knowing about it in advance. Normally I can't keep a secret for toffee but somehow I managed to pull off a full holiday without giving the game away. The people, for the most part, were friendly, and everything we visited was absolutely worth it. I can see why people go back – we've only scratched the surface of what the city has to offer.

We'd move there in a heartbeat save for the fact that a decent flat in a nice area is over a million quid and well, we don't have that sort of money hidden down the sofa (feel free to buy more copies of this book though, it might pay for a lamp or something). I think my favourite day, of all of them, was walking around Central Park – nothing much happened but it was so beautiful and *so* New York.

We travelled with Virgin Trains (reasonable), British Airways (excellent) and stayed at the Wyndham New Yorker (lovely, but ask for a newer room – our room was a bit old-fashioned and stuffy. We liked it, but you might not).

Onto the next holiday…

twochubbycubs on: paul realises he's fat

James is running late, he rang me from inside the multi-storey car park shouting and bawling about the barrier being broken – I could barely hear him over the sound of his car, his rage and my Now That's What I Call Soviet National Anthems CD. I made out the words '...'king sick of this cun...' and 'as much fucking use as a sandpaper tampon' then he cut out. He'll be home soon, but I thought I'd do a blog entry for once. Poor guy. Poor you lot.

This week I managed to find a major motivator to lose weight in somewhere that I least suspected – clothes. That's right. Despite being two of the most uninterested people in fashion as well as being the most unfashionable people out there, it was trying to find a nice suit for a job interview that really hit home how much we need to lose weight.

I have more trouble than James on this front – despite him being a good few stone heavier than me he's also got another half a foot, so his chub is much more easily spread out – he's like a wardrobe – whereas I'm more like a chest of drawers. Or imagine sputnik balanced on a chubby pair of thighs. It's a bloody nightmare to find anything that fits properly, if at all. It's like trying to dress a car accident.

As we've previously touched upon, we've finally found somewhere that caters to our needs that doesn't result in 100% polyester or finding them between rows of Pringles – except for a Jacamo run on payday we often find ourselves strutting around a local garden centre and a franchise of Cotton Traders. I know, I know, we're not on deaths door or enfeebled but the stuff fits. Well, it fits James – I have to make do with a chequered bit of cotton that sits over my belly but results in the breast pocket being underneath my tit, and the bottom of the shirt floating around near my knees, which if I don't tuck in ends up billowing about like a curtain in a Celine Dion video.

So it all came to a head when I needed a nice suit for a job interview – there's a few suits in our wardrobe but they're all suspiciously high in acrylic (it came to a point a few weeks ago that we had to chuck a few out because every time we swished open the floor to ceiling wardrobe door, there'd be a smell of plastic burning and an alarming amount of smoke). Plus, naturally, they are all far too small (keep hold of them...we'll fit into them eventually, we say...).

Seeing as though I actually *wanted* this job we decided to splurge out on a reasonably priced one. So, being fat fucks and the garden centre of no use we went online to Jacamo and ordered a few, in different sizes so I could try one or the other and make a choice but all to no avail. I just cannot look good in a suit. At all. It feels like the shoulder pads are jutting out like I'm the sexiest milkmaid ever and I have to swing my arms around like a wind turbine to stop the sleeves from flapping about. It's an absolute mare.

And, naturally, because it was something nice, the cats immediately took a dislike and left me looking like Grizabella with just a quick vag-flash and an ankle rub. So that was no good. I did manage, however, to hang on to the waistcoat which didn't do too much of a bad job. It did make me look as though I was presenting Big Break alongside Professional Shitrat Jim Davison, but hey, you can't have it all.

Perhaps I do need to lose weight then. I would love to be able to get something without schlepping out to a place where I can also get barbecue tongs and a lavender plant. As convenient as it is.

twochubbycubs on: the elderly

You know what really boils my piss? Being told my opinion is invalid because I'm 'young'. For a start, let's be frank, given my diet, years of smoking and tendency to mainline gin after a hard day at work, I'm probably comfortably into the dotage of my life. I'm about two doddery steps away from putting a tartan blanket over my legs and calling it a day. I mean, I've already mentioned that I enjoy The Archers, but did you know I've also developed a tic of making proper old man noises when I get up from a chair? The noise isn't just air escaping from my blubber, either, it's a proper 'oooooof'. There's no hope. So I'm certainly not 'young'.

The reason I mention all of this is due to yet another facebook argument I've been having with the elders of the town where I live. I joined a facebook group full of people discussing the current events around our town and it is absolutely awash with bloody moaners. I live in a great place but seemingly every Tom, Dickhead and Harry who would previously moan to their wives behind the net curtains has joined to put in their thoughts. It's full of people looking at their shoes and feeling sorry for themselves because 'our town doesn't get this' and 'that town gets that and we get nothing'. If there was an emoji of someone twisting a cloth cap between their hands with watery, sad eyes, it's all you'd see on this group. I can't stand it. Despite my constant moaning on here, I'm a pretty chipper person and certainly a firm believer in making do with what you've got.

So, naturally, I end up bickering. I point out that we're unlikely to get a leisure centre of our own given there's one within four miles of us in each compass direction, but that's not good enough. I explain that we don't have a swimming pool because there's bloody five within a ten-minute drive – that's me being unreasonable. I mentioned that another town near us pays a tonne more council tax, has more residents and thus, has a tennis court, and you'd think I'd shat on their Wiltshire Farm Foods blended lasagne. I'll have a discussion back and forth with anyone and I'm always unfailingly polite, even if I did get a stern lecture of swearing from one of the crinklies when I used the word bloody. But they always play the trump card: 'you're young, you don't understand'.

Paul tells me that my retaliation of: 'you're old, you'll be dead soon enough and you can't get a coffin down a water-slide' is churlish at best. I agree, so I merely think it to myself. But see it really does vex me that my opinion is apparently worth less because I'm 'young'. I may be young, but I own my own house, I've worked since I was 16, I'm sensible and eloquent and I try my best not to fart in committee meetings. My opinion is as valid as someone who can't type for their bottom lip hitting the keyboard.

Manners between the old and the young seem to be a

very one-way street. We hear a lot about how rude kids are and how badly treated old folk are (and I hasten to add – anyone who is rude to an old person is an arsehole, absolutely) but never the other way around. I've had plenty of experiences with old folk pushing into queues with that resolute cats-arse-lips-face that says don't fuck with me, I've got razor sharp shards of glacier mints in my winceyette cardigan.

I've been sworn at by old ladies during bingo. When I worked at BT in the complaints department, it was the elderly who had the most entitled, brusque manners. I was told by someone to stick my '1471 up my arse' when I had the temerity to tell her it cost money to press 5 and call back. Charming! I hold doors open only to be met with glazed eyes, a stern look and zero thanks. Hell, I've stopped my car in the street to let some whiskery-chinned charmer cross the road with her Zimmer without the threat of being turned into lavender jam, only for her to shuffle over the road like an Edinburgh Woollen Mill sponsored snail without so much as a shaky nod of thanks in my direction. Bah.

Perhaps I was spoiled, I don't know. My own dear nana was a proper nana – she baked scones and played her television so loud that you could solve the Countdown Conundrum on the drive over to see her. She used to take such a large intake of breath when I mouthed the word 'vacuum' at Paul that I'm surprised she didn't get the bends. We used to go over for an hour or so to hear who had died in the village (which she always spoke of with barely hidden relish, the auld ghoul), how she was getting on never taking her tablets (100% record) and to fix all the incorrect answers in her Puzzler.

I do find myself thinking of her a lot in summer, weirdly. It's been over a year since she died (that entry makes me feel sad, so I don't read it) and Paul and I are always laughing about things she'd come out with. The reason I think of her in summer is because, despite the glorious sunshine and thirty-degree heat, you'd walk into her living room and she'd have her coal fire blazing away, with the rug in front of it always just on the cusp of catching alight. She'd complain she was cold despite us being able to hear the bacon frying in the fridge. Funny what you remember. She'd never shoot your opinion down and always listened. I say listened, she couldn't hear a bloody thing, so the polite nodding and murmurs of assent were probably just a touch of Parkinsons.

Eee, I'd give anything to have her back.

Anyway, come on, I wasn't meaning to end on a miserable note. She was always laughing and she'd have loved this blog, despite not being able to understand what the hell I was going on about when I explained the Internet. She thought it consisted purely of people making telephone calls to each other and stealing money. Which I mean it does, but there's also a lot of pornography too. Tsk.

twochubbycubs on: a trip to the seaside

Let's begin with Naked Attraction on Channel 4. Ostensibly a dating show, it's a crude little performance masquerading as a serious look at attraction. To put it succinctly, it's an excuse for everyone to gawk at a few cocks for 60 minutes. Listen, it's not like I'm averse to that, I love my daily intake of Vitamin D, but haway, on the telly? The only time I want to see an engorged prick when I turn the TV on is when Owen Smith hands in his resignation. Boom: biting political satire. The problem with this show is that there's really no such thing as an attractive cock when it's on the flop. If the guy isn't packing heat, it ends up looking like one of those lugworm piles you see on the beach when the tide goes out. Like a walnut whip left in a slightly warm room. Similarly, if he's a shower, it just looks like someone's stuck a googly-eye on a length of intestine. A penis is a wonderful thing, regardless of whether it's compact, coupe or stretch, and yes, it's the motion not the meat, but please, erect only.

Damn, I actually *should* do a full article on the above. So many thoughts.

We had a trip out in the car yesterday to Seahouses, North Northumberland's premier tat-shop hotspot. It was literally a trip in the car, because, after driving for what felt like eight hours behind some lovely old dear in a Fiat Euthanised doing about 6mph and throwing the brakes on every time the air over her chin-whiskers got a bit much. I reckon it would have been quicker for me to park up, jump into the North Sea and swim up the coast – I'd have done that but I didn't want a human turd in my 99. By the time we had arrived in fair Seahouses, the car was actually running on the steam from my ears. When will people learn that it is just as dangerous to drive too bloody slow than it is to drive too fast? If I was PM, I'd make it legal to give these tiny, slow cars a gentle nudge into a layby or say, a combine harvester. I can't imagine she was enjoying listening to Paul and I bewailing our way through We Don't Need Another Hero that much.

Seahouses was a bust. When I was young it was the go-to place for my parents to take me and my sister – it had the dual advantage that they could furnish us with a few quid and we'd look after ourselves in the arcades for a couple of hours whilst they sat outside and smoked. Sometimes they smoked inside for a change of scenery. It's a perfect example of a town that should be so much more. For a start, it's in an absolutely beautiful part of the country – fantastic beaches, amazing castles (Dunstanburgh, Bamburgh, Chillingham – all very different experiences and all marvellous), great food and the majesty of the North Sea.

I remember great places to eat, chips on the pier, rock-pooling, playing that shitty bingo above the arcades where you slid a plastic door over the numbers as they were called and won a packet of J-Cloths for a full house. Now there's a Co-op, a litany of awful trying-to-be-upmarket gift shops, an expensive fish-and-chips place and a sense of general ennui. I took the jackpot out of a Deal or no Deal fruitie on the seafront and I genuinely thought I was going to get stabbed on the way out. I'd have had less eyes on me if I'd stripped naked and given Paul a rim-job over the Grace Darling commemorative buoy.

There used to be a brilliant arcade full of sit-on-rides and proper funfair type games – that's gone – replaced by soulless, identikit apartment blocks that no doubt don't have enough room to nudge-nudge-nudge your lemon in. Yeah, some rich la-de-dah has a sea-view and somewhere to put those awful inspirational-shite-on-a-piece-of-driftwood wall-art that you can see fading in every gift-shop within flying distance from a seaside town, but where's my chance to win an asbestos-stuffed Sanic the Hodgeheg from a fixed claw machine? Eh?

I should have learned my lesson from the last time we visited – this time with Paul's severely autistic brother. He disliked the place so much he got himself worked up into a sulk and wouldn't get out of the car for love nor money. He had the right idea. We should follow his sage advice – my favourite story ever involves him asking his mother to buy that tea-tree and mint Original Source shampoo because 'it makes my head feel like it's sucking on a giant mint Polo'. I love that, he's brilliant.

I'm perhaps doing the place a disservice for the sake of a tongue-in-cheek blog entry. It's still worth a visit. Remember, I have rose-tinted (well, more nicotine-stained) glasses from childhood visits with school and family. As a returning adult, I see all that has disappeared and wince at what has replaced it. Perhaps it was the fact we arrived at 3pm on a Saturday (to be fair, we'd set off at 5pm on Tuesday but thanks to that auld cow in the Fiat...) but it was all very meh.

One glimmer of hope, though: ONE of the tat-shops remains. I think it's called Farne Gift Shop but don't rely on that, I saw the name through a red-mist of pure rage as I drove in. It hasn't changed a jot – it was a relief to find that the giant pencil with 'SEAHOUSES AND BAMBRUGH' smeared down the side in lead paint was still tucked away on the shelf where I regrettably left it when I was 8. It's literally a shop full of tat: tea-towels with a 'HERE'S TO A HAPPY FUTURE' message for Charles and Diana, jigsaw boxes devoid of all colour from being left in the sun for eighty-seven years, sticks of rock to prise your fillings up and tonnes of other nonsense. I loved it.

We had a moment of hilarity when Paul discovered something which he'd been referencing for years: a donkey which shits out cigarettes. Apparently his mother had one, along with a toilet ashtray which dispensed a little bit of sand to snuff out your fag – and

I'd never believed such a thing existed. Well, here we had one – I wanted to buy one to really class up our living room but Paul pointed out that a) neither of us smoke and b) our furnishings aren't being paid for in weekly instalments. Spoil-sport.

What I love about that listing is that it's filed under 'Cigar Accessories', as though it's a classy humidor or a tasteful engraved ashtray like the one that did Saskia in. I can't imagine ever having a conversation where I'm offering someone a Colorado Maduro and when they gratefully accept, waving their hand away and saying 'but wait, watch it emerge from a donkey's arse!'. Actually, that's a filthy lie. I totally can.

No, do give Seahouses a go. If you've never been, have a weekend away on our coast. It's amazing. I'm planning a proper paean in the future to the wonderful world where I live, so keep an eye out for that, but in short, come see the castles, have a trip out on the boats to Holy Island, enjoy our beautiful beaches and have some cinder toffee. Just understand that if you get in front of me on the roads and your car has dust on all the numbers above 25 on the speedometer, you'll get three minutes of me smiling at you politely before I drive into your boot and throttle you with my bare hands. I'll do it, prison holds no fear for me.

twochubbycubs on: oh, mother

I went over to visit The Progenitors this evening to make

sure that a) they're still kicking about and b) to casually remind them that there really is no better time to make a will than right now, and yes, don't worry I'll share. They're in rude health as ever, and although I got roundly admonished for proclaiming that 'the iPad can't sense through leather' when my mum told me her iPad wasn't recognising her fingerprint, all was well. However, my mother has two messages for the blog which I feel I must pass on, at the very least to ensure that the flow of newly-laid eggs keeps coming my way.

First: she's taken umbrage with the fact that I like to portray my childhood as some kind of Catherine Cookson-esque, poverty-stricken wasteland of bland meals and stolen potatoes. Well, obviously that wasn't the case. We didn't have much money but my sister and I never went without – we always had good food in our bellies, clothes on our backs and all the second-hand Lambert and Butler smoke a child could want. I reckon I was on ten fags a day by proxy by the age of ten. I've certainly inherited my lack of worry from them – they're both very down-to-earth, decent people – just because my mother can drink like a sailor and my dad uses flatulence like one might use a full-stop doesn't change that.

No, look, I do jest, and I do like to make gags about growing up, but I couldn't have wished for better parents and when I listen to them now, bickering on at each other and twisting their faces, there's still so much love there, it's marvellous. They've been married for absolutely bloody ages and it's quite inspiring to think you can make small-talk with the same person over dinner for thirty years and not want to stab them in the eye. It's all I can do not to set myself on fire if I pass the same person on the stairs twice in one day. I think the anniversary gift for 30 years is pearl, and I'm definitely not going to mention that to my parents because, Christ, if you think I'm bad for smut and innuendo, you haven't seen anything yet...

The second public service announcement from Mother Cub is a new gadget. See, since buying hens she has been awash with more eggs than she knows what to do with. My poor dad has had fried eggs, cubed eggs, boiled eggs, poached eggs, eggs eleven, eggy-eggs, eggy-bread and god knows what else. Anyway, my mum has found this on Amazon and it filled her with so much excitement it was the third thing she said to me after I stepped through her door (after DON'T GO STRAIGHT TO THE FRIDGE and CAN YOU JUST HAVE A LOOK AT SOMETHING ON THE COMPUTER FOR ME).

It's a three-way egg-slicer. For when cutting with a knife won't do, but then, nor will boring old slices. This one makes perfectly chunked egg mayo, wonderfully measured egg slices and, for that decadent touch, egg quarters. Whilst admittedly it's quite literally the only time I ever want to hear about my mother having a three-way in the kitchen, it's a gadget too much for me. I'll say this though – the egg mayo sandwich that she made me was terrific. I've never had such uniform egg-based texture.

This makes enough for two big fatties to shovel in as dinner. So, just enough for me and Paul. So let's say three syns per serving, but remember, it's a giant bloody serving. I do like how the Amazon picture above already has the nicotine mottled-effect that most things in my parent's house have. I'm joking again, just to be clear. Anyway, it's on Amazon for only a few quid, so if you're looking for a slicer that will blow your mind, go for it!

Anyway, that's quite enough from Eva Braun, this is my blog, damn it.

Before we get to the sausage, fennel and pesto pasta, I have a quick question. I listen to The Archers. Love it. Don't care that it's a fuddy-duddy programme, I like how relaxing it all is. I've probably been listening for a year now – I tuned in when Rob Bastard started terrorising poor Helen and she stabbed him over the burst custard. But three questions:

- am I ever going to get to the point where I recognise who is talking and who is related to who – I'm currently treating it like a white noise machine but I reckon I'd get more out of it if I actually understood the characters. But see, I go onto the Radio 4 website, read up on them, and then instantly forget everything I read, like my brain is trying to save me from premature old age;

- is that young Johnny fella ever going to boff that other one (Josh?) – I feel like they've been building to A Beautiful Thing, but maybe that's just me; and

- am I wrong for getting teary-eyed over poor Scruff? SOB.

Now, you might be scoffing and tittering into your hand about my love of The Archers at the age of 31, but you know what, I don't care. Not after poor Scruff's death! LIFE'S TOO SHORT.

twochubbycubs on: the gullible and the greedy

How do people keep falling for Facebook scams? It's beyond me. I get it, people are keen for a bargain and would snatch the skin off your face if it meant getting 25% discount at Aldi, but please, exercise just a modicum of common sense. Tesco aren't giving away 500 gift-cards with £500 quid on them because they've turned 50. You can tell that because a) Tesco wouldn't give away a quarter of a million quid via stay-at-home-mums on facebook 'buy 'n' sell' pages (the 'n' stands for not having THAT in my house because it's *fucking gopping)* and b) Tesco wouldn't give you the steam off its piss.

I only mention it because Alton Towers have had to issue a statement explicitly stating that they're not running a promotion for five free tickets for each person who shares some crappy low-res and clearly photoshopped picture of a ticket. I just find it perplexing that people get suckered in by crap like that. Surely at some point during the 'complete X surveys' and 'submit your Paypal account details here' an alarm bell must ring, and presumably that bell is going to be bloody loud because it's got no brain to muffle the sound? Pfft. If I was in charge of Alton Towers, I'd honour the crummy tickets and put all the people most vocal about it straight on The Smiler – and I'd put the work experience kid in front of the controls. I mean

HONESTLY.

This wouldn't have caused me so much ire if Alton Tower's official status on Facebook wasn't awash with people who immediately started twisting their gobs about how Alton Towers had a duty to provide free tickets as compensation. Com-pen-bloody-sation! Listen, you should get compensation if you have your legs blown off by faulty wiring or your eyes smacked from your skull from a falling crane, you don't deserve compensation just because you got your juicebox in a froth thinking you'd get a free ticket because of some barely literate sharing on Facebook.

Anyway, the last time I went to Alton Towers I had a very reasonable time. Make of that what you will. I enjoyed waiting in the queues for a one-minute ride, I loved looking at the delicate displays of litter and wasps and found the experience of applying for a loan just to buy a small fries and hotdog to be remarkably thrilling. I love theme parks but I've been utterly spoiled by spending a month in Florida, with the added bonus of not being the fattest person in the park.

My mind boggles.

Speaking of mind boggling, you need to give Stranger Things a go. It was recommended by a friend, who, to her credit, is normally fairly spot-on with her recommendations and tea-making. It's sublime. Wonderfully shot, gorgeously scored, tightly plotted and just something so unusual on TV these days – a real rare treat. It's on Netflix and I can't, in turn, recommend it highly enough. Who knew Winona Ryder (Ryder? I barely knew her!) could act? She's a revelation. Even the kids can act! How comes whenever we see children on UK television they're always that unique breed of smug, breathy annoyances with a know-it-all attitude and a name like an old Victoria affliction. OH LITTLE DROPSY, DO COME ALONG, YOU'LL BE LATE FOR YOUR MANDARIN CLASS. That kind of shite.

If it helps sweeten the deal, there's a policeman in there with a strong jaw and a mean attitude, so at least you're guaranteed a bit of rain at Fort Bushy.

twochubbycubs on: caravans

Something awful happened yesterday.

I didn't want to write about it because I felt so bad. I'm not a man who easily shames – I'd need the priest to cancel his summer if I ever went into a confessions box – and I'm very much a 'meh' person when it comes to morality and decency, but sometimes even I feel penitent. I need to apologise genuinely to everyone out there who thought I was a decent person. Let me explain, OK?

Naturally, because I'm a gobshite, I'll need to set the scene. It was a glorious summer day – the type of Sunday afternoon that is just fizzing with possibility – do you spend all day watching Four in a Bed re-runs on More 4 or the Come Dine With Me omnibus on 4OD? Due to the weather being so damn warm we were at serious risk of bonding directly with our leather sofa so we decided, after peeling ourselves off the leather with a loud, wet fart, to 'go for a drive'. My parents used to take me and my sister out to go 'there and back to see how far it is', and that's exactly what we planned to do. An amble out in the car to shout loudly at the back of caravans and the front of BMWs.

As you may or may not know, we live near the Northumbrian coast, and it was a matter of minutes before we were beetling up the coast road, with Paul's terrible taste in music playing loudly through the speakers of my car. That's the deal. If we take my (better) car he gets to choose the music, meaning eight hours of Tracy Chapman Sucks The Joy Out Of Every Conceivable Situation. Meh, I like doing the driving so I let it slide. Anyway, we had only been going for about fifteen minutes when he turned the music off and turned to me, mischief writ large on his already burning, doughy moon-face, and suggested we go and look at caravans.

Well, I was shocked, let me tell you — Paul has all of his own teeth and isn't unemployed, so why suggest a caravan? He explained that he didn't want to buy a caravan, rather just have a nosey around, and that he had seen a sign for an 'open day' at a nearby caravan park but a few moments ago. I can't say no to Paul — one look at his rheumy, beady eyes and I'll give him the world. Caravans have never appealed to me — I don't see the joy in dashing away on holiday to look at the same four walls you've previously looked at for a long wet week. The ones I have been in always start of smelling of foist and sex and end up smelling of farts and shame, which perhaps says more about me. I'm not a snob, I'm sure there are some lovely models out there that don't come in discharge-beige, but they're just not my scene.

Nevertheless, I turned the car around under the guise of humouring Paul but really wanting to have a nose myself. I've always wanted to see how someone could find sweating in a plastic box so inviting. We pulled in at around 1pm with the idea that we would have a gander around a couple of caravans, maybe swear at some children in the bar and buy some cinder toffee for the drive home.

WE WERE THERE FOUR FUCKING HOURS. FOUR! Why? Well, this is the bit I feel I have to apologise for. We had no sooner walked in when some wonderful, charming, effortlessly polite young man hustled over in a veritable cloud of Lynx Africa and sat us down in a comfy chair. I immediately started mouthing DON'T SAY ANYTHING to Paul but he had his eyes on both ends of an eight-berth caravan with balcony and when asked if we'd like a coffee, said yes please. I could see at this point we'd be there a while NOW MY HUSBAND HAS COMMITTED US. Yep.

The guy was charm himself and I didn't want to feel like we were wasting his time so when asked whether we were thinking about buying, I issued a vague 'we've come into a bit of money but can't commit today' in the hope of appeasing him and getting away sharp. No. No, he couldn't have had a firmer grip on me if he'd sunk his teeth into my scrotum. He promised us a look around, asked a few questions which Paul, lost in a reverie thanks to his machine-brewed cappuccino, left me to deal with. I floundered but still the salesman pressed on. He asked us how often we would be visiting (never), what attracted us to caravans (nothing) (perhaps maybe the swinging), how long we'd been together, who held the purse-strings...

Out we went. We were treated to an almost two-hour tour of the facilities. As caravan parks go I'm sure it was lovely, but I just can't relax when a good half of the men walking about look like they're going to kick your teeth out through your arsehole and their wives have more writing on their knuckles than on the work experience bit of their CVs. We wandered down to the beach which afforded us wonderful views – and that part is true, I've never seen an aluminium smelter glint in the sunlight with such beauty – but listen, I know what gets discharged into the North Sea (hell, I'm responsible for the worst of it) and I don't fancy bobbing out of the water with a turd-cigar in my mouth.

Actually, that point was highlighted a little later with the appearance of a 'secret beach', a little sandy cove hidden out of sight by virtue of a bit of marshland and the flats of the dried-up river-bed. Nothing says 'enjoy a summer picnic with me darling' like watching two seagulls fighting in the carcass of a bloated cat and a rat trying to free itself from a spent condom.

All through the tour the sense of feeling shit for wasting this guy's time was growing, but we thought he'd be finished in no time and then we could slip away before most of his afternoon was wasted. But he just kept going with his endless energy. I don't know who his girlfriend is but I bet she walks around with a huge smile and two pairs of chapped lips.

So much time passed that we couldn't in all good conscience tell him we had only wanted to look around a caravan and nothing more. He extolled the virtues of the site-wide Wi-Fi (because we would definitely want to be on the same network as some of the guys we'd spotted looking mournfully from their caravan windows, yessir), the on-site entertainment and the swimming pool. Actually, the pool looked great – it's been ages since I'd had a verruca to pick at. I'm not going to fib though – whether it was the heat of the day, my body expressing shock at moving more than 100 yards under my own steam or just his excellent sales patter, the idea of owning a caravan here was starting to look more tempting. If only so I could lie down and scratch my feet with a match-box.

We finished the afternoon with the most awkward hour of my life – looking someone in the eye who was so keen for a sale that he skipped over my obvious attempts at deflection – we're gay, Paul's an arsonist, I have bail conditions banning me from being near old folk – with that deft, assured mannerism that must come from months of getting people off the fence and into caravan ownership. He asked for a number to contact me on and in my haste to get away I gave him the right number – which he then called a day or two later – thus this being the first instance of me giving my number of a guy and him not immediately scribbling it on a toilet wall with the annotation 'CAN TAKE THREE AT ONCE'. We discussed finance packages, we discussed carpet options, whether I'd bring my own gas from home (I always do, I chortled, and the crowd went mild), park rules (which essentially boiled down to not nicking the copper from the exchange box and not being a grass), whether my parents would be interested and whether we'd need a two double-bed set-up. I exclaimed that we weren't that fat which finally seemed to kill the mood and, after many promises that we would be in touch, we were able to slink away.

Paul made to put his Tracy Chapman music back on once we were in the car but I slapped his hand away and reminded him that as his cappuccino had almost cost us £30,000 in 6540 crippling monthly payments, I'd choose the music. Our salesman called us a few days later and we explained that my parents hadn't quite died just yet and that we'd be in contact and do you know, he was so nice – said no worries, thanked us for a lovely afternoon and bid us goodbye. I was so stricken with guilt that I immediately called back and asked if I could send a letter in about his wonderful customer service (and it really was – fair enough he chewed my ears off but he was polite, courteous and charming to an absolute fault) but he said we didn't need to, as long as we kept him in mind if we ever wanted a caravan. I felt like I'd kicked a begging dog to death.

So, my apology then. A big, heartfelt genuine apology to

the poor lad who showed us around for an entire afternoon with the impression we were going to buy a caravan. We weren't. We had gone in just to have a nose about and were too cowardly to say we were just nebbing. In our defence, we did try to make it obvious we couldn't commit, but you were so impassioned by your job that we didn't want to break your spirit. There comes a point a couple of hours in when it's too late to back out and we hit that point around the time of the secret beach. But: you were great, you really were, and if we ever do decide that we want to give up on life and get a caravan, we'll come to you. I hope we're forgiven. I still think of you when I get stuck behind a Shitcabin Deluxe-3000 on the A69 and even now the remorse is raw. Goodbye, Mr Caravan Man.

twochubbycubs on: pokemon go and cats

As I type, there are four people who, given they look as though they've been carved out of milk we can safely assume have never been outside before, fussing around at the bottom of our garden with their phones. I think we can safely rule out them being paparazzi, though if a slot-shot appears on the Daily Mail side-bar of my hairy arse-crack taken as I put the bins out in my Luigi dressing gown, I'll take the credit. No, I think they're playing Pokemon Go, and good luck to them – anything that gets young'uns out into the fresh air and away from the TV can't be a bad thing. It's not for me, though. That's not to say that the idea of coming across a Jigglypuff in the woods doesn't appeal to me – hell, that was my Facebook status for a good two years – but the whole thing is just too active and sociable. I'd be terrified of having to make small talk with someone.

Plus, on an entirely shallow note, I went along to a 'gamers' meet-up many moons ago (I'm big into video games, thought it would be good to meet up with some fellow players) and I'm barely exaggerating when I say you could have chewed the BO that hung in the air. Perhaps it's a lazy stereotype but good lord, waft a stick of Mum under your pits and fuck the fuck off. Oh and brush your bloody teeth – there's no excuse for teeth that look as though they've been whittled from margarine. I didn't so much beat a retreat as swim away through the waves of stink.

Maybe I'm just being miserable. Remember my elation at the fact we've managed to source a wonderful garden table after two years of trying to find one we liked that a) wasn't made of plastic and b) could withstand a couple of years of our giant arses pressing down on it? Well, whoop-de-whoo, too good to be true. First it was delayed, then delayed again, then delivered with a chunk missing, then the replacement bits didn't turn up on time. As melodramatic as it might seem, I'm so pissed off with it that I'm returning the lot and it's back to the drawing board. It's only because their customer service people were so pleasant to deal with that I'm not naming the company, but it's such a bloody shame! Our neighbours are doubtless thankful that their summer isn't going to be full of images of Paul and I reclining in the sun like butter on a crumpet, but hey.

Anyway, that's quite enough negativity. Let's have some positivity!

You may remember a while ago we visited Mog on the Tyne and had a lovely time, surrounded by cats whilst we had our lunch? Well, I recently discovered that there's another café down on the Quayside, and a good friend suggested we go for lunch. Actually, that's a fib, she made some terrible joke about eating out and pussy, and when she'd brought me around with the smelling salts, we both agreed to would be an excellent way to spend a lunch hour. Certainly better than trying to wrest a meal-deal sandwich from the hands of other office-workers in our local Sainsbury's. I'd kick someone to death for taking the last brie and grape sandwich, just saying.

Well, it was wonderful. If you're unfamiliar with the concept of a cat café, they're small rooms filled with cat furniture, cat scratching posts and lots of dogs. Obviously not. No, cats. No good if you've got allergies but if that's the case, have a Piriton and suck it up. Whilst the cats at Mog on the Tyne are all sorts of rescue cats and gorgeous kitties, Catpawcino has rare breeds and unusual looking delights. The food is typical little café fare but done well – paninis, sandwiches, cupcakes, that sort of thing. Let's be honest though, no-one goes to these places to critique the sandwiches. It was all about the cats.

twochubbycubs on: our dislikes: round two

Now, long time readers may remember I did an article way back in February of last year called james vs paul and it consisted of five things that annoyed him about me and five things that annoyed me about him. If you haven't committed our various faults to memory – and if not, why not – you can find it here, together with a delicious recipe for chicken chow mein. Yeah, that's right. Anyway, it's due a sequel. You'll be glad to know that we both still do every single thing that previously annoyed the other, but hey, fuck it, that's marriage. Here's five more – and, just like before, I've got right to reply on Paul's critiques of me. Why? Because I have no gag reflex, and frankly if he wants to take advantage of that going forward, he has to let me reply...mahaha! Plus, I get the right to expand on my annoyances too. What a cad!

Paul's five things that rile him about me:

there's always coat hangers in our bed

aye, it's a fair cop this one. See, I get ready for work about ten minutes after Paul, because bless, he has to get up and put the coffee on and turn the shower on for me. My reward for his wonderful kindness is to litter his side of the bed with coat-hangers from where I'm trying to decide what shirt to wear in the morning – the shirts then get put over the top of the door rather than hung up. I think Paul's getting a complex that I'm trying to do him a mischief when every time he climbs into bed he gets prodded with the coat-hanger, but in my defence, they're velvet

james never put liners in the tiny kitchen bin

meh. I can see Paul's point, no-one wants smears of cat-food and whatnot on the inside of the bin. Fair enough. But Paul insists on buying a) tiny bins and b) massive bin liners. I wanted a lovely massive Brabantia bin but Paul knocked that idea on the head saying that we'd never empty it and we'd have what amounted to a vertical skip in the kitchen. Hmm. But then see he buys bin liners that you could drive a car through, meaning I've got to spend ten minutes flapping them out and trying to get them to sit in the tiny bin without just filling up the bloody container in the first place. It's an ongoing, very middle-class problem, and it threatens to tear us apart at times

everything electrical is going to burst into flames unless it's unplugged when not in use

again, I think this is unfair! I grew up on a diet of 999 and with parents who had a very casual attitude to fire safety and thus I think my fears are entirely reasonable. I'm a catastrophic thinker – if I leave a box of matches on the side, I'll spend the day envisioning various ways that the cats will knock them to the floor, followed by them knocking on the gas-oven in fear, followed by spiders skittering around on the sulphur of the scattered matches, igniting and destroying my home. That sounds fair enough until you realise we don't have a gas oven

socks, socks everywhere, as far as the eye can see

not fair: they're not just my socks. For two tidy, professional men, we don't half have a habit of leaving our socks scattered about in unusual places, and not just because they're the wanksocks, we're not 14 anymore. I don't think I owned a pair of socks that didn't crunch and crackle between the age of 12 and 19. But see in my haste to have my feet rubbed and squeezed (despite Paul's entirely baseless remonstrations that it makes his hands smell like Roquefort), my socks will often just get discarded and forgotten until either Paul or the cleaner finds them

james' genuine concern and worry whenever I hurt myself in a clumsy, hilarious manner

I may have reworded that a little. Paul is taking umbrage at the fact that when he hurts himself by a) tumbling over in that way only fat men can, b) burning his mouth because he's so keen to eat he doesn't let his food cool down or c) cuts himself on his edgy political analysis, I immediately respond by fussing over him and saying 'what's the matter' eighteen times a second. Hmph. I think that shows only love and concern for my precious, gorgeous husband, frankly.

Hmm. Seems fair. Now it's my turn. Because I'm the writer, I get to say what annoys me about Paul AND expand on it too. What annoys me about Paul?

WELL.

James' five things that annoy him about Paul

he can't hoover to save his life

let me explain, as that seems a trifle extreme — we've got one of those fancy-dan digital Dyson vacuums that sit on the wall charging up until it's needed, then you have exactly six minutes to flounce around the house shrieking whilst it vacuums at full power. That in itself is a mere inconvenience. No, it only becomes a problem because Paul vacuums up every single fucking thing on the floor rather than picking up the bigger bits — whole pasta twists, cable ties, shoes, you name it Paul's tried to suck it up into the tiny drum and then spent 5 minutes gawping and swearing at the vacuum whilst it chugs and splutters because the tube is blocked. I swear, I spend more time poking around in the drum with a chopstick trying to dislodge errant nonsense than I do breathing in and out. I half expect to walk into our utility room to find our full-sized tom cat squeezed into the tiny plastic drum of the vacuum, mewing pitifully through a mouthful of dust and ped-egged-foot-skin

he always wants his back scratched

doesn't matter where we are, I can blink and when I open my eyes, his shirt will be hoisted up over his tits and his back will be looming towards me with his plaintive cries of 'up a bit down a bit go mad NO NOT THAT HARD' filling the air – if I had the money, I'd get a HappyCow machine installed – you need to stop reading this right now and look that machine up – it will fill your wee heart with joy

he can't handle Sky Digital

we've been together nine years and still whenever we're recording and watching The Today Show and recording Panorama, he'll attempt to turn the telly over onto a third channel and then act perplexed when the TV says no. He also can't fast-forward through breaks – it's like he has a tremor when he presses the button during Hotel Inspector and suddenly everything is 30x the speed and unpaused just as Alex Polizzi's giant smile is filling the screen and she's climbing back into her Audi

he maintains that his Smart car is a sensible choice despite massive evidence to the contrary

I go to this well a lot and I don't care. Going to buy anything bigger than a Rubik's cube? Paul will spend ten minutes assuring me it'll fit despite me advising him that the rules of physics still apply even if his car is the colour of a baked bean. Of course, once we've bought the BBQ / new SONOS soundbar / sack of potatoes and made our way back to the car park, he'll realise that, whilst it does fit – just – there's no space for me, leaving me standing in the car park cursing his name whilst he races home in the car at its top speed of 32mph before returning to pick me up not even a little bit contrite. We've had many a terse conversation whilst making our way slowly and uncomfortably back home, I can assure you

he wakes me up by farting, but not in the way you might expect

we both find farting absolutely hilarious – there's few things funnier to our juvenile minds than a good *taint-stainer, plea for help from Sir Knobbly-Brown, misguided burp, creeping hisser, floorboard troubler* or an extended moment of *steam-pressing your knickers,* so that doesn't trouble me in the slightest. No, if I'm woken up by a loud fart, I'll spend the day chuckling. It only becomes a problem because we tend to spoon when we're asleep in the morning and Paul manages to turn whatever food he's had the night before – no matter how fine the ingredients, no matter how dainty the amounts – into concentrated pure death. I can't tell you the amount of times I've been woken up in the morning by what smells like concentrated hate not so much filling my nostrils as filing them, peeling off skin and various bits of my olfactory system. It's a bad job when you wake up gagging and reminiscing with longing for the smell of burning cows from the Foot and Mouth days. I grew up right next door to the farm that started it all and they said it could never happen again. Well it is – in Paul's arse at 5.45am.

Mahaha. Hey, listen, those are his faults. But for all of those minor things, he's still the man who I've only spent 6 nights away from and who makes me laugh right from the get-go as soon as I come through the door. There's no regrets here and there's not many couples who can say that!

twochubbycubs on: a productive day

Today has been a day of **getting shit done**.

So what have we managed to get done today? Well, I pressure washed everything we owned that was looking a little bit grubby: outdoor furniture, fence panels, the blood stains on the front of my car, the hair and scalp in the tyre-wells, the paving slabs and the gate. There's something amazingly satisfying about watching a tiny jet of water blast away years of accumulated dirt and filth. If I didn't think it would tear straight through his small intestine I'd have a crack at blasting Paul's *out-pipe*. It'd be like pressure-washing a hot Malteaser. It goes without saying that I blasted several choice swearwords into the path but Paul made me remove them – apparently it doesn't *do* for folks who visit to be greeted by an increasingly-vile set of phrases culminating in mingetacular. Pffft.

When I was putting away the pressure washer into the let's-tell-Paul-I'll-use-it-all-the-time-but-then-never-use-it-again pile in our shed, I realised that one of our cats had disappeared under the various detritus on the shed floor and was mewing pitifully. After digging through and locating her and putting her outside the shed (to which point she immediately came back in through the cat-flap to get lost again) (I was all, alright love, you're not on fucking Fun House here, I haven't just tagged you back in), I realised it was time to clear out the shed.

I know, this is truly riveting reading, but please, bear with me. See, I've mentioned before that we turned our giant outdoor shed into a Cat Hotel / stockpile room (hence the cat-flap on a shed, see — it gives them somewhere to go when it's raining and they can sleep on the cat tree in there). Recently the shed has become a depository for remnants of abandoned hobbies (GPS units from geocaching, walking boots, an unused tent, lightshade made of human skin), stuff from the kitchen which we're keeping in case we need it (Nutribullet box, ice-cream maker, pickled knees) and well, all sort of other shite. It was chaos, but after two hours and several trips to the tip (mainly because Paul insisted on taking his Smart car rather than my car, limiting us to taking two Rizla papers and a discarded screw at a time), we could see the carpet again.

Yeah, carpet, we can't have the cats getting cold feet.

As an aside, the men at our nearest tip are a delight, and I'm not just saying that because they wear those fancy hi-vis boiler-suits and I want to be roughly groped behind the oil-disposal drums (though it would be fitting). It's rare to find folks who seem happy in their job and who are keen to help, pointing us in the direction of the appropriate skip and masking their disapproval of the fact we couldn't be arsed to separate our garden waste from our general waste. I know, we deserve to be bricked up in a tomb somewhere for killing the Earth, but honestly, Paul's arse does more damage to the environment and I don't run the risk of pricking my fingers when I handle that. It's a far cry from the roughly-hewn grunters at our previous Newcastle tip. I honestly thought I was going to have my face slashed with a shard of a broken Pyrex dish for having the temerity to ask which bin to put hedge clippings in. I mean, I apologised for interrupting their blistering chatter about which bird (sorry: boord) they'd fuck out of the Daily Sport. Pfft.

After clearing the shelves and vacuuming about half a tonne of dried rosemary out of the carpet (hang it in the shed he said...we'll use it all the time he said...) we had a clear shed and a clear mind. This meant only one thing: time to restock. See, Slimming World and life in general can be expensive but if you buy the staples you use in bulk, you'll save cold hard cash, and that's good for everyone, not least because it means you can buy a few more raffle tickets in class and keep Queen Mags in Cheeky Vimtos and Cutter's Choice. We buy food like beans, chopped tomatoes, passata, pasta and rice in massive bags and store it in the shed, meaning if we're ever stuck we can throw something together in the blink of an eye. Off we went to B&Ms to replenish.

Now listen, I know B&Ms is like Mecca to some folk, but I just can't bear it. It's full of people who dawdle and who hold up a jar of Nescafe in one hand and a jar of Blue Mountain in the other, looking dead behind the eyes whilst their spittle pools around their feet. The aisles are littered with ladies who look like they could punch an articulated lorry to death. It's awash with screaming children and bright lights and too many not-quite products to bear. We filled our trolley with dishwasher tablets, coal tar soap and oops-sorry-Mags a box of Lucky Charms and hurtled through the checkout. The charming lass behind the counter carried on a conversation with her co-worker the entire time and spoke only to spit the price out at us. Never again. I never learn, I always think 'let's save some money' but then I end up stuck in an aisle with mirrors with the Playboy logo on them whilst Paul holds himself up crying next to the locked display of perfumes featuring classics such as I've Just Come by Mark Wright or Gonorrhoea by someone who came second in I'm a Celebrity in 2009.

Celebrity scents confuse me at the best of times – I've never in my entire life looked at someone famous and thought by Christ I wish I smelled like them – but even more so when it's a non-entity from a reality show on ITV Be (Thankful You Can Turn It Over, presumably). I imagine that smells like pure shame.

The good news is the shed is all stocked up. The bad news, if you're a picker at the Tesco in Kingston Park, I've just put an order in for 96 bottles of various mixers to fill up our mixer shelves. If you want, crack open a bottle of the diet ginger ale because that belongs to Paul and I know he'll spare it. Touch my tonic with a hint of cucumber and I'll turn your delivery truck over. Obviously I'm kidding, but seriously now. Paul did suggest we go and pick up the drinks ourselves but frankly, if we took his car, we'd only have enough for one of those tiny tins of Coke you used to buy from Woolworths. The jokes about his Smart car will never, ever end, you realise. Even he's accepted that, answering me with a chuckle that says 'oh my' and eyes that say 'fuck you'. Ah well.

twochubbycubs on: internet trolls

It's a shame that Leslie Jones has been getting shit thrown at her on Twitter as a result of being in the Ghostbusters movie. She's been called all sorts of vile things for simply putting herself forward and making people laugh. It's depressing, and it's not as though the world isn't depressing enough as it is. It's getting to the point where I could open my curtains in the morning and notice a mushroom cloud billowing towards me and I'd shrug and meh and go back to watching whatever atrocity is blazing across the TV.

That's the problem with the Internet, it gives a voice to all those gimps with no self-confidence and no tact. I should know, I've made a healthy sideline from it. You see the vilest of comments left on the most innocuous of posts and articles – I've seen someone wish another woman a miscarriage because they disagreed over how much sweetener to put in a recipe, for goodness sake – and the answer to that one, by the way, is none at all. You have people who wouldn't say boo to a goose blurting out vile rhetoric and for what? No other reason than to wound and upset. I genuinely don't understand the mentality, and I love a sly dig every now and then – but I couldn't take pleasure in actually breaking someone's spirit.

We have a local paper up here called the Evening Chronicle, and it really is the go-to paper if you want to know who someone from Geordie Shore had up her snatch the previous day or perhaps a picture of a local councillor pointing furiously at some potholes with a face like he's trying desperately not to shit himself on camera It's entirely pointless but generally harmless, although they're not averse to strumming up a bit of racial tension to get their comments counter overflowing. Anyway, they posted a story about some poor bugger who had climbed up an electricity pylon and was threatening to hurl himself onto the live wires. He was suicidal and as a result, the power folks had to turn off the juice. The story was full of comments like 'shocking behaviour' and 'I hope he was charged', which, whilst crass and insensitive, is harmless enough. We're all guilty of a bit of black humour. However, topping off the comments was 'So glad it didn't hit my area I'd be raging if I'f missed the soaps!!'. For fucks sake. We're not talking about someone nicking a bit of copper wire, we're talking about someone being so fucked in the head that they think the best option is the pain of burning alive, and this claybrained footlicker is more concerned about missing Eastenders.

I despair. Not in a sanctimonious oh-aren't-I-wonderful way but just as a human, how can you lack the compassion? Also, as an adult, how the fuck do you not know that it is I'd not i'f — and that's *after* editing her comments. Urgh.

twochubbycubs on: the 90s

I've discovered a new past-time. Admittedly it's one that shows off my mean, vexing side, but I don't care. I <3 looking through and commenting on the Facebook 'buy and sell' groups in our local area. Honestly, the tat people try and sell is just beyond me. Plus, you get the bonus of looking at pictures of people's houses and getting to suck air over my teeth at the state of the wallpaper or the "canvas art" littering every room. If I see another KEEP CALM AND DRINK PROSECCO poster I'm going to find a way to reach through the atoms on my iPad screen and torch their house.

As an aside, Paul used to know someone who drank from a cup that said 'KEEP CALM AND GO MENTAL' on the side. I rather think it remains to his credit that he didn't smash it over her head.

I recently got into a spat with some orange harridan with a face like a rushed omelette who accused me of being a bald fat fuck because I accused her '100% NOT FAKE' Calvin Klein dress as being fake. First of all, you can't insult me by calling me a bald fat fuck because, if you remove the spaces from that and add slut, that's my Grindr name, and secondly, I don't think Calvin's knocking out dresses under the name Calvan Kline. Calvan Kline sounds like a ski village in Norway, for one thing. Anyway, spluttering ill-conceived and predominately vowel-less insults at me has no effect. It rolls off me like gravy off a fat duck's back.

Just an aside, I'm not always mean. I've bitten my tongue all weekend after seeing a PicCollage (it's always a fucking PicCollage) recipe for '**Hawaiian** BBQ chicken'. **Hawaiian**? That's how a Geordie mother calls her children in off the street.

Now, a lovely bit of news. You may remember from previous posts that we are part of something called the Reddit Gift Exchange? In short, you pick one of the monthly themes (for example, The Simpsons, or The 90s) and you're matched with a complete stranger from somewhere else in the UK. You then buy this person a gift pertaining to the theme and send it to them. It's a giant Secret Santa. You're guaranteed a present in return from someone else and it's all very jolly-hockey-sticks and amazing. We *love* it. In the twelve months we have been doing it we've had some genuinely brilliant gifts – homemade cookbooks, a massive box of 'tourist' paraphernalia from Scarborough, posters and gaming kit and plenty of others too numerous and marvellous to mention. I do love a Secret Santa, although I did once get my ex-boss a duck for her bath without realising it was a vibrator. That caused much embarrassment, especially when she tried it out in the office no-she-didn't-don't-worry. We didn't have a bath!

So the theme this month was favourite decade and for both Paul and I this was definitely the 90s. It had it all – great TV in the shape of The Crystal Maze, 999 and dinnerladies, superb music (aside from Eiffel 65, fuck those guys) and proper morning-piss yellow Sunny Delight. Though for the record, remember we didn't have much money and so branded radioactive drinks were out – the best we had was a bottle of Overcast Ennui in our lunchbox. What a time to be alive.

Anyway, our Secret Santa totally knocked it out of the park with their selection of 90s goods – there were three CDs which I used to own and absolutely fucking love, a packet of Nintendo Playing Cards, two Tamagotchi's, some Hot-Wheels and a proper little watch. There was also a lovely card. But good lord, what a perfect selection of 90s goodness – I had such a rush of nostalgia that my pubes disappeared and my voice unbroke. I know that's not a word, squiggly-red-line, but it makes sense in this sentence.

I was always very lucky in that I didn't go through the whole protracted stage of my voice breaking – I went to bed one night with a voice like Joe Pasquale and a scrotum like a tangerine, woke up the next morning sounding like Isaac Hayes and had a ballsack like a Bassett Hound's ear. Perhaps it didn't go quite as deep as Isaac but certainly I avoided all the squeaking and dropping that so many teenage lads seem to experience.

It was the Pogs that really sent us both whooshing back into memory land though. I absolutely **loved** them. God knows why, it's just some natty coloured cardboard discs, but something about the simplicity really won me over. Paul and I tried to have a quick game only to send them tumbling all over the kitchen floor so god knows what has happened since, but back in the day, I was the King of Pogs. Well, perhaps the Queen of Pogs. I had the full set, a fluorescent green Pog holder and a slammer which was really just a massive, heavy-duty washer that my dad brought home from work. The Pogs epidemic swept through our school like the norovirus, with fights and scuffles leading to the outright ban of Pog battles in the playground. Didn't stop us – we used to just play out of the sight of teachers. Honestly, you wouldn't believe the amount of lads I beat off behind the sheds when no-one was looking. Some things never change, eh.

I reckon Pogs was also the first flirtation with crime for both me and my sister. We had been dragged along to a car-boot sale somewhere inexplicable and indoors and were bored shitless. Parents, don't take your kids to car boot sales. They're full of things other people don't need or want and anything interesting a kid finds is always met with a 'WE DON'T NEED THAT' from the parents. Oh, but we *do* need a VHS of Beverley Callard's Fitness First and a giant glass ashtray, apparently.

We had spotted a Pog stand full of slammers that looked like something out of Saw and not-quite-Pogs that were possibly printed at home. Didn't matter. All about volume in those days, see. Anyway, I distracted the lady behind the decorating table by commenting on how fine her moustache was or something whilst my sister proceeded to fill her trousers with Pogs, all held in by virtue of her Adidas Poppers had been tucked into her socks. Genius right? We were like the Krays of South Northumberland.

Don't judge us too keenly, we were young and bored. Karma got us back anyway because the Pogs were of such bad quality that the ink ran and they were ruined by the heat of a rustling shellsuit. I'm sure my sister probably has a faint imprint of a Tazmanian Devil somewhere on her ankle even now.

Mind, as an aside, Pogs were nothing compared to the thrill of completing a Panini Premiership sticker book. Seeing Alan Shearer's smug, insufferable face sliding out of the packet on a shiny backing meant being King of All Things, if only for a day. Nevermind the arguments that Pogs caused, I've seen fights that looked like when The Bride battles the Crazy 88 in Kill Bill 1 over a four inch by two-inch sticker of Tino Asprilla. No amount of trading Paul-Furlong-for-Kevin-Pressman-and-the-Nottingham-Forest-logo is worth having your first adult tooth kicked clean out of your mouth for.

Dangerous times indeed!

twochubbycubs on: the DVLA

I'm fizzing with anger! Remember we traded in the tiny Micra way back in March for an even smaller Smart car (next year we're trading the Smart car in for a Little Tikes Cozy Coupe and some magic beans)? Well, we did all of the paperwork to switch the ownership of the Micra only to receive a stern letter from the DVLA telling us that we were breaking the law because GASP the Micra was uninsured despite a) us not owning it anymore and b) I'm fairly sure it's a fucking cube of metal the size of a box of Swan Vestas by now.

I had the joy of speaking to someone so thick she'd struggle to look through a ladder who, after much umming, aahing and dribbling into the microphone so it sounded like she was in a washing machine, told me to send a letter in proving we had indeed sold the car. I did this promptly, without delay, and with only minimum amount of swearing. Hell, I even used my full name on the letter because it sounds lovely and posh. Then I, comfortable in the knowledge that the good folk at the DVLA were sorting it, immediately forgot about it and moved on with my life, which has recently consisted of looking at and ruling out garden furniture for 23 hours a day.

Until today when lo and behold I get a fucking penalty in the post for having an uninsured bloody car! Great! I'd understand if the penalty was for reasons of bad taste because we bought an orange Smart car that looks like we're driving around in a Fruitella but no! AARGH man. Now I've got to send another letter with further proof and I've been told, via another wonderful customer service adviser who was also knitting with one needle, that I'll still need to pay the fine regardless. Honestly, I almost did a proper Jeremy Kyle punch through the wall, though knowing my current luck this would result in a penalty from More Than for unauthorised household alterations.

Why are these things so difficult? We live in a world where, if I wanted to, I could nip onto the Internet and show my button off in glorious 1080p to some pervy old masochist in Canberra, but we seemingly can't invent a system where we can submit our documents online in a safe and secure fashion. No, I have to leave important financial documentation to the idiosyncrasies of the Royal Bloody Mail, who currently have a 0% success rate with me. Perhaps I had a dyslexic postman who thought I meant VLAD instead of DVLA and is currently hiking his way through deepest Transylvania with a furrowed brow and a garlic necklace. Who knows.

Samsung was another experience – product still in warranty, had to call six times before I got through to someone who dared break the script in front of them and even then, still got absolutely nowhere until I complained via Twitter and got you lovely folks to chip in. In the end we had our hob fixed for free and the chap dealing with it was lovely but why make me jump through so many hoops? I mean COME ON I'm morbidly obese, jumping through hoops makes my ankles splinter. PAH. Nevermind.

Just as an update on the garden furniture situation – because I know you lot will have been gasping awake in the night with fret and worry about whether we've got somewhere to bronze our bitch-titties this summer – we found the table we want only to discover we'd need to hire a bloody crane to get it into the garden. Paul and I both agreed that this would be fine only on the basis that the fat builder from the moneysupermarket adverts was the crane operator, and oopsy-daisy-let-me-get-that-wet-hi-vis-off-you-oh-goodness-me-my-cock-fell-out, but they couldn't guarantee this., the unreasonable swines. So we're back to square one. Great!

twochubbycubs on: our old pets

I'd love chickens of my own but we have the type of neighbours (some of them) who probably have a stack of photocopied letters to the council just ready to go with any possible infraction of the law of the land. You may recollect a moment from last year when we were accosted on our own doorstep by a man whose face was, somewhat coincidentally, the colour of a beetroot egg. He shouted at us for not mowing our garden enough despite our gardener doing it once a week. We're still cleaning spittle off the front door. So understand, we might want chickens, but we also don't want angry letters.

I'm very jealous though – growing up we had chickens when I was a wee'un but they mysteriously went to live on a farm when we moved house. What was even more weird was the fact we had roast chicken for dinner eight nights on the trot and I remember the meat being particular succulent, but I suppose that'll have been the tears splashing down on it.

Thinking back, we've had quite the menagerie – our first pet was a giant rough long-hair collie called Shannon who I have two single memories of – one of our cousins came to stay for the summer and, whilst walking up the lane to our house, was met with the sight of a dog twice as big as her who tumbled her over and bit her on the arm. Ooops. Don't worry, it's not as bad as it sounds, we added a bit of Listerine into the dog's water and he was fine. I jest I jest. The other memory is a sad one though (sob) – poor Shannon got loose into the back fields and suffered a nasty chemical burn and was put down. What can I say, living in Bhopal was tough. Nah, it was some weird pesticide, the poor bugger.

We had cats a-plenty – Smokey with the loudest purr who lived a happy life until he decided that the A69 at rush hour was an appropriate place to stop and lick his balls. There was Cleo (went missing) and Tabitha (attacked by foxes). Listen, we grew up in the countryside, these were hard cats but nature always prevails. We did manage to have two cats make it to dotage though, thankfully, despite the efforts of God himself. Salem was my favourite as he was quite genuinely the laziest cat as could be. He had masses of long black hair (hence Salem) and would never clean himself, which, when combined with his tendency to *download his Whiskas* all over the place without bothering to see if had tangled into the hair on the back of his legs, meant many a fun evening for my mum and the cat hairbrush. She used to throw half a cat's worth of matted poo-hair onto the coal fire and Christ, you've never smelled anything like it in your life. Even now if I take a deep breath I can still smell it.

Speaking of cat-fires, I was watching a film one night when a spark from a crackling log leapt out of the fire and nestled neatly on the cat's flank. By the time I'd untangled myself from my blanket and leapt as only a fat man can do from the sofa, there was quite a considerable amount of smoke rising from him. Just as I bounded over he rose to his feet more akin to a cat stretching on a summer's day and barely looked bothered as I beat his sides to extinguish the fire. He had the same expression as I lowered him into a cold bath to ensure he hadn't been burnt. He had a great life mind, as all countryside cats do, and died at 15, buried in the garden for ever more. I reckon by now he's nothing more than bones and a few giant clumps of matted poo-hair.

Salem was joined by Misty a little into his life, and she was an entirely unremarkable but lovely cat who spent most of the time outside, deigning only to visit us when she was hungry, when she was cold or, once, alarmingly, when she was pregnant. We had no idea she was up the cat-duff and it was only when a load of tiny squeaking started up behind an armchair that we realised she was having kittens, and even that was after ten minutes of my dad trying to adjust the telly because he thought the sound on You Bet was playing up. She also lived a long and happy life and padded off around 14 years.

Shannon the dog was replaced by Bracken, who was a discarded greyhound who leapt into my mum's car on her way back from the Spar shop. We tried giving him away to a farm (he was too athletic to be a house-dog) but apparently the nicotine withdrawals from not passively-chain-smoking 40 Lambert and Butlers a day meant he had to come back. I've never seen a dog with a yellow fringe before. Oh Christ before I get the RSPCA on the phone (although let's be honest, they'd only be ringing to ask me to donate to their new director's Bentley fund), the dog was given away and finished out his days running around chasing chickens. That's not even a fib I was told to make me feel better, he went to the farm a few doors down!

Bracken was replaced by Oscar, a ginger border collie who was thick as mince and the bane of my life (though I loved him dearly). When I used to take him for walks over the fields and let him off, he'd immediately turn around and belt for home. Every. Single. Time. This would invariably lead to me trying to run (bear in mind I'm fat) after him and catching him just the moment before my ankles snapped. He did calm down a bit and could be trusted to run on his own after a while, but as soon as he heard one of the many bird-scarers go off in the fields away he'd be again, destined for home. It's a wonder I was so fat as a kid given I spent so much time chasing him.

He wasn't just dense outside the home, either, oh no. He used to try and shag Salem, the aforementioned tom-cat, who would be wearing the same non-plussed expression noted above even when he had a 20kg dog thrusting its lipstick up and down his back, smearing his back like a slug. My parents thought it was horrible but looking back, what a terribly progressive household we had. I should start a Tumblr about it.

My favourite memory of Oscar was something he did all through his life, though – we would let him out into the garden for a poo, and, after ten minutes of turning around, sniffing, shaking and finally doing that thousand-yard-stare-whilst-defecating, he'd crimp one off. He'd then go absolutely bloody manic, hurtling back into the house and round and round the sofa, almost literally running along the walls like a motorcyclist in a Wall of Death, with the biggest dog-grin you can imagine. I don't know whether it was sheer relief at passing a stool he was feeling, but Christ, my mother was feeding him Pedigree Chum, not ball-bearings and cement. He did that up until the date of his death at 15, where the poor little bugger had a heart-attack on my parent's bathroom floor.

To be fair, I grew up walking into the bathroom after my parents, I'm not surprised he had a bloody heart-attack.

Naturally, we had a range of hamsters (Boris, Truffles, Snowy, then we stopped naming them as they invariably escaped and disappeared into the walls) and rabbits. We used to build massive runs for the hamster from Lego until one hamster started filling his cheeks with Lego bricks which put paid to any future construction. Hell, if it hadn't been for that hamster I could have been the next Frank Gehry. Still, if ifs and buts were sweets and nuts, we'd all have a lot to eat.

twochubbycubs on: workmen and drivers

Ah, autumn. It's finally arrived. You know how you know autumn has truly arrived? It's really very simple – it's not the leaves on the trees turning russet and golden, nor is the first icy chill in the air oh no, it's when you first spot the first sharing of 'MUSLIMS WANT 2 BAN THE POPEYE LIKE IF U THINK THIS ISA DISC RACE IGKNORR IF U H8 EVRY1' on facebook.

Just for the record, this is a disc race. The word you're aiming for is a **disgrace**, as in 'I am a **disgrace** to my peers for sharing this hateful nonsense'. Twat. I've had my first one already this year. Don't share hatred!

Anyway, not sure where that little nugget of anger popped from, as I'm actually feeling quite laid back. Apologies that we stopped posting for a bit but well, we're busy folk and plus, in all honesty, it's hard to eke out 700 exciting words about doing very little thanks to ear infections, busy work and house problems. Some random thoughts, though.

Paul pointed out that I must have come across as a right unsympathetic arse with the guy who comes around and cleans my car, and not least because the poor sod has to sit in a mist of my farts, Haribo wrappers and chest hair whilst he scrubs away at my accelerator and that weird second pedal in the middle that I have no idea what purpose it solves. See, he was supposed to be at ours last weekend and failed to turn up, leaving me seething and sighing dramatically to the point where Paul diagnosed me with COPD and put me on an oxygen feed. He texted a few hours later to say his mother had been taken into hospital, hence no contact, and I said it was fine, no worries, we can re-arrange. See, I'm not a complete bastard.

If I was a bastard I'd have driven to the hospital, unplugged her life-support and plugged in the little handheld hoover so he could give my gearstick bag a good suck, but I digress.

He turned up yesterday full of unnecessary apologies and set to work. I asked if he wanted a coffee to keep him warm then promptly forgot about it and went about my business. It was only after spotting him looking forlorn across the garden that I remembered and hastened out with a piping cup of the Blue Mountain that we keep for guests. However, Paul pointed out afterwards that I'd served his coffee in one of our Modern Toss cups, namely the one that says "I don't feel like turning up for work today, so fuck off". I hope he doesn't think I'm being passive aggressive and refuse to polish my rims. Just once I'd like a workman to leave this house and actually want to come back.

Ah! You know how people always say there's never a policeman around when you need one? Well, after five years of driving, it finally happened for me – I was beetling along a dual carriageway in the right hand land, unable to pull over into the left lane as there was slower traffic, when some wankstain in a Vauxhall Insignia came so far up my arse that I almost unrolled a condom as force of habit. He was doing the usual – giant hand gestures, yelling incoherently, wanker signs – I'm not sure if he had realised that I literally couldn't go anywhere as my DS3 was unlikely to squeeze into the passenger seat of the Fiat 500 to the left of me. Cock. I drove on, keeping to the speed limit and putting my hand on my chest and shaking my head ruefully in a very British 'what am I like' gesture, which only served to make him angrier.

However, once I *could* get over, I *did* move over, not least because his face had turned into a mewling over-ripe strawberry at that point and I didn't want the fucker to stroke-out and need mouth to mouth by the side of the road. I rather expected his lips would taste of sweat, cheap cigars and Lynx Atlantis. He sped past, gesticulating all the while, and I promptly forgot about him, the very same way I imagine all his friends and family do at a social occasion. Five minutes later, at the end of the dual carriageway, there he was getting talked to by a very butch looking policeman. Ah, lovely. I made absolutely damn sure I slowed down as I went past but didn't manage to catch his eye – however, he saw me on my fourth trip around the roundabout, and I was sure to give him the tinkliest, most coquettish little way as I trundled past.

Finally, it's been a while since we discussed the

neighbours and that's for a good reason — all bar one have turned into decent human beings. We still have the one who won't talk to us unless he's blowing spittle in our face and complaining about our cats, but then he's also the one who bemoaned to our other neighbours that having two gay men on the street would bring the house prices down, so you can imagine how much we value his opinion. Everyone knows that having a gay couple only improves the house prices because there's no screaming children kicking about and well, we're hardly likely to put a trampoline on our immaculate lawn, are we? The stupid fart.

Anyway, the reason I mention the neighbours is that we're coming up to Christmas cards buying time (sorry!) and we still haven't solved the problem from last year — we realised that we have a couple called Pat and Les on the street but no fucking clue which is which. I know it doesn't matter but I hate not knowing, not least because they're decent people and always make a point of saying 'morning **James**, you're looking slim' or "sorry **Paul**, can you come and retrieve your car, a slight gust has blown it into our lobelia", to which I can only stutter and say 'howdo...my love' or similar. Is it Patrick and Lesley? Patricia and Les? Bah. At least we know what to call the homophobic neighbour, although, as he's deaf, he's must be mystified as to why we call him a Count as he walks past scowling at our cats.

twochubbycubs on: family BBQs

Can I just get the ultimate first world problem out of the way first, in the hope that someone out there can solve it for me? Every time I switch my Mac on to write I have to clart about in the system settings to make the Caps Lock key active as soon as I start to type. Why? Why can't it come on the second I press it? I know using the Caps Lock key to capitalise letters as you type is just one level above running your fingers under words as you read but I don't care, I was too busy wiping smudged ink off my left hand in school to properly type. Not even a euphemism – being left-handed in a school where you have to write in proper ink was a nightmare.

Speaking of solving problems, I'll say no more than how excellent the DVLA are at dealing with complaints and really, they employ the most terrific staff. I rescind everything I said in my previous post and really, can't say enough about how good they are. Yep, they have sorted out the issue with the shitbiscuit Micra and now I'm good to go! Thank you, Guardian Angel. I know, I've got more faces than the town clock, and each one of them is putting things in its mouth that it shouldn't.

So, BBQs then. Let's be frank – no-one wants to sit nibbling away at a limp bit of lettuce whilst people shove more meat into their mouths than an eager lady on a football bus.

You have no idea how much stress I went through trying

to decide on the correct spelling of barbeque. It's acceptable with either a Q or a C, so if anyone is feeling they want to comment telling me it is wrong, I invite them to go find a church and sit on the steeple. Can you tell I'm cranky?

BBQs were always a mixed affair in our families. In my house barbecues consisted of enough black smoke to warrant someone knocking on the door and asking my dad if he was burning tyres in the back garden, a chicken breast that had the unique feature of being pure carbon on the outside and still clucking on the inside and running around the garden until the shits kicked in and then it was twenty minutes sitting on the toilet crying. My parents hosted barbeques of an evening for adults only, where all us kids could do is look mournfully from our bedroom windows like the children in Flowers in the Attic whilst everyone chomped party food under a solid ceiling of Lambert and Butler smoke. I did once light the barbeque at 5am in the morning when my parents were away and I had people over, although the bewhiskered chin of our neighbour appearing and tutting at us soon put paid to that fancy. To be fair, who *does* want to be woken up by some posh bird from Hexham screeching her way through the opening of B*Witched's C'est La Vie with her knickers around her ankles? Not me.

Paul confirms that his barbecue experiences were much the same, save for a time when someone enlivened proceedings by accidentally kicking a gas canister into the fire. I've always wondered why Paul always looks so shiny and surprised, now we know. He was fed 'Mum salad' which consisted of lettuce (iceberg, heaven forbid there would be flavour), chopped tomato (always almost green, heaven forbid there would be flavour) and cucumber (yeah, you get it). This would all be put in neat vinegar and served with a healthy side of coughing. I do love it when Paul tells me stories of his childhood, it's always like a Catherine Cookson novel but with more knock-off fag brands. There'd always be a bowl of microwaved-to-fuckery golden rice which was served in the same bowl used if anyone needed to vomit, oh, and this bit I love because we had exactly the same — a french stick from that bakery in the Co-op whose name escapes me cut into discs and buttered.

Truly, those were golden times.

twochubbycubs on: swimming

We've been swimming. Good god I know. Normally we confine getting our tits out to times when we're at least two large water masses away from the UK, but balls to that – literally buoyed up with goodwill from the gym, we thought we'd dip our toe in the water, not least before all the swimming pools in the United Kingdom get filled up with cement and turned into posh hat shops. Anyway, look at the state of us – at least you know we're going to float with all the blubber.

I love the thought of swimming – I enjoy thinking about getting up early, getting myself a nice fresh towel, driving myself to the baths and doing a few luxurious lengths of the pool before laughing gaily in the changing rooms and talking of times past with some accountant with a verruca. It never happens though. It's probably the early morning – we have four alarms in the morning and it's only the fourth, an exceptionally loud chorus of Peter Andre's Mysterious Girl playing through every speaker in the house, that gets us up. There's a lot to be said for having a fancy connected house sound-system but having that tangerine-faced little shit-tickler caterwauling throughout until you get to the iPad and turn him off isn't one of them.

I did used to swim with my old flatmate, Mary, but she stopped going when she thought the chlorinated water was giving her cystitis. Not the regular parade of blokes you understand, but the mild waters of Hexham baths. She'd put on a coach over the weekend. I've always fancied having a pop at wild swimming, which, from what I understand from the Guardian, is where lots of people whose first name ends in a -reh or a -rah sound get together, show off their varicose veins, swim in a river and then stop for an elderflower press on the way home. That's fine but my closest river is the Wansbeck and I don't fancy swimming using someone else's recently passed stool as earplugs. Plus, remember, I'm scared of dams and sluices and grates and weirs. I'd wind up having a panic attack in the water near a sewage pipe and end up with Michael Buerk narrating my dramatic rescue, with candid overhead shots of me being winched into the helicopter on a slab of tarpauline like the time that poor whale got stuck in the Thames. Fuck that.

Now, the last time we *did* venture into a swimming pool that we hadn't rented all to ourselves was at David Lloyd, where the pool comes with a steam room that makes you smell like oranges. Which is great, given a lot of the ladies (and indeed most of the men) had the skin colour of a bottle of Tropicana as it was. We didn't enjoy it because there were so many beady eyes watching us attempt to swim, so we sat in the Jacuzzi farting just as hard as we could. If you're going to be snooty with me, Madam, you can enjoy the smell of pizza stuffed meatloaf dispersed through so many jets of bubbles.

So anyway, it was at 8am on Saturday morning that found us pouring into Paul's Smart car, destined for the salubrious wonderland that is Morpeth Riverside Leisure Centre. See, Morpeth is canny posh and we thought most of the residents would be too busy making soufflé or beating their help to be bearing witness to our attempts. The morning hadn't started well – the swimming shorts that I had previously worn in Corsica had somehow shrunk in the wash (yes, that was it) meaning the netting inside pressed right up against my *clockweights*, giving them the impression of an overstuffed tangerine bag. Paul was fine, his *elephant's elbow* was tucked away neatly. I cut out the netting, thinking at least I'd be able to use him like a rudder if the water was warm.

It wasn't, by the way.

But I will say this – it was very enjoyable! Yes, you've got to get changed in front of everyone else, and yes, there's always one man see-sawing a towel in his arse-crack like he's rubbing out an error in an exam, and yes, everything jiggles, but once you're in the water and swimming, it's actually very pleasant. Burns about 500 calories an hour if you swim slowly, though let's be realistic. Unless you're committed, you'll do one length and then fart about in the shallow end for an hour before it's a reasonable time to get out and get a Mars bar from the vending machine. Paul likes me to go underwater and swim between his legs, but I've stopped doing that since he left a racing stripe on my freshly-shaved head. We will definitely be talking about going back.

twochubbycubs on: perception

Here's an odd thing. There seems to be a rash of people posting pictures of themselves in dresses on facebook and then asking total strangers how they look, only with the caveat of 'no nasty comments' but 'honest replies please'. How does that work? For a start, don't ask strangers how you look because frankly, there's too many arseholes out there who will be cruel just for the sake of it. But, if you are going to seek the validation of strangers you'll never meet then at least be prepared to accept that some people will have different opinions and that they aren't the Devil Incarnate for saying your dress is a bit tight under the gunt.

Personally, I couldn't give a flying toss what people think I look like – I described my own body as looking like a landslide of hairy Trex just the other day – and it's a very liberating place to be. I spent years hidden behind a giant black coat like the Scottish fucking Widow when I was younger because I was ashamed of my man-boobs and having to buy my school clothes from the adult section in BHS. But life's too short to care – no-one ever, in the throes of death, turns to their loved one and says '**yes, but Suzanne from Warrington thought I looked fab-hun-xox in my Primark bikini**', after all.

That said, I did have a rather mortifying moment the other night when Paul, in his haste to get all of our holidays photos on Facebook, accidentally uploaded a completely nude photo of me getting into an outside bath in Cornwall which sat in our photo albums before the sound of retching from all around the North East finally reached us and I hastily deleted it. Not because I'm ashamed as such but really, I could do without my friends and co-workers knowing that my arse-cheeks look like someone stood on a pumpkin and rolled it in cat-hair.

Not that such privacy is everyone's concern, though. I had to remove a couple of distant friends from my facebook because every nuance of their tedious lives was played out via passive aggressive memes, hospital check-ins and barely legible statuses about 'standin on mi one agin'. The hospital check-in is the most baffling – big status about waiting in A&E or 'PRAY FOR MY LITTLE MONIQUA-MARIELEIGH' then, when people invariably comment asking what's wrong (*whts up hun??*) they are either ignored or worse, the old '*inbox uz hun*'. I hate it – mostly because it's just attention-seeking, but also because I'm incredibly nosy and not finding out leaves me massively unsatisfied, like being interrupted by someone coming home unexpectedly just as you reach Batter Splatter Point. One for the gentlemen, that.

God, I miss the heady days of logging in and out of ICQ (3536698204, oh yes*) to get someone to notice you, or changing the MSN Messenger tagline to some kind of meaningful lyric to really show you meant business. Such innocent times indeed.

Anyway, enough reminiscing. I wanted to do something with a rainbow theme as it's Gay Pride month and well, after my post last week was followed up by the absolutely awful events in Orlando, I thought it might be a nice idea. So many lives lost because some knobhead couldn't handle the fact he liked a bit of cock. Great work, you callous shitbag. I hope the 72 virgins waiting for you are all rough, hairy powertops with vein-canes like those snake draught excluders nanas used to put under the door.

Actually, you know, it's shit like that that reinforces what I was saying about not caring what others think of you – life's too bloody short. You never know what's coming round the corner.

twochubbycubs on: local celebrities

'tis a lovely day. Now see, whenever Saturday comes around, I always think we should fill it with fun activities and marvellous days out because within the blink of an eye it'll be Monday again and I'll be sick of my life. There's only so much enthusiasm one can fake for getting into a car and looking at the back of some cockknocker in an Audi for forty-five minutes on a Monday morning. But invariably it'll get to noon, Paul will peel himself out of the soggy patch, make the bacon sandwiches and we'll spend two hours farting about doing fuck all. Then really it's getting on for being too late to go out and make a day of it, so instead we end up watching X-Files and turning pale from the lack of sunlight. In my defence, I was going to spend the day weeding the flower-beds but one of the litters of flimflam up the street are having a BBQ and I can't concentrate for the smell of Iceland sausages not being cooked correctly and the tinny sound of Now That's What I Call Inevitable Domestic Violence playing over cheap speakers. I stepped outside to hang out some shirts and someone was loudly discussing Crocs as if they were anything other than fit for a bonfire so I came straight back in. Pfft.

I suppose I could entertain myself by watching the football but really, no. I can't see the appeal. I see grown men crying (possibly because of the tear gas) on the television and feel nothing but cold embarrassment.

I'm not afraid to show my emotions but I can't leak over someone not kicking something else into a football net. I don't feel national pride stirring when Rooney lumbers out looking like someone shaved Susan Boyle and spun her through Sports Direct and it annoys me more than avocado being synned that none of the players sing the national anthem properly, instead choosing to mouth the approximate sounds and keep their heads buried into their dandruff-free shoulders. I come from Newcastle, a city known for its enthusiastic football supporters, but I confess the only reason I own a football shirt is because my ex used to like using it for role play. I still don't know who Jimmy Five Bellies is.

And it's not as if many people haven't tried to get me into football. My parents used to have loads of people around to watch the matches back in the day when Newcastle United were half-decent. I used to watch every other match that I could but it wasn't out of interest or passion, oh no, it was more for the opportunity to try name-brand buffet food – Pringles instead of Stackers and Diet Coke instead of Påpsi Mild. The luxury! This was when football would be faintly interesting, too – when Newcastle beat Manchester United 5-1 or when Kevin Keegan was blowing spittle into the camera on Sky Sports. I could name you more players from 1996-1999 than I could modern day footballers, but I suppose that's because you rarely see their faces given they're always rolling around on the grass clutching their ankles.

Darren Peacock used to have a lovely home in the village that I grew up in, and he'll remain my favourite player ever simply by virtue of giving us all a tin of Quality Street each for Hallowe'en – and this was before the tin was the size of an engagement ring box. I've met Alan Shearer twice in my career and each time he's been nothing short of an arse – entitled, self-aggrandising and absolutely in love with himself. Honestly, if you're going to pick a Geordie to make you wet, don't make it him with his baldy heed and face that looks like he's always trying to remember if he's switched the iron off. I appreciate that there aren't many other Geordies to choose from that'll make your Birth Cannon tingle. Jimmy Nail looks like a donkey being told bad news. Robson Green is 2ft tall and apparently suffers from the same arse-ache as Shearer. Sting would be too busy cooing at his own reflection to satisfy you and well, you can't have Ant without Dec.

We did give the world Charlie Hunnam though, so you can thank us later for that.

twochubbycubs on: homosexuality

I was talking with a colleague yesterday about the hanky code. For those who don't get the gay newsletter, the hanky code was/is a system used mainly by gay blokes back in the seventies and eighties to subtly clue in possible paramours (for those less classy: shags) as to their sexual predilections. A dark blue hanky in the right back pocket meant you preferred being the garage rather than the car. Grey meant you liked light bondage, black meant you liked extremely heavy BDSM and pain, like being made to sit through The X-Factor without having a mallet to repeatedly set about your skull with. Somewhat disconcertingly, the hanky for a chap who likes men who smokes cigars is described as 'tan', whereas the colour for someone who wants to act as a *full* toilet (i.e. someone who fancies a Hot Karl: don't fucking google it) is 'brown'. I genuinely don't think I could tell you the difference between brown and tan, and imagine the horror of going back to someone's house for a Montecristo and a chat about socio-economics only to be confronted with them squatting over you with a determined gurn on their face. YIKES.

And anyway, it wouldn't work for me – I have trouble spotting Paul in a room, and he's the size of a family tent. Trying to get me to differentiate colours, especially when blood is rushing to a head on my body that doesn't contain my brain, is just asking for trouble.

It's almost a shame that the hanky code has died off, I reckon it would be interesting if we all, quite literally, nailed our colours to the mast. We certainly live in a time where people are open and being gay is so much more accepted. It's brilliant. I was driving home the other day past a school (this isn't as Operation Yewtree as it might sound) and there was a young lad walking up the street, surrounded by girls, as flamboyant and camp as you like – more mince than even our fabulous Musclefood deal (BEST LINK EVER). No attempt to hide it – and why should he – and whilst he might have just been a colourful young straight lad, my gaydar pinged and I thought it marvellous. I reckon we're about twenty years from it just not being a thing at all, I reckon.

I've certainly been lucky, having never experienced any kind of homophobia. There's been jokes about my sphericalness and god knows I endured many a crack about my long black hair, but never the fact I'm a backdoor betty. Perhaps because I've always been hard to push over, who knows? I've never hidden Paul away – I'd need a fucking big piece of camouflage netting for one – and although I like playing the 'partner' game when I meet someone new (i.e. using non-gender specific terms of endearment when talking about Paul – my partner, Fats Waller, my bitch, slave), I'm always proud to say I'm a gay man.

I have my own feelings about the ever-increasing list of

genders and sexualities which I won't share here, only to say I genuinely struggle to understand some of the more far out terms and, personally, I think there's a chance that identity problems won't be taken as seriously when someone describes themselves as identifying as an otherkin or as a ze (someone who believes 'he' has negative connotations of gender, apparently). I get gender fluidity, I think (i.e. I think I understand it) but when someone describes as a non-cis pivotgender being, it just makes my head hurt. To be quite honest, it makes me feel old and confused. Perhaps that's my own ignorance though. Hmm.

Anyway look, I'm not here to reflect on my life as a shirtlifter. I really just wanted to crack a joke about tan/brown hankies! Let's get the recipe out!

twochubbycubs and Helen G on: online dating

Paul and I are out and about tonight, so I'm going to bring in a guest writer for tonight's post, who is going to talk to us all about online dating. This isn't an area I've had much experience in – see when I was growing up, it was just a case of logging into gay.com, putting 14/m/newc in and twenty minutes later I was being bundled into a transit van for puppies and sweets. I'm kidding, I was legal age and too fat to bundle anyway. Roll, perhaps. I had an awkward date with someone who bought me a necklace from Argos and then didn't say a bloody word as we tortured ourselves through a Pizza Hut buffet. Paul had someone give him a £20 Argos gift-card with £4.98 left on it. Still, both of our gentleman suitors received anal in exchange. We don't fuck about at twochubbycubs! Over to our guest writer, then. As usual, because I'm a big egotistical horror, I'll be butting in, and also, please remember that these guest writer articles give someone a chance to tell a story – don't be mean! Lots of feedback please! All those who have submitted articles, we're aiming for one a week and I'm drawing randomly. If you've sent in stuff and haven't made it online, don't cut yourself, you'll be cubbed up soon enough. Anyone else who wants a go leave it in the comments below. I'll be the only one to see it, don't worry!

Our guest writer tonight is Helen "Whistling Canyon" G. I asked her what her party trick was and she replied something incoherent about a Premier Inn and a hockey team, so who knows...?

clicking – by Helen "Whistlin' Canyon" G

I ventured into the world of online dating for six months a few years ago, this was before the days of Tinder mind, so I have no idea about this swiping left or right stuff. I'd only swipe left and right when I was alone in the bath. Like rubbing ink off a hand. Back when I was doing online dating you simply messaged someone and hoped they replied, and then didn't turn out to be a weirdo / murderer. Sadly, they often do, but ah well, needs must.

My first date was only a couple of days after I joined, and I was surprised. I had thought nobody would message a fatty like me! The guy seemed OK, we had a couple of coffee dates, and a couple of nights out for drinks at country pubs. All seemed OK. Then he asked me did I want to come to his house and he would cook for me – and I could stay over. I figured, yeah go on then – I had only been single a couple of months after a long term relationship and I had no idea what was the decent amount of time these days before someone gets a look at your bits. (**James: it's usually about fifteen seconds, just enough to shake the drips off**)

He picked me up and said we would call at the supermarket on the way to his for the ingredients and some wine. Perfect – though it would mean a lot of 'no no, put it back, I don't eat chocolate' and fakery. Plus, what if he took me down the lube and condoms aisle and spent ten minutes giving me knowing winks and leers? As long as he didn't pick up a box of Trim, I didn't care. Hell, if he picked up a box of Magnum XXL I'd have let him ravish me amongst the frozen peas. Anyway, off we went, with me full of excitement for what treats awaited me...and he proceeded to buy reduced chicken breast – you know the ones with the yellow stickers on that need to go now before they go off in the next few hours? Yep, them. The ones that cause fights amongst the blue-haired, yellow-chinned folk. And then we went to the wine aisle and he told me to choose anything from the three for a tenner deal. Charming. I'm not a snob but surely the first time you cook for someone new you would at least let them feel they are worth full price chicken? Or if you really want to buy a bargain, don't take them with you? Swap them out into a Waitrose bag and make your date feel like a queen? He also bought two apples for pudding. Hmm. **(James: to be fair, I used to buy oranges before a hot date. Keeps them quiet if you jam one in their gob. If you've got a fat date, make it a chocolate orange. It's like poppers for us chunkers)**

We got to his house and I soon noticed none of the door frames had doors attached. I mentioned this and he said he didn't like doors and he liked his cat to have free run of the house. Fine, but this included the toilet. No door on the toilet – fuck that! I'm all for being open but no-one needs to see me grunting away like Mel Smith solving a wordsearch as I have a crap. Plus, he was always kissing his cat and then trying to kiss me with an inch of cat hair stuck to his stubble. I'm not going to lie, I did envision to start with that he might end up with hairs from a pussy caught in his stubble, but not this way. NOT THIS WAY. No offence to cat owners by the way. I would feel the same if it was dogs, horses, sheep – anything. Needless to say that didn't really go anywhere.

My next date was with a guy who spent two weeks asking me to go on a date with him, then not being able to make it, so rearranging – when we finally went out we had an alright night but he didn't look at all like his photos and his craic was shit! Then he told me he was moving to France so wasn't looking for anything serious but he would very much like to see the inside of my flat. He claimed it wasn't a euphemism but I've seen a barely disguised stiffy before. No thanks pal.

Next up was a fellow divorcee. Nice guy, had a great time both times we went out then the third time let him stay over and then discovered he had thought my first name was something completely different to what it is, and I just thought, if you can't even be arsed to learn my name, you can do one as well mate!

Then was the guy who smoked a joint on our first (and only) date on a Saturday afternoon in a beer garden. Of a family pub. See ya!

Then the penultimate guy was someone I knew from years ago and used to have a crush on. I was so looking forward to the date, as he was the guy EVERYONE fancied back in the day. Well, I don't know what happened in the 15 years in between but he was not that guy. He lectured me all the way through our food about being a vegetarian and how bad I was for eating meat. I still ate all my chicken like. He was wasting his breath. He also told me he didn't have a TV as he believes that aliens can spy on us through the aerials so he only has it hooked up to a PlayStation to watch Blu-Rays on. He was writing a conspiracy play and was hoping to take it to LA and become famous. Honestly was expecting him to whip out a tin foil hat at any moment. There were a few awkward silences which he proceeded to fill by asking me more about what I eat in a typical day and criticising me for having jacket potato several times a week. But he lived on veggie pizzas. So, ya know – he knows all about good nutrition clearly. Bell-end. Incidentally, he texted me a month later after complete silence and said "how about that second date?" Hahaha as if! Then THREE YEARS later he texted me asking for another chance. I didn't even know who it was! Who does that?

James edit: I remember! I did have ONE bad date. We went back to his after a movie and I went to the bathroom to prepare myself and managed to completely block his toilet. He didn't have a brush or anything to swoosh it away with so I had to break it up

with the bottom of a bottle of Radox. The smell was unbearable and, with the mood killed (at least for me, he was 'waiting') I walked right past his bedroom and out of the door into the night. To be fair, I had a lucky escape, as I heard from another acquaintance that he was very much a one-spurt-Burt.

It's not all bad though. I was just about to delete my profile forever when a guy I had approached replied to me apologising for the delayed response but he had been working away and hadn't had access to the Internet. I had messaged him as a long shot as he was a fair bit younger than me and had not expected him to reply. We chatted a bit, exchanged numbers and then after a couple of weeks of texting while he was working away again we eventually managed to squeeze in a last minute date one Sunday afternoon. I was so unprepared, I had been visiting my mam in hospital and it was a boiling hot day and you know hospitals are the hottest places on Earth at the best of times, so I was a right sweaty mess but I went anyway. The rest is history, as they say. We now have a beautiful 2-year-old daughter and live together. So, he was kinda worth wading through all that shit for. And he still fancies me even though I am fat. So, yay!

Aaah, I do love a happy ending, and seemingly the fragrant Helen likes dishing them out.

twochubbycubs on: bloody summer

It's too hot. It's too hot for a long post so damn it, I'm going to post a recipe for six smoothies and go lie down in our air-conditioned bedroom, wailing and calling for Paul to turn me away from the sun.

I hate the hot weather. I really do. I can't be done with it. I'm sweating like a cat burying a shit on a concrete floor. Yes, that's tasteful enough to put in. You should have heard the three I *didn't* put in. I've always been envious of those folk who can seemingly bask in sunlight and thoroughly enjoy it. You have no idea how much I want to take my shirt off and eat ice-cream in the centre of town, but I genuinely think it would cause a riot. Whilst I'm not a *huge* fan of the type of bloke who goes topless the very second the ice warning dings off in his car, it must be a nice feeling. Perhaps I should get a copperplate-writing tattoo on my neck and turn my shoulders red. It ruins every aspect of anything enjoyable – good hearty stews get pushed to one side and replaced with salad, more salad, salad with a bit of salad on the side and salad-salad. I can't face toiling in the kitchen for hours – even by proxy, given Paul is the one who does the cooking – so meals tend to get repetitive. Sex becomes a chore with everything sticking to each other like pulling warm bacon rashers apart. The roads become full of stupidly big cars trundling along at 25 miles an hour with a big plastic shitheap being towed behind them. I know it's terribly fashionable to hate on caravans but look, they're bloody ugly things and almost (unless YOU'RE a driver, you're fine) always pulled by the type of people you know read the Daily Express, furiously circling the word immigrants in thick red pen with spittle on their lips. The men who are more nose-hair than bellend.

Pub gardens become full of braying donkeys taaaalking like thaaas and coughing at people for having the temerity to light up a fag. Beaches become awash with badly parked Dacia Dusters, dog poo and poorly buried Poundland BBQs with a half-life longer than Tellerium-128 just waiting to slice your foot open. You can't open the windows because all of the neighbours are cutting their grass to the exact millimetre meaning the air is so thick with pollen I've only got to sniff daintily at it to make everything inside my face swell-up and turn me into John Merrick's fun-house reflection. Birds singing from 3am in the morning until 2.58am the next day means only one thing – endless half-chewed birds being dragged through the cat-flap and deposited somewhere where I'm absolutely guaranteed to stand during the night when I get up for a piss. You've never known revulsion until you've felt half a sparrow crunch under your toes in a twilit bathroom.

But you know what really fills me with unbridled fury? When people say 'OH BUT YOU'LL MISS THE HEAT WHEN WINTER COMES'. No! No I absolutely fucking won't. I have never turned around in December and said 'well yes Marie, this Christmas vista **is** quite charming but it could only be improved with the top of my head being sweaty, extensive chub-rub on my legs and sinuses like cocktail sticks'. I bloody love the winter! If I'm cold, I can put a jacket on. Well no, I'm Geordie, so I might deign to put a thin t-shirt on if the ends of my fingers turn black. There's nothing you can do when you're too hot except gripe, moan and whinge about it, even when you say you're not going to do a long post. But god it felt good getting all that off my chest.

twochubbycubs go to Peterborough: part one

Normally at this point I'd apologise for being cruel in anticipation of the angry emails and comments I'll get about slagging off a town, but I'm not actually convinced Peterborough has electricity, nevermind the internet, so I shan't bother.

It's all Paul's fault. His family are all from down South whereas my family are from The North. Thus, he sees a lot of my family and only rarely does he venture down South to see his. He hasn't fallen out with them, you understand, but we're talking about a man for whom turning over in the bath to wash himself is an effort — the thought of driving however many miles and spending a weekend nodding at nonsense is beyond him. It's certainly beyond me and that's why whenever Paul has previously slopped family-bound down the A1, I've stayed at home eating delicious food and idly masturbating. It's what every single guy does when his partner leaves and if you're sitting there thinking that your partner doesn't, then you're in for a very rude awakening when you find all the crusty hand smears down the side of the mattress.

Oops, I got diverted. It began a couple of weeks ago when Paul turned to me, ashen-faced, and told me it was time we both went to see his family. I'd have been less frightened, alarmed and upset if he had sent me a letter explaining he was Patient Zero of that antibiotic-resistant gonorrhoea and I could expect a cock like a dripping nose within a week. However, because I'm a gentleman, I acquiesced – not least because Paul's had ten years of trying to decipher my Dad's Geordie accent and eight years of my nana force-feeding him butter sandwiches like he was a foie-gras duck, so me visiting his relatives seemed fair enough.

Just so you're aware, I have visited Peterborough once before – we stayed at Orton Hall and visited the cathedral. It was mildly diverting in the same way a repeat episode of your third favourite TV show may hold your attention. We got drunk with a friend of his and ended up sat in a Vauxhall Nova in a McDonalds car park eating chips. I've literally never felt more street in my life. So we weren't in a rush to repeat that and decided to book a nice hotel on the outskirts. Finding a decent hotel that wasn't massively overpriced turned into such an insurmountable challenge that I threw a sulk once we reached Nottingham on the map and demanded that we just check into the first Premier Inn that came up on the map. We later found out that the Burghley Horse Trials were on and that explained – apparently – why all the hotels were booked up. Personally, I hope all the horses were found guilty.

We agreed that we'd drive down to Peterborough on the Saturday morning in our rented Ford Tedium and despite willing my liver to rupture, I was unable to get out of it. Actually, nevermind getting out of it, I could barely get into our rented car. Perhaps you've been in a Ford Fiesta – do you find the doors ridiculously small and low down? I had to fold myself like an accordion of chafed skin just to get inside. I haven't quite reached the stage where I can't physically fit into a car (probably a few pounds away) but this was a nightmare. I actually think I cracked a rib jumping in after I'd filled the bugger up.

To make my joy complete, Paul decided that he would be the one to drive most of the journey, leaving me to sit in the passenger sit twisting my face and eating crisps. I did spot that, being a fancy new model, I could text the car and it would read out a message for Paul. You may have seen the advert on TV where some spurned husband has the car read out a heart-warming apology and they laugh gaily at one another and ruefully shake their heads? Yeah, well, I got the car to say 'Paul, stop driving like a c*nt' – bet they don't put that in their adverts.

The drive down was spectacularly uneventful – the usual parade of stopping to have a piss in amongst the poo-cloud of eight hundred harried dads and children, paying way over the odds for a cup of tea and moaning about it for ten minutes in the car, spending too much money on the fruit machines in the vain hope I'd win the jackpot and I could whisk Paul away somewhere exotic and full of promise, like Norwich. Nope. We arrived at his mother's house at 11am.

I had a cup of tea. It was nice.

Twenty minutes later we agreed to take his brother out for lunch. I love Paul's brother – he's a proper gentle giant and really knows his stuff. He has severe autism which leads to moments of slight awkwardness when he blurts out to a waitress that she's gorgeous and can share his milkshake. Or, memorably, when he whistled at a poor woman in Seahouses literally three inches from her face as he walked past. He just says what we're all thinking. Anyway, a quick look at decent places to eat nearby turned up absolutely nothing and anyway, he wanted to go to a Bella Italia, so off we went to an industrial estate to have a meal that was about as Italian as I am a Calvin Klein model with a cock like a roll of wallpaper.

I'm not going to review the place in depth because well, it was a Bella Italia for goodness sake, but understand that it was a dismal meal in dismal surroundings for £90. Until that day I would never have thought a pizza could actually look bored but there we have it. We asked for a quiet table away from any noise and the prissy little manager who seated us looked like I'd personally walked into the kitchen and shat in the carbonara. When I first typed that I typoed walked as wanked – that also works, so pick one. He sat us next to the bar with a fetching giant cylinder of blue-roll to sit with. Perhaps he thought we could snack on that in the vain hunt for flavour.

Our starter was described on the menu as a 'real taste of Italy'. Who knew that Italy tasted like a third of those continental sliced meat platters you get in ASDA sweated behind the radiator for an hour or so? It did come with shaved fennel and orange segments but there's only so much excitement you can wring from such a lacklustre repast. Between the three of us we had it finished before the bubbles on my diet coke had come to the surface. Naturally, it cost £15.

We had a pizza each (at £15 a pop) which tasted like a carpet tile smeared with passata and shunned by society. At one point I nearly gave up and smeared the blue roll with tomato sauce to get my money's worth. The sides consisted of six onion rings for £4. 66p an onion ring. I did want to enquire whether or not Gino d'Campo was slicing them personally with a diamond but Paul shook his head at me and said no. Oh and the drinks! The diet coke came in a glass that Thumbelina herself would have considered meagre and, as usual, was more ice than drink. They were £2.60 a time, non-refillable. From my vantage point I was afforded the sight of the barman preparing a 'fresh apple juice' by opening a carton of Tesco Value apple juice and pouring it into a tiny milk bottle. That cost £2.50, by the way.

Desserts were a little better. Paul's brother wanted ice-cream but also wanted to pick the flavours – his treat, so why not. The waitress had the good grace not to vomit into her mouth when he ordered a mixture of rum and raisin, chocolate and bubblegum ice-cream all topped with limoncello sauce and crushed almond biscuits. Paul and I ordered a Mean Joe between us which is apparently:

"Nutty fudge brownies, vanilla and chocolate gelato, chocolate sauce, fresh cream, popping candy, dark chocolate tagliatelle and a wafer curl. He's got it sorted!"

What we got was four scoops of chocolate ice-cream, a brownie that could have been used to chock the tyres of a runaway bus and a shitty look. I've had more delightful desserts free from the Chinese takeaway. Paul's brother gamely ate all of his ice-cream and we settled the bill. You know what stung the most? Our waitress was lovely and I couldn't not tip her, so the meal actually ended up costing £100 in total. Imagine my delight. We bundled Paul's brother back into the car and made our way back to his mother's house to drop him off before the sugar kicked in.

I stroked a dog. It was nice. Paul had threatened in the car to make me laugh by pulling faces at me whilst his mother made conversation with me but that never happened.

We made our way to the Premier Inn, at least comforted by the fact we'd get a good night's sleep, guaranteed. Things got off to a shaky start when Paul realised that the guy checking us in was his mortal enemy from school who had told everyone he was better than everyone else and was off to New York to pursue a music career. Seemingly the bus to the airport terminates at Junction 16 of the A1. Who knew? I had noticed that our welcome was a tad frostier than normal but it was only when Paul explained in the corridor – and I had ascertained that he hadn't actually sucked him off at some point (which, to be fair to me, seemingly applies to anything with testosterone within a 60-mile blast radius of Peterborough) that it all became clear.

The Premier Inn itself wasn't bad, but meh. We were put into a weird extension bit which required trundling down an endless corridor of foist and extra-marital-sex-stink and our room eschewed curtains, instead sealing out the light with a huge set of sliding wooden doors. This mean the room was hot and tiny, the two worst things for two fat blokes. We freshened up (i.e. Paul immediately had an introductory thundering crap in the toilet like he does in EVERY SINGLE HOTEL ROOM WE EVER, EVER BOOK) and set out for his dad's place, a little bit further down the A1.

Well, this was actually lovely. His dad and his partner are lovely, funny folk with witty conversation and big warm hearts. I'm not even being sarcastic (I know!) – we stayed for two hours and it felt like minutes. I'm actually quite a shy person and find making conversation tricky with people I don't know but it was wonderfully easy and I was sad to leave. We did manage to subscribe them to the blog so, if you're reading this Mrs A, take comfort in the fact that you both were a bright spot in an otherwise relentlessly grim weekend!

After leaving we did a cursory glance on Tripadvisor for a delicious place to eat, realised we'd have more marginally more success finding someone with a complete set of teeth and instead decamped to Tesco, where our Saturday night was made complete with a few packets of Cup-a-Soups and some crisps. We both fell asleep in front of the X-Factor, wishing for death.

twochubbycubs go to Peterborough: part two

Where were we...

Ah yes. The charming Norman Cross Premier Inn. After a night spent sweating, tossing and peeling our back fat away from each other with loud slurps, we woke bright and breezy. We decided that we'd take care of our ablutions and then see about getting some breakfast. Can I let you in on a mortifying secret? We chose **not** to get the Premier Inn breakfast that we normally do because it wasn't an unlimited buffet. How greedy, I know. Technically it *was* unlimited in the sense that I could ask the waiter to bring me more bacon, more eggs, more sausages and a portable ECG monitor, but I'm always too shy.

We like our breakfast to spread far beyond what the eyes can see and frankly, if I'm not clutching my chest, hoisting my fat-arse out of my chair and walking to a tureen of beans with the barely-disguised disgusted whispers of the other occupants of the hotel, I'm not interested. We made do with a Twirl from the vending machines and that was that.

We stopped by reception to ask if we could change rooms. I explained that the room was too hot and that Paul's genitals now looked like a trio of celebration balloons left tied to a fence for a week, and the receptionist promised that she would arrange a new room for us once we returned from our day out. The charmer from the day before was obviously off meeting with Big Men in New York. We decamped back to our sweatbox so Paul could slide the chocolate bolt across, giving me time to plan our day.

I logged onto tripadvisor to find something to do. When the third or fourth suggestion is a chain cinema, you know you're in trouble. I searched High Wycombe and Lowestoft (sorry, I'm so proud of that laboured joke that it's staying in) and there was absolutely bot-all to do that didn't require an outrageous drive and the threat of growing old prematurely by osmosis due to close proximity of coach tours.

Eventually Paul's voice piped up from the thunderbox to tell me Bletchley Park (home of the codebreakers during WW2) was about an hour away. Shamefully, my reaction was meh, but faced with the prospect of X-Factor repeats and turning into a prune in the hotel room, we agreed that Milton Keynes our best chance of happiness – something which I'm fairly sure has never, ever been said about Milton Keynes before. Before we yawned our way down the A1 we needed fuel, and thanks to the good folk at the Mace garage in Yaxley, even that turned into a right song and dance.

See, Paul got out, put the nozzle in and clicked the handle. The pump dispensed about 4p worth of fuel then shut off. The lady behind the counter looked grimly at him through the window and ignored his plight – he kept clicking, the fuel would dribble out enough fuel to get us approximately 4ft off the forecourt and then shut off. I'm sitting in the car effing and jeffing because I'd spotted an Esso literally over the road and Paul's clicking away like he's a farmer counting his sheep.

Eventually, the Queen of the Pumps spots something is awry and comes out. What followed was an excruciating exchange where she just didn't accept it was her fuel pump that was broken. No, Paul hadn't 'put it in right' (I find that easy to believe, given the years and years of 'up a bit, down a bit, up a bit more, push forward – honestly, sometimes gay sex is like I'm guiding someone in Knightmare – SIDESTEP LEFT), then he 'wasn't clicking hard enough'. In a gesture that speaks volumes about his character, he decided against going all No Country For Old Men on her and smiled politely throughout. IT TOOK TEN MINUTES. I mean, God loves a trier, but we know how to use a bloody petrol pump for goodness sake, we're not on the fucking Krypton Factor.

She went in and reset the pumps about a dozen times before asking whether we'd like to switch to another problem. Guessing that the second pump would probably require us to solve a cryptic crossword and a complex Sudoko we politely declined and went on our way over the road, where only a packet of Cadbury's Snacks could calm our ire. I wouldn't have minded so much but Paul actually went in and paid the £2.10 of fuel we eventually got. Bah.

Driving in Milton Keynes is an adventure, isn't it? Bill Bryson absolutely hated the place and whilst I thought it looked alright from the car, I had no desire to step out and trip the light fantastic myself. Things became tense when we realised the Sat-Nav, built into the car with no obvious way to turn her down, was having a complete shitfit over the amount of roundabouts. If the British government ever need to break a terrorist, they need only to strap them into a Ford Fiesta and let them endure 20 minutes of 'AT THE NEXT ROUNDABOUT TAKE THE SECOND LEFT AT THE NEXT ROUNDABOUT TAKE THE THIRD EXIT AT THE NEXT ROUNDABOUT TAKE THE THIRD ROUNDABOUT TAKE THE JUNCTION TAKE TAKE TAKE ROUNDABOUT ROUNDABOUT ROUNDABOUT'. I felt like I was being driven by Johnny 5 in the throes of a nervous breakdown.

We arrived at Bletchley Park with only mild tinnitus and discovered a small computer museum at the arse-end of the car-park. Being giant geeks we were very excited, and, being giant geeks, we waddled breathlessly to the entrance just as the volunteer flipped the open sign over and opened the door. Hooray! We immediately got stuck behind a visitor who thought he was God's Gift to comedy, every line to the cashier was a 'joke' and bit of patter. It was just awful. I had a thought that it must be what it is like to be stuck behind me in Tesco but I quickly tucked that thought away into the same mind-folder where the 'I bet that ingrown toenail goes septic and you lose your foot' and 'is your heart supposed to go boom-badum-boom-badum-BOOM-whoo when you climb stairs'.

The computer museum was a treat. It was a pleasure to be somewhere which wasn't full of screaming children getting their arses smacked and stupid interactive displays that don't work. No, this museum was decidedly (and fittingly) old school – full of amazing old computers and genuine pieces of history like the Tunny machines and Colossus, which were both instrumental in helping decipher secret messages during World War Two. We revelled at the old computers from times way past and then were horrified to find that computers we remembered from our youth were classed as 'retro'. I've never felt so old. A lot of the old machines were switched on and I couldn't resist typing

HELLO SORRI HUNS MI APP IS DOWN HOW MANI SUNS IN ALDI YOGURTS PLEASE XOXOXO

into an old ICL DRS6000. I know, I'm a stinker. We did want to sit and play on the old BBC computers (I've never finished Granny's Garden and god-damnit, I still remember where the magic tree is) but there was a group of three lads in the room spraying spittle through their braces and chuckling loudly about frame-rates. Is there a word for intimidation mixed with pity? I bet there's a German word. Regardless, we moved on and after a quick fanny about with a few knobs in the classroom (oh that takes me back) we were done. We left a lovely positive Tripadvisor report and made our way down to the actual Bletchley Park estate.

Now, something to annoy you, due to ongoing issues with the managements of both attractions, you pay twice – once to visit the Computing Museum (block H of the estate) and once more to visit the rest of the estate. Hmm. Naturally, because the estate had a few interactive boards and a video tour, the price for entry is £34.50 for the two of us. Bah. However, this too was a lovely few hours – we wandered around at our own pace, taking in the interesting stories and displays, and credit where it's due, the attraction does an excellent job of celebrating the amazing work that folks like Alan Turing did. I confess to a little bit of museum-fatigue: there's only so many times you can walk into a hut, look at a map on a table and nod appreciatively. It also gave us both pause to think that only 64 years ago being gay was cause enough to lock someone up for gross indecency. How far we've come, eh.

twochubbycubs go to Peterborough: part three

When you left us we were just finishing up Bletchley Park and steeling ourselves for the journey back to the hotel. Despite the sat-nav's attempts to make our head explode scanner style by repeating roundabout over and over, it was a pleasant enough journey and we were back at the hotel in no time at all. True to their word, they had switched our rooms to an altogether more charming one (although Paul's face was ashen when he realised it was up a flight of stairs, the poor lamb). They told us to nip back to the old room and pack our things, which we promptly did.

On our thigh-chaffing walk to the old room, Paul pushed me out of the way and hurtled ahead. Turns out that his ashen-face was more down to the immediate and pressing need to dispose of the World's Shittiest Italian Meal from the day before. I, being a thoughtful chap, told him that he'd need to hold it in because the housekeepers would be waiting for us to leave so they could clean the room and there was no way I was adding 'walking into a deathcloud of barely digested pancetta' onto their list of reasons to hate life. So began the quickest debate you've ever seen, with Paul dancing back and forth on his feet and me being firm and telling him he had to hold it. I only relented when he said it was either the toilet of the old room or the hood on my hoodie in the corridor.

Well, you can't argue with that. I stepped aside. There was a lot of noise and motion.

Of course, it smelt like someone had died, meaning we had to stay in the room for twenty minutes frantically wafting the curtains and flapping the duvet to try and get the stench to dissipate. I don't want a mark on my Premier Inn record that states we leave the room smelling like someone has burnt a tyre full of human hair. Having done the best we could, with me liberally sprinkling Rive D'Ambre everywhere (and that stuff is £170 a bottle, just saying: we're fat, it's the only designer thing we can wear), we switched rooms.

Why is it, no matter what time of the day or night it is, you can turn E4 or More4 or 4Skin or 4goodnesssakepickaname on, there's always a Come Dine with Me quintet to watch? At the very last there's a Four in the Bed chain to work through. Having realised that there was absolutely bot-all-else to do on a Sunday in fair Peterborough, we settled down with vending machine snacks and a tiny cup of Barely Grey and made the best of it. Naturally, we fell asleep. Say what you want about Premier Inn, they do make a damn comfy bed. I should know, we've got one installed.

We woke up at 7, full of piss and vinegar for falling asleep and wasting our evening, only to realise that there was nowhere in Peterborough that caught our eye. Paul did suggest a visit to a floating boat which served Chinese food but then we bought realised we didn't fancy stopping every ten minutes on the way home to revisit our dinner. Casting our net a little wider we eventually spotted somewhere that *did* take our fancy – Stilton, just over the roundabout. Lovely. I made to make a reservation at a lovely looking place that I can't remember the name of (Bell Inn?) but Paul reminded me of something.

See, my lovely, confident husband frets something chronic about going to 'nice places' to eat. He has an inferiority complex – he absolutely shouldn't, he's wonderful, but he thinks he is going to make an arse of himself. I reassured him that he amazing in every way and so we made a reservation and set off.

Well, honestly. It was a gorgeous little pub and the menu sounded great. We were given a seat on a tiny table by the fire (not a criticism mind) and ordered our food. Paul was a little on edge but we got through the starters without any difficulties. The mains arrived and we got stuck in. Everything was going just so until Paul illustrated a particularly bold point with an expansive sweep of his arm, which pushed his pint of Pepsi off the table and down the wall. Nobody noticed, thankfully, despite the pool of Pepsi around my feet. Fair enough, everyone's allowed one. I went to take a bite of my burger – one of those overly stuffed, towering piles of meat that are the style these days – only to have the cheese covered meat slide out and cascade down my pink shirt. Great! All equal.

Naturally, Paul had to one-up me. He'd ordered pork belly which came with a smashing bit of crackling which, try as he might, Paul couldn't crack into small enough bits of eat. He couldn't very well pick it up and eat it with his hands so he tried many different ways to get into it. No joy. I suggested using the knife as a chisel and to tap it from the top with his hands, like hammering a nail. I thought he'd be careful. Of course not. The ham-fisted dolt hit his knife so hard that it not only shot through the crackling but also cleaved his dinner plate in two. He very much won that round. We finished our meal, polished off a cheese-board, paid the bill and left a hearty tip before we were asked to leave. It was a gorgeous meal and a lovely place, mind.

We stopped at the hotel 'bar' for a gin and tonic – me resisting the urge to ask if he'd gone to press the juniper berries himself he was gone that long. We won £7 from the Itbox and made for bed, safe and snug in the knowledge that we'd be home in the morning.

We woke at eight, peeling ourselves apart once more like two flip-flops in the sun due to the room being the temperature of lava. I walked around in the shower for ten minutes until I was wet enough to clean myself and then we made for the car. It was here we made a rash decision. You need to understand we were motivated purely by hunger at this point.

We went to a Toby Carvery for our breakfast.

I know, we're monsters. I'd seen an advert somewhere and it seemed like a filthy proposition – and as I've mentioned before, we do love a buffet breakfast.

I barely need to tell you how awful it was. It was foul. I could talk about the fact we were having breakfast on an industrial estate. I could describe the food: baked beans cooked last November, bacon you could reupholster a settee with, sausages with less meat content than a butcher's pencil, eggs that I'm still working through my teeth now. Hell, I could go on about the fact that they advertise the fact they have 'special breakfast Yorkshire puddings' (i.e. the Yorkshire puddings they didn't sell in the roast dinner the day before that were so hard I could have used them to stop a runaway train) or the 'cheese and potato hash' (i.e. the roast potatoes that didn't get used the day before with a bit of Primula added) or even the 'special breakfast gravy' which was yesterday's gravy with some tomato ketchup in it. This gravy didn't so much have a skin as a coat of fucking armour. I've never had to slice gravy before, I can tell you.

No, what put me off (after all that, shocking!) was the sheer, unadulterated, naked greed from the person sitting a couple of tables away. Everyone makes a pig of themselves at a buffet, yes, but this guy deserved a gold medal. Three plates of breakfast, each heaped like a mini cowpat of excess. He ate and he ate and he ate without barely drawing breath – which was in itself not such a bad thing because when he did breathe it sounded like someone hoovering up a pile of rubber gloves. When he did stop he burped, and it wasn't a polite wee burp into a hand like decent folk, but a really resounding *baaaarp* like he was clearing out just another pocket to cram breakfast into. Bleurgh.

I must be clear: I adore a buffet, I'm capable of great amounts of eating, but have a bit of fucking decorum. When your chin is more bacon fat than skin, stop. This is why we don't do those all-you-can-eat Chinese buffets in town – you always get someone who treats it as though it's their last meal and I'm sorry, it makes me feel queasy.

We drove home, ashamed of ourselves for the breakfast and full of regrets that we'd spent as much money as we did on an awful weekend. It was lovely meeting Paul's brother and Paul's dad and his partner, but those were the only high points in an otherwise dismal 72 hours. Paul chastised me constantly for driving at 90mph all the way home but in my defence, it was the fear of breaking down and the car having to be towed back to Peterborough that kept my foot firmly on the accelerator. Never again.

We nipped back home to pick up my car and then made our way back to the car rental. Paul, naturally, forgot to have the windows down on the drive over so when the rental guy bent down to check the interior of the car for cleanliness, he visibly paled. I'm surprised he didn't charge us for making vegetable soup in the boot. Paul also helpfully forgot to un-sync his phone from the car's entertainment system so when the guy started the car back up, it reconnected with Paul's phone and started blasting the chorus from Big Girls Don't Cry by Lolly. A fitting end.

Naturally, upon our return, the cats paid entirely no attention to us and carried on licking their bottoms. We did have a moment of hilarity when we realised we'd accidentally packed the little purple Premier Inn branded bed-runner into our suitcase. I confessed our accidental theft on Twitter and they kindly told us to keep it. I put it on the bed for ten minutes, Paul chortled, then we both realised exactly how many different accountants and salesmen must have wiped their cocks on it. We've packed it away in the cupboard for when his mother comes over.

And that's that. I was disappointed but Paul even more so – he remembered growing up in a place with lots to do. Heraclitus wrote that 'it is impossible to step into the same river twice', and no more so is that true then when you go 'home'. Bah.

twochubbycubs and Vicky M on sticks and stones

Partially because I'm too lazy to type and also because tonight's guest writer Vicky looks the sort to smash your knees in over an unpaid catalogue debt, I'm going to hand you over to her. Vicky would like to talk about something not normally mentioned on this blog – being thin. Let's go. Mind, because I'm an egotistical terror, I'll be butting in throughout. REMEMBER, these articles are done by people who fancy taking a stab at writing but don't have an outlet. If you can't say anything nice, keep it schtum. For me! FAIR WARNING: there's a lot of blue language in this post!

---

sticks and stones – by Vicky "Thundergash" M

So – James has invited us mere mortals to write in his blog – I feel like I've been invited to have tea with the Queen. Except it's a Queen that swears a lot and slugs gin like a menopausal housewife. (**James: our Queen does have a much better beard, mind**)

We've been advised that we should write about what we know. Hmm. I don't know loads – I'm just a normal 35-year-old mum of 2 kids.

I do know about weight though. Oh, I know a hell of a lot about weight, on both ends of the scale (scale, geddit?) (**James: I'll do the jokes, please**) (**I'm kidding**)

Firstly – I have Marfan syndrome (look it up if you want to be nosey) – it basically means I have long skinny limbs and according to textbooks I should be as skinny as a beanpole. Pfft. I was, as a kid. Skinny jokes were all I heard growing up and I absolutely hated my body. I was the tall gangly kid and to this day it annoys me that people can be told *"you're too skinny – you need to eat"* yet fat comments are a no-no. Why can't people just not comment at all? Wankers. I seem to have slipped from one end of the fat-scale to the other. I had legs like string – no, not those slender, sexy legs that people gaze lustfully upon. I'm talking bony with knobbly knees that invite cat calls of *"oy Wednesday legs! Wednesday gonna snap?"*

(**James: I feel really bad for laughing at that one, but see I'm a huge fan of word-play. Also, I didn't need to look up Marfan syndrome – one of my exes had it bad. Now normally I wouldn't say anything bad about anyone with a disability but fuck it, he was an absolute shitbiscuit, so I'll say this now – if you ever want to experience seventeen seconds of sex that feels like you're wrestling a human-sized Daddy Longlegs with a shit haircut and a willy like those long matches posh people use to light the Aga, give Neil from Northumberland a call**).

Yep – being skinny was a fucking ball (a ball of shite more like) now I know I'm meant to say "embrace your body sisters (and brothers) love every part of yourself!" but try telling a 15-year-old girl that. I hated my body. One day I hit puberty and widened. It seemed to happen overnight. I looked like an HGV reversing up a back lane. I got hips, thighs, an arse you could hide Shergar in and stretch marks all over – on my shoulders, my hips, my bastard thighs – you name it.

My mum would tut and kindly say "those jeans would look great if your hips were smaller" (cheers ma!)

as I got into my twenties (after giving birth to a 10lb 12oz baby) I looked like a road map naked, or perhaps a saddened zebra, with my big massive tits resting kindly on my deflated belly. Gorgeous eh? Anyway, here's my point. I'm a size 16 or on a good day a generous size 14. To this day I get told "there's nothing on you! I'd love your figure!" cos I do now have decent legs (ha! take that bullies!) but I still hate what I see in the mirror. No amount of dieting and exercise can hide my saggy tits, my C-section scar and how Mother Nature decided to gift my skin with probably 40% of it covered in stretchmarks.

What annoys me is the "I'd love your body" comments. No, no you wouldn't. I dislike my body and massive hips just as much as the next woman.

Did I mention that I recently got engaged? I finally met a man who loves me and my dodgy bod. Does it matter that whilst I'm naked I often have "how can he stay hard when he's looking at this?!" running through my head? Not to him. He's 17 stone (**James: pffft amateur!**) and loves cake and bread. I LOVE his pot belly, I wouldn't change a thing on him and sometimes (on a good day) I let it sink in that he feels the same way about me.

I suppose I should be happy and if this was a film I'd discover a way to love myself. But I'm not in a film. Haven't been since 'Vixen Vicky and the Broken Down Rugby Coach 8: Fill 'Er Up.' Reality isn't like that is it? I know that if I won the lottery and could afford new tits and a new belly, I'd never be fully happy with myself. I did however discover shirt dresses and that belts create a waist. A decent bra can hide a multitude of syns. I'll never have a bikini bod but a cute swimming costume with a little ruffle skirt can hide my thighs and the stretchmarks. I suppose I may not be happy with what I'm working with – but I can dress to create a way to carry it off, and unless someone's looking fabulous and mentions it themselves never EVER tell someone they need to "lose a few pounds" to look good in their jeans or to eat more as they're too skinny. You never know what they're facing.

Just be kind to people.

Oh and enjoy your syns – that's what they're there for!

I'd like to applaud Vicky for her honesty and her very Radio 4 way of putting things. That's if Radio 4 was hosted by Jordan and consisted solely of her gargling semen down the microphone for eight hours. I wish people did love themselves more. Without wanting to be all claphappy, everyone looks beautiful in some way. Even if you've got a face like a prolapsed anus, you might still have nice fingers. Teeth like a downed aircraft? Bet you've got a shapely bottom. Everyone has something good about them and I tell you now, from someone who spends a lot of time people watching, those who walk with confidence aren't always the skinny, toned folk you might assume. I've given up caring what people think – I've met my husband, I'm happy with my lot, so now when I go to a beach I'll pay no second thought to getting out my hairy back and my wobbling Mitchell Brothers titties. If you don't like it, that's tough banana. I like to feel the sun on my tyres as much as the next guy.

twochubbycubs on: pyramid schemes

STRONG WARNING: if you're a seller of Juice Plus or Forever Living, let's just assume that you're the exception to prove the rule rather than someone who is guilty of the below. No need to get uppity, I know there's some good in all scams. Even a stopped clock is right twice a day.

We all know how I feel about Juice Plus. It's worthless powder pressed into pills and shakes designed to be sold to vulnerable folk by desperate pushers who care not about the health risks but more about lining their pockets. The company actively encourages reps to post via Facebook slimming groups and pretend that they tell people off for it when they don't. Meh. I've talked about them plenty of times and frankly, if you're a Juice Plus seller, I think you're a parasite.

No, Forever Living entered my orbit recently (lots of things tend to do this – when you're the size of a horse-box you tend to have your own slight gravitational pull) because I, out of nosiness, responded to a post on a Slimming World group from someone who said '**they desperately needed help**'. Actually, it was more like *'CAN ANI1 HELP PLZ I DESPRATLY KNEED HELP PLZ MESSURJ ME'*. Sorry, no, forgive me, it was more like *'CAN ANI1 HELP PLZ I DESPRATLY KNEED HELP PLZ MESSURJ ME* x**X**x**X**x**X**x'. That kind of shit typing that makes you feel like you're being inadvertently groomed by Dark Justice. Anyway, being a kind soul and/or nosy, I messaged to find out if she was OK, only for her to launch into her sales pitch about Forever Living and how wonderful the products were and she just needed people to try the products and they could solve eczema and depression and MS and aches and pains and first world melancholy and the Times Cryptic Crossword blindfolded. I responded that it was a load of horse shit and she promptly blocked me. I was annoyed simply because she'd made out like she was in trouble or needed support and it was just a ploy to get caring folk to message her so she could exploit them to pay off her Brighthouse sofa. Or rather, pay off her leader's Brighthouse sofa. Which you just know will be 90% highly-flammable Taiwanese foam and have built-in speakers. The worst part is that I know some poor sap will end up buying her products, losing their money and feeling blue. Nice one!

Anyway, I let that lie, but seemingly because I'd mentioned the words Forever Living on Facebook, the sponsored ads threw up an intriguing proposition that I should get in contact with a 'Global Home Business Manager', accompanied by the kind of graphic someone disinterested in Media Studies might put together in MS Paint in order to stop failing a class. The kind of poster you see in church halls advertising beetle drives and jumble sales. The type of advert that gets filed under 'God bless them, they're trying'. It was the 'Global Home Business Manager' bit that made me intrigued –

not because I want to work from home, but it's such a clash of words that it really struck me. Many things do at 7.30am in the morning over my bran flakes. What is a Global Home Business Manager? To me it sounds like the kind of absolute nonsense title that people who sit in front of Jeremy Kyle recruiting other people to help live the dream give themselves to justify their existence, but no, turns out it's the title given to the next tier up in the Forever Living pyramid, presumably because Chief Shill isn't quite positive enough. A quick look at the profile for this 'Global Home Business Manager' reveals all the usual tricks – the rent-a-quote images about 'BEING MY OWN BOSS' and 'YOU CAN DO IT TOO', all the positive reinforcement messages lifted verbatim from 1000 other Forever Living profiles.

There's no doubt you can do well from it, absolutely no doubt. Problem is, you have to turn into one of those annoying folk who piss off their friends, families and neighbours with constant and endless pushing of your tat. How come if it is such a great product it can't be bought in shops but rather needs to be peddled via a network of recruits on facebook? People describe themselves as business owners but that's a complete misnomer – you're a modern day Avon lady, only you're an Avon lady who rings the doorbell every ten minutes and shouts through the letterbox about the benefit of smearing aloe vera on your 'gina to clear up your cystitis. You'll sharp notice that people stop answering the door too, the more you pester them. I left a comment on this sponsored advert asking why there is never any mention of the folks who buy into the whole Forever Living scam and then lose all their money, or about the dubious marketing, or the fact that it's a giant fucking racket. I didn't swear, but the comments were deleted immediately and I got a snooty, patronising private message from someone with a dreadful haircut advising me that 'they felt sorry for me for not being able to see the benefits of such a fantastic product'. You can imagine how grief-stricken I was by such a retort, but typical that the negative comments get deleted. People looking for the champagne lifestyle – which such a tiny amount of sellers will achieve, and even then it's only with the ill-gotten gains of those below them – are likely to be suckered in. It's a mess.

I think what gets me most of all, though, is the fact they prey upon the desperate. Officially, they're told they're not allowed to say that these products help with illnesses, but I know from personal experience – many, many times over – that the reps say whatever they can in order to gain a sale. I'm lucky that aside from being outrageously handsome and ever so slightly overweight, there's nowt much wrong with me. I play along, though – I make out I've got disease XYZ just to see if they ever back down and say no, this product isn't for you. They never do. It's always 'oooh yes, this can help with your illness' as though they have the cure to all known disease in a box in their bedroom as opposed to a few sachets of knock-off tat. They don't give a flying fuck whether these crappy, untested products make a disease worse or the pain that you might go through, they care about one thing only: your money in their pockets. Well, a tiny bit of your money in their pockets and the rest in their leader's pockets. They are arseholes of the highest order.

Listen, as you can imagine, the Internet does a much better job of explaining this. Take a look at this article on cracked.com or this (god-forbid) recount of an ex-rep on the Daily Mail (I know I know). Have a gander on Mumsnet for some honest opinion of what people think of the sellers or take a read of the many, many discussion threads out there on it. If you've got someone with white teeth and whistling ears trying to sell you a magic potion or worse still, trying to recruit you, ask yourself three questions:

- why can't I buy these wonderful products in a shop or why aren't they prescribed by a doctor;
- what has this person got to gain by promoting such a 'wonderful' lifestyle; and
- who do I trust more – science, the NHS, doctors and medical studies – or the badly-typed words of someone with a BTEC in Travel and Tourism and debts to pay off?

Exactly.

twochubbycubs and Clarabell on: thrush

Tonight's entry is by the charming Clarabell, who lists the ability to say the alphabet backwards and having a creepy double-jointed hand as her party trick. Don't believe me? Take a look!

Goodness. Least she never struggles to get the last Pringle out of the tube, eh? I'd better make sure that isn't the image that shows up when you post this to facebook. Over to Clarabell...

---

sweatbox: a tale by Clarabell

Now, we're all used to the candid craic from James and Paul about douche bulbs, all things in the downstairs department, and of course the post that mentioned bukkake...which I had to google. On a work laptop. Upon which I forgot to delete the history. Cheers guys! So I figured that with a gaggle of MAINLY female readers that my post would have to be about some nether region tale of the female variety. Something we've probably all experienced at one point. Perhaps not James and Paul. *(James edit: NOT TRUE! I've been there and it was all very charming, but not for me. That's what keeps the world interesting, different opinions, apropos of nothing I don't like potted ox tongue either).*

I've been fed up lately, I've been getting bouts of cystitis, antibiotics, thrush, cystitis....repeat. I've had a scan and there's nothing wrong with me other than I don't drink enough water, and have self-created this cycle of misery.

Resigned to buying the thrush cream, after the standard tactic of 'ignore it and it might not be there' stopped working, off I went to the local shopping centre, my purse hovering on the thick air in front of me. I'm in Asda but I can't see what I want on the shelves, and I'm quickly narked that the chemist is the other side of the centre, only because when your regions are on fire, that's a long walk to do, simultaneously avoiding the urge for a scratch, and walking like there's stones in your shoes. But! In a flash of delight, I remember that they took out half of the checkouts, to make an optician that no-one goes in, and.... a PHARMACY! Whoop! There's nothing like the delight of knowing you can get minge cream at the same time as your linguine.

I approach the counter, there's a pharmacist (identifiable by not being in day-glo Asda attire) fannying on with those little plastic mesh baskets that the prescriptions are homed in before dispensing, and very engrossed in it HE is too. Yes, he's a he. Urgh. Oh well, in the spirit of "he's heard it *ALL* before", I man up and he eventually stops fussing and walks over, asking the age old idiot question *"are you being seen to?"*...am I being seen to?! By who?! Unless you've started employing invisible colleagues, then no...there's only you there, and only me this side of the counter, and so no, I am not being seen to! Shop assistants, bartenders and pharmacists really need to drop the "are you being seen to?" line. What we all know is that you are trying to feign perplexion at my presence, as some sort for cover for the fact that you effectively ignored me for a good few minutes whilst procrastinating at your work – in this case the vital work of rearranging plastic baskets.

"I'd like some Canesten Oral Duo" I say bravely– pointing to the bottom shelf. Worryingly, he looks like he doesn't have a clue what I'm asking for. He follows my finger to the bottom shelf, and picks up some Sea Legs, examines box, puts it back and repeats – he does this a few times with a box of Rennie, and some headlice solution, and eventually comes across the thrush 'range' glowing on the shelf like a barber's pole in full red and white glory. I'm wondering at this point if he is the pharmacist, or whether he's mugged the rightful medicine man of his Asda badge and strolled behind the desk in the manner of an imposter, hoping to get first nab of the nearby 'Whoops' range, but he comes across the requested item at last. Not literally, you'd really struggle to pick the box up if he did that.

"Is it for you?" he asks. Christ on a bike...look mate, it's fifteen flaming quid...I am not about to raffle it off in the Slimmer of the Week basket I don't say this, instead I go with "**yes**" and 100% resting bitch face. Oh but he isn't finished, *"have you used it before?"*...panic! What's the correct answer to this? 'Yes' and appear like some serial offender, someone who can't control their rancid ways and lifting minnie?! Or 'no' and risk a declined purchase, or worse, some sort of lecture on best application practice and/or side effects?! I go with "yes" quickly followed up with "a while ago..." He gives a small nod. He knows I'm baking bread. Phew, home and dry, which is good because another customer has joined me and she has the smug privacy of a prescription, which is her ticket to a no question transaction. What is it with these useless questions?

However, there can be none more useless than the question I once got asked buying antihistamines for hayfever, "drowsy or non-drowsy" I was asked! Really?! Erm..let me check my diary...nope, nothing on the afternoon, drowsy for me please, I'm fine to lounge around spaced out and sleepy, I was not planning on driving and the only 'machinery' I'll be operating will be the telly, so yup, drowsy will do just do fine...ah wait, no consuming alcohol? Poop.

Anyway, Ahmed walks to the till, and promptly stops and stands above it doing jazz hands, and of course he just remembered he doesn't know how to use it. Suddenly, *"Doreen!"* he shouts WAVING THE CANESTEN BOX IN THE AIR! *"Doreen, can you ring this in for me please"*! I swear the smug-prescription-holder does the smirking shimmy, that tiny little wobble that comes only with an inner titter. I throw her some side-ways shade, which is code for 'look lady, we've all been there, and you will one day (maybe soon after that prescription for antibiotics teehee!) also have to stand here and deal with this lovely bloke, showing the world his arm pit sweat patch whilst at the same time holding aloft the solution to your itchy snatch'.

Goodness me! I once had a flatmate who had perpetual thrush, brought on by the fact her extra-endowed boyfriend seemed hellbent on hammering her cervix over her back-teeth. Not even kidding there, she showed me a photo he'd sent and what I thought was his arm holding the camera definitely wasn't. At one point our fridge was more cranberry juice than anything else. I still can't have a cranberry sour without thinking of her undercarriage. I remember we once had a full stand-up row over the fact I refused to boil tea-towels in a saucepan on the hob to sterilise them. Awfully judgemental for someone with a little too much glue on their envelope.

Now listen, before anyone starts writing their 'ANGRY OF TUNBRIDGE WELLS' letters and getting themselves in a tizz, don't. I know it's perfectly natural and I know people get all sorts of things but do you know, if we can't laugh at ourselves, what can we do? Let's not live in a joyless vacuum.

twochubbycubs on: celebrity injunctions

Tonight is a super-quick post because it's Friday, I want to sit back, put my cankles up and rest my weary hide. I'm lucky in that I enjoy my job, god knows what it must be like if you hate it. Paul watches a lot of How It's Made on the TV (really getting the use out of our Sky subscription, because who *doesn't* want to know how pencil sharpeners are made or how they deliver 24,000 cherry Bakewell's a day?) and you'll often see, amongst the fantastic machinery and wonderfully clever mechanical systems some little old dear spending eight hours troubling her sciatica and screwing toothpaste caps on or holding over a sheet of pastry. I'm not knocking anyone's job because well, a job is a job, but goodness me, how do they do it? I get bored if I have to type the same word twice – I treat my emails like a round of Just a Minute. No repetition, hesitation or deviation.

I confess myself a little ticked off because I went to fill the car and promptly filled it full of Supreme Diesel. My car is diesel, so what's the problem? Well, it offends my meanness to pay extra for something that I can't see the benefit of. Nevertheless, I went in, handed over my monthly pay and the cashier, clearly sensing my distress, offered me a free copy of the Sun. I joked that since we fitted a cat-flap we don't need to line the cat litter tray and thus I didn't need the Sun, but I could tell from his ashen face that my joke wasn't welcomed. He was clearly having a bad day. I took one, but only to be polite, the way someone at a buffet may take a spoonful of potato salad that the host has made only to drop it into a plant pot when their back was turned.

What a rag, though. Read what you like, it's your life, but look at the front cover today – it's not filled with the sad news that a plane crashed into the Mediterranean killing 66 poor buggers in what could be another frightening turn of terrorism, oh no, it's got a mock-up of an olive-oil filled paddling pool with the frothy headline 'The Day Free Speech Drowned' and a couple of subheadings about how it goes against common sensibility. That should tell you everything you need to know about this shitrag.

We all know who it is, so please don't be a funny bugger and comment on this saying 'OMG ITZ THINGY' because, well, don't. What I can't fathom is why anyone cares. The visual is troubling enough but can anyone genuinely say that the fact some happily married man and his husband had sex with another man? Why is it news? No-one was hurt (although they'll be smelling like a Greek salad left out in the sun for a few days), no laws were broken, it wasn't even a Boy George whoopsy-daisy-chained-an-escort-to-a-wall moment. Some mouthbreathing anus from (I think) The Sun was on Radio 4 on this morning saying that it's in the public interest because this artist is in the public eye. Well, here's the thing, unless he's felching someone out on my front lawn, I couldn't give a toss – and even then I'd only mind because he'd be flattening our new grass. The journalist went on to say 'AND HE HAS KIDS' like having kids immediately renders it illegal to have sex and fun with your partner, which is ridiculous, and there was more than a hint of the kids being exposed to their seedy lifestyle.

Of course, the media printing the name of the children's fathers and explicit, in-depth detail of their olive-oil-orgasms isn't exposing them, oh no no no. That's in the public interest.

Honestly, they're a bunch of twats. Feel free to print that, you Tiddler-Riddler-haired witch.

twochubbycubs on: the NHS

Today's post isn't going to be played for laughs because something is on my mind. The NHS. Yes, today we're not going to so much as wander off the path as set camp in the forest. See, I was driving home listening to Professional Chode Jeremy Hunt gabbling away in that smug, shit-eating way of his about reaching a deal with the junior doctors. I can't *abide* the man. You know when someone is described as making your skin crawl? He makes me turn inside out like a salt-covered slug with shyness issues. I'm unapologetic in my view. He represents the very worst – perhaps second only to George Osborne, a man so smug that he probably has a Fleshlight designed in the vision of his own face delivering bad news – of what is wrong with who is running the country. But that's another rant for another time.

See, I love the NHS. I truly do. I've mentioned before that I've had previous bouts of health anxiety and whilst that's under control, it's also meant I've had many trips to the doctors in my time. I've also got a dicky ticker to boot. Every single time I've been into hospital I've been treated with the utmost respect by all of the staff, who wear their smiles wide and work hard to bring reassurance and comfort to all. I was in there this morning for physiotherapy on my Klicker-Klacker neck. The doctor who I saw was wonderful, knew about my anxiety, took the time to explain what the problem was (and more importantly, what it wasn't!) and even had the good grace not to recoil when I took my shirt off. I wasn't rushed, I wasn't made to feel like I was inconveniencing them, and I was told just to call up if things got worse.

I hasten to clarify something – I've only been into hospital when I've actually had something wrong – I'm not a timewaster (though I'll say this – don't dismiss anyone with health anxiety as being a timewaster – take a moment to ponder what it must actually be like worrying and fretting that they're dying). I've never had a single bad experience with the NHS, and it breaks my heart (just what I need) to see the systematic dismantling of it coming in via the back door.

And listen – I normally love things coming in via the back door. Of course there could be improvements, but what massive organisation can't stand to lose a little fat? Plus, if I have to sit through one more 'GO YOU' video in the waiting room where positive messages are beamed at me by someone more tooth than human I'll cut myself. Least I'll be in the right place. I'm going to hand over the typing to Paul, who can put our feelings in much better terms. Over to you, Fatty.

All we ever really hear about the NHS is that it's awful, things are going wrong, mistakes are happening – I can only disagree with that entirely both with my own experiences and those I've seen of others (as a spectator and a cog in the machine itself).

It's pretty amazing to think of this giant institution being there in the background which we all take for granted. Can you imagine having to dole out some cash every time you wanted to see the doctor? I had a taste of it when we last went to Florida and suffered from a simple perforated eardrum. It cost nearly £500 for ten minutes with a mardy quack and a Tiny-Tears bottle of ear drops. £500! James started clutching his heart until I reminded him we'd need to mortgage the house to pay for the defibrillator. We paid it because I needed it – I was in agony and due to fly back, and fortunately had some travel insurance to cover it, but to imagine having that sort of thing drop into my lap on a normal day beggars belief and needless to say would mean I'd probably have to self-medicate with whinging and attention-seeking, and probably some Ben & Jerry's too.

This whole idea of the value of the NHS hit me today just as I was sorting out our diary – I've got a few medical appointments coming up with my GP and at the hospital (we're at that age, you know) that are for things that are all down to my fatness, and James had a quick rub-down by the physio today for his wonky neck. I did a quick bit of googling about the subject and to have all of these things without the NHS (i.e. like in America) would have cost nearly £3,000. Isn't that astonishing? I know there's insurance and various schemes but overall, what a mess.

Isn't it great that all these services are offered for nowt, all because of our NHS. Now, I know – I annoy myself with these things – all this treatment is entirely my own fault and completely avoidable, and I am a little ashamed to have to be using up the resources of the NHS on me being too greedy, but on the other hand what a fantastic public service it is – to know that all of us, whoever we are, where we come from, what we do, can have the most fundamental thing – our continued survival – at our disposal. And, what a thing it is that we can be so lucky to have something so grand and wonderful that we take it for granted.

So I made myself a commitment today – to look-up to the NHS and champion it, and also defend it. James will be rolling his eyes at this (he hates it when I get political) (**James edit:** no I don't, I just find it hard to get it up when you wear your Thatcher wig and flat shoes) so I'll maybe soften it a bit – but we ALL need to defend it from those that want to take it away. It is OURS and we must keep it OURS and so we must all do what we can to cherish it, use it, and make sure it's there for others in the future. So, from today, I'll continue my weight loss journey so that I can get healthy but also reduce the strain on the NHS in the future – today it's a fatty liver but if I keep on at the rate I am there will be all sorts of obesity-related conditions that come knocking at my creaky door (and knees – and I need them for....things...), and make sure I do all I can to protect and defend the NHS when I can. Not just in a rabble-rousing way but also to defend the very essence of the NHS and the culture that comes with it, because god knows we'll miss it when it's gone.

Phew. All better.

twochubbycubs on: taster nights and Eurovision

Nothing seems to strike fear into slimmers at Slimming World more than *'we're having a party next week, bring something along'*. Well, perhaps the words *'let's split the room in half, someone keep points, we're going to do group activities'*. God I hate that. I'm too antisocial at the best of times but being forced to come up with a witty team name and shout out speed foods makes my throat hitch. For those not in the Cult of Mags, a taster night is where everyone is expected to bring along some food to share with the rest of the class and usually results in about twenty quiches and a box of grapes bought from the Co-op over the road by the lady who forgot it was on.

I struggle with taster nights because, as previously mentioned, I don't like eating food when I don't know how clean the kitchen it's coming from is. Luckily I'm in a class now with people who do look familiar with a bottle of Ajax, but Christ, some of the sights I've seen in other classes, well I wouldn't eat what came out of their kitchens even if it contained the antidote to a life-threatening poison I'd accidentally ingested. I don't mind a slice of Slimming World quiche, I just don't like to be twanging cat hair out of my teeth for the following week. Anyway, as 'what can I make for taster night' and 'slimming world snacks' appear quite regularly on the little index of what people search for to find this blog.

Well, it can't all be 'chubby cub cum explosion' (can't remember that recipe?) and 'fat men fuking' (masturbation is no excuse for poor spelling, chaps).

Oh! A quick word. When a buffet is served up in class, try and allow the meek amongst us access to the food. A couple of years ago, in a class in Wakefield no less, Paul and I didn't get any food because half the class — not the better half — dashed forward as soon as the 'party' began and formed one giant body of impassable bulk. It was like the Berlin Wall, only smelling faintly of chips. I've never seen food shovelled and devoured with such ferocity and I've seen Sicilian wild boars being fed. All I wanted was a (nothing-like-a) Ferrero Rocher and a few 'JUST LIKE DORITOS' crisps that I could have planed a door with. I had my revenge anyway — the wasabi peas that I put on the table thinking they were syn-free were actually about eight syns a handful. What can I say? My knowledge of the Mandarin language is a little rusty.

So, with all the above in mind, we decided to do a post on snacks, also fuelled by the fact it was Eurovision last night and we like to have a trough of food to work through whilst we watch our entry get annihilated. Before anyone says the UK will never win because 'it's too political' and 'no-one votes for us because of the war', that was relevant maybe ten years ago and certainly isn't now. Russia almost won it and well, that Putin's been a bit of a tinker this year, has he not? We don't win because we send absolute shite – po-faced, dreary, period-pain music with insipid staging and crap tunes. No doubt that Aldi Jedward can sing a tune and strum a guitar but they lost a singing competition where literally tens of people voted for someone else to be a winner. Why would that translate to success in the Eurovision Song Contest? EH? We need to send something amazing, with a massive chorus and an uplifting melody, not a song that would barely make its way onto the second CD in the Now That's What I Call White Noise 87 compilation.

I was just sore because I had Poland and Italy in the sweepstakes, and did you catch them? Poland came dancing out like a crystal-meth Cheryl Cole and Italy's act was so boring that I forgot about it whilst she was singing the words, which is quite something. I wanted Russia to win. That stage, that song (You Are The Obi Wan, You're My Obi Wan...) and gasp, when that screen spun around...well, I loved it. Plus, one of my work colleagues had Russia in the sweepstakes and I just know he's going to be spend his winnings on delicious things for the entire floor. That's right, isn't it Alan? SHOUT-OUT FOR ALAN. Mahaha. Paul threw his weight behind Sweden, who I can't really be mean about because the singer was only 8 and he has the angst of puberty to get through. He's no Eric Saade (2011) with his exploding glass cages though.

As it happens, one of the worst songs managed to win –

Kate Bush's stunt double caterwauling about politics — and Ukraine took the prize, meaning Russia will be hosting the Eurovision next year. Boom boom. We've said it every year — we should go to the next Eurovision — and the fact that it is being held in Ukraine only sweetens the deal. If it had been Russia we'd have been conflicted — on one hand, we love the idea of a night of catchy tunes surrounded by every other gay man in existence, but on the other hand I prefer not to have my teeth kicked down my throat because I'm a rampant bummer. Ah yes.

twochubbycubs on: hallowe'en 2016

Hallowe'en has been and gone, and hopefully the only fright you've experienced is the site of your own toes as your gunt shrinks ever inwards.

For the first time in ten years since Paul and I got together, we decided to embrace Hallowe'en instead of spending the evening sat behind the sofa with the lights off, watching Coronation Street on the iPad with the brightness and volume turned right down. No, in the spirit (oh h oho) of taking part, we stuck up some perfunctory bits of tat from Poundland (probably getting lead poisoning whilst doing so) and put a pumpkin outside, shockingly not with the word C*NT carved in it. We're getting better at this being social lark.

We wanted trick-or-treaters to knock on the door and take our chocolate. Perhaps that's too far – we certainly had chocolate, but Paul had eyes like a kicked dog when I told him they were for any guests. That didn't stop me eating three Freddos and a Fudge when he went to the bog, though. We didn't dress up because apparently my suggestion of answering the door as Fred and Rose West was a little too "near-the-knuckle". I'm not sure what Paul's problem is; I've got a pair of my nan's Blanche Hunt glasses that would have looked resplendent on him.

Best of all, we ever went to the trouble of setting up a

light system for the house – all of our outdoor lighting is controllable by colour and timers so we had the house flickering like a fire with occasional bursts of white light like a lightning bolt. It was all very brilliant and took an hour of tinkering with our router and swearing incoherently at the iPad to get it all set up.

So, what did we get, perched as we are on a lovely corner of a cul-de-sac full of expensive houses all ripe for trick or treaters? Absolutely zip. Bugger all. Sweet fanny adams.

Actually, that's not entirely true, we did get two teenage girls (very rough – they looked like they were on their third pregnancy of the year but only their first toothbrush) who stuck their hands out and said 'trick or treat' – a quick glance revealed that they hadn't bothered with any sort of costume bar eight inches of poorly-applied foundation. We asked for trick and they kissed their teeth at us and tramped away over our lawn.

There were several children in groups who visited the streets but avoided our house altogether. I admit to being distraught. It was all I could do to choke down every last bit of chocolate and sour jellies that was left in our fruit-bowl.

Of course, like all things, Hallowe'en was a lot different when I was young. Because money was tight, my costume was a bin-liner (because nothing says BOO like

'NO HOT ASHES' spread across my arse) and my pumpkin was a turnip. Have you ever tried to carve a turnip? It's like cutting a diamond with a butter knife. It's why I associate Hallowe'en with carpal tunnel syndrome. My sister wore a bed-sheet with some red paint on it. Back in modern time, Paul and I couldn't use our black bedsheets because people would think we'd come dressed as a badly tuned TV channel.

Most of the people in our village were knocking on 90 and thus, no sweets, fucks or hearing were given, but we always hit the jackpot when we visited the only footballer in our village, who gave us all a tub of Quality Street each. It's tantamount to my obesity that this remains one of the fondest memories I have of growing up in Backwater, Northumberland.

Back in the now, I did find it interesting that after all the gash-crashing and naval-gazing that's been happening over the 'terror clowns' 'epidemic' recently that so many parents thought it would be wise to dress their children up as frightening beasts to terrorise the neighbours, mind you. What's good for the goose is good for the gander, after all.

I'd welcome a clown jumping out at me to give me a fright — I just don't shock that way. They'd get an entirely non-plussed reaction and a shoulder-shrug. No, if you really want to scare me, dress up as my bank manager and tell me Paul's spending on the First Direct card. You'd need to bring me around with salts. I'd love to have a flasher jump out of the bushes, too, if only so I could ask if he wanted me to blow it or smoke it. Nothing cuts a man down quicker than a jibe at his wee-willy-winky.

The idea of ghosts certainly doesn't scare me because I don't believe in such a thing. I think, once you die, that's it, though I've already told Paul that if the afterlife does exist I'll be haunting him relentlessly – whooing and booing every time he reaches for some consolation ice-cream or, worse, a new lover. I've told him to at least let the sheets cool first, though I don't doubt he'll be asking the funeral procession to pull into a layby on the A19 on the way to the crem to take care of a lorry driver.

You know why I don't think ghosts exist? Simple. If you could bring comfort by letting folks know you're in a better place, why wouldn't you just do it? Why go through the rigmarole of knocking over vases? Worse, why would you deliver your message through rancid vile grief-exploiters like Sally Morgan or other psychic mediums? I don't know about you, but I'd want my comforting messages to be passed directly to the target rather than over the lips of some permatanned Liverpudlian on Living TV. I'd love to think my dear nana is giving us a sign – perhaps that whistling in my ears and high-pitched ringing isn't tinnitus after all but rather the ghost of her 1980s NHS hearing aid coming over time and space? Doctor Eeee-No. Bless her.

twochubbycubs on: car boot sales

Batch-cooking: it only works if you don't have a freezer that looks like an Iceland lorry crashed down an embankment. We must be the only couple in Britain whose freezer is 50% Häagen-Dazs, 50% good intentions.

However, we thought we'd try batch-cooking and make a chilli. Plus, we wanted to have something warm and comforting to come back to after nipping out last night to watch the fireworks at Hexham. I know I've waffled previously at length about firework displays – in short, I thoroughly enjoy the spectacle but not the a) crowds b) thought of wasting so much money and c) did I mention the crowds? And of course, the main problem with Hexham fireworks is that the whoooooosh and squeeeeeeeee of the fireworks is almost drowned out by the braying and neighing of all the posh, chinless lot scrabbling around in their Hunter wellies and desperately unhappy marriages. I've never seen so many children dressed like accountants and stable-hands squealing and yelling. Still, the fireworks were really very good, and the hour or so we spent trying to get out of the overflow carpark in a sea of BMWs, Range Rovers and other shitcarriages gave me plenty of time to practice my swearing and make adamantly clear to Paul that we'll never have a child. To be fair, I think that's rather a moot point, I can't envision Paul ever telling me ashen-faced that he's managed to get someone pregnant. I mean, we've been trying for ten years…

Oddly, it's not the first time this month that I've been sliding around in a muddy field. No, for whatever god-knows-reason, we decided to go along to the local car boot sale a week or so ago. I didn't take much persuasion, but then I never do when it comes to being in a dimly-lit field surrounded by men with their car doors open flashing their wares. My DS3 is possibly the only model out there whose interior lights don't so much blink on and off as actually strobe. Ah well. We are what we are. No, I rather relished the chance to revisit a bit of my youth, spending many Sundays way-back-when as a boy at the Corbridge car boots. I remember it fondly – lots of colourful board games, piles of NES cartridges, stopping at the mobile hot-dog van for a small saveloy and severe gastroenteritis. I did once find a set of James Herriot books which came in useful 20 years later propping up my broken bed, so that was useful.

We piled into the car at ungodly'o'clock on the Sunday morning (by ungodly, I mean before dusk) and beetled up the dual carriageway, giving my nana's old house a friendly wave as we chugged past. She was always such a big part of our Sundays that, even now, it feels odd driving through the village where she used to be. Any soft feelings of nostalgia were eventually swapped with mild anger as, upon getting to the general area of the car boot sale, we joined a queue of waiting traffic. I couldn't believe it. I thought we were the odds ones for going but here we were, part of an eager mass of beige coloured cars, cardigans and fingernails. I touched Paul's hand and asked if they were giving out free blowjobs and chocolate but nope, these were just folk wanting a ratch about. What had we become?

We were shown to an overflow car-park by an officious looking tit with a poor attitude and dandruff – the exact type of person who you know came a bit when he was given a hi-ves jacket and a clipboard. He told me off for going around the overflow car park in the wrong direction as though I'd killed the second coming of Princess Diana and then scuttled off to harass some poor old biddy in her Fiat Pubis. With heavy hearts, we trooped in.

What's to say? It was awful as I expected. Look, I know that so many of you will get a lot out of a car boot sale, I really do, but it definitely wasn't for us. For a start, the absolute fucking tut on display was second to none. I wanted to see if I could find any decent N64 games and, whilst I managed to locate a small cache of them, the owner wanted way more than I'd pay for them on eBay. I tried haggling – I'm not shy – but I would have had more success arguing with the decorating table he had spread his wares on. Someone else seemed to have brought everything from her home that wasn't fastened down – books (fine), dirty cups (dubious) and various magazines, including last week's What's On TV? Why? Who needs that? I'd cheerfully bet my house that there hasn't been a single instance of someone sitting bolt upright in bed in the dead of night clamouring to read the synopsis of what's happening in Eastenders a week ago.

The same bewhiskered dolt was also selling a selection of used ashtrays. We're not, as you might expect, talking tasteful art-deco pieces here, no no, just those awful pub style ashtrays with XXXX on the side, with lots of burns and ash-marks on them. Here's the thing. If you smoke, you're going to already have an ashtray, unless you're a common slattern who puts her ash on the carpet and hey, you laugh, but I know of at least **two** blood relatives who do this. I fell over in their living room once and came up with my hair looking like Doc Brown from Back to the Future. Returning back to the point, who did she think was going to buy these ashtrays? It's not like they could be roughly distressed by some twat in a lumberjack shirt who has set about it with a power sander. I find it all very odd. We moved on.

I wish I could say we had at least some success, but nah. Stalls full of unwanted nonsense, committed (at least, they fucking should be) car-booters all scrabbling around and being rude, rubbish fast-food options – we won't be going back. We did make a purchase, though, in the vain hope that they could at least look good in our games room – a battered box with some Super Mario rollerskates. Great! No, sorry, not great – shit. When we got back to the sealed box that was our car, we realised that they'd clearly come from a house where it was obligatory to smoke forty Capstan Full Strength tabs before dinner, meaning they're now in our shed gathering dust and wheezing gently. We should have returned them – I was half-tempted to nip back to the old lady's stall and buy the Rollerskates Family a few ashtrays as a pointed joke – but the clipboard man was looking furiously at us again so we drove away. All in all – a failure. Nothing of interest and a new bit of shite that will clutter up our lovely shed.

Of course, where there's muck there's money – perhaps next week Paul and I should load our car with all of *our* tat (my car, not his: it would be a bit of a shit display if we used his car, given we could only fit a tie-pin and a sachet of coffee into his car) and go and sell it. I couldn't, though. For a start, I wouldn't be able to deal with hagglers – I'd take it as the purest insult if someone tried to suggest my slightly-wrong-colour-Le-Creuset cups weren't worth full price, for example. Then, if we didn't sell, I'd fall into a deep self-doubt – *I* thought the giant lava lamp was tasteful – why didn't Elsie and Eric want it for their caravan? The soft light would really diffuse the harsh blue veins of a swinging party, for example. Ah well.

twochubbycubs on: cinema and a Chinese

Can I just take a moment to say I thoroughly enjoyed Batman v Superman? I just like to think that Ben Affleck is probably reading this blog, dying to know how to turn ASDA beef chunks into something palatable, and after all of the criticism he's faced over his boring film, this might cheer him up. Plus, Paul and I both agree that you have quite an impressive knob in Gone Girl, and I'm not talking about Rosamund Pike. I went to see Batman vs Superman with an old friend (literally, she's well old) and it was all very enjoyable, even in blurry 3D-vision. I'm a fan of 3D if done well (Saw 3D, of all things, was fun) but not if it's just to make the odd leaf or snowflake look like it's coming towards you. No amount of blistering 3D detail is going to make me think I'm right there in Gothametroplis (right?) – my arse-cheeks turning to concrete on the rock-hard cinema seats keep me grounded.

Oh, that and the little shits along the row who, along with their father, spent every other minute looking at their phones and being unnecessarily rambunctious. Naturally, as a Brit, I tutted and sighed for two hours until I was on the verge of hyperventilating and had to blow into my pic-and-mix bag for comfort. The father took a bloody phone call at one point! Unless it's a doctor ringing up to tell you that "yes, Mr Smith, we've found you a brain, you'll need to come in for fitting immediately" you **don't** take a bloody phone call in the cinema. If I had my way, everyone would have their hands stapled to the arm-rest and if your phone rang or you needed a poo, well tough titty. The cherry on the cake was towards the end I went to get the last sour apple snake from my bag (not a euphemism) (also, yes, hypocritical) when one of the children sighed like he was blowing out the candles on a birthday cake and said '**I CAN'T WATCH THE FILM IF PEOPLE ARE TRYING TO RUIN IT**'. I've never felt so chagrined.

Anyway, today we've said at least two things that hammer home how old we're getting – first, Paul suggested we go out *"for a drive in the car"* which wouldn't have been too bad until we bumped into our octogenarian neighbours getting in their cars (they're still getting in as we speak) and they said that they too *"were going out for a drive"*. I don't know why we do it, we invariably get stuck behind someone for whom the fourth gear is uncharted territory and I end up going apocalyptic behind them trying to overtake. I have to come home and punch a brick wall to calm down. The second line that tumbled from my ageing lips was the clincher though – when Paul mentioned that our home town could do with some decent flowers being planted (in itself a very Disgusted of Tunbridge Wells thing to say), I replied by saying *'yes, but the young'uns would just pull them up and cause a mess'*.

May I remind you I'm 31.

Goodness me. I almost stopped at the Lloyds Pharmacy

on my left there and then for a hearing test and a fitting for Tena for Men but well, it would take a while to get parked and with my aching hips, getting out of the car is too much of a chore. So instead we drove to the beach and ate sandwiches in the car whilst listening to Gardeners' Question Time and nodding at nothing in particular.

Ah well, to the satay! It's something I always order whenever we get a takeaway, though sadly our favourite local takeaway seems to have closed down. I like to think they couldn't keep up with our demands. I've definitely had more than eight *'it's my birthday, can we have a free giant spring rolls please thanks'* events this year. I certainly hope it hasn't been closed down by the council because that would bring our total of 'favourite then condemned' eateries to three. We used to have a Chinese takeaway literally across the street from us when we lived in Gosforth (more Kenton actually, but Gosforth sounds posher and well, we didn't have a trampoline or discarded mattress in our front garden, so we didn't belong in Kenton*) which was fantastic.

Paul was confused when he first went to order because the tiny, very Chinese looking lady behind the counter spoke with a Geordie accent that sounded like she was possessed by Tim Healy. And he's not even dead. It really didn't gel with her beautiful cheongsam dress and I-kid-you-not chopsticks in her hair bun.

Still, the food was delicious and tasty up until the point the 'Scores on the Doors' folk came around and rated them zero out of five for cleanliness, food safety and hygiene. Nothing says did you enjoy your chow-mein like seeing it again two minutes after eating from one end or twenty minutes from the other. I must have a stomach of asbestos though as so few things ever upset my natural balance.

We now get our Chinese food from a car-park in Morpeth. So far, so good – they certainly don't seem to be using the same microfibre cloth to wipe their work-surfaces and their bumholes, so they're already up on the Gosforth Chinese.

* Kenton is lovely really. Please don't firebomb my house or spray me with Greggs crumbs as you refute my jokey aspersions.

twochubbycubs on: getting stuck

you won't have so much to read through tonight to get to the recipe because, to use a Geordieism, I'm STOTTIN' MAD. It took me two hours to exit the multi-storey car-park this evening – not because I fell down the stairs or I got lost trying to find my car, no, because some bumhole thought it would be a smashing idea to block the one-way road off with roadworks and then not put any provisions for people wanting to leave in place, leading to about 300 office workers all trying to leave at once from eight different directions down a one-way street. All it would have taken is some preferably-fit bloke in a hi-vis to guide the traffic out or indeed, a set of traffic lights, but no.

To make things worse, I got into my car at 5.05pm and needed a piss by 5.07pm. Of course, I was in a completely static line of traffic so I probably had enough time to get out, go home, have a piss, send that away for testing, discuss why it sometimes smells of coconut with a doctor and then begin a course of antibiotics, but I couldn't take the risk that as soon as I stepped away and nipped to the gents that the line of traffic wouldn't start up and I'd end up with a ticket for abandoning my car.

Have you ever had to look around your car and gauge what you could realistically piss in? I have, and let me tell you, in a reasonably clean DS3, there's not many options. There's an ashtray and an oversized glove box, and neither of them are waterproof. A Doritos bag seemed like the only option but even then, I'd need both hands to turn the tight corners and I didn't want a crisp packet of urine balanced on my dash. I knew there was an empty Orangina bottle in the boot but I couldn't remember if it was glass or plastic, and well, I've spent my life avoiding getting a gash on my helmet, let's not start tonight.

Nevermind, I managed to hold it in, and after an extended period of muttering away to myself in a very British fashion and embarrassing my friend on the radio, I managed to get away, although not after losing my temper with some doddery old bugger who pretty much reversed into my car in his haste to try and cut in front of me. It's surprisingly awkward when you shout at someone and then have to sit in front of them for another forty minutes, trying desperately not to meet the eye of the old bugger you yelled at in haste.

twochubbycubs on: our masochistic cats

Can I just start by saying that I'm glad that I *didn't* have a piss in my car the other day as I previously mentioned, as we now have a strapping young man giving both of our cars a deep clean. I'm just glad he turned up – his message to me was that he'd be here for dinner time. Now to me as a Geordie dinner means 12-2pm and tea is 6-8pm. However, I was fretting that he might be like Paul (i.e. a big Southern shandy-drinking Nancy) and believe that dinner is an evening meal and he'll rock up at 6pm after I've spent six hours looking mournfully out of the window like James Stewart in Rear Window. I do feel sorry for him – Paul's been farting so much in his tiny little Smart car that when you open the door it hisses like the door on The Crystal Dome. I might go and check he's not face-down on his industrial pressure washer after I've typed this.

Nah, he's fine. My angst at having people I don't know touching my things or being in my house has been well-documented, but I'm just about managing to cope without blurting at him whether he'd like a tup of key or a handjob instead of hand-gel. I did notice that my car seat has an unfortunate white stain right where my crotch is and I don't feel I know him well enough for him to believe me when I tell him it was a dollop of McFlurry and not jism. One look at me and you'd know I'd never miss a mouthful of McFlurry. Then again, one look at me and you'd know I'd never miss a mouthful of...and we'll stop right there, thank you.

Anyway, today is to be spent out in the garden, walking around, occasionally picking up a spade, putting it down again and ringing the gardener. This probably sounds like the height of laziness but listen, I feel like life is too short to be clarting about hoeing and weeding and strimming. We've got all the tools — we inherited a fantastic shed full of manly things (which we naturally turned into a cat-house and a place to store our many, many tins of beans) when we were given our house — but I can't find the inclination. That said, I do like growing vegetables and this year's theme is weird and wonderful — unusual colours and types of vegetables, including black tomatoes and rainbow carrots. Our neighbour (one of the decent ones) came over this morning to give me five tomato plants so I'm sure that'll keep me busy. See, if I buy them myself and forget about them, I've let no-one down, but because he's given the plants to me I feel duty-bound to be out at all hours watering and tending to their every whim. It is worth it, everything tastes nicer when you grow and nurture it yourself (except, say, vaginal thrush), but I find it all very stressful making sure everything is watered and happy. I only need to spend fifteen minutes extra in bed on a Saturday for everything to turn yellow and die off in a huff.

We did go and get weighed on Thursday and although we both put on (2lb each!) that's more than fair enough

– we've had my birthday, Easter, two meals out, drinks and the Bank Holiday to contend with. I admit that we're struggling to fit Slimming World into our life at the moment – we're eating healthily when we can but I can't go out to a restaurant and be that guy who orders a salad with a pot of dressing on the side and eight hankies to wipe my tears away with, plus, let's be honest, a night out isn't the same unless you're on the hard stuff and finishing off with something slopped from a takeaway van that practically walks on its own steam. I've got our end of year party at work next week followed by a Fizzy Friday after that, Paul's going down to Peterborough to see friends and to wash the sheen of nicotine off his mother and then we've got a holiday booked for the last week in April! How am I supposed to diet around that lot? I bought Slimming World's magazine for tips and inspiration but it made all my teeth rot away with the sugariness of it all. Actually, I suppose that does help. I did enjoy how one of the few pages dedicated to men was about looking after your prostate. Very important indeed, but the guide made it sound like it was a Tamagotchi from the nineties and well, just like the plants, I killed all of my Tamagotchi's through sheer idleness. You've never known terror until someone has told you to look after their Tamagotchi whilst they're away and you check and find two piles of poo and a skull icon. Oops!

So, aside from that, just a lazy weekend ahead. That's the joy of having no children or commitments see, it's perfectly acceptable to stay in your dressing gown watching Netflix, only moving to put some coffee on or to open a window. I often ask what people are doing at the weekend and it's invariably full of a list of wholesome children activities that make my eyes glaze over – taking them swimming, taking them to parties, taking them to soft-play, driving them to a friend's house. That's why I couldn't have children, far too much of a constraint on my time. If only they came with batteries that you could remove and bundle them into a cupboard so you could do all of the exciting things like take them to Disneyworld or have an amazing Christmas without dealing with all the poos and strops and tantrums, I'd have several, possibly in a range of different shapes and sizes. But until that day, it's just me, Paul and the cats, and even they are playing up lately, with the cat who likes being spanked getting way out of hand. I half expect to see her pressing her nipsy up against a hot radiator and meowing 'OOOH I'M A FILTHY SLAG' in cat-speak. She won't stop mewing and showing off her minnie-moo, she even did it when the car-wash man came to the door earlier. She's lucky he didn't use her to hold his chamois.

twochubbycubs on: school detentions

Apologies that I forgot to post the last couple of days but well, I've been busy with work. For the first time in so long I'm actually *learning* something new and it's great fun. If you knew what it was I was learning you'd probably think it was deathly dull but honestly, it's nice to use my mind for something other than fart-gags and thinking about what to cook for dinner (**not** Paul's willy).

I've never been the best learner mind. I did very well at school despite my very best efforts not to and although I didn't go to university (a decision I don't regret), my grades have steered me where I want to go. I always wanted to be one of those people who could make snappy little flash cards and a schedule for revisions but my exam preparation happened to coincide with the arrival of broadband in our sleepy village, and let's just say it wasn't the books I was bashing. It's lucky I only use my left hand for writing otherwise I'd have really been fucked in my English literature exam.

I've just asked Paul what his favourite lesson was and he replied 'science', which seems like a bit of a catch-all. Personally, I never had much truck with science – my physics teacher had a voice like a dying bee and made everything sound dull and our biology teacher made us watch a video of a baby being born which I think may have at least strengthened, if not concreted, my homosexuality. Chemistry was fun only because we had a teacher who looked like Professor Weetos and who you could genuinely imagine blowing a crater into the Earth. He once set the ceiling on fire during an experiment and given it was a) a bit of a run-down school and b) just before health and safety kicked in, the resulting toxic plastic smoke was rather spectacular. If I cough hard enough now I still get polystyrene flecks.

No, my favourite lesson was English (hence all the writing I do now, I suppose) but that's mainly due to the succession of genuinely excellent teachers I had. My AS level teacher was also a friend of Dorothy and I used to try and shoehorn in as many references to me being gay in an unproductive attempt to be 'asked to stay behind'. He was ever the professional. All those hormones. He could have *split my complex sentence* at any time.

I've already talked about the time I ran out of the PE changing rooms shouting 'I'VE GOT DIARRHOEA' thinking it would get me out of cross-country only for the sadist midget (and mind, he was both) to order me back and tell me 'IT'LL MAKE YOU RUN FASTER'. He wasn't wrong. Nothing gets you around the back of Newcastle Airport like the threat of filling your Diadora Borgs with yesterday's school dinner. He once threw a blackboard eraser at someone so hard that it cracked a chunk of plaster (probably asbestos, actually) out of the wall behind. How he kept his job I do not know, although I'm sure the same school's headteacher got fired for putting the naughty children UNDER THE STAGE when Ofsted came around, so I'm sure there's a reason there.

I, rather disappointedly, only remember getting four detentions. One was for carrying a knife around school, which of course makes me sound all hard and dangerous until you realise it wasn't a knife, it was a tiny gouging tool used to make a pattern in cork tiles during art class, and I only had that with me because I snapped the blade and didn't want to get wrong off the teacher because he used to whistle through his teeth when he talked and it made it difficult not to laugh in his face. Well fuck me, you'd think I was walking round the school like the Zodiac Killer the way I was yelled at and threatened with permanent expulsion. It's a bit hard to shank someone with a tool you could barely use to clean behind your nails with.

Another detention – very unjust – was for suggesting a condom was a sensible thing to take on a survival course. My reasoning (which I learned from my little SAS Survival Book) was that it can carry up to two litres of water. Why, incidentally? Unless you're rolling it onto a bull, why does it need to hold that much? Anyway, the home economics teacher (who I might add was the wife of the PE teacher, and clearly used the same razor he did to shave her top lip) threw me out for being vulgar. It wasn't like I offered to put one on to demonstrate.

Detention number three was another injustice – I

dropped a three-tier, full size wooden xylophone down two flights of stairs in a genuine accident. Of course Mrs Jinks didn't believe me, put me in detention and didn't even get me a credit for the fabulous melody it made as it clattered down the stairs and turned to matchsticks. Of course nowadays I'd be given a badge for displaying artistic integrity, which is certainly more than the xylophone did.

Finally, detention number four was a doozy – we used to have big jugs of fresh water on the table during lunch see, to help take away the taste of the horse arseholes they put in the stew. Anyway, someone stole my Pogs and put them in the water jug. My measured reaction was to turn around and punch him on the jaw, shaking a tooth loose. I wouldn't care, but they were my duplicate Pogs and a shit slammer to boot, so really I suppose that detention was fair enough. Still, never disturb a fat man when he's eating, it's like poking a sleeping dog. Funny what writing this blog does – for years I've been confidently saying I've only ever been in one fight (and even that was over nothing – someone stood deliberately on my ankle during rugby, so I stood deliberately on his head) but now I can add this one to the mix. What larks.

twochubbycubs on: our poor cat's va-jay-jay

Before I even start, I need to regale you with a bit of hilarity. We've been wrapping presents in the utility room this afternoon and we're just sitting down with a totally syn-free Baileys Hot Chocolate when our cat came steaming into the living room. Nothing unusual in that, you might think, only she was scooting across the living room carpet at a rate of knots on her arsehole, pulling herself forward with her feet. She looked like a determined, furry Roomba, only leaving a faint hiss of digested Whiskas for good measure on our fancy black carpet. Naturally we were full of concern and once we'd stopped laughing (laughing to the point Paul actually fell off the sofa) we managed to catch her and check her over. Turns out she'd got a piece of double-sized tape stuck just above her minnie-moo and was pulling herself along to try and get rid of it. I spent a minute very carefully pulling it away, being treated to a far more detailed view of my cat's vagina than I could have ever hoped to see on a Saturday evening, and she was back on her way, ignoring us evermore. I'm sure she will take her revenge tomorrow once we put the tree up. We once came home to find the entire tree tipped over which, when you consider it was standing in one of those tree-gripper thingies.

Speaking of my cat's vagina (because why not?) I remember when we first got Sola, our queen. We saw an ad online from some rough trollop in nearby Blyth who was giving cats away because she didn't want them anymore. So aghast was I by the state of the living room in the photos of the cats that I told Paul we had to rescue the littlest one at the very least and so it was that we ended up in a derelict car park at 10pm at night picking up a cat. It was like Breaking Bad, only with more mincing. She was the tiniest little thing and we spoilt her rotten until one day she broke. Yes, broke.

We awoke to the most horrifying sound imaginable – like she was meowing into a hoover tube, all distressed and unhappy. We hastened out of bed and found her lying in the hallway, at which point she immediately stopped meowing and started purring all content as could be. As soon as we stepped away the awful meowing would start up again. Surely she hadn't fallen in love with us so hard that our absence from her field of vision caused her such suffering? We were perplexed and it was only after 20 minutes of googling and ringing my mother that we found out what was wrong – she was horny.

Which, to be fair, explained why every time we looked in her direction she was lying on her front with her fadge raised up into the air.

It was awful. We couldn't take her to get spayed because most vets won't do it when the cat has come on, so we had to wait for her kitten-bajingo to cool off and calm the fuck down, meaning we were subjected to almost a week of her caterwauling, licking away at her privates and backing herself up against the front door for every passing tom. She was like Paul when the binmen turn up to take our bins away. At one point I came through the front door just as she was pressing herself against it and I swear she ended up like those stick-on-Garfield's you used to get on car windows. We had her spayed the very second we were able to (presumably when the vet's scalpel wouldn't come out looking like someone had sneezed on it) and all was well again. We were given strict instructions not to let her jump up anywhere in case her stitches burst open and her innards came tumbling out, so we took turns sleeping with her in the spare bedroom. That week, post operation, was the nicest she's ever been to us – all nuzzling and warm and friendly. Since then, she'll give us the occasional moment of civility in amongst all the hissing, scratching and ignoring she manages to throw at us, but that's alright, I'm a big lad, I can take it.

There's no secret that we love Christmas – it's the best time of year for both of us, even if last Christmas we ended up so ill we spent three days on the sofa snoring and sniffing and farting and only moving to nip to ASDA for tonic water and more gin. I don't think one single hour passed that Christmas that wasn't punctuated with the sound of Paul slicing a lime or the hiss of a tonic. This year we plan to push the boat out a little and have lots of decorations, including getting our Christmas tree nice and early as opposed to waiting until December 24th to buy a tree with as much foliage as a

12-year-old boy's top lip.

One new thing this year that we've just finished doing is putting up lights *outside*. Every year we fill our windows with twinkling beauties but this year, thanks to us having the foresight to arrange for some thick-fingered electrician to come around and fit us outdoor sockets, we can finally light up Chubby Towers the way it was meant to be. We nipped onto eBay, researched the brightest possible LED Christmas lights available and naturally, bought two sets. It looks *tremendous*. Best part? It'll wind up the one neighbour who hates us. Everyone else in the street is lovely bar the arse who thought the gays would bring the house-prices down. You can imagine how distressed I am at the thought of him being inconvenienced by our lights. I hope a plane attempts to land in his front garden — it'll give him a distraction from our cat pooing in there.

twochubbycubs on: getting a Christmas tree

Remember when the Spice Girls released that god-awful version of that god-awful 'Christmas favourite' song, Christmas Wrapping? Wasn't it just awful? We'd be shit Spice Girls, though I've got the bust to carry off a Union Jack leotard. I could be Grindr Spice – guaranteed to blow your mind *and* your cock. Paul would be Spherical Spice, or Mmmmace for short. Anyway, that's quite the digression for an opening paragraph, isn't it?

We have our tree! It's beautiful. 7ft of glorious Nordmann fir, equal branches, lovely deep green, smells like a taxi-cab office. We flirted with the idea of buying a really good fake tree but do you know, it just wouldn't be Christmas unless a good couple of hours was spent with us furiously trying to squeeze a 7ft tree into a 7ft car. Paul suggested taking the Smart car and simply strapping the tree on the top but come on. It would be like using a Little Tikes Cosy Coupe to tow a friggin' plane down an icy runway. One of Paul's friends has a fake tree which she last decorated back in 2008 and all she does after Christmas is wrap the whole tree in cling film – lights, baubles and tinsel still in situ – and then bungs it up in her loft.

I like her style, but such shenanigans wouldn't work for us, not least because we have a new theme every year. We're not one of those sentimental (for sentimental, read classy) couples who buy a tasteful decoration every time we go somewhere fancy and then spend hours at Christmas reminiscing and smiling at each other over memories past. No, every single Christmas since we've been together Paul has decided that the last decorations were old-hat and that we needed to buy new ones because what previously looked amazing now looks drab and tired. We've had a snow theme. We've had a rainbow theme. We've had a chuck-everything-on-there-at-once-theme. I suggested a budget theme where we don't dress the fucker at all but that was shot down for being grinch like. My second suggestion of a retro-theme where, god forbid, we actually use the same decorations as before, was met with a look like I'd just shat in his coffee.

However, Paul doesn't cause me too much fuss, so I tend to just retire to the Xbox and let him crack on with decorating it. He does a grand job, to be fair, even if there is an unusual amount of swearing during the decorating process and far too much Mariah Carey for my liking. I get to come and appraise his efforts, drink Baileys and turn on the lights, which every year fills me with so much angst because I've seen 999 and I know my Christmas tree is just *itching* to burst into flames.

Anyway, perhaps we should have exercised a modicum of common sense when it came to picking the tree because getting it home was an adventure in itself – whilst we did indeed manage to squeeze it into the car, it meant driving the fifteen miles or so home without any visibility behind me, the ability to see any of my mirrors and great difficulty in changing the gears because the car at this point was 85% fir needles. I had to rely on Paul to check his side when we were pulling out of junctions and this is a man who gets distracted wiping his own arse. I've never feared for my life more behind the wheel. Imagine having a crash and the ambulance men not being able to get at your prone body because you have a £70 tree through your face. Goodness.

We made it home – obviously – and the next part of the struggle took place: trying to get it back out of the car. It was wedged in so tight that it had almost become a feature of the car itself and it was only after twenty minutes of jimmying it every which way that we were able to get it free, stumble across the lawn and into our house. Paul took great care to make sure every possible wall received a scratch or a bit of mud which resulted in me getting one of the eighteen tester pots of paint out to gussy the place back up. Final insult? The bloody thing wouldn't go into the tree-stand from last year because the trunk is too thick. Pfft. Listen, if being a gay man has taught me anything, is that you'd be surprised at what you can slide into a very small hole if you just take your time and apply enough gentle force. Fifteen minutes of wrestling back and forth was rewarded with the trunk sliding in with a satisfying pop. I'd have offered the tree a cigarette afterwards but see above re: fire risk.

And there it stays. Paul will decorate it tomorrow once it has dried out, leaving a 24-hour window for the cats to climb all over it and scratch away at the trunk. Hell, I'd hate to feel like they were left out. Sola might have enjoyed the Christmas experience so much yesterday having wrapping tape stuck to her bajingo that she's become a full Christmas convert.

twochubbycubs on: a Christmas ouch

Our tree is up! But let me tell you: blood was almost shed. Let me paint you a picture. There's me, in the bath, luxuriating / basking in a sea of Molton Brown bubbles and The Archers omnibus playing in the background. Paul was in the living room fussing about the tree like a make-up artist at a wedding. I could hear the occasional shout and strop but hey, the bath was lovely. After an hour or so a plaintive cry came from the living room for me to come and help — his tiny Nick-Nack legs didn't quite afford him the height needed to pop our furry star on top of the tree. Fair enough — the tree is 7ft and Paul drives a Smart-car.

I clamber out, the bubbles caressing my every curve. It was exactly like the bit in Casino Royale when Daniel Craig emerges from the sea in his little blue knickers, only with far more heart disease and loud straining. I mince into the living room and exclaim at how pretty the tree is before immediately fretting as to whether our Dyson Digital can cope with the quarter-tonne of pine needles that already litter the floor. Completely nude, I lean into the tree to make the final adjustment, to adorn it with the shiny star of Christmas, and how was I rewarded?

With a fucking pine needle right down my hog's eye. My beef bullet was speared by the cold fingers of Christmas present. I know that a lot of you ladies out there will have been through child birth but honestly, that would have been like ripping off a wet plaster compared to this. I don't like to exaggerate but it was literally the worst pain in the world. There's places that nothing should ever venture and a gentleman's scrotum-totem is one of these. I since looked it up on the internet only to find it's an actual fetish, with people putting all sorts of things down there. Internet: what is wrong with you?

Anyway, you'll be relieved to know that he's fine and still in working order. Phew, right?

twochubbycubs on: Christmas parties

Tomorrow is our office Christmas party. I'm excited, but saying as I was one of the four who organised it, there's a certain air of 'phew, we made it' to the whole affair. Who knew that organising shenanigans for 150 people could be so exhausting? Thankfully I work for a company with some flair and imagination so it'll be a bit more than a few Tesco quiches and a glass of warm piss – party on!

I'm not exactly a social butterfly when it comes to work parties but I always make the Christmas one. There's been some absolute corkers. Back in the heady days of a Labour government I used to work for a quango (long since shut down) doing a very important job – literally no-one else could use the photocopier. No, I was a secretary, but my boss was this amazingly posh woman with a filthy sense of humour and the rest of the team were equally as fun. It was a fantastic place to work – you'd turn up whenever you fancied in the morning, fanny about a bit with some papers and then fuck off home at around half past two. We spent more time outside dicking about at the smoking shelter than upstairs working and at one point the entire team hid in a meeting room for a surprise 70s buffet, emerging several hours later pissed on Babycham. In retrospect, it's not difficult to see why the government shut us down. Maha.

Anyway, the Christmas parties were immense – starting at 10am with drinks in the office, followed by a rude secret santa, followed by the entire department going out for 'Christmas team lunch' and staying out until 3am in the morning. Hilariously, we worked right next door to the HR team who were led by a manager who had never known joy. Her PA used to log what times we'd all rock into the office and send us prim notes which we'd all ignore and go smoke instead. One especially messy Christmas party saw our Head Boss get so bladdered that we had to bundle her onto the last train back home into rural North Northumberland only for her to promptly fall asleep missing her stop. This then meant her husband had to chase the train to Edinburgh to pick her up, scattered as she was with her knickers around her ankles. That was after the point where I'd received a drunken lap-dance from her, I hasten to add. There were some exceptionally sore heads the next day.

Oh, and we got asked to leave a pub for failing to realise that every time we nipped out the back door for a smoke that we were setting off the fire alarms for the entire pub. Oops. We weren't to know, surely. Also, at some point, someone set themselves on fire by accident. All every eventful. Oh and one more addendum to this little tale: I accidentally bought said boss a vibrator for the secret santa. In my defence I thought it was a little duck for the bath – turns out it was, but with an especially-shaped beak that vibrated. She loved it though and any embarrassment was soon put to bed when the next person along opened a book of sex positions and a half-used jar of Vaseline. Seriously, that jar looked like the one in Kill Bill 2.

Ah, truly halcyon days. I love where I am now, don't get me wrong, I do, but you never know what you've had until it's taken away thanks to budget cuts!

Conversely, my worst Christmas party was at BT, where our team manager had promised to take us out for dinner and a piss-up if we met our sales targets. We worked our arses off for weeks pushing 1471 onto folks who didn't need it and 'accidentally' putting people on Option 4 broadband (£7 commission!) knowing that they'd always be able to cancel it later. I know, that's awful behaviour, but to be fair, I was pretty much permanently stoned during that job. You had to be, dealing with so many complaints. Hell, I went outside for a smoke during a quiet time and was approached by someone in another team selling speed to get through 'the difficult calls'. I politely demurred, given my dicky ticker, but that should give you an insight to why people are often so peppy in a call centre. Smile when you dial...

Anyway, Christmas rocked around and we were told he was putting on a bus (which we had to chip in for) to take us to a country pub. He did, fair enough, but after charging us £10 a time for the bus and then putting no fucking money behind the bar for food and drink, well, that put a bit of a downer on things. We worked out later he'd actually made a profit on the coach, too, the oily-skinned fucker. We made the best of a bad day but most of us just buggered off home after an hour or so of strained conversation about sales targets. The manager clearly knew he'd upset us as we returned to find a selection box each on our desk. Most of the team left them on a point of principle – as did I – but I made sure to nip around and get all the Double Deckers out of them first.

twochubbycubs on: Christmas 2016

I had a genuinely lovely Christmas – Paul and I woke around 9am, realised it was a god-awful time to be alive and went straight back to sleep, snoring and farting and grunting our way to 11am, at which time the world seemed a lot more welcoming. I dispatched him straight to the kitchen to make bacon sandwiches (cheese topped roll, tomato chutney, bacon with so much fat on it that Sharshina Bramwell would explode in a fit of hair lacquer and half-smoked Carltons that you *know* she keeps tucked behind her ear) whilst I dozed for a bit longer. We had our sandwiches and exchanged presents in front of a Crystal Maze repeat. We both (unusually) stuck to our agreed present limits but somehow I managed to justify buying a new bottle of Tom Ford Oud Wood "for the house", the way that others may buy a new candle or a doormat. What-am-I-like. We then wrapped up* the quarter-tonne of presents we'd bought our nephew (honestly, I felt like Challenge Anneka when she used to turn up at the orphanage with a lorry of gifts) and then made our way over to our parents where we opened all of our gifts and immediately set about fattening ourselves up.

* I say *we* wrapped presents. What actually happened was Paul was on sellotape duty whilst I farted about doing all of the folding and wrapping and cutting. I hate wrapping presents. I do! If it was socially acceptable to hand over gifts in a Netto bag with their name scrawled

haphazardly over the top in Sharpie I'd do exactly that. I was furious inside watching my nephew tearing away at my delicate wrapping – I missed most of the industrial zone wrapping that Kinetic Sand, you little stinker.

My parents had built a grotto in the garden for the benefit of my nephew – this being the first Christmas he'll remember – and actually, despite my cynicism about these things, it was really lovely. Pine trees, twinkling lights, a heated gazebo, music playing – a fantastic effort. Even my cold, icy heart melted. Christmas last year felt slightly off because my nana wasn't at the table proclaiming that 'this'll be my last Christmas' and 'I'm not going to make another year' – you know, the cheery statements of the elderly. She had the last laugh though – two years ago she was bang on the money. Christmas isn't the same without having to repeat what you say four times over until you're bellowing like you're caught in a house fire and she's holding the phone. Christ, I remember one Christmas a couple of years ago when she slumped dramatically in her chair and we all looked aghast at each other thinking she'd died in the middle of eating her one sprout and chipolata ("that'll do for me Christine, I'm not a big eater"). It was like Helen Daniels all over again, only Paul was too fat to play Hannah.

Turns out she'd just dozed off and, because she had one of those fabulous NHS hearing aids that was of equal use to her whether she was wearing it or had left it at home, couldn't hear our plaintive cries to wake her. She was lucky – the way my dad with clearing up she was fortunate not be have been buried in the garden "to save time" before the cheeseboard came around.

One thing I can take away from yesterday is that my mother is turning into my nana, at least on the food front. As usual with Christmas, everyone buys enough food to last us through a nuclear winter, nevermind a British one. I can't open a cupboard without eight hundred gaily-decorated packets of crackers and biscuits and crisps and oatcakes and pickles and nuts and Pringles and sweets and mints and Bombay mix and tinned olives and breadsticks and chocolates cascading down onto me like I'm in Fun House: Obesity Edition. Christmas dinner was the usual spread of gorgeous food all shovelled down with booze and er, in my case, Vimto. I was driving, and anyway, when do you ever get a chance to have Vimto? Mother's gone to Farmfoods! I'd no sooner managed to see my plate through my pile of food then my mum started piping up with 'have a bit more turkey' or 'have another tureen of veg, it'll not get eaten'. I swear, for all her concerned protestations that Paul and I are looking fat, she was determined to have us break at least one wooden chair before we left.

Christmas pudding followed, accompanied by cream and more food-pushing (have a bit of tiramisu, have some profiteroles, have some more cream) and then, just as I was fully expecting to start leaking mashed potatoes from my ears and start coughing up barely digested sprouts, out comes the cheese platter. Now listen, Paul and I love a cheese-board. We do. We *may* have accidentally worked our way through a six-person cheeseboard from Marks and Spencers only the night before. But we have limits, and frankly, when I've eaten so much cheese that my poo is coming out the same colour, consistency and indeed smell as a Cheesestring, we need to rest. But no! Old Mother Cub (?) was cutting off a bit of this for us and a bit of that for us and try this relish and have some crackers. Most people like to finish a good meal with coffee and perhaps a cigar – my mother seems to think a meal isn't complete without one of her guests being ambulanced to hospital with chest pains. I was as full as a fat man's sock.

Final thought from the day? I look at my nephew now, all full of chatter and wonder, and think that I'd like a child for the house. Don't get me wrong, I'd tire of any child after thirty minutes and sadly, it isn't like you can pack them away in a cupboard anymore, but it would be fun to see Christmas and Easter and all that fun stuff through their eyes. Towards the end of the day he had managed to find and consume an entire family-sized bag of sugary sour worms and it was as all that sugar was kicking in that we bid our goodbyes. My sister, an excellent, patient mum who thankfully has managed to evade the temptation to change her name on FB to Deborah 'Mammyofspecialone' Surname, had that joy to deal with. Mahaha! We get to be the fun uncles who swoop in with gifts, e-numbers and presents and then get to leave just as the Kinetic sand is being trod into the carpet and he's doing a loud, continuous impression of a police car.

It really was a great day. We came home, watched Doctor Who (pap), Eastenders (rubbish) and then fell asleep during Corrie. We don't watch the soaps during the year so god-knows why we inflict them upon ourselves at Christmas but see, that's exactly why – because it's Christmas. I hope you all had a lovely one!

a few closing words

What does the next year hold for us? Well, look, we really do need to lose some weight. I'm sick of everything I sit on creaking like an arthritic thumb. I'm tired of only being able to buy my clothes from Jacamo. Paul's getting to the point where he has a nap before going to bed. I know we've said it so many times before but if we carry on, we'll die!

The plan for the blog is to carry on with our nonsense but as it is our tenth anniversary in 2017, we plan to take 10 holidays – the idea being that we'll diet like mad up until our holiday, then eat what we like. It'll hopefully provide focus and alleviate all the joint pain. Plus, we love writing the 'holiday entries' so there will be plenty more of those! Oh and of course, the recipes will continue. Sometimes we forget that the core of the blog is the delicious food...

If we've left you satisfied and smiling please take a moment to leave us a review on Amazon! If you're feeling especially keen, make sure you recommend us to your friends! It would make us beam.

Finally, a huge thank you. We do it all for you – and we'll keep going for another year!

James and Paul

x

JAMES AND PAUL ANDERSON

23502776R00264

Printed in Great Britain
by Amazon